The Ugly Sister

by Gila Berkowitz

Cover art: Pencil drawing, "Ausziehen!" ("Strip!") 1945-1949, by
Ella Liebermann-Shiber (1927-1998). By permission of Art
Collection, The Ghetto Fighters' House Museum, Western
Galilee, Israel.

FOR THE SURVIVORS
especially my parents,
Mendel Berkowitz 1909-1998 and Margit Berkowitz 1912-

AND THE MARTYRS

AND YOU WHO CLING TO THE LORD YOUR GOD ARE ALIVE, EVERY
ONE OF YOU, TODAY.

—Deuteronomy 4:4

CHAPTER ONE

September, 1936. Kosice, Czechoslovakia

The laughter stopped.

The sharp knock came again. All six sisters tensed. Sari, the eldest, went to the door. A beggar stood there, hugging himself in a threadbare coat.

"Madame," he began, but Sari cut him off.

"Please come in, sir."

"The menfolk are in the House of Study," Eva said drily. It was a place where a pauper was welcome to lie down on a bench for the night.

"I...I don't want charity. I can pay."

"Nonsense!" said Martha. Helen was already at the stove, heating up the left-over goulash. Renee was slicing bread. Kitty, the youngest, sprang up and set the table.

The beggar insisted. "I have a gift—rather, a curse. I can read the future from the palm of the hand."

"The future! You mean like fortunetelling?" Kitty's eyes widened.

"What next?" smirked Eva. "Gypsy women studying Talmud?"

"'You shall not suffer a witch to live,'" cited Sari.

"Please don't misunderstand, Madame. I don't deal in black arts."

"Hoodwinking the gullible is as sinful as idolatry," Sari lectured.

"If I charged money for it, would I look like this?" the stranger asked miserably.

"Oh, Sari," said Kitty, "don't be so pious. Let's hear what he has to say."

Sari shrugged and folded her hands under her arms. What was there for her to learn from a fortuneteller? In twenty years of marriage she had never been pregnant.

"Well then," said Martha, the next oldest, "I'll go first."

She extended her hands, pushing her pregnant belly against the table. The stranger used the handle of a fork to trace the lines across her palms. His face was very sober.

"Well? Will it be a boy or a girl?" Martha's adored children; she would welcome either answer.

"Boy," he said.

Martha beamed triumphantly. She already had three boys and three girls. She extended her hands further toward the stranger. "How many children will I have altogether?"

"These seven," said the stranger flatly.

"Oh, just seven? But will they be healthy?"

"Yes."

"Thank heaven!"

The stranger drew back from the table but Martha bent further toward him. She blushed. "What about grandchildren?"

The sisters hooted with laughter.

"No. No grandchildren."

The laughter trickled dry.

"But how can that be?" Martha touched her stomach protectively.

Sari stepped in. "That's enough for Martha. Give the others a turn." What a ninny Martha was, taking this hobo for some sort of seer.

Helen came next. She took Martha's seat and opened her fists as if in a dare. The sisters readied for confrontation. Behind her back they called her "HeLenin."

"And how many children will I have?" she asked, looking slyly at the beggar.

Helen and her husband weren't Orthodox any more and had decided two children were enough. They had obtained a birth control device.

"Two," said the fortuneteller.

Helen's eye twitched. It seemed so final.

The stranger jumped up. "My God, it doesn't matter. I can't bear this anymore." Sobs rumbled from his chest.

"What is the problem, Reb Yid?" said Sari, her disdain for the fortuneteller erased by pity.

The man raked his face with his nails, pulling hair from his beard.

"There is a terrible... time...a terrible thing…coming."

Renee raised a clenched fist. "He's right! The world is bristling with arms, and we're whistling pretty little tunes of peace and justice. It's about time we Jews made our own destiny."

"But we live peacefully with our neighbors," Martha insisted.

"And how long will that last?" Renee asked darkly.

Kitty piped up. "My teacher, Mr. Bernstein, says the worst is already over in Germany." She didn't really see why, but she wanted to add an authoritative opinion to the adult conversation.

"Really?" said Renee. "Why shouldn't we believe what the Germans say about wiping the Jews off the face of Europe?"

"Girls! Stop fighting." Sari turned to the stranger. "I'm afraid we've had enough of your 'gift,' sir."

"What about me?" pouted Eva. Rings and bracelets jangled and clacked as she lay her hands, palms up, on the table. Eva's in-laws had gone into debt to buy the jewelry.

The beggar examined her hands. Suddenly, he bucked in his seat and made a gagging noise.

"How many children will *I* have?"

He took a moment to compose himself. "One."

Eva smiled. A single child seemed so elegant, so modern.

"Will I be rich?"

"No."

Eva snatched her hands back. "Liar! Faker!"

The stranger rose suddenly. He threw the fork to the table and it bounced and clattered to the floor.

"You don't understand," he said shaking with frustration. His hands tore at his collar, as if he were trying to choke himself. "Run, Jews, run! What's coming is more awful than anything that has ever happened. More horrible than the pogroms, than the Crusades. Worse than the destruction of Jerusalem."

"Another glass of tea, sir?" asked Sari. The fellow was a lunatic, but he was still their guest. "Girls, is there any cinnamon cake left?"

"Please, you must believe me. I see it all the time, in every Jewish hand. I keep hoping that someone will have lines that cancel it out. But no one does. We have to get away."

"Czechoslovakia is our dream come true," said Martha gently. "The Great War is over and a new world is rising from the ashes. We've never had it this good."

"No, no," the man shook his head hopelessly. "It isn't safe, it won't be safe."

"Our guest is right!" said Renee stoutly. "The place for all Jews is Eretz Yisrael. We must go home to Zion."

"It isn't possible," moaned the stranger. "The British will not let us into Palestine. They will have no mercy. No one will. Not even the Americans."

Several sisters pursed their lips. If the man wasn't crazy he was a fool. America had been a blessed refuge for the tortured Jews of Czarist Russia. Possibly, it was the answer to the troubles of the German Jews, who were more Gentile than Jewish anyway. But for people like themselves, people of learning and culture, of integrity, could soul-sucking America ever be an option?

The man got up to go.

"Mister, mister. What about me?" Kitty stretched her small, agile hands across the table.

Sari threw herself on the girl. "No, darling, don't. It's silly."

"Please Sari, just for fun."

"No, no, it's...sinful."

Sari was afraid for her youngest sister. It was one thing to make apocalyptic prophecies, but what if the stranger made a *really* hurtful prediction. What if he said Kitty would be left an old maid.

Poor Kitty was so plain. The five of them resembled their mother— Mother before tuberculosis. They were tall, broad-shouldered, big-eyed, fair-skinned, and blond. But Kitty took after Father. She was short, noodle-thin, and olive-skinned. There were almost no lashes around her brown eyes. Her hair was thin, straggly, and dark as earth.

"I have an idea," said Kitty. Her hands were on her hips, her eyes sparkling with mischief. "The gentleman will read my palms, and if he finds a terrible future there, we will all agree that he's an awful liar and a sorcerer. *But* if he finds true love, and treasure, and adventure, we'll declare him a prophet like Isaiah!"

Kitty had the sisters smiling again. The visitor, tears still on his cheeks, agreed to one last reading.

Kitty's feet left the floor when she leaned over the table to extend her hands. The stranger looked at one palm, then the other, then he returned to the first palm, and shook his head.

His face seemed at war with itself, as confusion, doubt, and hope passed over it.

"I don't understand," he muttered. "I've never seen anything like this.

"One hand is like everyone else's; there is death, obliteration from the face of the earth. But the other..."

"Hold your tongue!" Sari shouted.

But he didn't hear her. He raised Kitty's right hand, which was oddly unlined, like the hand of a cloth doll.

"The other promises love, beauty, and rebirth."

CHAPTER TWO

"Big harvest this year," Sari said, gingerly. "Joseph will need my help." Sari's husband's job was buying bruised fruit from farmers, which he delivered to distilleries to make liqueur.

"Great. When will you be leaving?" Kitty finished her homework, dotting a sentence with finality.

Sari didn't answer. Kitty looked up and smiled at her sister's beauty.

"We will be leaving in two weeks."

"I'll miss you and Joseph."

"But you're coming with us," Sari said, putting a hand on Kitty's.

Kitty shook off the hand, and capped her pen. Then she noticed the hurt on Sari's face. "I want to go with you but after the school year. I'll join you for the summer, after graduation."

"You'll finish in Janace, darling."

Kitty grimaced. Janace was not much better than a village. Kosice, on the other hand, was one of the largest and most cultured cities in Czechoslovakia.

"But Dr. Francova will be disappointed." The principal of her school was a national figure, a feminist, a protégée of Masaryk, the Washington of Czechoslovakia. Kitty was one of her pets.

"She's a great woman. But you, well, you know we can't be like that."

Kitty set her lips. Who was Sari to judge? Sari, fiercely proud of her own learning, had been educated, in the days before public schools, in a *convent*.

"Even Jewish girls have choices today. I don't necessarily see myself marrying a Hasid, the way you did."

"I married the man I loved. He just happened to be a Hasid."

"Oh, I know that. I love Joseph! But there's less than a year left 'till graduation. Can't we discuss the future afterwards?"

Sari shook her head. "We have to leave the house."

"What?" The house had been in their family for generations.

"It's been sold."

"Sold? Why on earth?"

Sari licked her lip nervously. "It made sense. Joseph and I have our home in Janace. Martha and her family live way off in Ruhigbad. Helen and her family don't need a big house. And as soon as Renee and Eva get their emigration visas to Palestine, they'll be gone."

"What about me? When I get married, I want to stay here. That way you'll all have this house to come back to. We'll always be able to come *home*."

"Really, Kitty. How would it look for a young girl to be living alone in a big house? Besides," Sari looked at the floor, "the house is sold."

Kitty frowned. Sari, despite donning Mother's mantle, would never have considered selling the house on her own. Who put her up to it?

It wouldn't be Joseph, that gentle, humble man. Martha? Martha wouldn't buy a soup ladle without consulting the whole family. Helen and Thomas couldn't have done it, either. Those impractical intellectuals deplored capitalism.

Renee and Eva? But they were just a few years older than she was. Their husbands wouldn't have dared propose such an action to a family they had just joined.

So who *had* sold the house? And what had become of the money?

Janace, eastern Slovakia

"What do you miss most about Kosice, Kitty?"

Rachel-Leah, Joseph's niece, was Kitty's new best friend. The same age as Kitty, she was already engaged to a Hasid.

"Mostly school. Also, the movie theaters, the department stores, the Speakers' Corner at the park..."

"Janace must be terribly boring for you."

"It has its charms. In Janace everyone seems to have the time to stop and talk. And there's you, Rachel-Leah."

"I'm just a dummy. I left school ages ago."

"You're smart enough to run a household. Twelve brothers and sisters, and you can take over your mother's job without breathing hard. That's no dummy."

Rachel-Leah smiled proudly. "Still, I'm glad you're here, Miss Sophistication. How could I have bought a chic trousseau without you?"

"I should thank you. Now every mother-of-the-bride in town is asking me to help with her daughter's wedding—and paying me."

"Yes! You'll be rich."

"Hardly. But it's nice to have some money for shoes and fabric and permanent waves, and not have to ask Sari for an allowance."

"I'm not pleased with Kitty's new 'business,'" Sari complained to Joseph. "None of us ever worked before marriage, not even in Father's store."

"Oh, Sari, she enjoys it."

"People will think she's a poor girl trying to scrape together money to buy pots and linens. It gives the wrong impression to matchmakers and possible suitors."

"Quite the contrary. What is more desirable than a wife who is handy, clever, energetic, able to help support her family whatever the future brings?"

Rich and beautiful, thought Sari.

Joseph read her thought. "My angel, you worry too much about Kitty. There's a girl who can take care of herself. I know you promised your parents that you would see each of your sisters settled. Renee and Eva were not easy, Heaven knows. But I have a feeling that Kitty will be different. She'll find herself a good husband, I'll bet. And he will be a lucky man."

"May God will it," said Sari, sighing.

CHAPTER THREE

Janace, eastern Slovakia

The Hasidic men rose early for Sabbath prayer in the synagogue. But for women the day of rest meant lolling in bed, reading magazines. The most pious prayed at home, but the others luxuriated in their free time until the men returned from services.

Holidays were different. Particularly on those days when the memorial prayer for the dead was said, every woman made an appearance in the synagogue, dressed as well as her wit and her income allowed.

In early summer Sari invited Renee, Eva, and their husbands to Janace for the festival of Shavuos. She wanted to show off her three youngest sisters the way her peers were showing off their daughters.

The four sisters gathered to inspect one another before heading off late, but not too late, for services.

"You're letting Kitty go like *that*?" Eva said to Sari.

Sari jumped at the accusation that she had failed a responsibility. She scrutinized Kitty's outfit. The dress, on which they had spent many hours, was a triumph of tailoring. They had bias-cut the silk crepe, slashing triangles of fabric that were caught up in five big bow-knots. The bows were sewn precisely where they would fill out Kitty's scant bosom and hips. The hem moved sinuously around Kitty's slim calves.

Was the skirt too short? No. Kitty had lobbied for raising the hem. Her legs were her most attractive feature and the fashion experts were predicting shorter skirts. But Sari insisted that the rumor from Paris was unsubstantiated. The hem remained at eight inches from the ground. Kitty wore sheer "blond" hose, but there was nothing radical about those. Except for Hasidic women, almost everyone had switched to sheer, more natural-looking stockings.

"What's wrong with what she's wearing?"

"Look at the color of her dress. It's a scandal."

"What do you mean, Eva? It's that Schiaparelli pink. 'Shocking,' they call it, but that's just a figure of speech. It's a bit much on us, but it flatters brunettes."

"It flatters prostitutes."

Sari gasped. Decent women didn't use such words. She checked Kitty again. A bit of, well, *spice*, didn't hurt a plain girl. "Kitty looks lovely," she insisted.

Eva fell slightly behind, her eyes shooting daggers into her sisters' backs. *It was always the same. Poor little Kitty gets away with murder, while she— all of two years older—can't breach a single silly custom without a tongue-lashing from Sari.*

And it had always been that way. When mother was sick, the poor little baby had to be coddled, while Eva had to buck up and be a big girl. Poor homely Kitty could dress like a slut, and she was to be penalized for her beauty!

Oblivious to any dissension, Sari admired her troops as they marched to the synagogue in the bright morning sunlight.

Eva wore an ice-blue shantung suit. Her gloves were chamois and her veiled hat covered all but a bit of her hair, as was the custom for a married Jewish woman. Everything about her said expensive, chic, and proper.

Of all the sisters Renee had the best figure. It made the most of her simply tailored navy-blue suit. She had a Tyrolean hat and low-heeled shoes to match. These days Renee sewed and bought only those items that would wear well in rugged Palestine, but the sturdy clothing only accentuated her loveliness.

Kitty's outfit was softened by a straw hat trimmed with flowers. The magazines were always advising things like "do decorate an inexpensive chapeau with fresh blossoms," but Kitty was the only one who actually picked weeds and pinned them on a cheap gardening hat. The flowers were drooping now, but that only made the effect more charming.

For her part, Kitty sized up Sari with satisfaction. "My summer wool will do fine for at least another year," Sari had insisted. So Kitty had secretly dug the old coat-dress out of the closet, replaced collar and cuffs with white satin, and sewn on mother-of-pearl buttons. Now, even with the thick black stockings and tight turban of the Hasidic matron, Sari looked stylish.

When the Lebow sisters entered the women's balcony of the synagogue, only those totally immersed in prayer failed to look up. Sari sat down in her customary seat, and Renee and Eva found places in the back among the visitors.

In the front row Rachel-Leah stood up, turned around and beckoned Kitty over, wildly waving her arms. She had reserved room for Kitty by flinging her suit jacket across a seat. Kitty blushed. The front row was reserved for the rabbi's wife, the head of the women's burial society, and other elderly worthies.

Rachel-Leah had brazenly taken the seats because they afforded an unimpeded view of the men's section. "There's my Chaim," she whispered, "left of the ark."

Kitty looked, finding a snowy white prayer shawl among the older, yellowed ones. That would be Chaim. A prayer shawl was a traditional wedding gift from a young man's in-laws.

Her guess was verified when Chaim turned around, instantly spotted his wife, and gave her a smile as dazzling as his prayer shawl. In response, Rachel-Leah almost fell off the balcony railing.

The couple's marriage had been arranged. They had met three times before the wedding, but always in the company of relatives and matchmakers. They had been shy then and managed only to mumble a few words, and exchange furtive glances. But once married they became besotted.

Chaim was exceptionally homely, Kitty thought. Short and dumpy, the fringes of his prayer shawl dragged on the floor. But when he smiled at Rachel-Leah, the cheeks above his thick beard plumped up like apples, and his eyes danced in the light of the synagogue chandelier. Rachel-Leah was no beauty, either. Her figure promised to turn into a cylinder by three years or three babies, whichever came first. But right then, the balcony might have belonged to Shakespeare's Juliet.

Chaim turned back to the service. Rachel-Leah soon grew bored of her prayer-book. "Kitty, see the guy three back from Chaim? Isn't he gorgeous? That's the Baron, the best-looking man in Janace." She checked herself. "Oh, but he's not for you, Kitty."

The director of the Committee for Visiting the Sick glared at Rachel-Leah. "Shh! This is a synagogue, not a coffee house!"

Kitty seethed in silence. So, she was too plain for an aristocrat! Says who? Why didn't she deserve a handsome man? A rich man? The best man?

But her anger evaporated. Grudges were a waste of time. She opened her mouth to ask Rachel-Leah more about the unsuitable young man, but the head of the Sabbath Supporters League—which provided weekly food packages for the poor—gave her a warning look.

Kitty leaned over the railing and looked for the Baron. It was easy to find the bachelors; they didn't wear prayer shawls. The Baron was of medium height, but well-built. He wore a beautifully cut suit, in which he moved gracefully. His black fedora was tilted just so, but he was deeply immersed in prayer and never looked up to the balcony.

A Jewish aristocrat was the rarest of birds. There were the Rothschilds of course, and the Emperor Franz Joseph had been kind to Jews, even elevating a few to the peerage. But what was a noble doing in little Janace?

The memorial service was announced. Everyone whose parents were alive left the synagogue. Rachel-Leah took her jacket and dashed off. She was meeting Chaim in the courtyard. Most of the young people exited, and Kitty was left with the stuffy old ladies in the front row.

The Baron turned to leave. The sight of his face ransomed her breath. He was more than handsome; he was beautiful! She'd never seen anything like him, not even in the movies.

If the Baron was leaving the synagogue it meant his parents were still alive. So how did he get the title? He must have earned it himself. What a man of uncommon accomplishments!

Kitty had been present at the memorial service for several rounds. It had been years since Father's death, and even Mother's passing was no longer a fresh wound.

But this is no place for me. I should be out in the courtyard, chatting with my friends, flirting with the Baron. What am I doing with these people?

She wondered what Father and Mother were up to in heaven, now that they no longer had a family to care for or work to do. It was said the righteous spent all eternity basking in the glory of the Holy Throne, like rich people sunbathing on the Riviera.

Father, Mother, it's time to speak with the Almighty about me. It's the Baron I want. Please order the Baron for my husband.

At the end of the service Kitty felt relieved. In life, her father and mother had never denied a reasonable request. Why should they do so after death? Also, it was well known that, of all petitioners, God answers orphans first.

After the prayer, the younger worshipers filed back, and Rachel-Leah took her seat. She did not immediately resume gossiping with Kitty. The aura of death, like some noxious mist, lingered in the synagogue.

Before long it was time for the blessing of the priests. In the rear, Renee perked up. She wasn't much for prayers in general, but this one intrigued her. In the land of Israel the priests blessed the people every day. Only here, in the cold Diaspora, was it distributed stingily only on festivals.

Now the priests stood up before the Holy Ark. They covered themselves with prayer shawls, as did the men of the congregation, because the prayer was considered so powerful that neither the priests, conduits for the blessing, nor the congregation being blessed, dared look directly upon the act.

In the women's balcony the ladies turned their heads to the rear, or hid their faces with hat brims and prayer books. Rachel-Leah took one last look at Chaim's back, then covered her eyes with her hands.

Kitty remembered how, as a little girl, she took refuge in Father's prayer shawl. She loved the masculine smells of starched shirts and snuff and old wool. In the holy white tent, she felt so protected. Never again would she feel that safe, she thought, and tears came to her eyes. Now she felt Father's absence more than she had during the memorial service.

The priests began: "Blessed is the King of the Universe, who has endowed us with the holiness of Aaron and commanded us to bless your people Israel, in love."

The congregation roared "Amen."

Although the men's section wasn't visible from where they stood, the women in the back also covered their eyes.

"What stupid superstition," Eva whispered to Renee. "Do they think they'll go blind if they look?"

"Go ahead and look," said Renee, "you're already blind."

Now the cantor called out each word in a soft voice, and the priests responded by repeating them in a primeval ululation.

"THE LORD."

"BLESS YOU."

"AND KEEP YOU."

Joseph Wassermann loved the priestly blessing above all prayers. God was blessing them for no reason at all, just the simple love of a parent for children.

"THE LORD"

"SHINE."

"HIS FACE."

"UPON YOU."

"AND GIVE YOU GRACE."

Benny Fruchter, Renee's husband, was in a quandary. Should he tell his wife now, or should he wait for when the visas arrived? Either way, it would be an unpleasant scene. But they were certainly not going to

Palestine. Really, it had always been a ridiculous notion.

He had been a member of the same Zionist youth group as Renee and they had sung the beautiful ballads about the Land, they had had their dreams. But now they were adults, a married couple. Time to get down to earth, which was not the same as The Land.

Palestine! The place was a pit, a malarial swamp. For two thousand years many great empires had ruled it and it was still just a junkyard. And they—a bunch of Jews from Europe—were supposed to make it another Greece or Portugal? What a joke.

In Czechoslovakia, with its decent government and free economy, his prospects were excellent. It would be a hundred years before the Jews had it this good in Eretz Yisrael. Plus, he was an only son. What was he supposed to do with his parents, bring them into some desert full of wild Arabs?

No, he would have to lay down the law to Renee. He was the man of the house, she was obliged to go with his decision. Still, it would be unpleasant. But maybe the British would save him yet. They were getting more miserly with those visas to Palestine.

"THE LORD."

"LIFT."

"HIS FACE."

"TOWARDS YOU."

"AND GIVE YOU..."

Martin Blumenthal asked God to hurry those visas. He didn't know how much longer he could hold out. Eva had made him promise that if they didn't come by August, they would move to Ruhigbad, where her rich sister Martha lived.

Martin dreaded the thought. Ruhigbad was a beautiful resort city but it was so far west, practically Germany.

What would he do there? Martha's husband, Ignatz Rosen, had offered him a job, but he hated the idea of working for relatives. He wanted to work The Land.

Once a lecturer had told the Zionist club about aquaculture, growing fish in artificial ponds! Martin liked that. He stared into his prayer shawl and imagined a white lake sparkling with silver fish.

"PEACE!"

Sari hastened to wipe the tears away before the blessing was over and everyone came up for air. You weren't supposed to cry on a holiday, but she couldn't help it.

Why? She begged and pleaded with God for the millionth time. What have I done? How have I sinned?

Oh, God, answer me!

Help me! I never ask you for anything but this. Oh God, all I ever ask for is a *baby*.

"AMEN."

The prayer shawls were lifted off, the faces beamed out, and the synagogue noise reached its highest level.

"So," said Kitty to Rachel-Leah, "you think I'm not good enough for this Baron."

"What? You're *too* good for him."

"You put your foot in your mouth and now you're trying to weasel out of it."

"I am not."

"Come on, admit it. You don't think I stand a chance with a rich, handsome guy like that."

"Rich? Who said anything about rich?"

"Well, he's a baron, isn't he?"

Rachel-Leah whooped with laughter. Now the rabbi's wife was steaming. "The service isn't over yet, girls. Can you hold your brilliant remarks for a few more minutes?"

Rachel-Leah leaned over and whispered. "He's not a real baron—it's a nickname. Everybody makes fun of his fancy taste."

"His taste in clothing is exquisite."

"Too exquisite. If Alexander Halter can't get the best, he'd rather do without. So he usually goes without. Oy, is that family poor.

"And that's why you don't think he's right for me?"

"Not just that. He's got a terrible reputation. You know, he broke the hearts of the Minsky triplets."

Rachel-Leah indicated the sisters Minsky. Kitty saw not three but four young matrons with good jewelry. They did not look heartbroken.

"They're second cousins of Sender's, and they were all madly in love with him. A good suitor came and took the eldest. The second gave up and left the field open to the third. She held out for the longest time, but in the end also gave up, and married someone else."

"What about the fourth one?"

"That's a younger sister. She never even bothered."

"Well, I can't say I blame them for trying. The 'Baron' is, as you said, gorgeous."

"Shh," said Rachel-Leah, "time to say the Order of the Incense."

"Huh?" The Order was an esoteric debate in the Talmud about the formula for the Temple incense. Most people thought it an opportune time to button their jackets and pack up their prayer books. "*Now* you're starting to pray?" said Kitty.

"Listen, the Order of Incense is the formula to find and keep your true love."

"Oh, please."

"Really. The incense was what the Bride Israel perfumed herself with for God, her Divine Lover."

Kitty re-opened the prayer book. "Balm, cloves, galbanum, and frankincense, seventy parts each; myrrh, cassia, spikenard, and saffron, sixteen parts each...Whoever adds honey renders it unfit. Whoever omits an ingredient incurs the death penalty..."

Was there a prescription for love, too? Did every element have to be there in the right proportions, with no extras?

Rich or poor, baron or commoner, didn't matter. Kitty was certain she'd found the right recipe for her.

CHAPTER FOUR

Alma's was the most elegant dress shop in Janace. At its door, Kitty breathed deeply and squared her shoulders. She looked all right. Not fabulous—that wouldn't do for a salesgirl—but all right. She carried the expensive leather purse that Joseph had given Sari for their last anniversary. Her white gloves were immaculate.

An elderly saleswoman was speaking with two customers. Kitty stood in the back, waiting patiently until the saleswoman approached her.

"I'm here about the opening for a shop assistant."

"Oh, wonderful," said the woman eyeing Kitty's dress with appreciation. "Mr. Nagy would like to fill it as soon as possible."

Kitty was shown the office in the back, and introduced to the proprietor.

"Won't you have a seat," he said graciously.

Kitty sat, arranging her legs to best advantage. Mr. Nagy took it all in: the legs, the shoes, the purse, the cut of her dress.

"Well, then, have you any experience, Miss Lebow?"

"Oh, yes, Mr. Nagy. I have been employed at Mrs. Kandinsky's hat shop, in both design and sales. I have also worked for some time as an advisor to brides in selecting their trousseaux."

"Excellent, excellent. And do you speak foreign languages?" Even small towns like Janace received visitors from the many countries bordering Czechoslovakia .

"Yes, sir. Besides Slovak and Hungarian, I know Czech, Russian, and Polish. And I'm fluent in German." And Yiddish, of course, but she wasn't about to say so.

"Fluent?" These Jewish girls had the idea their Yiddish would pass, thought Nagy, until they actually spoke to a German. That could kill a sale faster than anything.

"Yes, sir. We used to spend summers in Vienna with my mother's family."

"Marvelous. And can you calculate the bills and write receipts?"

"Absolutely. I was first in my class in mathematics."

The interview was going well. He told her the salary and asked if it would do. Kitty's heart leaped. It was twice what she was making at Mrs. Kandinsky's.

Mr. Nagy asked when she could start, and when Kitty said immediately, he smiled.

"Well, I think that covers it all. Unless you can think of something, Miss Lebow. Otherwise, see you tomorrow morning."

Now. She had to tell him now. "Well, there is one thing, Mr. Nagy."

She swallowed, searching for the easiest words.

"Yes, Miss Lebow," said Nagy impatiently.

"I, I can't work on Saturdays."

"Saturdays? But that's impossible. Everyone works on Saturdays."

"Well, it's my Sabbath. But I can work extra hours every day. I can even come in on Sunday and clean up and do inventory. I can work twice as hard..."

"I'm sorry, but..."

"You can deduct a day—two days—from my salary..."

"Thank you for coming in, Miss Lebow, but this won't do. Should you decide to drop those silly old customs, please come by again."

Outside the shop, Kitty took off her gloves and dropped them in the purse. They soiled so easily, and never looked quite the same after you cleaned them.

She wanted to cry. It was so hard to be a Jew.

That year the New Bridge was completed. The Old Bridge was as sturdy as ever, but the New Bridge would lead Janace into the modern era of motorcars and trucks. The whole town was excited about the christening.

There was a nervous moment when the contractors couldn't finish their work within budget. But the merchants' association came to the rescue and paid the difference. The festivities were on. Then, disappointment: the ribbon-cutting was scheduled for a Saturday.

It had been a deliberate decision. The old mayor, who had led the town since Joseph's youth, was also the head of Janace's Anti-Semitic League. He figured the Jews wouldn't come on their rest day.

But they did come. They poured out of the synagogues and, dressed in Sabbath finery, arrived by the hundreds to the banks of the river.

The mayor surveyed the crowd of Jews and stamped his foot. "I won't have it!" he roared. "I'll stand here until I freeze to death, but I won't open this bridge until the Jews are gone from here."

Humiliated, the Jews went to their homes.

That night the merchants' association met in special session. Before the Great War the group had accepted no Jewish members, but after independence it was forced open to anyone who qualified. Once the Jews got in, though, the Gentiles left. Now the association was all Jewish.

Mechel Halter, a prominent bedding manufacturer, was furious. "This is intolerable! Who does that bastard mayor think he is? We Jews paid for that bridge!"

"Calm down, said Schneider, proprietor of a large tailor shop. "All the citizens of Janace have shared in this great project with their taxes."

"Hah!" said Halter. "Who pays the lion's share of taxes? And who made up the deficit?"

"No, no. The merchants' association is not a Jewish group," Schneider insisted. "Anyone can join. And I'm sure you remember, Mechel, the bad days, when we weren't allowed to. Be a little grateful."

"I tell you, we are paying to be insulted," growled Halter.

The mollifiers won out. The merchants' association never lodged a protest. On the contrary, it sent a congratulatory letter to the town council.

No reason to rock the boat, the merchants decided. After all, Jews had survived in Janace for hundreds of years, some of them horrific. Now, when things were so much better, why fuss over a trivial matter? Their neighbors would appreciate their humility. Surely it was worth the good will of the Christians in the years and decades to come.

"The truck is making a funny sound. I better take it in to the garage," said Joseph. The Ford was fifteen years old but in perfect condition, thanks to Joseph's careful maintenance. It had been bought with the money from Sari's dowry, and was their most valuable asset.

Kitty's eyes widened. "I'll come with you, Joseph. It's a fine day for a drive."

It was indeed a fine day, and the cab of the truck smelled pleasantly of apricots. Joseph talked about the Torah portion of the week, as he did with his wife.

Whenever Sari and Joseph rode together, he would talk about his constant studies, and she would analyze her secular readings. The couple spent their days in a private garden of the intellect. Kitty felt a bit out of place, and usually had no idea what they were talking about!

Joseph paused, as if to get Kitty's response to something. But her mind had wandered, and she said nothing. She snapped to. Her brother-in-law must think her an idiot.

He changed topics, smiling. Joseph thought: one could not wish for more in a daughter.

When they got to the garage, Sender Halter was just finishing up with a customer. Joseph got out and opened the cab door for Kitty.

A very high-heeled shoe appeared on the running board. Kitty's other leg slowly stretched down to reach the ground, revealing shapely calves, a tantalizing bit of thigh, and a pert bottom snugly encased in silk.

Suddenly, there were three mechanics present to attend to the truck. The biggest one pushed the others aside. "What's the problem here?"

Joseph looked toward Sender, who usually worked on the truck, but the beefy mechanic had been first, so it was only right to deal with him.

"Well, it's been making these flopping noises."

The mechanic leered at Kitty. Moving closer, he leaned over her. His very bulk was menacing. "Yeah, isn't it a pain when they make noise."

Kitty stood her ground as if her high heels had sunk into the cement floor. She held on to her hat as she looked up, glaring at the mechanic.

"If this job is too menial for you…"

The big mechanic swaggered over to Joseph's truck and opened the hood. Seconds later he was back. He ogled Kitty again, but then spoke over her head to Joseph, as if she didn't exist. "Looks bad. It's gonna cost you."

Joseph sighed in resignation.

"What, exactly, is the problem?" asked Kitty.

The mechanic had an ugly smile. "Well," he said suggestively, "want to come with me and look?"

"Sure," she snapped, "and afterwards we can go sew some ribbons onto my hats."

Joseph stepped in quickly. "Would you please explain the problem to me?"

The mechanic snorted, then spat to the side, barely missing Kitty's shoe. "Your torsion belt is shot."

Joseph frowned. "Excuse me. I haven't heard of this torsion belt before. Would it be possible for Mr. Halter to explain…"

Sender was now standing at his side.

"You don't need the Jew mechanic for your Jew truck."

"No?" said Kitty. "Are you sure this 'torsion belt' isn't unique to Jews? Like a ram's horn or a Torah scroll?"

In the mechanic's face lust melted into rage. He lifted a clenched fist.

Sender quickly put his arm out to take the blow, but the bully bowed out.

"Bitch," he growled, slinking away.

Sender stepped back, relieved that there had been no physical confrontation, but Kitty had still not moved from her place.

What courage! That lout hadn't even made her flinch.

When he greeted Joseph Wasserman, she did not step back meekly, the way other girls did. She was modest—her chic outfit was in keeping with Jewish tradition—yet she was so close to him that he was dizzy with the scent of citrus cologne and apricots.

Joseph shook Sender's hand with both of his.

"Good to see you, too, Reb Joseph." Sender managed to stammer, "And how is Mrs. Wassermann?"

Kitty looked over "Baron Alexander" while the men talked. His eyes were as blue as wood violets, bristled with black lashes, circumflexed by strong, arched brows. His mechanic's overalls were spotlessly clean. Sender's voice was musical, and his Yiddish refined and sweet.

"My Sari is fine, thank God. May I introduce my sister-in-law, Kitty. She's the youngest of the famous Lebow sisters. 'Last of all, beloved of all,'" Joseph said in Hebrew, beaming. "Kitty, meet the best mechanic in Czechoslovakia."

"How do you do?" she said. Her voice was throaty, confident.

Kitty's broad-brimmed hat now covered everything but the tip of her nose and her lips, shiny with raisin-colored lipstick. Her skin—what Sender could see of it—was smooth and matte. Throughout the nasty exchange with the brutish mechanic, she hadn't even perspired!

Words were spoken, but Sender couldn't register what was said. No doubt something about the truck. He hoped he wasn't making a fool of himself to Wassermann.

It was a relief to be able to duck his head under the truck's hood and take some time to collect his thoughts. Unfortunately, there wasn't much wrong with the vehicle. He had to get back out.

She was nearby, smoothing out her skirt. How tiny and trim she was, yet fully a woman. In his mind's eye she seemed to take up all the space, as if the physical Kitty was just a small core of a big, radiant being. Sender's throat felt raw, as if he had inhaled diesel fumes.

"So the 'torsion' is all right?" she said with mock gravity.

He chuckled. This Kitty was not only fearless, she saw the humor in a situation that would have depressed almost anyone else. Sender thought of the biblical Woman of Valor: "she is dressed in strength and glory, and laughs at the days to come."

Reluctantly, he turned to Joseph. "My colleague must have made a mistake. It's just a slipped fan belt." His eyes moved involuntarily to Kitty, and he thought: I've got to get a look under that hat brim or...

"Thank God. What do I owe you, Sender?"

"It was really nothing, no parts, no real adjustments. The shop charges a one crown minimum for service, but really, this was more of a social call." *And then I'll be obliged to return it.*

"No, no Sender. We don't want to antagonize the boss. A crown is fine, and a lot less than I expected. You fixed it so I can use the truck today so that's worth money right there. And peace of mind."

"I won't take money for your peace of mind. That's my obligation to you, according to the Torah."

"I insist you take the money."

Joseph and Kitty got back in the truck. Sender stared at Kitty's leg, revealed again, just as it was when she alighted. He clutched a wrench as hard as he could.

In the truck Kitty said "That's quite unusual, isn't it, a Jewish mechanic?"

"And a God-fearing Jew, too."

"It must be a pretty good line of work. There are more and more cars all the time. Soon it'll be just like in America, with every family owning one of its own."

"Not so fast, Kitty. I, for one, still miss the old days with horses and wagons. Maybe they'll come back."

Sari had told her that when Joseph sold the horses he had cried. So Kitty refrained from saying how ridiculous it was to expect the world to reverse itself. "Whatever the future, an expert mechanic should be able to make a good living."

"You would think. But poor Sender has held the same position at the garage for years, while less qualified men move up."

"Why is that?"

"At least two reasons. One, he is too honest."

"And the other?"

Joseph smiled sadly at the injustice of the Diaspora.

A man like Sender should have his own shop, Kitty thought. An honest mechanic would win customers in the long run, not just Jews but Gentiles, too. Her dowry would make a down-payment on a garage. Not a huge one, but one that...Especially if she ran the office, handled the books. They could make a fine living. They might well prosper.

Kitty leaned back in her seat and enjoyed the passing view. Joseph dropped her off at the house.

"You have regards from Sender Halter," Kitty told Sari.

"How nice. He is the sweetest boy. And so handsome."

"Yes, that's what I thought," Kitty said carefully.

"Oh no. Get him out of your mind, darling. He's not for you."

What was this, a conspiracy?

"Really? I thought he rather liked me. And Joseph sings his praises."

"I've got nothing against him. But his family's in a difficult situation. He's in no position to support a wife."

"What? But he's an expert mechanic, and experienced."

"I hate to gossip, but Kitty, you need to know the facts about the Halters. Sender has two older sisters. When it was time for them to marry, the parents found two wonderful boys, real stars, brilliant, learned young men. The parents were determined to get them for sons-in-law. And they did."

"So what's the problem?"

"Such stars are meant for the daughters of rich men, and there were other, wealthy families bidding for the same two fellows. The Halters hadn't saved that sort of money for dowries, so they borrowed. That's always a mistake. At the time the father had a good job as a supervisor at the brick works, and the mother brings in a few crowns selling healing herbs. They expected to pay off the debts in five or so years.

"Unfortunately, the father had a heart attack. He's had to take light work that barely puts food on the table. Sender is the main support of the family, and his younger brother also helps out, but it will be a long time before the debts are paid."

"That's sad, but it sounds like they have the problem under control. Eventually, the debt will be paid off. Meanwhile, they just live a little more frugally."

"No, there's more. The oldest in the family is a brother, and he got divorced."

"Goodness! Why?"

"Who knows. You never get a straight answer to that question. Meanwhile, not only is it a shame on the family, but he had to give her dowry back when they divorced, so he's in financial trouble, too. Plus, while he lives at his parents' house he still has to support his ex-wife and children. It's a nightmare."

"It is sad. But I don't see what's so impossible about Sender's marrying. It would just mean another cup of water in the soup."

"Not quite. There's a younger sister, too. When—I'd hate to say if— they pay off the debt, they will have to start saving up for her dowry. It won't be what the sisters got, but still, a girl needs *something*. As it stands, she doesn't have a penny. And they'd never let one of the boys marry before the sister is married off. They're respectable people, after all."

CHAPTER FIVE

It was Sunday and raining hard. Joseph was in the House of Study and Sari was wrapped in a comforter, reading Kant. Kitty had planned to go to Rachel-Leah's but the weather was so foul she stayed home and sewed for charity instead.

The Society for Honoring the Bride provided for poor girls who could not afford to get married. They had asked Kitty to sew some nightgowns for an orphan bride marrying an orphan groom. Kitty had been given money for cotton flannel, but when she got to the fabric shop, she was struck by the beauty of a bolt of shimmering silk. Deciding to make the bride one truly magnificent nightgown, Kitty bought the silk with her own money.

In keeping with the rules of the Society, Kitty didn't know the bride's identity, but aqua was a color that suited almost everyone. She smiled as she sewed, fantasizing the young couple feeling the delicious charmeuse between their bodies.

She bit off a thread. Why, she wondered, didn't the Halters avail themselves of the services of the Society to marry off their youngest daughter? Probably too proud, she concluded. The Baron did not spring from common stock. Even so, pride is a poor substitute for a husband.

Sari and Kitty both heard the car pull up in a great splash of rainwater. They dropped what they were doing and ran to the window. It was a taxi, a rare sight on their street. A black umbrella fanned out at the taxi's door, shrouding the woman who emerged and headed straight for their house. The wind slapped the umbrella in her face, and forced her to struggle forward. At last she reached the front steps. Before she had a chance to knock, Sari and Kitty flung open the door.

"Renee!" they shouted simultaneously. They gripped her in a pincer embrace and kissed her wet face.

"I'll tell the driver to bring in your bags," said Sari. "Kitty, put up some tea."

"No, no," Renee said. "There's no time. I've only come to say goodbye."

"Goodbye?" said Kitty. "But where are you going?"

"To Israel!" said Renee, and the word made her face shine.

"So the visas finally came through!" said Sari. "Give thanks to the Almighty!"

Renee's face darkened. "No. They never came."

"I don't understand. No visas? But then how can you go?"

"There is a group of us, mostly from the movement, but some German Jews as well. We've chartered a fishing boat from Marseilles."

"Marseilles," Sari repeated, as if in a spelling bee. "But where does it go?"

"I can't tell you exactly. Somewhere north of Tel Aviv. A coastal inlet poorly patrolled by the British."

"You mean illegally?" asked Kitty. What a thrilling plan!

"That is simply insane," said Sari.

"There is no other way."

"What do you mean? Where's the fire? Why can't you wait for the visas like a normal person?"

"Where's the fire? All of Europe will soon be burning. There's no time to lose. Oh, Sari, you've all got to come with me too!"

"You're out of your head."

"Then Kitty. Let Kitty come with me."

"I don't want to go," Kitty said immediately. Leave Czechoslovakia? Leave her family and friends? Leave her job? Did they even have hat shops in Palestine? To say nothing of a certain beautiful baron.

"What does Benny say about this craziness?" said Sari. "Where is Benny, anyway? Why isn't he with you?"

"Benny Fruchter is no longer my husband."

Sari staggered back, as if she'd been punched. "Kitty," she croaked, "go to your room."

Kitty left immediately. In her room she had discovered a hidden alcove. She had cleaned it out and found that it ended in a grilled opening right over the nexus of living room, dining room, and kitchen.

Kitty wiggled up the alcove and looked down through the grill. From this vantage she could see and hear without being seen. It was even better than being present at the conversation. Sari and Renee, without her young ears to protect, would speak freely.

"Now let me get this straight. You and Benny had a spat, right? My dear, it happens in every marriage."

"We've had no spat. I've always made it plain that I would go to Eretz Yisrael. Benny said he shared that goal, so we married. He lied, and the marriage is dissolved."

"He's only being reasonable, Renee. He loves the Land of Israel, just as you do. When the visas come through, he'll go. And Eva and Martin, too, so you'll have kinfolk to help you. It's hard enough to settle in Palestine with family, but at least it's a possibility. On your own you are doomed to failure. You can't blame Benny for not joining you in this scatterbrained scheme."

"You needn't defend him, Sari. He did well enough defending himself."

"I'm not taking his part. It's you I care about. How can you break up a marriage on such flippant grounds? God himself weeps over a divorcing couple."

"I'm sure he cries more about stubbornness and self-destruction."

"Renee, Renee. Tell me, sister, can you really give up love for politics?"

"It's a little late in the game for you to speak of love, Sari," Renee said.

In the alcove, Kitty held her breath. Renee and Martin Blumenthal had been friends since childhood, and then co-leaders of the Zionist club. They had been of one mind about the world and the future. Everyone always assumed that Renee and Martin would marry.

But then came the biggest shock to the family since Father's sudden death. Martin asked to marry not Renee but Eva! Eva, who didn't even attend Zionist meetings, whose interests were comfort and luxury, not pioneering utopias. And she was younger than Renee, too.

The family was thrust into chaos. With Father dead and Mother very ill, it fell to Sari to marry her sisters off properly. Sari, Martha, and Helen had all had rational, old-fashioned marriages, with parents and matchmakers finding just the right lid for each oddly shaped pot. But how was Sari to work out a solution from the tangled skein of the younger girls' love lives?

Fortunately, Benny Fruchter was waiting in the wings. He too had been a Zionist, faithfully attending meetings, adoring Renee from afar, although he knew he had no chance of coming between the club's co-presidents. Now he was provided a perfect opportunity. Sari quickly arranged the match with Benny, and Renee did not protest. Finally, to Sari's great relief, both sisters were married, in proper age order.

"Come, come Renee. You know Benny loves you, as you love him."

"Love me? No, I don't think he ever did. He worshipped me from a distance because someone else had me. He wanted a Lebow girl, wanted to be a Lebow's husband. You know, we always get best in class. You've got Joseph, the most learned in Torah, Martha has Ignatz, the richest, Helen has Thomas, the smartest. Benny wanted to be part of us. But I don't call that love.

"As for me, I don't think I've ever loved any man. No, not really. I've known real love, I love the Land, but I've never loved a man like that."

"Never? Not even...Martin?"

"No, not Martin. I realize that now. I was lucky not to get him. Martin is a weak man, and weak men cannot survive as Jews."

"Then it's not as if your heart belonged to another. You can forget past foolishness, go back to Benny, start fresh, build a life together."

"You aren't listening to me, Sari. The divorce is done. I have the writ in hand." Renee reached for her purse.

Sari put her hand over the clasp. "You can still reconcile."

"No, my path is clear. It leads forward, not back to Benny."

"Please, Renee, divorce is horribly destructive. You'll never live it down."

"I don't care. I know what I have to do, and I am doing it."

"If you won't consider yourself, consider the family. No Lebow has ever been divorced, nor anyone from Mother's family, either. This will be an indelible stain on our honor. Think of Kitty. Who will marry her, with this blight on her background?"

In the alcove Kitty thought: some fellow with a divorced sibling of his own.

"And surely she already has enough strikes against her in finding a husband."

The grate burned across Kitty's cheek like a branding iron.

"I suppose she'll have to find a man who will value her for her own sake. I love her, but I can't exchange my life for hers."

"Your life? What sort of life can you lead? How long do you think the dowry money will last you?"

"There is no dowry money. I didn't get it back."

"What are you saying? Everyone gets dowry money back in a divorce. Unless they committed adul..."

Sari fainted dead away. Kitty jumped and was about to run down to help, but Renee quickly revived Sari and got her some water.

"No, I'm not an adulteress. Just the victim of extortion, I'm afraid. Benny was so angry, he threatened to contest. And his parents egged him on, too."

"Renee, tell me." Kitty had to strain to hear Sari. "He didn't give *anything* back?"

"No. Nothing. The devil take him. I don't care for myself, but when I think how Father and Mother saved for us..."

"Listen, Renee, there is something I have to tell you. When we arranged the wedding, Benny's parents...they wanted more."

"More money? But it was a very generous dowry!"

"Still. They threatened to call off the whole thing. We had to give them what they asked for. To avoid a scandal. To avoid destroying your happiness, and Eva's."

"But Father was already dead, and he'd left us each an equal portion. What more could you give the Fruchters?"

Sari looked as if she would faint again. "The house," she whispered, but Kitty could hear all too well. "We gave them the proceeds from the house."

"I think I'll have that tea after all," said Renee. She went to the kitchen and came back with steaming cups. They sipped in silence for a while.

Sari put the warm cup to her temple, then the other. "So you see, honey, you must go back."

"No. I'm horrified and I'm sorry, but this changes nothing. I can't go back to Benny."

"At least return to Kosice and petition the rabbinical court. They will certainly rule for you about the money."

"Yes, in five years, or ten. I can't wait. I'm leaving on that ship from Marseilles."

"Selfish! Stubborn! Don't you understand what this family sacrificed for you? Can't you even spare a few months, a year or two? How can you be so disloyal?"

Renee put on her coat and gathered her still-dripping umbrella.

"There's nothing more to talk about. The taxi is waiting."

Suddenly Sari was standing at her full height. Her voice rang out with power. "If you leave now, Renee, I will never speak to you again as long as I live."

Renee walked slowly to the door. She turned and looked at her sister. "I'm sorry, Sari. Sorry for 'the sins of which we are aware, and for the sins of which we are unaware.'" It was the solemn confession from the service of the Day of Atonement.

It was a struggle to navigate through the wind to the taxi. Once

Renee got into the back seat, she was startled to find Kitty there.

"You're soaking little one, you'll catch your death of a cold."

"Here, Renee, take this." Kitty handed her a one-crown coin. "Give this or money of equal value to a poor person in the Holy Land."

Renee smiled and kissed her sister's wet head. It was an ancient custom to appoint a traveler as an agent of charity. According to the Talmud, "a holy messenger shall never be harmed."

Renee opened her purse and dug into it, but there was no money there other than the carefully counted bills for the taxi, the train, and ship's passage. In her coat pocket, however, she found two pennies.

"And you deliver these for me, Kitty. Please put these or money of equal value in the charity box—at the ritual bathhouse."

Kitty laughed with delight. The ritual bath was for married women.

Eva opened her sewing basket and took out a pair of pinking shears. Then she removed the top tray of thread spools. In the bottom of the box was a thick envelope postmarked Prague. The package was embossed with the royal coat of arms of England. It was still sealed.

Eva cut the envelope crudely with the heavy scissors, which were powerful and sharp, able to bite through several layers of the coarsest cloth. Paper and cardboard offered the shears little resistance.

A photograph of herself fell out of the mutilated envelope. Eva sighed. It was a flattering shot, so rare in passport pictures. But she couldn't risk keeping it. She cut the photo and the rest of the envelope and its contents into confetti-sized pieces.

After she was done, she carefully swept up the debris and deposited it in the stove. Then she lit the fire, and waited till the papers burned down to the coals. When she was satisfied that no shred remained, she closed the stove door.

She winced in annoyance. Her hands were filthy from the stove. In Ruhigbad she would get a maid to do this kind of dirty work.

CHAPTER SIX

Ruhigbad

"What are you doing?" asked Eva.

"What do you *think* I'm doing," Martin replied curtly. He was carrying a hammer, a box of nails, and several small brass tubes.

Eva let her big blue eyes fill up with tears, like an aquarium being replenished. "How can you speak to me in that tone of voice?"

Martin frowned. "We've lived here almost a month. We need to put up the *mezuzahs*." The tubes contained tiny parchment scrolls with passages from the Torah about God's unity. They belonged on every Jewish doorpost.

"Yes, yes, I know. But not on the front door. Please, Martin, not there."

"The front door is the most important. How else will people know this is a Jewish home?"

"That's it, Martin. This neighborhood is ninety percent German. We're the only Jews in sight. It's a provocation."

"It was your idea to live here. Do you think I like walking an hour to the synagogue? Having to take a tram to the House of Study?"

"I was only trying to save our money." The aquarium started to fill again. "An apartment in the Jewish neighborhood costs half again as much."

She sure is thrifty—with *her* money, Martin thought. Palestine or no Palestine, he'd never see a penny of that dowry. Meanwhile, she made his wages vanish like a magician's rabbit.

"Yes dear," he said. "I appreciate that. Sorry."

He said the blessing and put up the first mezuzah at the entrance to their bedroom. Then he put the others up. Finally he had just one left, and stood at the front door, hesitating.

"Please Martin-kins, don't put it up there."

Martin looked at the mezuzah in his hand. "Why can't we post it? Our ancestors did, everywhere in the world that they lived. And here we are in Czechoslovakia, a free country, and I have to be ashamed?"

"It's just a matter of courtesy to our neighbors, that's important too, according to the Torah. Isn't it?"

"Why should we be courteous to them? They're beasts." The week before he'd had to rescue a blind woman from some loutish youths who had tried to trick her into walking into traffic. That wasn't so remarkable in itself; teenage boys will act wild. But afterwards a whole mob of local shopkeepers and housewives came out and shouted curses at him. "Slav bastard," they screamed, "who are you to spoil our fun?"

And that was assuming he was a Czech. God knows what they would have done had they known he was a Jew.

"Oh, the Germans aren't so bad," said Eva.

No, he thought. Not to you. You look just like them, and with the Germans, looks are everything. Once he too had been mesmerized by her Aryan face, he thought, ashamed. Now he wondered why yellow hair and an upturned nose were supposed to be so beautiful. Who decided these things?

"The Kreutzers next door, for example. They're really sweet," Eva trilled.

Martin sighed. It couldn't be much longer before they'd get the British visas to Eretz Yisrael. He could hardly wait. In a Jewish country his neighbors wouldn't automatically be "sweet" just because they didn't participate in pogroms.

"Oh, Martin-kins, don't look so sour." Eva was standing in the doorway to the bedroom. She put up her hand to touch the newly posted mezuzah and brought it to her lips. Kissing the mezuzah was a gesture of the pious.

But instead of a reverent kiss, Eva licked her fingers lasciviously.

Martin pulled her into the bedroom and shut the door, hating himself.

Ignatz Rosen had learned the crafting of cloth from his father and expected to pass it on to his sons. The next generation would add to centuries of experience, he thought with pride. When the two eldest Rosen boys attended yeshiva they were able to illuminate the numerous Talmudic passages about the production of linen and of wool. Their knowledge of fabric and fibers, of weaving and dying, went beyond that of the sagest rabbis; it was in their bones.

Ignatz couldn't prove the family had been in textiles since Bible times, but he did have a letter from King Ottokar II, dated 1266, granting the Rosen's ancestor permission to operate a commercial loom in the nearby city of Cheb.

But over the centuries the Jews of the city were tormented, humiliated and slaughtered. Again and again they would be expelled, then grudgingly allowed to return. To this day the street running through the Jewish neighborhood was named Murder Lane.

The survivors of the first bloodbath were an elderly man and a middle-aged widow, who married and managed to produce a son, the progenitor of the Rosen clan. In 1364, the townspeople, after a period of economic depression, invited the family's return, along with other Jews. To show their good faith, they permitted the building of a synagogue and the establishment of a Jewish cemetery.

Finally, in the nineteenth century, the government promised some safety, but anti-Semitism remained so ingrained in the area that the Rosens cautiously built their new factories not in Cheb proper but in nearby areas. Their flagship was just outside the picturesque spa town of Ruhigbad. Somehow a resort seemed less forbidding, its citizens not quite as hard-hearted, as in industrial or rural areas.

Ignatz gave Martin a job as a bookkeeper in the accounting department. Martin had assumed he would loathe this work, but he quickly came to appreciate Ignatz's generosity. The job paid well and was mildly challenging, but not daunting. And neither his skill nor his ambitions were great enough to threaten the senior accountants.

Working in that department opened Martin's eyes to what was truly happening in the region. He was shocked to see that the company had not made a profit in over a decade, and that it was now operating at a loss.

The company had tried everything to keep afloat but who needed new clothing when there wasn't enough to eat? They produced cheaper and cheaper fabrics, they catered to the world's only growth industry, armies, by supplying uniforms for many of the countries created by the Great War. They experimented with the new man-made yarns. But all these efforts had little effect. All the other textile factories in the area had closed, and the future looked grim.

Martin was deeply concerned. Ignatz had treated him more than fairly; he was as warm as a brother. In the synagogue, where Ignatz was a respected officer, he was introduced as "my brother-in-law, the pioneer, preparing to go to the Holy Land." Ignatz made the departure for Palestine seem imminent, although Martin now despaired of ever receiving the visas.

"You know," Ignatz said, his arm around Martin's shoulder, a dreamy look in his eye, "if things go well in Palestine, maybe you can scout out a location for a branch of Rosen & Sons. Wouldn't that be something! Our own firm, in Eretz Yisrael."

Martin shook his head skeptically. "I don't know Ignatz. I don't think the British will allow Jewish investors. It annoys the Arabs."

"But we'd employ Arabs as well as Jews. Same as we employ Germans and Czechs and Jews here at home."

"Since when do Jew haters care about their own welfare, Ignatz?"

"You're too young to be so cynical, Martin. People are basically good at heart. Treat them with respect and they will return the favor."

Martin hoped that that was true, for Ignatz's sake. Rosen & Sons' policy was never to fire workers without cause. Nor were wages lowered as demand for product decreased and employees worked fewer hours. Ignatz said it had been the tradition of the family, a tradition based in Jewish law. They never, in all their history, had betrayed loyal workers. But Martin was sure it couldn't go on much longer.

Because of their distance from the synagogue, and the prohibition of travel on the Sabbath, Eva and Martin stayed at the Rosens' house every week. Martin, more than an ordinary worker, lived for the weekend.

"It's so kind of your sister and Ignatz to host us all the time."

"You're such a sucker, Martin. Martha is just showing off that big house."

"Come on, it's a lot of work for her. And every week..."

"What's the big deal? She has three maids."

"Just two maids and a part-time laundress. That's not so much, really, with seven children."

"The two older boys are in yeshiva all week. And the girls all help out."

"It's still a lot of work. And she does all the cooking, and cares for the babies by herself."

"Because she doesn't trust the Gentile help. Really! What are they going to do, shove the little ones into the oven, like in 'Hansel and Gretel?'"

"A Jewish woman should supervise the cooking and the children's care. You can't depend on a Gentile to follow the Torah; it's hard enough for us."

"Oh, Martha probably just wants to hang around the kitchen so she can eat. Did you see what a cow she's become?"

"Come on, Eva. She's almost forty, practically old enough to be a grandmother. And her cooking is delicious. Like yours." Luscious, spicy Austro-Hungarian kosher cuisine was admired by Jews everywhere, but lately Eva had been experimenting with the blander fare of the region. He wasn't happy about it.

"Anyway, please don't bad-mouth your sister. Martha's a fine woman of the old school. Like my mother was. And your mother, may they rest in peace."

"Martha certainly sees herself as Mother's heir. Did you notice her prayer book?"

"No. What's so special about it?"

"It's Mother's. The cover is real ivory, and the clasps are silver. Sari should have gotten it. She's the oldest. And the most pious. It wasn't right of Martha to grab it."

"Oh, I'm sure Sari didn't mind. Those heirlooms should be passed on for generations, mother to daughter. Like..." Martin thought of the fine china his mother had left his sister. Better not to mention it. Eva might figure out some way to lay claim to it.

Often the Blumenthals lingered at the Rosens through Sunday. One week, as usual, the two oldest boys left for the yeshiva and Ignatz and Martin sat smoking their pipes and talking politics. Malvine and Clara, fourteen and fifteen, were playing duets on the piano. Ten-year-old Vera, who resembled her mother in looks and personality, was entertaining the little boys with soap bubbles. Martha relaxed on a chaise, sighing happily at the domestic bliss around her.

Eva, thinking no one would miss her, went exploring. She had never been shown the master bedroom. It was enormous and airy looking, all gilded white furniture and pale blue draperies. The two beds were separated by a night table. How Orthodox, she thought, and snorted.

Eva sat down on the throne-like chair of the dressing table. *She* would have had a bedroom like this, if things had been different. If only Father and Mother had been around to arrange an advantageous marriage for her. Instead, she was left at the mercies of Sari and her fanatic husband. It was thanks to their stupidity that she had ended up married to a loser.

There was a velvet jewel case on the dresser. Eva opened it. It contained the ruby necklace and earrings that Martha had worn on the Sabbath. Eva put them on. The jewels glowered in the afternoon light.

She moved her head from side to side, admiring her appearance. People thought sapphires were best for blondes, but they were wrong.

Blood-red rubies made a more dramatic presentation against her porcelain skin.

Suddenly the door opened and Martha came in. Eva struggled to open the necklace clasp, and failing to do that, tried to hide the rubies with her arms.

"Oh, there you are," Martha laughed. "We've been looking all over for you." She laughed again. "Eva. You're just like my girls, always playing dress-up with my things." She kissed the top of Eva's head.

Eva recovered her breath. "You shouldn't leave valuables lying around where anyone could take them."

"You're right. Let me put them in the safe."

Martha removed a small painting to reveal a combination lock. "Come, Eva, you try it. I want you to memorize the numbers. We make all the children learn the combination as soon as they're old enough to take on the responsibility."

"You want *me* to learn it?"

"I think it's a good idea." Martha's face clouded. "They say there is war coming. Anything can happen. Teach Martin the combination, too. Just in case."

Eva thought her sister was insane, but she eagerly memorized the numbers. "All right, but nothing's happened. The door hasn't opened. Where *is* the door?"

Martha laughed mischievously, as if she were playing a game with the little boys. She walked over to a full-length mirror and moved it aside. There was the faintest outline of a door in the wall. Pressing the floorboards directly under it, Martha opened the safe. It was deep and dark, but Eva could see other velvet jewel boxes, and stacks of ingots, and bundles of American dollars.

"Isn't this ingenious?" said Martha. "Only the lock across the room will open it. Otherwise, you can't get at the safe unless you blast out the entire wall."

"May I come in Frau Kreutzer?"

"If you wish."

Eva admired her next-door neighbor's cool demeanor. Compared to the older woman, she must seem terribly florid and emotional. Terribly Jewish. "Oh, I see you're about to have dinner. I'm not disturbing you, am I?"

"No. Herr Kreutzer is finished with his meal and is taking a nap."

Eva thought Frau Kreutzer was charmingly old-fashioned. She had all these cute, country ways, like referring to her husband as "mister."

She also served Herr Kreutzer his meals, standing by until he was done. Only then did she eat herself.

"My, that looks delicious," said Eva. It didn't really, but she was making conversation. It took an effort. Frau Kreutzer was from rural Germany, and hadn't had the benefits of much education.

"Want some?"

"I've had lunch, but thank you, I will have a bite." Eva was so excited. After all these visits Frau Kreutzer was finally offering her food.

Frau Kreutzer cut a slice of meat and put it on a plate. "I'm kind of surprised that you'd take it, this being pork and all."

Eva stared at the food. So that's what it was! Her heart beat hard in her chest. She would try it at long last. Why not? All the world enjoyed this meat, but her people denied themselves for no reason at all. Well, she would break that chain of foolishness.

"Why wouldn't I take it?" asked Eva, pretending not to understand.

"Your being Jewish and all," said Frau Kreutzer.

"My *husband* is Jewish," said Eva. She cut a geometric piece of meat.

"Oh!" said Frau Kreutzer. "I *thought* you looked like an Aryan. I said to Herr Kreutzer, 'mark my words, that's not a real Jewess,' I said. And you speak such good German, too. But tell me, how did your parents let you marry one of them?"

"My parents are dead," said Eva, putting a forkful of pork in her mouth.

She chewed thoughtfully. Not bad. But not very good either. Bland, ordinary. Was this what all the fuss had been about?

"Ah, I understand," said Frau Kreutzer. "These are hard times. No one can blame you for doing what you did. Just the other week we had to turn away Herr Kreutzer's nephew Frederick from Pilsen. He just got married and came here looking for work. He applied at Rosen's, but of course the bloodsucking Jew turned him away. My husband said he wouldn't give the boy a penny. What a nerve to marry without a job. Let him lie in the bed he made."

Frau Kreutzer stabbed a piece of meat and chewed it hard. Eva wondered that she ate at all, she was so skinny. With her long, sharp nose and the wart on her chin, Frau Kreutzer lacked only a buckled hat to look like a character in the Brothers Grimm.

"What excellent pork," Eva lied. "You must tell me your butcher."

Frau Kreutzer shrugged. "Otto Schwartz. But keep an eye on him, he's a terrible thief." She clamped her mouth, finished eating, and took away the dishes, which she began washing immediately.

Eva smiled. How nice to just start and stop a meal as one pleased! At home there was washing and blessing, and then the long, long Grace after Meals.

Frau Kreutzer dried the dishes and placed them precisely into the cupboard. Eva watched with envy. What a pleasure to have only one set of dishes, not to have to separate constantly between dairy and meat.

Finally, Mrs. Kreutzer sat down. "I can't tell you what a relief it is to find out you're not a Jew," she said.

Eva cleared her throat. "And you, are you Catholic or Protestant, Mrs. Kreutzer?"

"A pox on the lot of them, Eva. We used to be faithful Catholics, not knowing any better. But when our Elsa died, the damn priest just didn't understand..."

Eva looked up in horror. "You had a child who...died?"

"Yes," said Frau Kreutzer.

"Oh, I'm so very sorry!"

Frau Kreutzer shrugged, her eyes dry. Eva was more impressed than ever. To remain so cool and collected in the face of catastrophe...

"Anyway, Christianity is just so much Jewish nonsense," said Frau Kreutzer. "We Nordic people must return to our roots, to the old ways."

"Something new for dinner?" asked Martin.

"Yes, veal."

"It's so expensive."

"I got it for half price!" Eva shouted, throwing down a dishtowel.

"Oh, I'm sure you did. Sorry. It's just that we should be saving up for Palestine..."

"Shut up and eat, I can't stand all this stupid talk during meals. Germans never do that. The Germans..."

"All right, all right. Sorry. You don't have to be so sensitive."

Eva thought she would explode with impatience as Martin washed and blessed and salted his bread and blessed and...

Finally, Martin took a bite of the meat. He moved it around in his mouth, washing away the sauce in which it was bathed. Suddenly, he spat the meat right onto the tablecloth.

"Martin! You're acting like an animal."

"This meat is spoiled. It's more than spoiled, it's rotten. Take it right back to the butcher tomorrow. It's an outrage. How can he sell such stuff?"

Eva took a quick bite. "I don't think there's anything wrong with it."

"Even at half-price, this veal..." There was a heavy self-imposed tax on kosher meat, which helped finance the needs of the town's Jewish community.

"You hate me! I try to do everything for you, to feed your stupid face the best dishes, but nothing pleases you, nothing. You just hate me!"

"Oh, no. No, don't say that, darling. I'm sorry, I..."

Martin picked up his fork and forced the stinking meat down his throat.

CHAPTER SEVEN

Janace

Rachel-Leah and Chaim were well into their honeymoon year and had never cooked a meal for a Sabbath or holiday. With large families offering invitations, there was no end in sight to this traditional privilege. But they pounced on Aunt Sari's invitation for Saturday dinner, although they had already eaten at her home several times. There was business to discuss.

Sari, Joseph, and Kitty raised their eyebrows. All work is prohibited on the Sabbath—except the teaching of children and the arrangement of matches. There were no kids in sight.

"Who?" asked Sari and Kitty in unison.

"Ladies, please," said Joseph, "Rachel-Leah and Chaim have barely been seated. Let's show a bit of hospitality."

"Oh, Uncle Joseph, I can barely hold it in," said Rachel-Leah.

"Well in that case..."

"It's Dr. Adler!"

"The dentist?" asked Joseph.

"No other."

"For Kitty?" asked Sari.

"No, for my grandmother. Of course for Kitty."

Kitty's heart said: If I can't have Sender, then I don't want anyone. Her mouth said, "You can't be serious, Rachel-Leah. What would Dr. Adler want with me?"

The dentist was Janace's most eligible bachelor. He was, of course, unusually bright. The Jewish quota at universities was extremely small. More amazing was that Dr. Adler was still an Orthodox Jew. It was a given that when a young man went off to university he was lost to assimilation. When Helen's husband, Thomas, was admitted to Heidelberg, both sets of parents forbade the move to Germany. Yet Adler had defied the odds. He had returned to Janace and to the ways of his people.

"What do you mean? You're perfect for him. You're bright, vivacious, from the very best of families—and the most stylish girl in town. Who would be more suitable for a God-fearing dentist's wife?"

"But you haven't actually spoken to him about me?"

"Kitty, I hardly speak of anything else. Not that it's easy, with drills in my mouth."

"Recently?"

Rachel-Leah groaned. She had terrible teeth. All but the front uppers were capped with gold crowns.

"My wife carries her dowry in her mouth," Chaim said, but in a way that implied this was some special talent. They gazed, liquid-eyed, at each other.

"So he asked about me?"

"Not only did he ask about you, but he wanted to know details about your father, may his memory be a blessing. And about what sort of men your sisters married."

"So everything is set," Kitty said evenly.

"Of course not, silly," said Rachel-Leah. "Even Hasidic people get to check out the 'merchandise' before the wedding."

"I meant for a meeting."

"Oh! Yes. He'll be here tomorrow afternoon, at three."

What was there to say about Dr. Adler? It wasn't as if there was anything glaringly wrong with him. It was the small annoyances that irritated Kitty.

Dr. Adler dressed no worse than any young fellow with no female to advise him, but it drove Kitty mad that he wore his pants tightly suspendered, like an old man holding up a pot belly. The dentist's looks were typical of redheads. Ginger hair, freckles, rust-colored eyes. For someone in love, those features might have seemed adorable, but Kitty was revolted. Adler didn't seem to notice, which infuriated Kitty all the more.

She tried to hint to Sari about her feelings. But Sari heard nothing, as if she herself were in love. She *was* in love—with the idea that Kitty and Dr. Adler were a celestially ordered pair. Sometimes Kitty felt that Joseph, though male, middle-aged, and old-fashioned, better intuited her mind than her own beloved sister.

There was no telling Rachel-Leah, either. How could she complain to her friend about Dr. Adler's looks? Compared to Chaim he was Gary Cooper. Besides, Rachel-Leah was now a firm believer in the inevitability of marriage first, love later.

And who was she, Kitty thought, to judge another by the yardstick of beauty?

Dr. Adler came calling, as regular as a tax collector. He took Kitty to what few cultural events were held in Janace. Mostly, they strolled on Main Street, the dentist and his beautifully dressed companion. He dispensed dignified nods to patients and acquaintances, stopping to charm the wealthy and prominent.

After several weeks of courting, Dr. Adler announced that he would be coming around the following day in his automobile.

"Imagine," breathed Sari, "a private car. Like a diplomat, or an American."

Adler opened the passenger door for Kitty. She had the feeling that it was as much to guard his car from what harm she could inflict as to show gallantry.

The dentist drove very slowly. They rode in silence.

"What's that?" said Kitty.

"What's what?"

"That sound."

"What sound?"

Kitty did an imitation of poor Mr. Hochberg whom she had tended recently on behalf of the Committee for Visiting the Sick. Mr. Hochberg, a retired coal delivery man, smoked Turkish tobacco and took snuff.

"I don't hear it."

Kitty said nothing. They rode again in silence. Suddenly Dr. Adler made an abrupt turn.

"Where are we going?"

"To the mechanic's."

"I thought you didn't hear anything."

"No, but you did. One can't be too careful."

It was one of the dentist's favorite sayings, and it particularly annoyed her. Why couldn't one be too careful? One could be too anything. Suddenly her annoyance faded and her heart fluttered. They were going to the *garage*.

Dr. Adler got out, seeking help, while Kitty stayed in the car. She scanned the lot like a bird of prey. She thought she saw a flash of clean overalls, but the dentist came back with another, dirtier mechanic.

The dentist pulled up the hood of the car, grimacing at the noisy, dirty, mysterious innards of the vehicle. The mechanic burrowed and tinkered for quite a while. While useless, Dr. Adler stayed outside the car, where masculine pride demanded grunting agreement with the incomprehensible comments of the mechanic.

Good, thought Kitty, the hours were passing. Soon it would be time to go home. Meanwhile, she yearned only for another flash of overalls, but even that modest hope was disappointed.

The repair—whatever it was—cost Adler a large sum of money, but he drove away in great satisfaction.

They entered the house and greeted Sari and Joseph.

"Reb Joseph, Mrs. Wassermann," said Dr. Adler, "I wonder if it would be convenient for me to call upon you on Wednesday. I have a matter of some importance to discuss with you," he said, winking at Kitty.

All that evening and the following day, Sari toiled at a new dress for Kitty and at baking fancy pastries. The procedure was for the suitor to request the hand of the young lady and iron out details with the parents, or, in this case, guardians. Afterwards, the new bride-to-be would be summoned, a toast offered, delicacies consumed. Later, relatives would be informed, and the news spread around town.

Kitty crushed her new dress as she wriggled through the alcove to the grate. It didn't matter. She hated the dress already and swore never to wear it again. The dentist had not yet arrived. He would be here exactly on the hour, just as he'd said.

Kitty bet herself that he would not drive the auto over. What for? He had already impressed everyone there was to impress, and there was no need to risk further injury to its poor, delicate body.

Oh, but that was cruel. That was no way to think of her husband. She shuddered. This couldn't be happening. On Shavuos, in the synagogue, she had been so sure...

Dr. Adler entered and shook Joseph's hand. He greeted Sari as if she were a rich lady with serious abscesses. He removed his hat and replaced it with a black velvet skullcap. Kitty craned to see better through the grate. Was that an incipient bald-spot?

The dentist directed his small talk towards Sari. She responded with desperate twitters. Poor Sari, thought Kitty. Inanities were hard for her. This was a woman who could get so engrossed in a book that she would walk out in the snow in house slippers.

"So, Dr. Adler, you honor us, closing the office early to call."

"Huh? Oh, no Mrs. Wassermann. We always close early on Wednesdays."

"Ah, well, how nice."

"Indeed, indeed."

Silence.

Finally, the dentist cleared his throat and turned to Joseph.

"Mr. Wassermann, I want you to know that I believe your sister-in-law is the finest, most gracious, most honorable..."

"Before we go any further, Dr. Adler, there is something you should know."

"Allow me, sir. I am fully informed as to the entire family..."

"Are you, Doctor? I think not."

Sari turned to her husband, amazed at his bluntness. What was he getting at?

"Did you know, Dr. Adler, that Kitty has no dowry."

"Jo..." Sari began, but Joseph clapped a warning hand down on hers. Kitty was astonished. The Hasidic way demanded extreme modesty in marital behavior. She had never seen Joseph and Sari touch each other in public.

The dentist just sat for a long time, as still and silent as a cast-iron pot. Then he opened his mouth and moved it several different ways before any words came out.

"No dowry?"

"No."

"Nothing?"

"Nothing."

Sari stared at Joseph, but he looked right back, certain and authoritative.

Adler blinked and spoke again. "How can this be? Wasn't Mr. Lebow a prosperous merchant?"

"Yes he was, may he rest in peace."

"And didn't he provide for all his daughters?"

"Yes, and provided well."

"Then why did he shortchange Kitty?"

"God forbid! Elchonon Lebow loved his children equally and treated them fairly."

"So, how...?"

"A family emergency arose, and Kitty's dowry was the only way to pay for it," Joseph explained, as if to a simpleton.

It was a lucky thing that there was a grate at the end of the alcove, or Kitty would have fallen straight down into the room.

Another silence fell, but this one was much shorter.

"I'm very sorry, Reb Joseph, but I'm afraid I must withdraw my request for your sister-in-law's hand."

It was a lucky thing that the alcove was so low, or Kitty would have jumped through the roof.

"And why is that, Dr. Adler?" Joseph asked, all innocence.

"Well, you see, I really must have a dowry. Really, I must."

"What for, if I might ask?"

"What for? Well, lots of things. My education was very expensive, you know."

"I'm sure it was. But surely you've paid for it all by now. You're the best dentist in town."

In fact Dr. Adler's only competition was from a fellow who believed that all teeth offended, and were best pulled and replaced by dentures.

"Well, yes, I am. But still there are expenses."

"Like what?"

"Like the office equipment."

"You haven't paid for it yet?"

"Well, yes, but still, there are other things."

"Such as?"

"Such as...the waiting room furniture."

"Oh! Mrs. Wassermann and I would be happy to lend you a few chairs."

"I've got plenty of chairs," Adler bustled. "But I should have some more elegant furnishings. Draperies. An Oriental carpet. Things that reflect my standing in society."

"Your standing couldn't be any higher. Why even rich men don't have a fine new automobile..."

"There. The automobile. That isn't paid for. I need money for that."

"You bought it...on credit?" Sari asked, as if it was an admission of larceny.

"Well," said Dr. Adler, grabbing his hat, "I really must be going. Please do convey my respects to Kitty...really is a wonderful girl...can't praise enough...if only I were in a position..." He was out the door and gone forever.

Kitty shimmied quickly out of the alcove. She dusted her dress off furiously. Well, it wasn't too badly bent out of shape. Nothing a hot iron couldn't fix. She'd get right to it. It was actually quite a fetching number.

Kitty poked her head around the door. "Is it safe to come in yet?"

"Oh Kitty!" Sari ran to her sister, held her tightly, and pressed her head into her bosom. "I'm so sorry, darling, so sorry."

Kitty could see Joseph over Sari's shoulder. Their eyes met. He winked.

"That wicked man!" said Sari. "All he cared about was money."

"He thought my dowry wasn't enough?" Kitty asked evenly.

Joseph and Sari exchanged glances. "Well," said Sari, "there was a family emergency and we had to tap the fund."

"What family emergency?"

"Never mind that. We'll talk about it some day when you have a family of your own. But don't worry, you'll be fully provided for, we've made sure of that."

"I don't understand."

"Joseph and I have saved up quite a bit, with no children to raise."

Kitty frowned. Joseph was a simple working man. They were a frugal couple and might have saved something, but not nearly a Lebow dowry.

"And," Sari continued, "Ignatz and Martha will make up the remainder. Of course they don't have cash in hand right now, the textile business is undergoing temporary hard times, but you may be sure that the Rosens are as good as their word. Even if worse comes to worst, there is money in the bank in Switzerland, to provide for you as surely as for their own daughters."

Sari addressed her husband. "Why didn't you tell that to the dentist? Why wouldn't you let me speak?"

"I just wanted to test his character," said Joseph. "A man's character is everything. And this fellow wasn't good enough. This Adler fellow is a show-off and a penny-pincher. Nowhere near good enough for our Kitty.

"Oh, no. Kitty could do a lot better. Starting tomorrow I intend to look seriously for a person of sterling character. You ladies can look around too. Recruit your friends. If we put our minds to it, we'll make the right match.

"And while we're at it, let's look for a fellow with a sense of style."

Kitty and Sari looked at Joseph in his sober Hasidic suit, and burst out laughing.

CHAPTER EIGHT

A thunderous roar snaked up the street. The neighbors came out and clustered in excited groups near the Wassermanns' house. What a sight, a Jew on a motorcycle! It was Sender Halter come to call on Kitty.

Kitty was already waiting outside. She had tried on every outfit in her wardrobe, made the agonizing decision about what to wear, and managed to reach her post outside the house with five minutes to spare.

Sender hopped off the motorcycle and approached the house. This was his sixth visit, so there was no need for more than brief pleasantries with Sari and Joseph.

But Sari couldn't manage a word. Not with a terrifying, snarling beast in her front yard! Why, Sender barely held it at bay.

"Is that...thing...yours?" It was a challenge. Had Sender answered "yes," or "it will be when it's paid for," Sari might have demanded an end to the romance right there.

But Sender said "No, I borrowed it from a fellow at the shop. I thought it would be fun for Kitty to take a ride." He pointed to the sidecar. "Something different, for a change." As if Kitty were in danger of being bored in his company.

Sari still looked dubious, but Kitty just pinned her hat on securely. With Sender she'd be willing to ride to hell on a rabid horse.

They were off in a roar. All through Janace children came out to see the sight, and adults pressed their noses to the windows. Alexander Halter, in a leather trenchcoat and rakishly slanted hat, and Kitty Lebow, head to toe in the last word from Paris. The town had never seen such glamour.

They reached the river at the edge of town. Sender leaned the motorcycle on an ancient oak and escorted Kitty, walking daintily on high heels, onto the Old Bridge.

Ever since the construction of the New Bridge, this one had been neglected. The bridge was still safe—the old stones had held true for almost six hundred years—but vines had taken root in its mortar, and wild ducks came to nest in its shadow. Sunlight moved rhythmically on the gentle flow of the river.

The bridge was a public, and therefore respectable, place. It was not indecent for an unmarried couple to spend time there together. But serious traffic had long since reverted to the New Bridge, with only an occasional horse and cart meandering over this one. Being Sunday, passers-by were few, and Kitty could hear nothing but the whispers of nature, and the loud sound of her own heartbeat.

Sender had brought along some leftover Sabbath challah bread, and Kitty tossed pieces to the ducks. Her mind was not on the task. She overshot the bank and the morsels hit deeper water. Attracted by the bread, a carp leaped up out of the river.

Kitty and Sender shouted out simultaneously at the silver flash of the fish.

"A fish means good luck," Kitty said.

Sender said, "There's lots of fish here, and sometimes you can see swans."

Kitty's smile faded. Sender seemed altogether too familiar with this bridge. "So, you've been here before?"

Sender shrugged. "Once or twice."

"With one of the Minsky triplets perhaps?"

"What? Why would I do that? They're only cousins."

"Weren't you courting them?"

"No. I never courted any of them. Or anyone else," he hesitated, "but you."

Kitty flushed. She was furious with herself for being jealous. "I only meant, how interesting that multiple births run in your family."

He was very still. "Yes," he said, whispering.

"Your little twin nieces," said Kitty, and when he didn't answer, "the ones with the braids." His oldest sister had twins whom he adored and who clearly adored him. Whenever he visited, he always brought colorful ribbons for their beautiful hair.

"There is something I must tell you about my family. Something that comes between us. It's a shameful secret. Can you keep it, Kitty?" Kitty tossed her head. They had been through all the divorces, the dowries, and the debts, and none of it had made a difference to either of them. Who cared about dusty skeletons in some forgotten closet?

He lowered his head. "No. I shouldn't burden you."

"If it's your burden, Sender, then I want to share it."

His eyes filled. Violets washed in April rain, thought Kitty deliriously. Then he blinked and they dried.

"I, too, am a twin."

"A twin!"

"Yes, identical."

Kitty laughed. The idea was too preposterously wonderful. Two Senders! Quickly, she hid her offending mouth. "Oh, I'm sorry. Is he dead?"

"No. He is alive, and living in Janace."

Kitty shook her head. "No, that can't be. Janace is a small town, and believe me, that's not something I would miss."

Sender sighed again, as if in apology. "It's a long story."

Kitty leaned back against the bridge. It was a comfortable pose, and, she knew, a flattering one. "Tell me."

He licked his lips, resigning himself to the telling. Then it poured out.

"We were fourteen, Anschel and I, in our last year of school. Father took sick the year before, so there was no possibility of our going on to study at yeshiva."

"But boys who are able are always provided for," Kitty protested. And you must have been among the brightest."

Sender smiled ruefully. "Anschel was brighter than me. But it wasn't a matter of tuition. Our earnings were needed for the family. You know why. Anyway, Anschel took it hard. I had accepted what fate brought me—I was even looking forward to apprenticing at the garage, but my brother couldn't get over his disappointment.

"Father had arranged for Anschel to train as a printer, which seemed like a good job, too. Printers get to read a lot of books and journals for free. But Anschel wasn't happy about it. His bitterness bubbled out of him like a poison.

"Anschel's main target was our teacher, Reb Meisels. Meisels was a bad teacher, and knew it. Anschel would make these cutting remarks that went right over Meisels' head. Later, Meisels would realize that Anschel had insulted him, but it would be too late for him to respond.

"Every so often, Meisels would beat Anschel. The teachers weren't supposed to hit boys past bar-mitzvah age, but Meisels couldn't control the class any other way. Anschel didn't care. We were already bigger than Meisels, besides, physical pain meant nothing to him.

"I'll never forget that day. It was a beautiful spring morning and the warm sun poured out of a window and fell right on me. I closed my eyes and thought about the coming summer and the start of my adult life.

Seeing me basking like that Meisels, naturally, called on me.

"'Halter! You, the mechanic.' He spoke sarcastically, as if there was something wrong with working with your hands, with machines. As if it was only decent to work with holy books, even if you made a lousy job of it.

"'So, Halter, what does this verse mean? Mr. Mechanic, do you know what verse I am referring to?' He stood there, arms akimbo, relishing the idea that I hadn't heard and would be punished. But I was listening on a superficial level, and I did know.

"'Yes, sir.' I said. 'The citation is "There is no luck in Israel." The fate of the Jewish people is determined by God every day, every minute.'

"I gave the right answer, as it happened, and Meisels was none too happy to hear it. Then someone in the room snickered softly. Meisels darted his head this way and that. The snickering grew louder. It was Anschel.

"Meisels was shaking as he called up my brother. He was so furious that he had to hold on to his desk to steady himself. 'Nu, Printer Halter, why don't you come up here and let us share in the joke.'

"A terrible fear came over me. I wasn't worried that Meisels would hit Anschel, he'd done that a hundred times before. Anschel considered a beating the price of a wisecrack, and well worth it. God forgive me, I was afraid Anschel would *blaspheme*.

"Anschel opened his mouth, but before a single word came out, Meisels reached behind him, to his desk, for his ruler. But the teacher didn't find a ruler or a pointer or a stick. He found a...a crochet needle."

"What?" Kitty said. "A crochet needle? What was that doing in a boys' school?"

Sender shook his head slowly. "I don't know. We never found out. Maybe a mother who'd come to speak with the teacher had forgotten it there.

"Anyway, Anschel forgot what he was about to say and started laughing. It was a ludicrous sight, the teacher with that lady's fancywork hook. The laughter made Meisels lose his mind. I'll never forget how his eyes rolled back in his head. He took the needle and he lunged with it. He stabbed it right up Anschel's nose.

"Blood poured out of my brother, but it wasn't a tremendous amount. Soon the nosebleed stopped. But then something else came out, thick, gray, mucous. It, it was part of his brain!"

Sender put his face in his hands and wept. Kitty wanted to touch and comfort him. Sender wiped his face with a handkerchief and recovered the thread of his story.

"My brother Anschel never laughed again. He never spoke again. It took another year to retrain him to use the privy. My mother goes to see him every day, but he doesn't recognize her. Sometimes I take a mirror and I show him how we look alike, but it makes no impression on him. He doesn't understand. His mind is gone."

"Where is he?" asked Kitty. Such a family member would have been discussed by everyone.

"Meisels. Reb Meisels took him in. He was a bad teacher, but he is not a bad man. When he realized what he had done, his remorse was as great as his rage had been. He quit teaching school. He has devoted his life to caring for Anschel.

"Please understand. Anschel couldn't come home."

Kitty did understand. If there was a mentally impaired child in the family, none of his siblings would ever be able to marry. Occasionally, in very wealthy families, some siblings might be married off. But these bought husbands and wives were considered worse than prostitutes. What sort of people would take the slightest risk of passing on retardation or insanity to their grandchildren? And the Halters were in no position to buy even the basest of spouses.

Poor Anschel had been the victim of a horrible accident and his tragedy was in no way familial, but that too would be overlooked by matchmakers and potential matches. Lunacy, idiocy, these were searing brands, and the siblings in a stricken family would suffer the consequences.

"So what does the teacher do for a living now?"

"He's forced to take the most menial jobs. Sometimes he works as a porter. That little man. And, of course, caring for Anschel is practically a full-time job."

"Doesn't he have a wife?"

"Yes. But Meisels tries not to have her take on too much of his responsibility. He destroyed Anschel's life, and he knows he's responsible, not his wife. Besides, the poor woman, they have four little ones of their own."

Kitty thought: with a retarded "son" in the house, they, too, would pay the price. "It must be very hard for them."

"It's terrible. And that leads me to another matter, Kitty, which concerns you. Every week I divide my salary in three. One third goes to my parents, to service their debts. One third to Meisels, to help support their family. If I were to marry..."

"Yes?"

"...We would be forced to make do on a third of my earnings."

"It can be done. It all depends on how frugal your wife would be. The right person could be rich with that third."

"Be realistic, my love. It would mean no house of our own, not for a long time."

"It's good for a family to be together," she said with false cheer. *If only Sari hadn't sold the house in Kosice.*

"Kitty. Does that mean you would have me, even with all my obligations and all my failings?"

"Oh, Sender. Yes, yes, a thousand times yes."

"Think carefully, Kitty. Can you resign yourself to such a fate, lifelong poverty?"

"Alexander Halter! Have you forgotten your own words? For us there is no fate. There is only God's will. And with him we can always negotiate."

CHAPTER NINE

Ruhigbad

It was the third time Eva had walked around the block, but she still couldn't find the ritual bathhouse. The neighborhood was unfamiliar, a deteriorated area from which the Jewish residents had long ago moved. The synagogue had been turned into a beer hall but the ritual bathhouse remained. They had to be built to exacting specifications and were too expensive to relocate.

Again she circled the area, in growing fury. Damn that modesty, of which Jewish women were supposed to be so proud. The ritual bath was never advertised, not even marked with a discreet name plate. She could never find the stupid place.

She stopped in front of the beer hall. A hearty roar came from its leaded windows. Eva licked her lips. She was awfully thirsty.

She would ask for a drink of water at the pub, then resume her search. But she hesitated. Preparing for ritual immersion meant taking off every drop of makeup. Her nails had been trimmed and the polish removed. She had left all her jewelry at home, even her earrings and her wedding ring. She had washed her hair, carefully combed out every knot, and slicked it back smoothly. Without adornment she felt practically naked.

Each month, when she got her period, she and Martin would separate. They wouldn't sleep together, or even kiss or hold hands. After she stopped bleeding, she would count seven clean days. That night she'd immerse in the ritual bath, and they would get back together again. That was the Law.

She'd thought it would be excruciating to go so long without sex. That was before marriage, when she'd craved Martin—when he was in love with Renee. Now things were different. She grimaced at the thought of his touch.

Eva tried as hard as she could to extend the separation. She pretended that her period went on and on. But inevitably, the night of immersion would come.

The day before was not so bad. Martin would always come home with some delicacy, or flowers. She would order him to change the sheets and clean the kitchen, and he would obey without complaint— with a silly grin on his face, in fact. She'd leave him more tasks to do while she went to the bathhouse.

The ritual bath itself wasn't so bad, either. She could luxuriate in the warm water, and then take her time doing her hair and putting on her face. There were often new perfumes and lotions to try—and stash in her purse—which some rich fool donated to the ritual bath association. But no matter how pleasantly the time passed, there was always the hour at which she'd have to return to Martin.

There was a large group of men in the beer hall. Eva took a seat at a far table. A barmaid instantly put a glass of beer at her place. It was cold and delicious. The region had the best beer in the world. She drank it down quickly and signaled for another. How nice to be able to sit here and drink like a normal person.

At the front of the beer hall there was a fellow giving a speech. Most of the men were clustered tightly around him, swilling enormous steins of beer.

Eva could barely hear what the lecture was about. Something about German nationalism. It was a typical self-pitying speech. She couldn't understand why the Germans did that. It seemed to her that with their beauty and strength and freedom, they should be the most contented people on earth. Yet they whined like Jews.

Eva had another beer. It was getting late, and the ritual bath would be closing soon. Then and there she made up her mind not to go. She wasn't ever going to go to that place again.

She despised Martin, but she was not about to leave him. Not like that idiot Renee who divorced her husband to end up penniless in some swamp in Palestine. There was altogether too much invested in Martin. Why throw her money and position away? But that didn't mean she had to agree to all his fanatical religious rituals. Why didn't *he* go to the stupid bath?

Eva moved her beer glass and studied the wet ring underneath. The Jews considered it important. The couple that slept together, unpurified, was to be cut off forever from the Jewish people. No descendants, and no future among the Jewish people.

Eva sneered. And that was bad?

Suddenly she was aware of a man standing beside her table. She noted his tight trousers and looked down in embarrassment. The pants were tucked into shiny boots. The man's wide belt matched his boots, and his shirt had many flaps and epaulets. He lacked only insignia and firearms to make a uniform. An illegal uniform.

The man was middle-aged but handsome in a dark, hairy way. His eyebrows almost met over black, clever eyes. She recognized the speaker who had been the center of the men's attention.

"May I introduce myself?" He clicked his heels and extended his hand. "Odilo Konrad."

Eva took it and felt pure sexual energy course up her arm. So that was why Hasidic men refused to shake hands with a woman.

"Elsa Kreutzer," she said.

"Permit me, Miss Kreutzer, to compliment you on your beauty."

Eva touched her simple bun, which was still wet. It was forward of the man to speak to her this way. But she didn't care.

"I'm not very glamorous tonight, I'm afraid." She had her cosmetics bag with her. If only she had gone to the ladies' room when she came in.

"No, no. I was just telling some of the comrades how refreshing it is to see an Aryan beauty in her purity. So many of our young women tart themselves up like Jewesses."

Konrad sat down at the table. This was more than forward, it bordered on insolence, but she said nothing. Perhaps he would order them a beer. Perhaps he would pay her bill. That would make it all right.

"You are new in these parts," said Konrad.

"Yes, I'm from the Harz Mountains."

That's where Frau Kreutzer came from. She had told Eva all about her childhood.

"Your accent is Austrian."

"I worked in Vienna for a while."

"And now you work for..."

"A Jewish family. The Rosens."

Konrad scowled, as if he'd tasted something bad. "You are a secretary?"

"No. A housemaid."

The answers came easily from Eva's lips. She realized that she had rehearsed these words. She had practiced this conversation for a long time.

Everything had been planned out. The name, the origins, the accent. The Rosens' house, so that he wouldn't try to contact her, or be suspicious if she was seen there. Housemaid was a job she could fake. After all, maids did the same work other women did, women who couldn't avoid it. And if she slipped and said something that smacked of Jewishness, well, servants often took on the mannerisms of their employers.

She had planned all this before even walking into the beer hall, before laying eyes on Odilo Konrad.

"And what do you do, sir?"

Konrad smiled half a smile, as if she were stupid not to know. "I, Fraulein, am director of the Ruhigbad chapter of the Sudeten-German Nationalist Front."

Eva shrugged. "I don't know much about politics." But she had heard of the Front. Of how they had gained increasing numbers of seats in the Czechoslovak parliament. Of how they frightened the Jews.

"Every son of the Fatherland must make himself political, as a duty of the blood."

"Obviously, I am no 'son,'" said Eva, batting her lashes.

"Obviously," said Odilo Konrad.

She didn't resist when he took her to a storage room at the back of the beer hall. There was an indentation in the wall, stacked with crates of liquor. Eva recognized this as the place where the holy Ark of the Law had been. When she lay down, she could see the part of the ceiling from which the Eternal Lamp had been removed.

Afterwards, Eva made sure she had all her things and left nothing behind. She dusted herself off and walked back through the beer hall. The tavern had emptied. There was no one left but die-hard members of the Front and old drunks, yet even these met her with knowing glances and snickers. She stared them down with a haughty look.

"Oh, Miss."

Eva turned around. It was the barmaid. Her face showed contempt.

Who was she to act superior, thought Eva. The girl was pretty, but not nearly as pretty as she was. What sort of girl worked in a bar, anyway. Eva narrowed her eyes at the dark roots of the barmaid's hair.

"Yes?"

"Your bill, Miss."

It was so late when Eva returned home, that Martin had already fallen asleep. She was pleased. Perhaps she could convince him the next morning that they'd been intimate, that he'd forgotten in the befuddlement of sleep. Having been with Odilo Konrad, she wanted Martin even less.

Eva undressed very quietly but it didn't help. Martin awakened with a start.

"You smell like..." his eyes widened, then blinked several times. "Like beer."

Eva considered apologizing, then thought better of it. Take a lesson from the Germans; attack is the best defense.

"How dare you complain! You, you lie here while I wander like an orphan in that horrid neighborhood looking for the ritual bath. And when I'm there, it takes an age, and they humiliate me, and I almost die of thirst. Do you consider my needs for even a minute? No! All you think of is the need of your disgusting...member."

She turned on her heels and went for the door.

"Eva! No, don't go. Where are you going? It's the middle of the night."

"I'm going to the Kreutzers."

"Don't. Wait for me. Let's discuss this."

But by the time Martin had put his pants on and found his slippers, Eva had gone next door. He arrived in time to hear the bolts click.

Martin knocked, but not too loudly, because it was so late. No one answered. After standing around in the cold for a few minutes, he went back to bed.

CHAPTER TEN

Janace

Sender was studying an annotated volume of the Book of Exodus by the light of a kerosene lamp. The Halters' home had electricity, but it was expensive and rarely used.

The other members of the household were asleep. Sender had had a long day at work, had called briefly on Kitty, and had visited his brother. He was too tired to go to the House of Study. But what sort of Jew went a day without reviewing Scripture?

From the outer gloom, his sister Bayla appeared, clutching an old robe around her. "Ah, you're home at last, Sender. I wanted to talk to you."

"Bayla! Have you been waiting up for me? That's terrible. Whatever it is can wait 'till morning. You need your sleep."

"I'll sleep enough in the grave," she said. A cliché, but jarring coming from a young woman. "I want to talk with you privately."

Sender's fatigue evaporated, and he gave her his full attention. He couldn't remember ever having a one-to-one conversation with Bayla.

Bayla was the youngest, and very quiet. She was thin and wraith-like, as if she were a shadow of a woman, or a child. Although she was healthy and normal in every way, everyone referred to her as "poor Bayla." The other members of the family, Sender realized with a pang of guilt, rarely spoke of the youngest sister at all.

"What is it, Bayla?" he said, putting the volume of Scripture aside, although he longed to finish the chapter and go to bed.

"I want to talk to you about Kitty."

"Oh," said Sender, "you do like her, don't you?"

"Of course. You really love her, don't you Sender?"

57

Sender blushed. "Yes, I do. I want to marry her. Someday." He spoke carefully. It was most inappropriate for a man to marry while an eligible sister remained at home. It seemed incredible, but Kitty and Bayla were the same age.

"Marry her now. As soon as possible," said Bayla.

Sender had never heard his younger sister speak with such conviction. "There's no rush. First we'll dance at your wedding."

"I will never marry."

"You're speaking nonsense, Bayla. Of course you'll marry. Any of a number of fellows have spoken to Papa already. It just takes a little time to find the right one." A good Jew, a decent man who isn't too particular about a dowry. Finding one would be difficult, but not impossible. One could make arrangements, one could compromise, one could confidentially call upon the Society for Honoring the Bride.

"No, it will never be. I've always known that. Sender, you shouldn't wait for me. You mustn't wait any longer."

"Bayla! Where do you get these ideas? Of course you'll marry. Girls in much worse circumstances marry all the time. And you're a beautiful girl."

She was beautiful. She had her brothers' blue eyes, although they were less vivid than Sender's, and the lustrous hair of her twin nieces. She looked like a doll, a breakable, sad-eyed doll.

"I don't want to talk about it anymore. I just want you to marry Kitty as soon as possible. Promise me, Sender." She squeezed her brother's arm. "Promise me."

"All right. I'll speak to the Wassermanns tomorrow."

Kitty was perched in her secret spot behind the grill. She was distressed because she was wearing a dress that Sender had already seen. There hadn't been enough time to bake cakes, much less sew a new dress.

Sender's back was to her, and she faced Sari and Joseph. Their faces glowed with such happiness that she would have married Sender if only to please *them*.

From the back, Sender didn't seem nervous. But then, a man that well dressed need never be nervous.

"Reb Joseph, Mrs. Wassermann, as you know, the Talmud states that 'he who has found a wife has found all goodness.' There could be no greater honor done to my family, nor any greater blessing upon me, than to have Kitty's hand in marriage."

Their acceptance was instant and joyful. "No, the honor is ours."

"No, ours."

"Give thanks to God! May such happiness be upon all Israel."

"Please, Mrs. Wassermann..."

"You must call me Sari from now on. All my dear brothers do."

"Mrs. Sari, won't you please call Kitty in now?"

Joseph cleared his throat. "In a moment. First, let's discuss practical matters."

"Oh, no need for that Reb Joseph. Kitty already told me there isn't any dowry. And I know she told you everything about my financial circumstances."

"Yes, she did," said Sari. "But the picture is not as bleak as you think, Alexander. It's true that Kitty's dowry...that she has no actual dowry now. However, Joseph and I have some savings, and no children of our own, so we want to offer that sum as a token.

"Also, we have spoken to my sister Martha and her husband, Ignatz Rosen, and they have promised the entire sum of the original dowry. However, because of temporary setbacks in their business, they are unable to advance it at this time. But they assure us that the money is not just a promise, it has been put aside, along with the dowries of their own daughters, in their bank in Switzerland."

Sender hung his head, as if he had heard bad news.

"Don't worry, Sender, their word is gold," Joseph said. "It's just that if they withdraw the money now, there would be stiff penalty charges. But as soon as the economy is back to normal, there will be plenty of cash on hand. We only mention the Swiss business to assure you that the sum is guaranteed."

Sender shook his head. "This is not acceptable."

Kitty, in her hiding place, was as shocked as the faces of her sister and brother-in-law showed them to be. Could they all have been mistaken? Was Sender really as greedy as Dr. Adler?"

"I'm afraid that's the best we can do," said Sari coldly.

"Well, it won't do at all," said Sender. "You and Reb Joseph may have been able to save up because you don't have children, but you also will need that money when you are old, for the same reason.

"Now Kitty and I would never let you want for life's necessities, of course, but by the time you retire we might well have children, God-willing, and other obligations. Surely you deserve to have some comforts, after working so hard for so long. We could not take a penny of your savings.

"As for the Rosens' funds...I don't know much about the economy and Swiss banks and such things, but I do know that they have plenty of worries on their heads and don't need us to add to them. We know they are good-hearted people, and generous. It might well be that some day Kitty and I would start a business and be in need of a loan, and then we'll see if they could help us out. But that's far in the future. Right now, we just want their blessings for our marriage."

Kitty wanted to cry out with pride. Sari thought about her promise to her parents, and wanted to weep with the joy of having fulfilled it. But it was Joseph who actually wiped away a tear, for God had finally given him a son.

If they were not to provide a dowry, the Wassermanns and the Rosens were determined to provide a beautiful wedding for the young couple

The wedding dress was of paramount importance. Sari and Kitty designed a gown, and Martha ordered materials from Budapest and Paris. Two full-time embroiderers were commissioned to work on the pattern. The hat shop's Mrs. Kandinsky presented the ladies with her best headpieces and veils.

The bridegroom's suit was a more pragmatic expense—it would serve as Sabbath best for years to come—but for Sender its construction would be no less painstaking than that of the bridal ensemble.

Kitty accompanied Sender to the tailor. The owner and his assistant were already aware of the date of the wedding and had arranged a display of fine fabrics for the couple's choosing.

Most young women did the actual selection of material, but Kitty merely approved Sender's choice, a wool imported from England. It furled from the bolt like silk, and felt like velvet to the hand.

As Sender was fitted, Kitty waited patiently, reveling in her new role. She listened to the conversation from the fitting room.

"Still the same measurements as ever, eh, Mr. Halter?"

"If you say so, Mr. Schneider."

"We'll leave a little extra around the middle. Just in case you expand like all the young husbands."

"I don't think so. You know how I like the fit, Mr. Schneider."

"Yes. Perfect."

"I was thinking trim, but all right, Mr. Schneider. Perfect will be close enough."

When it was time to pick up the suit, they brought along the new hat, shirt, tie, belt, and shoes that they had purchased together, a swatch of the suit material in hand.

Sender emerged from the fitting room. Kitty wanted to swoon. It was the Baron in all his splendor. He lacked nothing but a horse with a golden bridle.

Sender stared at himself in the mirror and frowned. "It doesn't fit," he said.

Kitty's mouth dropped open.

"Hmm," said the tailor. "We should take it in here, and here, and here."

Kitty watched in horror as the tailor violated the beautiful fabric with his chalk. Was she going blind? What on earth was wrong with the wonderful suit?

When they returned a few days later, Sender was still not pleased. "It doesn't fit," he repeated. This time the tailor did not agree. However, he marked the adjustments that Sender requested.

They returned to the shop yet again. The tailor beamed at the marvel of the suit, and called his assistant in to witness the artistry of his work.

Sender said nothing, but once they were a safe distance from the shop, he held up the bandbox and told Kitty, "It's still not right, but I didn't want to hurt Mr. Schneider's feelings. Frankly, I don't think he can do any better."

"My gown should look that good," said Kitty.

"No, no. I just can't wear that suit. Not the way it is now."

"There is nothing more to be done. Mr. Schneider is the best tailor in town."

"No, not exactly. There's old Mr. Nagy. He's retired, but maybe, for a price..."

"Who is that?"

"Do you know Alma's dress shop."

"Yes," said Kitty, her lips tightening.

"Mr. Nagy is Alma's widower. They worked together for years. Alma was the brains behind the business, but her husband was the master of style. Their son does everything now, but old Mr. Nagy will do my suit, for a price."

The Nagy house was done up in the garish style of Hungarian peasants. How could a person who lived in such a setting produce something of refinement, Kitty wondered skeptically.

While the men discussed the situation, Kitty looked around the room curiously. Ornate frames held oil paintings of the Nativity, the Last Supper, and the Crucifixion. Why was it that the biblical characters in Christian pictures never looked Jewish?

Mr. Nagy was ancient and barely coherent. Kitty had deep misgivings as his shaky hands fingered the wondrous material of the suit, but Sender displayed a respectful confidence.

Old Mr. Nagy's ministrations took two full weeks, but when he was done even Kitty could see the difference in the suit. It was now a work of art.

So when Sender quietly announced, "it still doesn't fit," Kitty felt a pang of doubt about her fiancé.

"Alexander, there is something wrong with you! It's just a piece of wool. And you paid a fortune for it! I don't mind scrimping and saving, but are we going to see every penny we put by washed away by some impossible ideal of yours?"

She didn't say it, but it was clear: I can't live with that.

Sender said nothing. He didn't like to fight, and he almost always let Kitty have her way.

Kitty was relieved to think that her display of temper had put an end to Sender's obsession, and that the suit would hang unmolested in the closet until their wedding day. But she was mistaken.

One day, only a month before the wedding, Sender announced, "My Uncle Mechel wants your permission to give the suit to Luckless Pollack."

Uncle Mechel was the Halters' single rich relative.

"Why would Uncle Mechel need my permission? Who is Luckless Pollack? And," Kitty gulped, "what suit are you talking about?"

Sender sat down. "You know Uncle Mechel's factory?"

Mechel Halter produced high-quality down comforters, mattresses, and pillows. He had already sent them several sets of heavenly bedding for a wedding present.

"I thought he was retired. Don't the sons run the factory now?"

"Yes. But back when Uncle Mechel was the boss, Luckless Pollack worked for him. If I'm not mistaken, Pollack's father was already Luckless. It seems to run in the family."

"What does?"

"Every illness and misfortune you can imagine. I don't know about the father, but this one has a crippled son, his only child. His wife died, their house burned down, and there were more tragedies that have mercifully slipped from my mind.

"Anyway, when Uncle Mechel retired, the sons didn't want to keep Pollack around anymore. He gummed things up in the factory. Everything he touched was ruined. 'You can't fire him,' Uncle Mechel protested, 'no one else will give him a job.'

"The sons begged him. 'We'll gladly support him with charity, but please don't make us keep him in the factory, Father.' Still, Mechel didn't like the idea. Being forced onto charity could kill a man. But Pollack's days in the factory were over.

"So Uncle Mechel made up some story, something about an early retirement scheme. At first, they sent him his old salary, but he'd always lose the money. So now Luckless Pollack comes to Uncle Mechel every week to pick up his 'pension.'"

"And?" said Kitty, tapping her foot. "Where is this leading?"

"Well, I was watching as Pollack came to my uncle's the other week, and I realized: he's just my size."

"Oh, Sender, no. You didn't."

"No, no. I didn't do anything. I mean, I approached Uncle Mechel and I told him, wouldn't it be a good idea, since I wasn't going to wear the suit anyway..."

"Oh, Sender!"

"Nothing happened, Kitty. Look, the suit's still at my house. Uncle Mechel said he wouldn't give it away unless you gave your permission. So it's all up to you."

"Fine. Since it's up to me, you'll wear the suit to the wedding and..."

"Just a minute, darling. With all due respect, I said it was up to you whether to give Pollack the suit, not whether I would wear it. That's for me to decide. And I won't."

"You won't? Not even to please me?"

"Kitty, I know it wouldn't please you for me to be miserable at our wedding. And that's what I would be in a suit that doesn't fit me properly."

"But what will you wear to the canopy?" Kitty asked plaintively. She knew from the tone in her own voice that she had already lost the case. "It's too late to order a new suit. Besides, we can't afford another round like this one."

Sender smiled. He had already thought this out. "My black with the fine gray pinstripe would be appropriate, and so would the solid navy blue.

"Either one, Kitty. It's your decision to make."

The following week Luckless Pollack came early to the home of Uncle Mechel. Sender and Kitty couldn't get out of the house without being seen, so Uncle Mechel rushed them to a little porch off his office.

"Sorry I'm early, Mr. Halter. My son was supposed to get some handwork at the mill so I took him there, but then it turned out that there was nothing..."

"Reb Shmuel, come in, come in. I have some good news for you."

"You do?" Pollack was not in the habit of hearing good news.

"Yes. A tailor paid a debt off to one of my sons with a suit, but of course my boys are Hasidim, and they don't wear 'modern' clothes. Perhaps you can try it on and see if it fits. It would be a shame to waste good clothing."

Kitty and Sender heard nothing more, and wondered if Luckless Pollack had fainted from the shock of a stroke of fortune. They stole a glance in the window.

Kitty immediately backed away. Pollack was trying on the suit.

"It's all right, Kitty," Sender whispered, "you can look now."

If clothes truly made the man, they would have to change the fellow's name to Lucky Pollack.

"There's a mirror in the hall, Reb Shmuel. Come take a look," said Uncle Mechel. When Pollack left the room he gestured to Kitty and Sender to come back into the house. They entered, rubbing their arms to warm up.

Suddenly, they heard terrible, heart-breaking crying.

"Reb Shmuel, what's the matter?" asked Uncle Mechel.

"I'm sorry, Mr. Halter. I thought there was nothing left in the world that could make me cry, but I couldn't help myself."

"But why? You should be happy. This suit looks wonderful on you."

"That's why I'm crying. I'm sixty-one years old and I've never owned a new suit. And now I have this one. I've never been so happy in my life."

CHAPTER ELEVEN

February 17, 1938

Kitty's wedding was not the extravaganza that Sari and Martha had planned. The Rebbe, the Hasidic chief rabbi of Janace, decreed a strict limit to the number of guests, and a maximum sum that could be spent on celebrations. Nothing antagonized the Gentiles more than an ostentatious Jewish wedding, the Rebbe said, and this was no time to provoke them.

War was in the air. Sender's older brother, Reuven, the grocer, told of a fellow who came into the store and declared loudly that the Jews were instigating war. They were always the ones behind wars, the customer said, they were the ones to profit.

"Right! We're always the ones gouging money," Reuven said in disgust. "Like I was raking in the crowns from his hundred grams of cheese. Let him go take his business elsewhere. Let the Gentile grocer give him credit for nothing. Let *him* have the big Jewish profits."

"Did you tell him, Daddy? Did you tell the Gentile off?"

Reuven looked abashed. "You can't do that, son. You can't criticize the Gentiles, no matter what lies they tell about us. It isn't safe. They can hurt us."

"Like Hitler?"

"Don't worry about that Hitler," said the head of the Men's Psalm Fellowship, a hearty fellow with a broad red beard. "We'll show him. He makes one move and we'll start reciting *twice* as many Psalms as we already do. Yessir! Hot tea and the Book of Psalms will cure anything nasty."

"Gentlemen, gentlemen," said Ignatz Rosen. "Is this any kind of talk at a wedding? Come, let's eat, let's dance." Rosen was secretly relieved by the rabbi's ruling. Their cash flow had almost completely dried up. He had finally broken down and described the dire situation to Martha.

She had responded not with tears, but with strength and an invigorating confidence. "Let's sell the ruby parure," she insisted.

He'd hated the idea. But in the end, that is what he'd done, and gotten a good price for the jewels too—another sign of impending war. But a big wedding would have put a dent in that sum. Dear God, where would it end?

The wedding was gracious if not lavish. Instead of a large hall, the House of Study served for the party. It was packed with guests. The Halters, despite their diminished finances, enjoyed a distinguished position in the community, the numerous Wassermanns were now considered kinfolk, and Lebow relatives had come in from around the country.

The main hall of the House of Study had been made into the bride's throne room. Kitty was seated on a raised stage in a peacock chair. Flanking her, on smaller chairs, were Sari and Sender's mother. Well-wishers had to shout to be heard above the lively sounds of the klezmer band.

In a smaller prayer room, the bridegroom sat at the head of the Groom's Table, which was laid with decanters of spirits, platters of cake, volumes of the Talmud, and a prettily illuminated document, the marriage contract.

Beggars were clustered at the doorway of the building. Joseph Wassermann handed out crowns and accepted the poor people's blessings for the happiness of the young couple. It was traditional for beggars to congregate at the entrance to a wedding party, but had there always been so many? It seemed that even as recently as Rachel-Leah's wedding there had been far fewer of them.

With feeling, he returned the beggars' blessings with blessings of his own.

Joseph invited the poor to return later for the leftover food, then headed for the bride's hall. He stopped within a few feet of the dais, grinning broadly. How he was enjoying his role, standing in for Kitty's father.

Kitty was a vision in a dress of crystal-encrusted silk. The gown's tight bodice emphasized her slim figure. A crown of myrtle and lily-of-the-valley held her veil in place. The details of finery were lost on Joseph, of course. All he knew was that he was the luckiest father-of-the-bride in all the Diaspora.

Kitty's smile widened at the sight of her brother-in-law, and her cheeks glowed pink. A pale face is the expected consequence of fasting on the wedding day, when God forgives all the sins of premarital life. Kitty's face was bright though; she was wearing all the makeup she liked, since Eva wasn't there to shame her out of it.

Eva was pregnant and feeling too delicate to travel. In her heart Kitty was glad. Eva always managed to take a bite out of everything joyous, and Kitty didn't want the day marred in any way.

Not that she wished her sister any ill. She was glad that Eva and Martin were having a baby. Perhaps it would help patch things up between them. Because obviously things were not right over in Ruhigbad. Martin was here at the wedding, by himself, and he wasn't even the blood relative. Kitty decided she would never let Sender leave her alone like that when she was pregnant.

But maybe she was being hasty. Poor Martin. He looked terrible. His thick black hair had turned quite gray and deep wrinkles carved up his face. It was hard to believe that he was the youngest of the brothers-in-law. Clearly he needed a vacation.

Most of the family did. Martha and Ignatz both looked harried, though they put on a great show of carefree good humor. Helen and Thomas also seemed drawn, and there was no mystery in that. Twice Thomas had been arrested at political demonstrations. Although quickly released on each occasion, there had to be trouble ahead if he kept this up. In the current tense climate, there would be less and less tolerance for non-conformity.

And Renee, oh, Renee, was less than a ghost, forgotten as one dead and buried. Worse. Never spoken of, her presence unmarked even by a memorial candle.

Kitty shivered slightly. She had failed to keep her promise. She had not put the two pennies in the charity box at the ritual bath.

Two days before, Sari, Martha, and Helen had accompanied her, all of them giggling like young girls. Kitty hadn't even brought her purse, just a case of cosmetics and hair things. Her sisters had paid the bill and tipped the attendant and provided her with everything she needed.

She was afraid to ask for the two pennies, reluctant to spoil the party by mentioning the lost sister, the one who had betrayed the family. But it wasn't right. She wished she could do it over again.

She'd have to remember to take along the coins the next time she went to the ritual bath. But what if she got pregnant tonight? Then she wouldn't be going for almost a year. What if she forgot...

Oh, here was Joseph approaching, the happiest she'd ever seen him. He and Sari were both ecstatic.

The crowd clapped rhythmically. With a flourish, Joseph removed his handkerchief and extended it to Kitty. She reached out and grasped it, to cheers. She had now appointed her brother-in-law to negotiate the marriage contract on her behalf. Joseph then repaired to the Groom's Table, a journey that took a full twenty minutes, as he had to shake hands with every man on the way.

Joseph, Sender, Sender's father, the Rebbe, all reviewed the marriage contract and indicated their approval. Two witnesses signed the document. All the while boisterous young Hasidim sang and stomped.

Joseph and Mr. Halter took Sender by the arms and escorted him to the main hall. All the men followed, singing at the top of their voices, clapping till their hands burned, and stamping their feet until the floorboards were ready to splinter. They drowned out the band and set the lamps flickering to a thrumming beat.

What a wedding! Afterwards, people said that such wild celebration hadn't been seen since King David brought the Ark of the Covenant up to Jerusalem.

The women parted to make way for the men, as much from fear of being trampled as for decorum. Finally, the entire assembly stood before the enthroned bride. Kitty's lids had been lowered in maidenly demureness, but now she couldn't help raising them up to look at Sender, whom she hadn't seen in a week.

He was glorious. His sartorial dilemma had been ingeniously resolved by the loan of a Hasidic outfit from a cousin. Sender wore a caftan of black silk jacquard, belted by a satin cord. A *shtreimel*, a velvet cap circled in sable, haloed his face. Luminous with fasting, his blue eyes looked down upon her.

Now everything was ready for the veiling ceremony. It was the oldest Jewish wedding custom. Ever since the experience of Jacob the patriarch, who was tricked into marrying Leah instead of his beloved Rachel, the bridegroom would make sure he had the right bride.

Sender was handed a veil, which he placed over Kitty's face. His duty done, he was shooed away by his female relatives, while Sari carefully pinned the cloth to Kitty's wreath.

The tumult of the men accompanying Sender increased on his way back to the Groom's Table. Kitty was taken by her sisters to a storage area that served as the bridal dressing room. There, Sari, Martha, and Helen untied all the knots on Kitty's costume: the bows on her gloves, the laces on her corset, even the braids of myrtle in her bouquet. Knots symbolized discord.

A hesitant knock at the door.

"Come in," they chorused.

Sender's mother stuck her thin, worn face into the room.

"Excuse me for intruding. May I come in? Just for a second? Please don't rise, Sari, dear. Oh, and certainly not you, Daughter! You're the Queen today. Forgive me, but I couldn't help noticing that on your beautiful gown there is not a snippet of red ribbon or red thread for warding off the evil eye.

"I know what it's like getting ready for a daughter's wedding. You're so lost, you'd forget your head if a kerchief wasn't tying it down. Fortunately, I found a red flower outside. Here, my darling, put it in your bouquet.

"I'll be waiting outside when you're ready." She bent to kiss Kitty on the cheek.

"Bless you, Mrs. Halter," said Sari. "Would you be kind enough to get the candles?"

"Oh, no," said Helen, when Sender's mother was gone, "not another ridiculous Hasidic superstition."

"I wonder where this red flower came from?" said Kitty. "It's dead winter out there, and we didn't order any from the florist."

"They say Mrs. Halter is a..." Martha faltered.

"An herbalist," snapped Kitty. "Not a witch."

"Oh, I didn't mean any such thing," said Martha. "Just that she knows where to find things like flowers."

Helen sniffed. "Don't pretend it's science. Herbalists, witches, Hasidim, they're all the same. A lot of superstition about evil eyes."

"I don't think it's superstition," said Sari. "It makes perfect theological sense. Somebody sees you in a moment of glory and thinks, 'who is she to have all this, while I have a feckless husband, or rags for clothes, or whatever.' If you accept the fact that God hears all prayers, then even that random envious thought creates a little prosecutor in heaven, to play down your merits and point out your sins."

"Oh? And a little red thread is supposed to fend off the heavenly tribunal?"

"No," said Sari. "But it does attract the eye. It might give the envious person pause. Enough time to remember that one shouldn't begrudge a friend's good fortune. God's blessings are unlimited, and he doesn't deny one to bless another."

"Apologetics," said Helen. "Apologetics for plain superstition."

Meanwhile, the guests had gone out to the courtyard. Boys held flaming torches to light the area and mitigate the cold. The snow had been swept from the ground and the chill seemed refreshing after the heat generated by the dancing crowd in the House of Study. A velvet canopy had been set up under the stars.

The cantor sang out "Blessed is he who comes," as Joseph and Mr. Halter, each holding a lighted taper, led Sender through the parting crowd. Sender was wearing a white robe over his clothes, to symbolize the purity of his new life as a married man, and, because the robe resembled shrouds, to impress upon him the gravity of his commitment.

The band's fiddler struck up a sweet, mournful tune as the bride came from the House of Study. Sari and Sender's mother led her by her elbows, the candles gripped tightly in their free hands. Their assistance was handy; the veil that Sender had placed on her face was opaque brocade. All Kitty could see was her bouquet of white flowers and myrtle, and the tops of her white pumps.

But she could hear perfectly well, and she noted with glee the gasps of the upright ladies. Shocking the traditionalists was her dress, which fell away from the knees to reveal her high-heeled slippers and her perfect legs, cased in silk stockings. A brilliant red blossom was tucked in one garter. The ladies rubbed their eyes. Perhaps they had imagined the scandalous show of leg, because, as Kitty passed, there was nothing but a luxurious length of train in her wake.

The three women approached the canopy. Kitty's bouquet was taken from her and Sari was leading her by the hand in the circling of the groom. Mrs. Halter bent down to pick up Kitty's train, symbolizing her acceptance of the bride's premier position in the life of her son.

After the ceremony, food and drink were served, and freshly refueled, the guests took to celebrating in earnest. The dancing, singing, joking, blessing, juggling, and rhyming came to a head.

The older people wore themselves into exhaustion and dropped out of the dancing circles, until only two circles were left. The young men shouted and stamped, raised the bride and groom on their chairs, and tossed them as if they were baskets of fruit. Kitty screamed in fear and delight.

In the women's circle there remained only a few young matrons, like Rachel-Leah, and the single girls, including Martha's daughters, Sender's raven-haired nieces, and Bayla. Most of the guests had been watching the muscular antics of the youths, but soon all moved over to the maidens' circle, as if drawn to a fire.

Bayla Halter was dancing like a piece of silk caught up in a whirlwind. Her body jerked and spun to the drummer's beat. Her eyes rolled, her mouth hung open. The pins in her hair flew out, but Bayla didn't stop to pick them up, and didn't smooth her coiffure. Instead the great black mass whipped round and round as she pulled the circle of girls in wild gyration.

Moved by the primal display, the guests on the sideline rejoined the young dancers. All but the oldest and the lamest danced with a manic energy, as if demons were prodding them with pitchforks. They danced all night, even after the beggars came back for the leftovers. They danced as if they would never dance again.

CHAPTER TWELVE

The Halters' neighbors woke to the sight of Kitty hanging laundry on the line. It was only a week after the wedding, and there she was in the freezing dawn, snapping out the linens like the banners of a conquering army.

Kitty had taken control of the household. Each member of the family had good reason to relinquish responsibility. Mr. Halter wasn't old but he was frail with worries, as well as with heart disease. Every day he came home early from work and went straight to bed. Later he might join the family for supper, but he could only muster the strength for a bowl of soup or a cup of hot milk. Kitty wanted to nurse him, pamper him, but Mr. Halter bristled at her efforts. He was not an invalid, he insisted, he just needed rest.

Sender's mother was a woman of high intelligence and inner strength, but unlike the matriarchs of many Jewish families, she did not step up to act as the head of the household. For years Mrs. Halter had supplemented the family's income with her earnings as an herbal healer. Local people, Jews and Gentiles alike, came to her for the treatment of ills, and her skills were such that rumors of witchcraft flitted around her. She might have grown prosperous from her practice but for two habits: the referral of patients to doctors when an illness seemed beyond her healing abilities, and the tendency to treat the poor for free.

Kitty had been raised on scary mother-in-law stories, and had been taught that it was wise to at least pretend submission. She was relieved to find that Mrs. Halter was the opposite of the domineering stereotype. Her mother-in-law liked her so much that she began talking of making Kitty her successor. Sender's mother did her best to teach Kitty the secrets of healing. But one plant or root looked exactly like another to Kitty. Worse, she had little patience for the whiny, demanding, uneducated people who made up Mrs. Halter's clientele.

But Sender's mother quickly ceded the household to Kitty. Kitty's gefilte fish was better than her own, she said, even though she had been making hers for decades. Kitty's way with a dustcloth, with a clothesline, with an iron (to say nothing of a needle) was superior to her own, she insisted.

Sari was grateful that her little sister was so well accepted in her new home. Sari did, however, whisper critical judgments in Kitty's ears. She thought Mrs. Halter something of a rebel, a "modern" woman who shied away from home and children to the greatest extent she could. What sort of woman would renounce her role as mistress of the house at the first opportunity? While admittedly hard-working and loving, Mrs. Halter was no "woman of valor" by Lebow standards, Sari said.

Free of those standards, Kitty could take to her new duties with gusto. Just keeping the Halter home tidy was no small thing. The building was large and well-built, a moss-overgrown memorial to a time long ago when the family enjoyed prosperity.

Kitty thought it an odd household. Bayla agreed to do any task she was asked to help with, but she never undertook anything on her own. And although her work was always acceptable, she worked so slowly that Kitty quickly became exasperated and the next time, rather than ask for help, Kitty did the job herself.

The life of Reuven, the oldest brother, was also strange. Every day, when the grocery he worked for closed for the afternoon break, he would go eat dinner at the house next door—which was occupied by his ex-wife and their three children. Every few days he would bring his dirty laundry, and his torn clothes, and return with clean, pressed and mended clothing. Once a week, when he received his wages, he would turn them over to his ex-wife. Every day, he helped the children with their homework, and attended to their discipline. He was, in all ways except one, a family man.

Kitty was baffled by this arrangement. The ex-wife was a cold woman, it was true, but decent enough. What could be so awful about her—or about Reuven—that they preferred this expensive, awkward, and humiliating set-up to an ordinary marriage?

Kalman, the younger brother, was good-natured—too much so. "Too good is also not good," she remembered her mother saying. That was true of Mrs. Halter and Kalman and, she feared, of Sender. She would have to be on guard to protect her beloved from the excesses of his own kind heart.

She was pleased, however, that Kalman worked as a printer. With the extras that Kalman and Reuven brought from their work, the Halter household was stocked with both physical food and food for thought.

"Kitty," Sender said one evening, "I'm going to visit Anschel. Do you want to come with me?"

"Of course."

"Are you sure? I can understand if you don't want to."

"Sender! Don't be silly. Anschel is a member of my family now. I want to meet him." Her enthusiasm was meant to convince herself as much as her husband. Dear God, she wondered, how dreadful would this be? What do you do when visiting the victim of such a tragedy? What do you say? God forgive me, what do you wear?

The first shock was the home of Reb Meisels, the remorse-stricken teacher who was now eking out a living as a day laborer. It was no more than a large shed, and it looked ready to collapse. Kitty twitched as the door was opened and then shut behind them. A good slam might bring the roof tumbling down on their heads.

It was bitter cold and dark inside the shack. A candle stub was lit in honor of the guests, allowing them to see what they might wish they could not. Sender introduced Kitty to Reb Meisels and his wife.

She shook hands with Mrs. Meisels and immediately looked down in shame. The woman's hand was the roughest and most swollen she had ever touched. Her own hands were softened with lotion, and the nails had been freshly lacquered.

Kitty's eyes fell on Mrs. Meisels' pregnant belly. It was covered by an apron with so many holes in it that it looked like a melon in a net.

Kitty noted that the place was absolutely clean; the poor family must have eaten every crumb, everything that could soil a surface. Tiny faces peered silently from under tattered quilts.

Sender and Kitty had brought along leftover food from the Seven Blessings, the week of fancy dinners that followed the wedding. The Meisels children tore the packages apart with their eyes.

Leading with the candle stub, Sender took Kitty into a second room. In the gloom a figure sat. Sender raised the dim candle to the figure's face. Kitty gasped.

"Hello, Anschel," Sender said softly.

Anschel smiled, but he had been smiling before, even, Kitty suspected, while sitting alone in the dark.

"This is Kitty," said Sender. "She's my wife."

Anschel didn't seem to hear. He found a loose thread on his sleeve and began to play with it in rapt attention.

"Look," said Sender, raising Anschel's chin with one hand and holding the candle up to Kitty's face with the other. "Isn't she pretty?"

Anschel continued to smile absently, but was more eager to return to his string. A silvery line of drool crept down his chin as he concentrated.

Kitty had always thought that Sender's physical beauty was a major reason that she had fallen in love with him. It was carnal and shallow of her, but there it was.

Now, however, she saw Sender's precise image in another man. It entered a hole in her heart and then exited. She felt nothing, not even the comfort of recognizing the familiar. Anschel was not Sender. Anschel was a cardboard image of Sender.

As they left the Meisels' house Kitty saw Sender's eyes water in the biting cold. His eyes had not watered on the way there, although it had been just as cold.

She could see that no matter how many times Sender had visited Anschel, no matter how often his dreams were dashed, he continued to hope that his brother would be just a little bit improved. And each time the facts hit him like fresh blows.

"Anschel looks well" said Kitty. "He's well fed, and his clothes are in good shape. It's clear the Meisels treat him with kindness. Better than their own kids."

"My mother comes every day. She feeds and bathes Anschel and keeps him neat. She doesn't think we know, but we all know. All of us come and all of us know about the others coming. But it's no use. No one makes a difference. Nothing helps."

Kitty took Sender's arm. "I know this sounds dreadful, honey, but, you know, in some ways Anschel is lucky. He is loved, and he is happy."

"How do you know? How could you possibly know that?"

Kitty knit her brow. "That smile. At first I thought it was a meaningless grimace, but I changed my mind. He's smiling because he's happy."

"You think so?"

"I know it," she said stoutly.

Sender considered her words and slowly, smiled.

Her heart leapt like a deer. This smile, *this* smile, was the light that had been extinguished in his brother.

Sender's tie to Anschel was a powerful one that held him to his natal family, but other ties began to weaken. The Baron began to turn from the past. While Sender continued working long hours in the heroic struggle to pay off the family debts, he was eager to finish this chapter of history and start fresh with his bride.

A few weeks after the wedding each of Sender's married sisters invited the couple for dinner. Theirs were indeed admirable families. The brothers-in-law sparkled with Torah learning, the children were well behaved. The twin nieces were little angels. The sisters and their families were, as Sari would say, aristocrats.

Neither of the families lived in luxury. They had modest homes and burgeoning numbers of children. But Kitty was keenly aware that both brothers-in-law had sat for years studying in yeshiva, supported by the hard-won dowries. And both families enjoyed steady income from the small businesses bought by the remainder. And both couples went to sleep each night untroubled by how they would pay the bills.

That peace, thought Kitty, was bought at the expense of the Halters, which now included herself. It wasn't fair! Why, her Sender was every bit as intelligent as the sisters' husbands, yet he was still toiling for the other men's studies. She and Sender were at least as capable of running a business as the two older couples, yet had no money to buy one. Did the sisters even realize who paid for their good fortune?

But Kitty said nothing to Sender. Sari had warned her before the wedding, "If you would be happily married, never, ever, criticize your in-laws to your husband."

Anyway, she was hardly in a position to call those kettles black, she thought angrily. Wasn't it her own dowry that was inexplicably missing? Neither Sari nor any of her other sisters had made a move to explain why. Kitty fumed. She was all grown up now, a married woman. But apparently that still wasn't mature enough to be told what had happened to the money.

What a hypocrite she was. She expected Sender to face up to his family, yet how timid she was about questioning her own. She'd just have to screw up her courage and confront Sari.

One of these days.

CHAPTER THIRTEEN

March, 1938.

A bare month after marrying, Kitty had the opportunity for a vacation. She was to accompany her best friend, Rachel-Leah, on a trip to Vienna. As both of their husbands were busy at work, the two young women would be traveling alone.

Rachel-Leah had been growing increasingly impatient with the fact that she had not yet gotten pregnant. The family doctor had recommended a simple procedure in his office, under local anesthesia. But Hasidic custom demanded that any surgery would be performed by the very best specialist. An appointment was made with one of the world's leading gynecologists, a professor at the University of Vienna.

With her fluent Austrian German, and an aunt in the city, Kitty took charge of the travel plans. Although intending to stay for less than a week, the two young matrons packed several suitcases with their most fashionable ensembles. They expected the medical part of the trip to be quickly concluded, leaving plenty of time for the good part: sightseeing and shopping.

The train ride itself, across half of Czechoslovakia, was an adventure. Kitty prepped Rachel-Leah about Viennese life, which she remembered warmly from the summers of her childhood.

"My relatives are not terribly religious, Rachel-Leah, but you needn't worry about the food. My aunt keeps a strictly kosher kitchen, of course.

"The problem is my Uncle Wilhelm. He was always a bad influence on my aunt. He's rather a pompous fellow. Never spent a day in yeshiva, but figures he knows more than any rabbi. He's a big success, though. He built a pencil factory up from nothing. And he is now the president of the Jewish Cultural Center.

"You're going to love my cousin Lotte. She is such fun! We're almost the same age. We spent so much time together, we were like twins. Until Mother got sick, of course." She turned her head to look at the passing scenery.

"What was she wearing at your wedding?" asked Rachel-Leah, trying to place Lotte.

"They weren't there. I've been wondering about that. It's not as if they couldn't afford the train fare."

Rachel-Leah had never seen a home as luxurious as Kitty's relatives' apartment. "It's like a palace," she breathed, reverently stroking plush velvet and golden tassels.

"We always thought it a bit much," whispered Kitty. "Helen called it ro-coo-coo.'"

They were four for dinner. Rachel-Leah gaped at the embroidered tablecloth laden with gilded porcelain and heavy silver flatware. A crystal chandelier hovered above them like a brilliant cloud.

"Where is Cousin Lotte?" asked Kitty. "I've been telling Rachel-Leah so much about her."

"Lotte's been spending some time in the country. Because of the political situation, you see," her aunt said.

"Oh, yes," said Rachel-Leah, "my husband says Hitler wants to annex Austria. If that happens, God forbid, what is to become of our people here?"

"You mustn't worry your pretty little heads about such nonsense, girls. The Austrians will resist the Germans to the last man. But even if Hitler were to weasel his way in, it would be very different from the situation in Germany. The Austrians are entirely independent types, you see. Live and let live—well! That's our motto, heh heh."

Uncle Wilhelm leaned back in his chair with a satisfying whoosh of upholstery. "The Austrian is calm, cultured, and he takes his Church seriously. Quite a contrast to those German boors!"

The appointment with the doctor was for the next afternoon. His office was located in one of the most elegant neighborhoods, so Kitty and Rachel-Leah decided to spend the morning touring the nearby promenades. The shops there were very expensive; they would have to content themselves with window-shopping.

They sighed with appreciation and longing at the beautiful clothes, jewels, and furniture. Soon, however, they began to notice certain disquieting signs. "This is an Aryan-owned concern," a posting stated in delicate lettering. The stores without the signs were empty.

The two friends paused for coffee at a sidewalk cafe. As they sipped, they noticed a commotion in the distance. Paying their bill, they walked over, joining a large, curious crowd.

At its center they saw a badly beaten man. His face was bruised and swollen as a ripe tomato. A pant leg was completely torn off and revealed a jagged bone sticking out of his shin. The man let out a terrible moan, and two teeth dropped from his mouth.

"My God," said Kitty to the woman next to her, who carried a crocodile purse. "Has someone called an ambulance?"

"Ambulance! I should say not. Communist! Let him die on the street like a dog."

Kitty pulled Rachel-Leah by the arm. "Let's get out of here. This is dangerous."

"But we're not communists. We're against communists. Aren't we?"

"Come on."

The great gynecologist's office overlooked a broad boulevard, whose trees were unfurling the first signs of green. Rachel-Leah had memorized her lines, speaking Yiddish-inflected German. "Herr Professor, please help me. I have been married for well over a year now and have yet to conceive."

"Really," he replied, "and you people generally breed so briskly."

Kitty stared at the doctor, but she could not read his eyes. His glasses were so highly polished that they were opaque, flat discs of light.

After examining Rachel-Leah, the professor recommended the same procedure as the doctor in Janace had.

"Would it be possible to get an appointment tomorrow, Herr Professor?" Kitty asked. "We'd like to get back to Czechoslovakia as soon as possible. Because of the political situation."

"Yes, indeed. And please pay the fee now. Because of the political situation."

When Kitty and Rachel-Leah returned to the apartment, there was a group of angry men there, raising their voices to Uncle Wilhelm.

"You can't just sit there. You've got to do something."

"Gentlemen, please. Why must there always be a hue and cry from the Jewish community? Let us show our Christian friends that we can be just as genteel and civilized as they. It will be to our advantage in the long run."

"What long run? German troops are massed on the border. They could move in any minute. They could be marching even as we speak."

"What can I do?" said Uncle Wilhelm, but he didn't look too perturbed.

"At least issue a statement on behalf of the community. Why do you think we elected you, anyway?"

"Well, I shall give the matter my most serious consideration. Excuse me, gentlemen. My supper is growing cold."

Rachel-Leah had been told to eat nothing before her operation, and Kitty was just as happy to go to bed immediately. This was not turning out to be the pleasure trip she had hoped for.

The next morning, as they went to the doctor, they noticed a festive mood outside. On the streetcar there were many children who ought to have been in school. Women carried bunches of flowers, and there was bunting around the poles of street lamps. Homemade swastika banners were displayed everywhere, although showing these was illegal.

At the doctor's office, a nurse prepared Rachel-Leah for surgery, while Kitty waited edgily in the waiting room. It was quiet, very quiet, but it was impossible to read.

Soon she noticed it was not as still as before. There was a distant, increasing growl. After a while it became a rhythmic cheer, like a large stadium of soccer fans welcoming a winning team.

"They're here! They're here!" A man burst into the waiting room. The Wehrmacht has entered Vienna!"

Except for Kitty, everyone else in the waiting room rose and applauded.

The nurse called Kitty into a consultation room. "Your friend is fine. The operation went as expected."

"Thank Heaven."

"Mrs. Halter, I'm sorry to have to say this. Ordinarily we like to observe the patient for a few hours after the procedure. But under the circumstances Herr Professor feels it would be best for you and your friend to leave as soon as she can get dressed."

The nurse left the door ajar as she went to help the doctor finish up. Kitty could hear their conversation clearly.

"She certainly was brave, that one. Not a peep out of her. Most of the girls cry and scream, even with anesthetic," said the nurse.

"You must understand, Sister," the doctor said, "that they don't feel pain the way we do."

Kitty wrapped Rachel-Leah in a coat and hustled her out of the building as quickly as she could.

"Are you all right? Can you walk?"

Rachel-Leah was bent almost double in pain. "Yes. There's a lot of bleeding, but the n-nurse gave me thick pads."

Kitty managed to steer her out the front door of the building. The sight that met them was not to be believed.

Thousands of people lined the sides of the boulevard. They were shouting themselves hoarse, waving handkerchiefs and silk scarves, and stabbing the air with the Hitler salute. The people were in ecstasy, although the Germans were not yet in sight.

"Try and walk a bit faster, Rachel-Leah. I'm sorry, but we must get out of this place. These people have gone insane."

"That's okay. I can walk as fast as we need to. I can do anything now." Her eyes gleamed. "The only thing that matters is, now I can have a baby."

Kitty steered Rachel-Leah around a corner, then another. Soon they were lost, but at least these streets were quiet. In fact, they were completely abandoned.

A single vehicle moved on the horizon, coming toward them. It was a taxi!

Kitty hailed it, and the cab came to a smart stop. She gathered Rachel-Leah onto the back seat and gave the driver her aunt's address.

"Oh, madam, it isn't wise to go there now. That's a Jewish neighborhood."

"Please, you must! We don't know anyone else in the city. And my friend is unwell."

The driver shrugged his shoulders and proceeded through back streets as best as he could. But after a while he was forced into larger throughways where traffic could barely move. Finally they came to a dead stop.

"It isn't far from here, madam, but I wouldn't advise your friend..."

Kitty got out of the taxi, leaving the door open. They were right in front of the beautiful Jewish Culture Center, a marble-faced building at a handsome plaza. The street was thronged.

In the center of the plaza was a middle-aged man on his hands and knees. Another middle-aged man was kicking him repeatedly in the buttocks. The victim did not rise, but continued to crawl forward on his elbows.

It was Uncle Wilhelm!

"What do you say, Jew-dog?" shouted the tormentor, as he gave Wilhelm another kick.

"Bow-wow," said her uncle.

"What?" Another kick.

"BOW-WOW!" Uncle Wilhelm was crying, and mucus was running from his nose.

"No!" shouted the other man, with a kick that flattened Wilhelm. "Say, please, sir, I'd like another one."

Wilhelm got back on his hands and knees. "Please, sir, I'd like another one."

The crowd roared with laughter, as if Chaplin was performing for them.

Kitty rushed back to the taxi, slamming the door, as if she could shut out the ugliness. Rachel-Leah was now white with loss of blood, and Kitty thought she herself must be just as white.

Kitty pressed her temples, she had to think.

"Driver, please take us to the train station. We are Czech citizens. We'll forget our luggage for now and go directly back home."

"That's not such a good idea, madam. The Germans are in complete control of the central train station."

Kitty fought to keep down panic. What should they do?

It was as if the cabby heard her. "May I suggest, madam, that I drive you ladies to the Czech border. It should be safe to take the train from there."

"But it's so far. We don't have enough money."

"Not to worry, madam."

Kitty did worry. If the driver didn't get money, what might he demand in payment? Perhaps they could offer him their wedding bands. No! Earrings? She sighed, whatever he would settle for. There was no alternative.

The taxi slipped magically out of the city. The roads around Vienna were nearly empty, and soon they were in the countryside, bursting with spring.

Rachel-Leah moaned long and deep. Kitty started. This was the first sound she had heard from her brave friend, who had not even cried out during surgery.

She moved Rachel-Leah over a bit, to what she hoped was a more comfortable position. It was then Kitty noticed that the seat was soaked with blood.

The taxi was speeding now, and had entered an uninhabited area. Modesty protected, Kitty shoved a fresh pad between Rachel-Leah's legs. The bleeding must have been stanched, because Rachel-Leah relaxed and fell asleep. Kitty too, closed her exhausted eyes. It was barely three in the afternoon.

She awoke with a scream. On both sides of the taxi were nightmare faces. About a dozen identical, grimacing gargoyles peered through the glass. The sound of a thousand crickets made her cringe. Kitty slipped to the floor.

"Don't be alarmed, madam. It's just a local custom in these parts. The townspeople dress up in costumes around this time of year to perform their ancient rituals. They shake their noisemakers to drive out the evil spirits of winter."

Kitty climbed back up on the seat. The figures had receded and she could now tell that they were men in ceremonial robes and masks. Their conical headdresses were like vividly colored clowns' hats, but there was something about their earnestness that was decidedly not funny.

"They take this seriously, don't they."

"Yes, madam, very seriously."

"But this area is Catholic, isn't it?"

"Yes, madam. Very religious."

"And doesn't the Church object? I mean, it's paganism."

The driver's back shrugged.

By the time they reached the station on the border, Kitty was calmer, and Rachel-Leah refreshed. Kitty was relieved to learn that a train was leaving for Bratislava in five minutes. There was always a convenient connecting train to Janace from there.

Fortunately, they had their passports and train tickets with them. After helping Rachel-Leah out of the car, Kitty pooled their remaining money. She went over to the driver's side of the taxi.

"We can never thank you enough, sir. I'm afraid this is all we have with us, but if you give me your address I promise to send the..."

But the taxi zoomed away, leaving a cloud of dust.

Back in Janace, Kitty waited several weeks for the return of her suitcases; they never arrived. This was most unlike her aunt, who was very correct about such matters.

Finally, she wrote a careful letter requesting the return of the items. She explained that Rachel-Leah's reaction to surgery had necessitated their hasty departure. She thanked the entire family for their hospitality. She did not mention the incident at the Jewish Culture Center. Perhaps Uncle Wilhelm had managed to hide what had happened from his wife.

Afterwards, Kitty wrote several more letters to her aunt, but neither she nor her sisters ever again heard from the family in Vienna.

CHAPTER FOURTEEN

Ruhigbad

Eva woke at noon, but pressed her head into the pillow, wishing she could sleep some more. She was so bored nowadays that sleep was her greatest diversion.

Ever since she had begun to show, Odilo had hardly spoken to her. At first she thought the reason was that he was afraid that she might press him into marriage. She assured him she wouldn't.

Instead of being pleased or relieved, he snapped, "I can't marry you anyway."

"That's all right," she said sportingly.

"I'm already married."

Eva didn't know why she was so shocked, considering she was married herself.

"You could divorce."

"On what grounds? My wife is a good German mother and homemaker. I am perfectly satisfied with her."

Eva swallowed hard, but the humiliation would not go down.

"At least provide me with a certificate of paternity. I want this child to be verified as a pure Aryan."

Odilo Konrad was now deputy commissioner of the Sudeten-Deutsch Home Front, the party representing the local German population. If, as was growing apparent, some sort of alliance with Germany was in the making, Odilo could make life very comfortable for her and the baby. One had to think ahead.

Konrad stroked his chin. "I have a better idea. Why don't you claim the child is Rosen's? Your Jew employer will pay you handsomely to keep your mouth shut."

Eva thought realistically about her brother-in-law. "Ignatz Rosen doesn't even look at the maids. He won't bite."

"Doesn't he have some sons, the heirs?"

"They're still schoolboys. And they're hardly ever home." The two oldest boys in yeshiva were very pious, too. Odilo obsessed about the richest Jew in town, but he didn't understand what an Orthodox family was like.

She'd let the matter rest. There would be time for discussions later, after the child was born. But she hadn't expected that Odilo would cool to her in the interim. He said he found a pregnant woman's body disgusting.

Martin had the opposite reaction. From the first missed period, the first swelling of her breasts, even the first retches of morning sickness, he had been mad with desire.

"Stay away from me," she warned, "it's bad for the baby."

"But darling, the Talmud says that relations during a healthy pregnancy are good for the baby and the mother, too. It doesn't say anything about the father, but I'm willing to take the risk."

"Very funny, Martin. My doctor says no. What are you going to follow, the advice of modern science, or that of some stupid old books?"

She had gone to a German doctor, although there were plenty of Jewish ones in this spa town, where many came from abroad for therapy. But she preferred to be patient "Elsa Kreutzer." She thrilled at playing another woman, another mother. She preferred the other, created, identity.

No sex, the doctor had insisted. "Only an ape would rut after it has been inseminated. And some lower order of human, perhaps."

So Martin, as always, agreed to abide by her decision. He grew chillier and more distant, especially after Kitty's wedding. He spent a lot of time away from the house, often eating his meals at Martha's. He no longer questioned her about her whereabouts, day or night. It was almost as if he were no longer a husband to her. That was fine with Eva. Martin was getting to be disgusting. His hair had gone completely white, and his skin sagged like an old man's.

She realized now that Martin would never make any serious money or achieve a position of power. Loser.

The major news from the wedding (she'd had no intention of going herself, all that bother, just to dance with some religious nuts?) was that Kitty had gotten herself a really good-looking fellow.

Cunning little Kitty, she sure was an operator. Eva wondered what

Kitty had had to do to trap the likes of Sender Halter.

She sighed. Things would have been a lot different had she stuck closer to Kitty than to Renee. She should have let Renee keep Martin, big bargain that he was. She should have let them all sail off to Palestine, off the edge of the earth, as far as she cared. Damned bad luck.

"Hello, Frau Kreutzer. What are you cooking? May I help?"

Frau Kreutzer was stretching out sausage skins. The kitchen was steamy and a tangy odor was in the air.

"I'm making black pudding."

"Black pudding? With chocolate?"

"No, no. You know, blood sausage."

"Oh, blood sausage. Why didn't you say so?" Eva's smile was a rictus. Blood was the ultimate Jewish food taboo. Pork had become routine. But blood?

"Yes. Didn't your mother ever make it?"

Eva suspected Frau Kreutzer was testing her.

"No, she never did." Eva remembered her mother baking a cake. Each egg was broken into a little cup and inspected for blood drops. If there was even a speck of red, you had to throw the egg out and then scour the cup. If you forgot and broke the tainted egg right into the batter, you'd have to throw the whole cake out.

"No, of course not. It's a country thing," said Frau Kreutzer. "There, the first batch is done. Have some."

Eva put a small slice of sausage in her mouth. This was no bland piece of ham; the flavor burst in her mouth like a grenade. Despite herself, her ears rang with biblical verses. *"But of the blood you shall not eat, for the blood is the LIFE of it."*

She cut another, larger piece and chewed on it thoughtfully. Then she ate more rapidly, finishing the sausage. Suddenly she felt free, free of the pounding verses, free of her parents, nagging even after death, free of the chains and constraints of centuries. She felt free and powerful and not bored any more.

"This is awfully good, Frau Kreutzer."

"You don't know the half of it. The secret is in the freshness. Schwartz the butcher swears he killed the hog this morning, but he's a liar as well as a thief. In the old days we used to say 'for a really fine black pudding, the pig has to dine with you.'"

"What does that mean?"

"It means you bleed the pig before you slaughter it. Live blood makes for a really fresh-tasting sausage."

Eva's eyes widened. Now they were talking not of the Jewish Law, of the endless splitting of moral hairs. On the table was a challenge to the Law of the Children of Noah, the basic rules of civilization for which all peoples were liable.

Eating "the limb of a living thing" was like murder or incest or idolatry.

Eva's heart filled with power, as never before. "Please, may I have another piece?"

"Certainly. Good for the little Jew you've got in your belly. Pardon me, half-Jew."

Eva wondered, what would Frau Kreutzer say if she knew that the baby was a half-Jew, but on its *mother's* side? But then, why should it have to be a Jew at all?

"Frau Kreutzer, I have a secret to tell you." The older woman moved her beaky head closer.

"This baby isn't my Jew husband's."

After the little story, cleaned up a bit for judgmental ears, Frau Kreutzer leaned across and squeezed Eva's hands. It was the first time the older woman had touched her.

Frau Kreutzer poured two large glasses of beer for them.

"Let us toast the child." She raised her glass. "May it be a son. May he be brave in battle, and a glory to his race."

Eva raised her glass higher. "To my warrior son!"

The following day Frau Kreutzer knocked on her door. Eva opened it wide. "What a pleasant surprise, please come in."

"No, no" said Frau Kreutzer. "You come over to my place. There is something you must see." Her eyes darted about fearfully. There were many alien, Jewish things to be seen in the parlor. Candlesticks, books. Lots of books.

Eva was just as glad. Mrs. Kreutzer would probably disapprove of her housekeeping, or rather, its absence. Why should she bother working hard, Martin didn't count, and no one else ever saw the place.

In the Kreutzer's kitchen was a folded newspaper. It was Der Sturmer, from Germany, Hitler's favorite periodical.

"Scientists Prove Christ's Pure Aryan Descent!" the headline read.

"This article?"

"Yes, yes. You'll be astounded, Eva."

The story, by a professor of Near Eastern Studies at the University of Berlin, described current "research" that showed that the Virgin Mary was not a Jewess but a Moabite. It also stated that Jesus' real father was a Germanic officer in the Roman army then occupying Judea, one Julius Pondera. Moreover, it claimed that Pondera's grave had been identified in Westphalia, and was now an official shrine of the Reich.

The article was somewhat fuzzy as to the significance of these "findings." On the one hand it took great pains to show that Jesus was in no way a Jew; on the other it decried the teachings of Jesus as a Jewish plot to emasculate Aryans with the corruptions of compassion and universal love.

Eva turned the page. There was a drawing of a horrendous fat Jew with a huge hook nose about to rape a young woman who looked amazingly like herself. She turned another page. Here was an article by a professor of African Studies informing readers of the special horrors of the Dark Continent. It was illustrated by a photograph of a gorilla-like creature, which was identified as the offspring of a Negro and an ape.

"Where did you get this?"

"Herr Kreutzer brings it home. He is of the opinion that we women should be informed about world events, same as the menfolk," she said proudly.

Frau Kreutzer folded the paper back to the original article. "Isn't that amazing?"

Eva shrugged.

"Think, Eva. Isn't that just like you?"

"What do you mean?"

"How you came to be impregnated by a clean-blooded German, instead of your Jew husband. Like the Madonna!"

Eva turned on her neighbor. "I said that was a secret! How dare you tell your husband. Who else did you tell? Spit it out!"

"No one, I swear it."

Frau Kreutzer was on the defensive, Eva realized happily.

"What an idiot. And I was a fool to tell you. You're jeopardizing my life!"

Frau Kreutzer turned pale. "Oh, no Eva. I would never do that. I told no one. Certainly not Herr Kreutzer. Why, we never talk about anything."

Eva grumbled. The Nazis were right about one thing: some were genetically destined to rule, others to be ruled. She was meant to stand over Frau Kreutzer, and other women like her, and rule with an iron hand.

"Look, Eva...Frau Blumenthal, I am honored to share your secret. Would that my daughter..." said Frau Kreutzer, but her eyes were dry.

"I, too, have a secret, and would be honored to share it with you."
Eva cocked her head.

"Since I was a little girl, I was consecrated to the Goddess Freya."
Eva blinked, uncomprehending.

"On the outside, we were good Catholics. But inside our hearts, and whenever we could, we followed the ancient ways, the ways of Odin and his companions."

"But that's so silly," Eva blurted. "These are modern times, the twentieth century. Gods and goddesses? No one believes in such things anymore."

"No, no. It is all true. Don't ask your brain, that's been tainted with Jewish thoughts. Ask your blood, your blood will verify that it is true. The Jews speak to us with words, but the gods speak to us on another level, on a level beyond logic."

That mouthful was certainly not coming from Frau Kreutzer's head. "Who told you these things?" she commanded.

"There are others, many others. The Fuhrer himself leads us and inspires us. You know the swastika is really Thor's hammer," she said, as if that was the most amazing coincidence.

"See here, Frau Blumenthal. This Saturday night is the Walpurgis. You will come with us. Then you will understand. And you will believe."

The Kreutzers were getting a ride up to the mountains with some other celebrants, and they had to leave early. It was Saturday and the Sabbath was not yet over, but that didn't matter. Martin had gone to the synagogue and would not be home until long after dark. He no longer waited for her before going to sleep.

It was utterly dark—the Jewish New Moon, by coincidence. How inefficient to have a midnight ceremony on a moonless night, Eva thought. Jewish festivals were always mid-month, with a full moon softening the darkness. But the Walpurgis had to be observed on the eve of Beltane, May Day. Besides, with dozens of young men carrying huge torches, they provided their own light.

The truck that had brought them could not proceed very far into the mountains, so they all got out and walked. Pregnant Eva and fat old Herr Kreutzer were quite winded by the climb. But Frau Kreutzer was already having a good time.

"Just think," she exulted, "in my youth Mother took me into the Harz Mountains to celebrate Walpurgis Night, and now I am taking you, Eva."

"Oh, hush up," Eva said under her breath.

"Yeah," said Herr Kreutzer, "shut your trap before I punch your face in for you."

Frau Kreutzer shrank back, and followed several paces behind them.

They came to a clearing within a copse of large old oaks, where torch-bearing youths formed a circle. The well-built young men were dressed like boy scouts.

Eva shrieked and pointed. Animals were swinging from the trees.

"Don't be frightened," laughed Frau Kreutzer. "Those are sacrifices to the gods."

Sheep, goats, pigs, a calf, a small colt, and a large dog were all hanged by their necks from nooses attached to sturdy limbs.

"In the old days—not that I saw, but Mother told me—there was always at least one man."

"Human sacrifices?" asked Eva, not believing.

"Oh, they were people who deserved to die. Criminals and such like."

She took Eva by the hand and led her to the edge of the clearing, where they sat on some rocks with other women. They stayed there for the rest of the night—only men were at the center of the ceremonies.

Some celebrants opened bottles of wine. Each one took a bottle and addressed a hanged animal carcass. Invoking one of the gods, the celebrant poured the wine over the animal, letting it pool below the beast. Then he nicked the groin of the animal, and its blood poured down, mingling with the wine.

At the center of the clearing the men dug holes in the ground and buried the bottles to the necks, forming a swastika.

Four men, moving clockwise, put shiny objects at each spoke of the swastika. To the north, a sickle, to the east, a spear, to the south, a sword, to the west, a horn.

The four men stood at attention and snapped their arms up in the Hitler salute. "Sieg heil!" they roared.

"Sieg heil!" the crowd roared back. So Eva did too.

After that everyone relaxed and sat down. Herr Kreutzer came over to them, rubbing his hands. "Now comes the sensible part of this thing," he said to Eva. She looked at him quizzically.

"You don't imagine anybody would drag themselves all the way up here just for this mumbo jumbo," he said.

Frau Kreutzer looked angry, but she did not dare contradict her husband.

Men rolled up barrels of beer and crates of wine and schnapps. Women brought smaller supplies of food—potatoes and sausages.

"This is the sumbel," Frau Kreutzer said, excited. "The drinking horn is filled with mead and passed around. Everybody gives a toast, or brags, or sings a song."

"Brags?"

"Yes. To brag is good, Bragi is the god of poetry. It's a good way of linking yourself to your ancestors." She frowned. "The Jews would have it that we take credit only for our own actions, but that is wrong. Let us boast of our ancestral deeds. We are our ancestors, and they are us. It's all in the blood."

The first man took a long swig of mead. "In me is the great wolf-god reincarnated! Holy is the tribe. Holy is the race."

The second man had to put his beer stein down to take up the horn. He drank deeply, and, considering that he was already drunk, spoke with surprising clarity.

"Duty to one's ancestors and kin is a holy duty that comes first. To hell with universalism, the teachings of Bolsheviks and Jews. Vikings, be true to your blood."

There were shouts of "Jawohl," which, as the night progressed, tended to become drunken grunts.

The horn passed to another. "I will now speak the praises of the gods," he said. "Odin, who breaks all the rules of 'civilization' to affirm his mastery of the universe."

Hoots of drunken approval. Another man indicated that he wanted the horn.

"To Thor, who indulges his appetites without shame or fear; so may we all."

Eva was astounded to see Frau Kreutzer waving for the mead horn. She was the first woman to do so. The men passed it over without hesitation.

"All hail the Sacred Sow! All praise the goddess who slakes her lust with her divine brother."

"Sieg heil!"

Another woman now felt free to take the horn. "Rejoice Freya, you who receives one half of all warriors fallen in battle. The day is coming when your halls will be overflowing with battle-bloodied soldiers."

"Sieg heil!"

A man, less drunk than the others, now took the cup. "May strength and ambition, pleasure and ferocity, never again be shackled by the chains of the Jews. Never again shall the mighty feel guilty for imposing their will!"

The words reverberated inside Eva. As Frau Kreutzer said, her blood recognized the truth. The spirits of her Aryan ancestors were born anew inside her...Yes, it was so. Somehow. Mother had been so tall and blond, somehow...perhaps Mother had also found an Aryan father for her children, because surely they were of icy, clean Nordic stock. All except Kitty. That scheming little Jewess was her father's daughter.

The mead horn had been refilled after every toast or two. Eva watched it go back and forth. She rose to her feet, and waved it over with a shaky arm. She had drunk more than she realized, and the horn spilled over as she raised it.

She held her hand over her stomach. "I swear by the wolf-child that grows within me," she began, to approving grunts, "I swear by the thunder gods and goddesses who spawned me. Guilt is the only evil. There is no sin. There is no God. There is no sin."

"Sieg heil!"

In the last months of pregnancy Eva agonized over the baby. What if it was a boy? She had to keep Martin from having it circumcised. But was that possible? The bris was no minor Jewish custom. She knew that Jews had it done even under pain of death. She wasn't sure that even her iron will and Martin's passivity would work this time. If worse came to worst, though, she would tell him the truth. She would not permit her pure, Nordic son to be mutilated.

Martha insisted that her own obstetrician attend the birth. "Nothing succeeds like success," she said cheerily. As if her herd of cattle was a "success," thought Eva. However, Martha also paid for the doctor, and for a baby nurse, so Eva agreed.

You were supposed to forget the pain of childbirth as soon as it was over, but Eva realized when labor began that she would never forget. And she would never forgive, either, and never have another baby, no matter who would be the father.

When she awoke, a nurse entered with a blanket-wrapped bundle, smiling. Smiling, as if there were nothing wrong, she placed the bundle near Eva's breast.

Eva removed the blanket from around the little face, then, quickly, uncovered its head. Shocked, furious, she ripped the blanket off its body, and despite its squalls, tore the diaper off, sending the pins flying.

She screamed.

It was a boy. A dark, dark boy.

The nurse rushed to take the baby away. A lot of them were like that, in the beginning, she thought. It took a while for the chemicals of mother-love to kick in.

For eight days Eva lay in bed. On the eighth was the circumcision, at Martha's house. Martha and her staff had been cooking and baking for all those eight days, and all the Jews in town were invited to the party.

"Aren't you coming, Little Mother?" said Martin.

Eva winced. "I've always been afraid of that ceremony."

"Me too. But we're not exactly the first Jewish parents to face the challenge."

"But it's so bloody and barbaric. You go ahead Martin. Tell them I'm resting."

"We'll be away a long time. Can you bear to leave the baby so long?"

"It's not as if he's nursing. He won't know the difference." She was bottle-feeding the baby. It was more modern.

Martin sighed, and left. The birth of the baby hadn't changed Eva, hadn't returned her to the way she had been before they were married.

As soon as Martin, the nurse, and the baby were gone, Eva got dressed and went to the stationery store, which had a telephone. She called Odilo at his office.

They agreed to meet at the old beer hall. Eva had lots of cash on hand to pay the nurse and buy things for the baby, so she took a taxi.

They met in the back room, as usual.

"Did you get rid of it?" he asked. Her stomach was flattening nicely.

"In a manner of speaking."

She looked closely at his face. He, too, was dark, every bit as dark as Martin. Yet the baby was darker than either of them! Was it Odilo's? Was it Martin's? Or was it some fiend that had crept full-formed into her womb?

For eight days she had pondered and pondered. Sometimes it looked like one man, and then, in a different light, from a different angle, it looked like the other. But now it no longer mattered. She would make no fuss.

Martin loved the baby, would love it even if she told him the truth. Odilo hated it. Even if it had piercing blue eyes and a little mustache, Odilo would hate it.

"It's good that you're back to your old self, Elsa," said Odilo.

He pushed her down on the floor and forced himself into her. She was still bleeding from the birth, and the stitches hurt like hell, but even so, she loved it.

"More," she said, gasping with passion and pain. "More."

CHAPTER FIFTEEN

The scene was like something from a movie: a tall, beautiful woman carrying a bouquet of drooping flowers wandered among the tombstones in a dense, cold fog.

The housekeeper saw her from a window of the rectory and called out, "Hullo there. Can I help you, miss?"

"Why, yes. Thank you. My name is Frau Kreutzer, from Pilsen. I recently married the nephew of Herr Kreutzer, of Linden Street..."

"I know them," the housekeeper snapped.

"Yes, well, my husband recalled his poor little cousin, gone these many years, and I thought I would bring some flowers to her grave. But I can't seem to find it. There are other Kreutzers, but no Elsa."

"You won't find grave or stone of her there, miss. The Kreutzers," she said the name as if it were something stuck in her throat, "would never spend the money. They buried the poor thing in the common plot."

"Oh, my goodness."

"Yes, indeed. And I hope your husband is nothing like his uncle and aunt. Godless trash, they are."

"Heavens! I can't believe we're talking about the same people. Are you sure? The little girl was named Elsa."

"I'm sure. I couldn't forget any of them if I tried. Murderers. And they'll have to answer to the Lord on Judgment Day, even if they got away with it this far."

"Whatever do you mean, ma'am?" Was there a possibility of blackmail here?

"That little Elsa, she was a hunchback. The Kreutzers hated her. They'd beat her and beat her, always on the hump. One time they cut right through it, and the hump became infected. They just kept beating her on it. Eventually she died, just as they'd hoped. They threw her in the pauper's ground there."

"Oh no. I simply can't believe that's true. I mean, they're a bit tight with their money, but such cruelty..."

"No? Come and see for yourself. I'll take you to the parish records. I'm really not supposed to show these without the priest's permission, but Father is busy..."

They went to the archives. The housekeeper pulled out the child's baptismal papers. Eva stared, memorizing the information. "Well, that's the girl, all right, but the death, the grave..."

"Here. Look at the death and burial certificates. It's all on paper."

"Oh, my. Oh, my." Eva extended the flowers. "I guess I won't be needing these, if she has no grave. Would you like them?"

The housekeeper brightened. "How nice. I'll just put them in water. Not for myself, for the Holy Mother."

As the housekeeper turned to find a vase, Eva stashed the death certificate inside her raincoat. When the housekeeper returned, she was filing the baptismal record. "I've put them all back in their place."

"Oh, thank you. How nice of you."

Back at home, Eva burned the death certificate in the stove. Perhaps there was a copy at the town hall, but the parish records were always the first to be checked. And Elsa Kreutzer, as far as the church was concerned, was alive and well, with neither death certificate nor gravestone to testify otherwise. This had worked out even better than she'd expected.

October 1, 1938

"I can't believe it. I can't believe that the British would betray us like this!"

It was the Rosen's junior maid, Anna, speaking. This was amazing enough. She was a Czech girl from a strict, reclusive Protestant sect, and she hardly ever ventured opinions about anything, certainly not politics.

But the situation was extraordinary, indeed, unbelievable. Neville Chamberlain had given—not negotiated, *given away*—a huge chunk of Czechoslovakia, the Sudetenland. This amputation of a democratic ally was done to buy "peace in our time."

All he wanted was Sudetenland, said Hitler, that's all. After that, he would never bother anyone again.

"You must leave!" Anna whispered fiercely to her mistress. "All the

Jewish people must leave right away."

"Yes, dear, I'm afraid we must," said Martha. "But not just yet. We have to pack. And Mr. Rosen needs to settle business matters. We must find someone to take care of the factory in his absence."

Anna wrung her hands, and immersed herself deep in her Bible.

It took only two weeks to prove Anna right, and the Rosens desperately wrong.

The Rosens, and Martin, were eating dinner. There was all the usual food, but the mood was worse than somber. Nazi thugs had broken into the factory offices that day and vandalized everything. They burned papers, broke typewriters, smashed telephones. Luckily, Ignatz had locked himself in the washroom until the Nazis left.

Most of the other Jews in town had fled east, to the territory still held by Czechoslovakia. After their country had made such a sacrifice for the free nations of the world, surely their friends would protect them from further predation by Germany.

This dinner was to be the last meal served by the Rosen's loyal staff. As of today, no non-Jews could be employed by Jews.

Anna placed the soup tureen at Martha's place. Martha stood, lifted the lid, and...

A rapping at the door. Thunderous, insistent.

Everyone froze.

The knockers were not patient. They broke down the door, took it off its hinges, and left it in splinters.

The Nazis came to the dinner table. They were beautifully barbered, polished, gleaming. As if the Grim Reaper was moonlighting as a theatrical costumer.

"Mr. Ignatz Rosen?"

No one moved.

The Nazis glared, then smiled. They relished the possibility of disobedience.

A chair scraped. Martin Blumenthal stood up.

"I am Ignatz Rosen."

Everyone else, Ignatz, Martha, the children, the servants, remained frozen.

The leader of the Nazis smiled warmly.

"Ah, very good. Well, sir, please take your coat and come with us. Just a few questions to ask."

The Nazi tipped his cap to Martha. "Your husband will be back in a little while, Frau Rosen. Nothing to worry about."

Martin went to the coatroom. Martha ran after him.

"Don't wait for me, get out tonight!" Martin whispered furiously. He threw his wallet out of his pocket.

"Martin, what are you doing?"

"They'll want the Swiss account numbers, and they will get it out of Ignatz. Believe me, they'll get it out of him."

"Martin! You're not to risk your life for money. No money on earth is worth it."

"Without money, none of you has a chance!"

"Martin, I refuse to let you do this. Think. The accounts are the same numbers as the combination on the house safe."

"What house safe? No, never mind. Don't tell me."

"The safe. Surely Eva told you."

"Eva." He laughed bitterly. "Martha, don't ever tell Eva anything. Don't trust her. She's poison."

"What do you..."

"Just leave her alone. Leave! Leave everything behind. Get to Switzerland, get the money out."

A rapping on the door again. "Now, now, lovebirds. There'll be plenty of time for all that when Ignatz gets back," the Nazi chuckled.

The office at the Gestapo headquarters was very bare. Later, equipment would be brought in as needed, equipment never seen in business offices before.

The interrogator slowly put on a pair of very soft leather gloves.

"We have a few questions to ask you, Mr. Rosen. You have a reputation for telling the truth."

"I swear I will answer everything I can."

The interrogator now had his gloves on. They were as tight and flexible as a surgeon's. "Good. Now about your Swiss accounts..."

Odilo Konrad came early the next morning.

"Well?"

The interrogator sprang to his feet and clicked his heels.

"I'm sorry, Herr Deputy. We got nothing."

"Nothing? How can that be?"

"I don't know, I..." The man's voice was tired, and there was an unaccustomed ring of self-doubt in it. He peeled off his gloves and dropped them into the wastebasket. "This has never happened before."

"What are you saying?" said Konrad. How could he not have talked?"

"I don't understand it myself, sir. He made up some ludicrous story about not being Rosen at all, about being some brother-in-law. And he stuck with it, stuck with it all the way through."

Odilo Konrad stamped his foot angrily. "You're incompetent! I'll get to the bottom of this. Where is he?"

The interrogator indicated the next room with his head. What Konrad found there couldn't be described as Ignatz Rosen—or any other man. The face and head were no longer recognizably human, and the genitals were such that no sex could be determined.

"He's dead, you idiot!" Konrad gave the corpse a kick in frustration, getting a greasy patch of flesh on his boot.

Two days later Martin had still not returned, and the Rosens knew the worst must have happened. Oddly, Eva had not called to inquire about him, so one of the older boys went to fetch her.

"What's all this about?"

"It's Martin," said Ignatz, crying. "He was taken by the Nazis. He has sacrificed his life for the family."

Eva absorbed this information for a few minutes, her face impassive. Finally, she spoke. "And what am I supposed to do now: no husband, no money, and with a starving child on my hands?" Eva wept, her tears half feigned, half genuine with self-pity.

"My poor, darling sister," Martha cried, embracing her.

Eva thought she would suffocate between Martha's big mammaries.

"Don't worry, dearest," said Martha. "The important thing is we are all together and we will all take care of each other. Tomorrow morning we are leaving for Janace. Of course you and the baby will come with us."

"No, I won't be coming with you. What is there for me in Janace? It's nothing but a Hasidic hick town."

"Unfortunately, there is no place to return to in Kosice," said Martha meaningfully.

Eva ignored her. "I have good neighbors here, the Kreutzers. They have agreed to shelter me and will vouch that I'm a Christian. But they won't take the child. They won't take a circumcised boy."

Martha was very quiet. Could any woman abandon her own child? It was unthinkable. Martin's terrible words about Eva echoed in her mind.

"Of course, we will take the baby. Tomorrow morning, bring his clothes and his bottles." She smiled wearily. "I always did want another one."

And welcome to it, thought Eva.

But the next morning, before Eva arrived, their plans were foiled. A truck came by, driven by German officers.

"All able-bodied Jewish men are to be conscripted into work camps. We've had enough of you lazy Jews, living off the labor of honest Aryans. It's time you did a day's work, for a change."

Ignatz (with Martin's papers) and the two oldest boys, were allowed one suitcase each. They would be leaving immediately, on the very truck parked before their house.

Martha thought she would die from the pain in her heart. In all the years of her marriage, she had never been parted from Ignatz for more than a week. And her two sons! Her sweet Torah scholars. Her glory.

"Don't worry about us, my love," said Ignatz. I'm in good shape for my age, and the boys are young. We can work hard."

"I'll wait here until you return home."

"No, love. Get yourself to Janace. You have two good sisters there."

He kissed her deeply. "Until we meet again."

An hour later, Eva showed up. Martha was crying so hard, she could not speak. The big girls, Malvine and Clara, told Eva what had happened.

"That's a pity. Well, here's the baby and its things."

"But Aunt Eva, we can't take him now. We don't know how we'll manage with our own little ones, now that there are no men around to care for us."

Eva was enraged. Her plans depended on this. "Martha! Stop crying. Get up. It's up to the family to live up to your promises."

"I'll take the baby."

They all turned. It was Anna, the young maid.

Martha got hold of herself. "Anna, dear, what a good heart you have. But how can you do that? Where will you take the child?"

"I'll take him back to the farm. I'll tell everybody he's my own."

Martha was stunned. Anna was a young girl with her whole life ahead of her, and she was sacrificing herself for the child. A Jewish child. "But your family is so religious. There will be a terrible scandal. They will throw you out."

"No. They will not condemn an innocent life that God has brought to earth."

It was decided then. Anna, who could not write too well, dictated her father's name, and directions to the farm, and Martha wrote everything on a paper, which she handed to Eva.

Eva hurried out of the house.

Martha looked longingly out the window. First her husband and sons, now her sister. God knew when she would see any of them again.

Her eyes widened as Eva crushed the paper into a ball and threw it in the gutter.

Eva stopped off at the stationery store with the telephone. "Odilo, get off your butt. You picked up the wrong man. The real Rosen is on the Jewish labor transport that left town this morning. You better find him and get those Swiss numbers."

There was a long, dead space on the line.

"I can't get anyone back from that transport. It's too late."

"Shit," said Eva.

"Yeah, shit."

She thought for a minute. "All right. I don't know what you've done with the men, but the rest of the Rosens are about to leave town, and they'll be taking treasure with them. Now listen carefully, and don't screw up this time. You've got to get to the safe in the master bedroom. Here's how it works..."

Eva walked home with stars in her eyes, and the vision of rubies cascading from her throat. She looked about the apartment. It was all hers now—without Martin, without the kid.

So what. Martha had never had to live in a dump like this. No, she had a beautiful mansion filled with gorgeous furniture. Well, that would change soon. The shoe was on the other foot.

Eva daydreamed about new color schemes. You could have whites and pastels with no kids to mess things up. They could redo the dining room. What a gracious hostess she would be. There would be parties, and dances, and the opera...

But meanwhile this apartment was only paid up until November fifteenth. So how to pay the rent? Martha would be no help. Odilo was probably on his way right now to clean her safe out completely.

A knock on the door.

"It's me, Frau Kreutzer."

Eva made no move to invite her in. The Kreutzers had served their purpose.

"It's so quiet here. Is anything wrong? I haven't seen Herr Blumenthal in days—or heard a peep out of the baby."

"I threw my husband out. All Aryans are supposed to get rid of their Jewish spouses. Haven't you heard? It's the law."

Frau Kreutzer's voice flattened with a stupid person's notion of irony. "What about your son? Did you throw out a future Reich soldier, too? What did you do with your pure little German?"

Martha leaned casually against the door post and folded her arms. "What did you do with yours?"

Frau Kreutzer jerked as if she had been slapped and slammed the door shut.

Eva fried up some pork sausage for lunch. She didn't have to hide anything anymore. Things were going well. However her dear "parents," the Kreutzers, were getting a little nosy. Would they play along when the authorities came to check up on them? At what price?

And the authorities would be coming. She had just applied for membership in the Nazi party.

CHAPTER SIXTEEN

November 10, 1938

Martha's family sat around the kitchen table. It was unbearable to eat in the dining room, with its four empty chairs. They had heard nothing from Ignatz and the boys; none of the remaining Jews in town had heard from their menfolk.

It was true that she had promised Ignatz that she would go to Janace, but there wasn't enough money for travel. The very day he and the boys were taken, German officers came and cleaned out the safe. It had taken only seconds for them to figure out the trick of it. And they had been so sure that the safe was foolproof!

How could the Nazis have known? There could be only one way. Martha tormented herself with the thought that the Germans had tortured Ignatz and the boys for the information. In that case, they would have gotten the money in Switzerland, as well. They were penniless.

Poverty was terrible, but bearable. Jews don't starve, not while another Jew anywhere has a piece of bread to share. But if the Nazis used torture on Ignatz and the boys, there were unthinkable implications. The question tormented her. *Were Ignatz and the boys even alive?*

Martha's usual confidence and cheer ebbed away, as if the Germans had taken her personality, as well as those she loved.

Fortunately, Malvine and Clara took up their mother's work, as well as that of the servants. The two teenage girls cleaned, cooked, and washed with great energy. Thrown out of school, they stayed home and supervised the studies of their younger sister, Vera, and the two little boys.

Those girls were Martha's consolation. What wonderful homemakers they will make someday, she thought. In a few years they would be ready to be married. But how could she do right by the girls, all by herself and without money?

Martha shook herself. Ignatz would be back; he would take care of everything.

The meal was really quite good. Cabbage with onions and potatoes dressed in sour cream. All their meals were dairy now; they'd had no meat or poultry since the annexation. Kosher slaughter was banned throughout the Reich. The Germans said it was cruel to animals.

Someone knocked at the kitchen door. Everybody's hair stood on end. These mealtime interruptions always brought evil.

"Frau Rosen, come quickly!" It was an elderly Jewish woman. "The synagogue is burning," she cried.

What remained of the Jewish community clung to habit. Trouble? Surely the Rosen family would take care of it. They always had.

Martha wanted to send the woman away, but how could she. "Malvine, Clara, you come with me. With no men around, we'll have to help the firemen. Vera, you stay home and watch the boys."

The glorious synagogue was the most graceful structure in the town. It had been dedicated only twenty years before, replacing a modest wooden building that the community, swollen by spa-goers, had outgrown. Ignatz's parents had been the major donors.

Martha and the girls had expected to see smoke rising from one or two locations, but they found the entire structure ringed in flames. Smoke puffed from its blasted windows. The cupola, painted in the Moorish style, was a ball of fire. The smell of gasoline saturated the air.

There were no firemen at the scene, but plenty of police. They were standing around, hands clasped behind their backs as if they were watching a parade. They let no one pass through to the synagogue, except for uniformed Hitler Youth. Clumps of Nazi teenagers, dressed in sporty short-pants uniforms, loitered nearby.

The mayor of the town stood facing the synagogue steps, arms folded over his immense belly. Martha knew the mayor well; he had been most cordial to Ignatz and her on the many occasions when the Rosens contributed to some public cause.

"Herr Mayor, please. Won't the police rescue the Torah scrolls, at least. They are very precious to us."

The mayor looked at her and smirked.

"You won't be smirking next election day," Martha snapped.

She looked around, expecting to get nods of approval from the outraged citizenry. But the onlookers—there were now hundreds of them—just gave her the same look as the mayor did.

"The Rosens don't run this town anymore," the Mayor declared.

"That's Rosen's wife? Are they still here?"

"I thought we'd gotten rid of all the Jews already."

"Not so easy to get rid of the Rosens."

Martha looked around. What was the matter with these people? Without Rosen & Sons a third of them would be unemployed. Annexation had emptied the spas, devastating the town's economy. Would they cut off their noses to spite their faces?

"Come on girls," she said, frightened, "let's go home."

"No, Mama, look," said Malvine. She pointed to a small building at the side of the main sanctuary. "The small chapel is all right. We can't get all the scrolls in there, but Clara and I could each carry one out."

Martha saw some Hitler Youth unloading fuel cans from a half-track. "Don't..."

But the two girls hadn't waited for her answer. They ran up the steps to the chapel. They never reached the landing.

The young Nazis fell upon them like raptor birds. Suddenly there were dozens and dozens of them.

One of them fell on Clara, ripping off her blouse and underwear with a single motion. There were others behind her, keeping her from covering herself or even falling down. Her breasts were revealed to the crowd, pink and perfect as June roses.

A great and primal instinct rose up in Martha. Her babies! Her daughters! The urge to protect them was so great that she thought no force on earth could keep her from roaring to their rescue.

But she was wrong. Two men, bystanders, were enough to prevent her from leaving the spot. They were enough, even, to keep her from averting her eyes; they held her head and forced her to look.

They all wanted her to see. These men, and the women, too, took pleasure in seeing a mother witness the monstrous rape of her daughters.

Rape wasn't enough for the Hitler Youth. One of them, having finished with Malvine, punched his fist up into her vagina, splattering his comrades with blood. They whooped as if champagne had overflowed.

Martha vomited on herself. The men holding her were not so disgusted as to loosen their hold. There would be more and they wanted her to see. The boys—they were boys, no older than Malvine and Clara themselves—looked around for other instruments to ram into their victims. Martha blacked out.

When she came to, the Hitler Youth and the men who had held her were gone, although there were still many civilians hanging around joking, smiling, relaxed.

"Serves you right, Jew bitches," said one, a middle-aged woman in fur.

Martha picked herself up and ran up the stairs. She carried Malvine down to where Clara was and sat down between them, stroking and soothing each in turn.

For the first time in her life, Martha thought she had too many children. How could she comfort Malvine and Clara at the same time? How, how?

Clara was sitting in an odd posture, her legs splayed like those of a broken doll. Malvine's hair had been pulled out of the entire left half of her head, so that she too looked like a discarded doll.

The girls' coats and shoes were gone, their dresses shredded. Martha put her coat over one daughter, then took her own blouse off and covered the other. Somehow she managed to get them up, and balancing them like a Dutch girl with water pails, led them down the street and toward home.

The people gathered round to get a better look, at the girls, and at Martha in her lacy slip. No one offered her a sweater or covering, much less assistance.

When they got home, Vera did not scream or cry or question them. Although she wasn't even twelve years old, she acted like the sanest and best trained of adults. She ran warm baths and brought clean towels. She found soft flannel nightgowns and fluffy socks. Having cared for her sisters, she tucked her mother and little brothers into bed, and then went to her room and wrote in her diary.

When she was done she took out a fresh sheet of paper and wrote a short letter. She crossed out and rewrote several phrases until the tone was just right: urgent but not alarming. The following morning she went to the telegraph office and sent it to her Aunt Sari in Janace.

For the residents of Eva's neighborhood, Kristallnacht had been something of a letdown. Yes, the synagogue and the Jewish library and the Jewish orphanage had been burned, but those were in the town center. In this dour suburb there weren't any fancy Jewish stores to loot, nor any public buildings to burn. There weren't even any Jewish houses whose windows they could smash.

Eva called Odilo Konrad from the stationery store.

"Darling, hasn't the Rosen house been evacuated yet?"

"Yes, it was."

"What's holding things up? I have no money left for rent. And I want a decent roof over my head. That Rosen house is rightly *my* home."

"We can't move in there."

"Well, what am I supposed to do? I'm tired of waiting."

"We'll find a place for you. Meet me at the beer hall in two hours."

Two hours were about right. She returned to her apartment and went through the liquor cabinet. There wasn't much there. Martin had bought a bottle of caraway spirits and one of peppermint schnapps, which he had used for religious ceremonies. They were open but almost full.

Eva took them over to the Kreutzers. "I'll be leaving soon, and I wanted to say goodbye. Can you use these? I'm afraid they'll spill if I try to take them with me."

The Kreutzers nodded, licking their lips.

Eva returned to her apartment and packed a few items in a small bag. She wouldn't be needing most of her things; they were nothing but junk. She could fix over some of Martha's clothes, which were too big but of excellent quality. Eventually, of course, she would be getting new things of her own.

The walls of the apartment were thin. She sat next to the one adjoining the Kreutzers and pressed a glass to the wall. Soon the sounds of their snores were so loud that she could hear them even without the glass. It was time.

Eva had barely lit the benzene heaters all season. There was plenty of fuel left in each of them. She poured the contents of a whole one on the wall, then spilled the other in the hallway, letting it pool at the Kreutzer's front door. The cheap apartments didn't have back doors. Then she lit a match and tossed it.

Out on the street she watched the flames lick up the apartment house, like a dog lapping water on a hot day. Farewell, Mr. and Mrs. Kreutzer, and goodbye Eva Lebow Blumenthal. Goodbye forever.

A man came by and yelled. "Help! Fire! Call the fire department!"

"Shut up, you fool," said Eva. "That's a Jewish house there."

So the man, and everyone else who came by, just watched the house burn.

The orders for Kristallnacht had been to guard all non-Jewish property from flame. But the fire brigade was needed for that, and no one had bothered to call it. This "action" was unofficial.

There were four other families in the burning building, including, Eva recalled, two with children. But that was just too bad. As the

Talmud said, "Woe to the wicked, and woe to their neighbors."

Odilo Konrad wasn't quite ready to bring her to her new home. There would be one more night in the back room of the beer hall. Eva had grown tired of this furtive aspect of their liaison. It wasn't that she wanted to marry; many high officers—Hitler himself—kept women with perfect respectability. But it was dirty and uncomfortable among the storage boxes. She couldn't wait to lie on Martha's ironed linen sheets. She couldn't wait to be mistress of her own fine home.

In the few hours she managed to sleep, Eva dreamed of a blissful night spent in her sister's bedroom. In the morning, she was awakened by a uniformed maid carrying a silver tray of fresh coffee and sweet rolls.

"These rolls are too crisp, overdone," she complained.

"I'll have Cook bake new ones," said the maid.

But when Eva woke up she was still in the storage room, dusty and disheveled, her mouth tasting of grit and old beer. Her eyes were grainy, and it hurt to look at the dawn. Odilo said he would have to go home and change; a German officer could not disgrace himself with a wrinkled uniform.

They drove up to the front of Odilo's new house. Eva recognized the place well.

"This isn't the Rosen's house," she said.

Odilo gave her a sharp little push that hurt more than it looked. "There's to be no more complaining, Elsa."

The pain and fear in her eyes placated him. "The Rosen house is reserved for the new regional Gauleiter, who is coming in from Berlin."

Odilo's house was the former residence of Dr. Gartenberg. It was large, but not as grand as the Rosens' place. Gartenberg, a shrewd and successful lawyer, had been among the first to leave Ruhigbad, and had managed to take almost everything with him.

They came into the front hall, which was empty except for carpet tacks scattered on the floor. Sunbeams poked like nosy neighbors through the tall, undraped windows.

Eva could remember the beautiful antiques that once graced this hall. She wondered if the study at the left, which Dr. Gartenberg had used to see those clients who demanded discretion, had been cleared of its files.

"Dagmar!" Konrad bellowed.

Dagmar?

"Dagmar, come here this instant!"

A woman came, hobbling in orthopedic shoes. She was simply but neatly dressed, and she must have been handsome a generation before.

A maiden aunt, thought Eva, or a trusted housekeeper, or just possibly, Odilo's mother.

"Sorry," the woman said. "Good morning, Herr Deputy."

Her first word had been an apology, and her eyes blinked too much. She was as wary as a dog with an unpredictable master.

"Elsa, this is Mrs. Konrad," Odilo said.

"Dagmar, this is the new maid."

CHAPTER SEVENTEEN

Janace

With the Rosens' arrival, Sari hoped to unite the family once again. It was tragic, of course, to see what had happened to the girls and to realize that the family had lost their home and all of their property. And she dared not even speculate about where Martha's husband and sons might be. Yet it was so good to have kin nearby, almost as it was in the old days.

Still, there were stresses. Sari found herself taking every opportunity to help out Joseph. The front seat of the truck had become a place of refuge from the fearful and wounded refugees from the Sudetenland.

Business was booming. There was nothing like economic fear and the specter of war to increase the consumption of alcoholic beverages. Joseph was grateful for her hands now, as well as her company.

Sari needed to make no excuses to add to the extended family's income. They now had eight mouths to feed; Martha had fled Ruhigbad with no more than toothbrushes and a few changes of underwear. The Rosens may or may not have had a fortune in Swiss banks, but at this time they had no access to it. They needed to find a certain Dr. Gartenberg, a lawyer who handled their banking affairs. But in the chaos of the expulsion, Gartenberg could have gone to any of thousands of places. There was also the possibility that the Germans had found him.

Her poor sister, once a proud mother, had become a shadow. All day Martha sat near the window, unmoving. Malvine and Clara, even more than the little boys, needed Martha, but their mother was lost in despair.

The teenage girls' physical wounds were healing, and Malvine's hair was growing back, but they had been severely damaged. They said nothing at all and clung like garden weeds to any adult female who came near them. If no woman was nearby, they clung to each other. The worst was that they did not speak. Not a word, not even to each other. That was so unusual in their chatty family.

Vera not only adjusted but thrived. She was a good-natured, and happy child, and she was lucky in that the family's arrival in Janace coincided with the opening of the local Beth Jacob, the first Torah school for girls.

Not only did she excel at her studies, both Jewish and secular, she founded and ran the Kindness Club. The club's volunteers were girls five to thirteen, whose aim was to put the Jewish ideals they studied at school into action

Late one evening Sender was nodding over a tome in the House of Study, when a strange individual walked in. The men were used to seeing some sad cases, but this man drew gawking stares.

Tall and hulking, he had a scraggly beard and wild hair and filthy clothes. He looked as if he had been living in a cave for weeks, which, in fact, he had been. But it was his eyes that were truly frightening, a madman's eyes.

"Is there anyone here who knows Mrs. Rosen?"

Sender jumped. "Who are you?"

"Mrs. Ignatz Rosen," said the crazy-eyed stranger. "I have urgent news for her."

"Come with me, please."

Sender walked home silently with the odd man. He wondered whether he should let him see his sister-in-law. God knew she didn't need any more to be upset about. He would ask Kitty.

Those members of the Halter family who were still awake welcomed the stranger as if he were a perfectly normal acquaintance. Reuven and Kalman put up another bed in their room. Mrs. Halter said casually, "I'd be pleased to draw a bath for you, sir. It can be so comforting after travel in the cold."

"Thank you, Ma'am. But I have to speak to Mrs. Rosen right away."

Kitty had been in bed reading. She dressed hurriedly.

"Do you really think we should take him to Martha?" Sender asked.

"Yes, of course. It sounds like he has information about Ignatz and the boys."

"Think, Kitty. It can't be good information, can it? An additional shock might send Martha over the edge."

"Martha needs to hear the truth. She's been living on fantasies, and they haven't helped her."

"Maybe we should warn the man about Martha's mental state, at least."

"What mental state? Martha is normal. Who wouldn't react the way she did to what she experienced? Let's not forget it's the Germans who are the maniacs."

"I don't know. I'm afraid for her."

"I'm afraid for all of us. As for Martha, she's stronger than anyone thinks."

The snow crunched loudly under their feet, announcing them even before Sender knocked softly.

Joseph shook the man's hand with warmth, and introduced himself, but the stranger ignored him.

"Is Mrs. Rosen here?" He would brook no more delays.

Sari led her sister into the room. Martha and the stranger stared at each other curiously. Neither registered any familiarity. They had never met before.

The stranger made no small talk.

"Mrs. Rosen?"

"Yes."

"Was your husband Ignatz Rosen?"

Martha paused. "Was?"

"Yes, ma'am. I'm sorry. He is dead."

A film appeared to slide off Martha's face. Her eyes were focused now, boring into the stranger.

"You saw it?"

"Yes, ma'am. He saved me. With his life he saved mine."

"What about my boys? Did you see my sons? Are they alive?"

"No. I did not see them, but there is no hope that they are alive."

"Was there pain. Did they die in pain?"

"No, ma'am."

Kitty, Sender, Sari, and Joseph could see how the man's eyes looked away when he said those words. But Martha did not see.

"So it is all over. Thank you for coming here to tell me. Won't you have something to eat?"

"No thank you. I have to be going."

Silence, like another midnight guest, settled in the room.

Martha closed her eyes for a moment, but when she opened them they were sharp and direct.

"Thank you, sir. Joseph, what is the law concerning mourning for me and the girls?" The complex rituals fluctuated, depending on factors such as the length of time from death to being informed.

"I am not certain, Martha. Tomorrow morning I will consult with the rabbi. For now, you'd best go to sleep.

"Yes, that makes sense. I'm very tired. Well, thanks again, Mister. Good-night, everyone."

They all held their breath, but it was clear that Martha was not going to break down. In fact, she sounded more stable than at any time since she had come to Janace.

They waited in silence until she was gone.

"Please tell us what happened," said Kitty.

The stranger's name was Zlotnik, and he came from the Sudeten town of Cheb, not far from Ruhigbad. After the town's Jewish men were marched into the countryside, they were joined by similar groups from nearby towns. Their numbers increased and then decreased, as the less hardy among them collapsed. They marched for two days without food or water. Whoever fell down or straggled was shot.

Finally, at the side of a sewage ditch leading into a culvert, they halted. The men's identification papers were collected and they were lined up single file at the side of the ditch. Shoulder to shoulder they formed a wall of exhaustion.

An officer went through the documents, carefully filing them in alphabetical order. He began calling out each name.

"Martin Blumenthal," he barked.

"Present," said the man beside Zlotnik.

Zlotnik turned his head. This man was not Blumenthal! He had known Martin well; they had met years ago at a Zionist youth convention.

"Who are you?" he whispered.

"I'm Ignatz Rosen," he said. Zlotnik had heard of Rosen, but it was hard to believe this bedraggled animal was the famous rich man.

"I've heard of your charitable works," Zlotnik whispered. "Honored to meet you."

Rosen smiled sadly. "If I die, please tell my wife, so she can marry again. Please, she will give you a generous reward."

"A reward for doing a Torah commandment? No thanks. I'll take mine from the Almighty."

Finally the German got to the Z's and Zlotnik responded. They were ordered to turn around and face the sewage ditch, with their hands behind their heads.

"Ready, aim..."

With his body, Ignatz pushed Zlotnik in front of him. A hail of bullets followed immediately. All the men fell into the ditch.

The barrage was followed by isolated moans and cries, begging for mercy. Apparently some men had survived, wounded. Ignatz was not one of them. Zlotnik could feel the body above him relax.

An argument ensued between the German officer and his men.

"You, you, and you. Into the ditch. Finish off the rest of the Jews."

"Apologies, sir, but I cannot go down there."

"This is an order!"

"It's filthy down there. It's a sewage canal, for Christ's sake."

"You are being insubordinate, soldier!"

"Call it what you will. I refuse to go into that mess."

"Me neither."

"And why should I go, what am I, the fall guy?"

It was quiet while the officer considered how to stanch the rebellion.

"Very well. You may shoot from the bank with your rifles."

This time the men followed orders immediately, picking off the survivors. The soft cries of the wounded were now replaced by the guffaws of the soldiers, who accompanied their work with coarse jokes.

"All right, all right," said the officer. "This is a work detail, not a party. Now cover up the carcasses. There are shovels in the truck."

"Begging pardon, sir. You want *us* to bury them?"

"You heard me, soldier."

"Sir, I for one did not join an elite unit to be a day laborer."

"The work isn't glamorous, but it has to be done. We can't leave bodies lying around. The locals will get nervous."

"Well, sir, then maybe the locals should be recruited to do the work."

"We should have left over a few Jews to fill in the ditch. It's a lot easier to dispose of ten Jews than a thousand," said another soldier.

"This whole operation's wasteful, with a bullet or more per Jew. Look, it's almost noon, and this is all we've gotten done today."

Zlotnik could hear the Germans moving off. He waited and waited. There might still be some soldiers around. But he couldn't wait too long. Someone would be coming back to fill in the ditch.

He knew he had to get out from under Ignatz Rosen. But then what? He could run into the woods. He would be safe in the woods. For years Zlotnik had been the scoutmaster for the Cheb troop of Religious Zionist Boy Scouts. He could make do in the woods.

Walking mostly at night, it took him one and a half days to reach the border. It was heavily patrolled on both sides. He hid in a cave for several weeks, watching patrol patterns. Finally, he made his way across.

113

In Slovakia he was still forced to travel by foot and at night, but at least there were Jewish homes where he could find rest. Everyone he asked gave him food and shelter, but no one, he soon found, believed his stories. "You must be exaggerating," the Jews said, or thought. "Even Germans, after all, are human beings."

At last he came to Kosice, and found the home of Helen and Thomas Gantz. The Gantzes were almost as incredulous, but, hearing of the death of their brother-in-law, were more sympathetic than most. Besides the usual hospitality, Thomas went out and bought Zlotnik a pair of excellent boots. That made the journey from Kosice to Janace practically luxurious.

Everyone looked down at Zlotnik's feet. They were encased in big, solid boots, the kind meant to last a peasant a decade or two.

"What's your occupation, Mr. Zlotnik?" asked Joseph. "We will try to find work for you." He was practically family now. They were responsible for him.

"Thank you, Mr. Wassermann, but I don't plan to stay long here."

"But where will you go?" asked Sari.

Zlotnik pointed to the eastern wall, where, as in many Jewish homes, an ornate sign indicated the way to Jerusalem.

"But it's dangerous there," she blurted. Then, realizing what that word meant to Zlotnik, put her hand on her mouth.

"How will you get to Palestine?" asked Kitty, practically. "You haven't any papers, and we can't give you much money."

"I go through the mountains, overland, by foot."

There was awestruck silence. Sender spoke for all of them. "That's impossible."

"No," said Zlotnik. "It's a one in a million chance for survival, worse for actually making it to the Land of Israel. But here, in Europe, it's truly impossible."

"Well," said Sender, "it's getting very late. You, Mr. Zlotnik need a good long rest. As for us, we've got a work day tomorrow. We'll talk more then."

"I'm sorry," said Zlotnik, but I will not be taking you up on your hospitality. I hope to reach the mountain pass before daybreak."

"Then let me pack something for your trip," said Sari. She went off to the kitchen.

With Sari out of the room, Kitty began talking quietly and quickly. "We have a sister in Palestine."

"Ah, yes. The one who married Martin Blumenthal. So, they reached the Land! That's the first good news I've heard in months."

"No, said Kitty. "This sister is divorced. Her name is Renee Fruchter. Or Lebow. Or maybe she has remarried."

"And sometimes Jews in the homeland take Hebrew names," said Sender.

"Ah, I see. So Martin..."

"Martin stands with Ignatz Rosen and his sons," said Kitty. "Before the Holy Throne. Pleading for us, the living."

Sari came in with a large, sturdily wrapped package. "Dried fruit leather," she said. "We always put some by for winter. It's good for traveling. Just a bite or two will refresh you and give you strength."

Joseph was writing something hurriedly. "These are the names of trustworthy farmers and woodsmen on the first leg of your route. They supply us with fruit and berries for the distillers. Tell them you are our relative. Just ask them for what you need, and I will pay them on my next visit."

Zlotnik thanked the Wassermanns. There were tears in his eyes, which looked less crazed than before.

"We have something for you, too," said Sender. "Please come back to our house. It isn't really out of your way."

Kitty wondered what Sender had in mind. The Baron had an overly developed sense of generosity—noblesse oblige—and she hated to be put in the position of the tightfisted shrew. She would not hesitate to put her foot down, though, if she found him shortchanging his own family to help a stranger. Zlotnik was a man of honor and decency, deserving their aid, but still, a stranger.

Everyone in the house was asleep. Sender disappeared. Kitty made Zlotnik another tightly-packed bundle and tied it to Sari's package. "Shelled nuts. They may get stale but they won't spoil. Very nutritious."

Sender came down with what looked like a large animal in his arms. It was a gigantic hooded sheepskin coat. The coat was given in payment by one of Mrs. Halter's patients. Cured after years of painful piles, the peasant gave Sender's mother his most valued possession, not realizing that she had no use for the big, smelly fur.

Zlotnik put on the coat. It covered him completely from his head to his sturdy new boots. "You've saved my life," he said to Sender.

"Not I," Sender shrugged.

Zlotnik shut his eyes in concentration, and said, "Blessed are you, Lord, our God, King of the Universe, who clothes the naked."

CHAPTER EIGHTEEN

The Rosen women observed a short mourning period, according to the rabbi's directions. At its end, Martha reverted to her competent and confident self.

She supervised her young sons, becoming one of the mothers who took up the slack, rather than added to it. She took Malvine and Clara in hand, and they improved. They never regained their speech, but they did become productive members of the household. With their mother, they did all the marketing, cleaning, and laundering, freeing Sari to work with Joseph, and, occasionally, to read her beloved books.

Using her excellent skills as a seamstress, and teaching them to her daughters, Martha began a little business out of the house, turning down old clothes. Since few people could afford new garments anymore, the Wassermann/ Rosen household became a little oasis of prosperity.

If Martha's heart was heavy with the loss of her husband and two sons, she let no one know it. She took pleasure in the progress made by Malvine and Clara, as well as in the achievements of her small sons. Outstanding Vera was her pride and joy. The nightmare began to recede.

With the end of mourning, Kitty and Sender relaxed too. It felt as if they were taking a honeymoon at last. Martha made a little party to celebrate Kitty and Sender's first anniversary, when the abhorred knock came at the door. No one moved.

At last Kitty went to open it.

"Good heavens! Look who's here," she called out in delight.

The assembled were so surprised not to be attacked that they remained glued to their seats. It was only when the guests entered—Helen and Thomas and their two children—that everyone jumped up and joined in shouts and embraces.

"But why didn't you tell us?" said Sari. "We would have made a special dinner and planned some outings."

"I'm afraid this is not a social visit, Sari. Frankly, we need your help."

"Anything, sister. Anything."

Thomas turned to his children. "Kids, help bring in the suitcases. Sari, Joseph, we hate to ask, but can we stay with you for a short while? We've been evicted."

"What sort of question is that?" asked Joseph. "You can stay here as long as you like."

Kitty said, "Evicted? But you'd never skip out on the rent. Did you lose your job, Thomas?"

"No, sales aren't very good, but I still make ends meet. And we pay the rent on time. The landlord just doesn't want us."

"Why not?" Most landlords these days were grateful to have decent tenants who could come up with the rent.

"Because we are socialists," said Helen, sticking her chin up, as if daring someone to contest her.

Sari and Kitty groaned. With war almost palpable, everyone was terrified of a connection to leftists of even the mildest sort. Helen and Thomas were so intelligent. Why didn't they have the sense to keep their mouths shut about politics?

The dining room table was pushed to a wall and bedding laid on the floor. It was the best they could do for now. The children were put to sleep and the men went off to the House of Study.

Sari, Martha, Helen, and Kitty finished tidying up in the kitchen. Despite hard realities, giggles overtook them. Sari threw down her dish towel and hugged her sisters.

"At least we're all together."

"By the way," said Helen, "I haven't heard from Eva in a long time. My letters to her are returned with 'addressee unknown' stamped on them. Where is she, Martha?"

Martha weighed her words carefully. When she first came to Janace, she hardly mentioned Eva. Martha had been "unwell," and neither Sari nor Kitty questioned her further. As long as Eva was alive, the sisters tended to leave well enough alone.

"You mustn't write to her anymore. It's dangerous. Eva is passing for Aryan. She has good German friends and they are hiding her."

"But why?" said Sari. "She could come here and be safe with her family."

Martha blinked. "The baby. You forget about him. She is doing it for the baby."

No one asked the obvious questions. What about the baby? How would pretending to be Aryan help him? How could Eva support him?

The next morning Thomas rose early, determined to look for a job. He had been modestly successful in Kosice as a sales representative for a publisher, but such work was not to be found in a small town. Thomas would have taken any kind of work, but so would the many other men, Janace natives, who were now unemployed. And the other men were not tainted by political sins.

Martha offered to share her work with Helen, so that the Gantzes would also have some money in their pockets. Helen was a gifted seamstress, like all the Lebow sisters, but political philosophy colored everything she did.

When one of the Minsky girls—having given birth to twins—came in with her entire pre-pregnancy wardrobe to be spruced up, Helen said, "How can you be so irresponsible as to spawn recklessly in times such as these? Have you no consideration for the common good? Don't you read the newspapers? Is there nothing that worries you other than being seen in—heaven forbid—the fashions of two years ago?"

The Minsky triplet burst into tears and left without placing an order.

"But Helen dear, people will have children, war or peace," Martha said.

"Hmmph. You're living in the middle ages. They need only have as many children as they plan for."

"Sometimes it's better to have as many as God plans for. Imagine where I would be if I had stopped after..." Her voice broke. She paused and collected herself. "Anyway, what's wrong with treating oneself to a little fashion? Is it such a sin to have something pretty in hard times? What next? Would you outlaw candy for children?"

The Minsky sister eventually returned and placed her order, and all was well. After that, Helen stayed in the kitchen, cooking and putting up preserves. She also spent time educating her children.

Her daughter, fourteen, and her son, twelve, did not attend school. The family in Janace was shocked to find that the children had virtually no Jewish education. It was one thing to be a freethinker and a socialist, quite another to be an ignoramus. The local public school system, increasingly right-wing, had barred the Gantz children from entering in mid-term. But no urging could get the Gantzes to enroll the children in the yeshiva or the Beth Jacob.

Vera, feeling sorry for her isolated and lonely girl cousin, tried to induct her into the Kindness Club. But her cousin's response was as sharp as a slap.

"Don't you understand that your club is making matters worse? By giving crumbs to the poor you're postponing the inevitable. It'll just take that much longer for them to recognize the truth and rise up against the capitalist oppressors!"

Meanwhile the boy was less than a year from his bar-mitzvah, when he would be called upon to fulfill all the obligations of an adult male, and he was as ignorant of Jewish law and ritual as a newborn. The child's parents did not seem to be concerned about the upcoming event, so Joseph and Sari came up with the money for his *tefillin*. The ritual boxes containing passages from the Torah, used by men in morning prayer, were expensive.

"I don't understand it," said Joseph in the privacy of their truck, "Thomas is such a learned man. When he enters the House of Study, people gravitate to him, waiting to hear the pearls drop from his mouth. And this is even knowing his lack of faith!"

Sari wrung her hands. "It's all my fault. Helen was always lax in religious matters, and I just let it go. We lived in a family, in a community that was so strong, it didn't matter if some people had a relaxed attitude in their observance or cracks in their faith, somehow they got pulled along. But times changed. I should have seen..."

"No, my darling, how could you have foreseen? You did what was best. Besides, you weren't responsible for raising Thomas."

Sari shook her head vigorously. "It's the woman who sets the spiritual tone for a family. I should have been a better example to Helen."

Joseph smiled, love in his eyes. "How could you have been a better model? You are as righteous as any woman who walks the earth."

On April first Martha received a letter that raised their hopes like a hot-air balloon. It was from Dr. Gartenberg, the Ruhigbad lawyer.

"My dearest Mrs. Rosen:

"What luck to hear that you are safe and sound with relatives! As you can see, Frau Dr. Gartenberg and I are here in Switzerland. Our family's health is as good as can be expected, considering the circumstances.

"I wonder if I might prevail upon you for a favor, Madame. Perhaps you have need of banking services at this time? A deposit to your Swiss accounts—or more likely, a withdrawal? Either way, I would be happy to serve you. You see, despite my assets the Swiss authorities insist that I prove that I can be self-supporting here, otherwise they will 'repatriate' our family.

"I should be glad to perform these duties at our old rate. Please forward the bank account numbers in the code which we have established.

"If you should know of the whereabouts of any of the following clients of mine, or their heirs, won't you please let them know my address, and my circumstances."

There followed a list of former Ruhigbad society, but Martha didn't know where anyone was now.

The next day Martha telegraphed Dr. Gartenberg with the information he had requested. She ordered him to clear out all of the family accounts. There was a fortune in them, enough to buy the whole family its freedom.

A week passed, and then a telegraph arrived from Dr. Gartenberg. She could picture the sweat on his bald head when he wrote it.

"Bank regrets cannot accept you as heir STOP Request copy of Ignatz Rosen death certificate STOP Will waive fee STOP."

The Western powers were mute when Germany took Czechoslovakia apart like a slice of stale bread. It tore off pieces and flung them to its favorites, as if to pigeons. A chunk containing Kosice went to Hungary. And Slovakia, including Janace, became an "independent" state, a fascist puppet of the Reich.

"You'll be happy to hear that we're finally going to move to our new home," announced Helen.

"Moving? But where? How?" asked Sari. Despite strenuous efforts Thomas had not found work. How could they move with no prospects in sight?

"To the Soviet Union," said Helen proudly.

"Oh my God," said Sari.

Martha put her hand to her throat as if she were choking.

Kitty said, "Have you gone crazy?"

"It's an excellent solution, we feel," said Helen.

"Helen, it's...it's Russia," breathed Martha, as if referring to a place so obscene, one dared not mention the name out loud.

"Ukraine, actually. Not very far from here really. Near the Polish border."

"A magical place," said Kitty dryly. "I understand entire populations disappear under Stalin's wand."

"That's nothing but fascist propaganda," Helen sniffed.

"Is it propaganda that there are no synagogues left in Russia?" Sari snapped. "No Jewish schools, no ritual baths. This Slovak state is not good news for us. It will be officially Catholic, and reactionary. Still,

Jews will be able to survive as Jews here. You are going out of the frying pan and into the fire."

"Nonsense. The city we're going to has been a major Jewish center for centuries. Besides, Thomas has a good government job. And I will be working in a bakery, which assures us of bread, come what may. Look how many Jews have lost their jobs here. Whatever will they do, eat Scripture and Psalms? In the Soviet Union everyone who wants to work can do so."

There was no reasoning with the Gantzes. They were determined to go. Sari and Joseph cornered Thomas alone.

"These are for your son, when he becomes bar-mitzvah."

Thomas took the blue velvet bag with the gold embroidery. "Tefillin."

He opened the bag and inspected the boxes, the leather straps. "A very fine pair. The ones I had were nowhere as good."

"You'll teach your son how to put them on, how to pray with them?"

"Sure."

"Please, Thomas. Please don't let this commandment pass out of our family."

"Oh, don't be morbid. There are Martha's little boys and Eva's baby, and Kitty hasn't even gotten a start yet."

"No one can predict the future, Thomas. Please, promise us to uphold this holy commandment."

"Very well. I promise."

The children had gone to sleep and now it was just Sari and Joseph, and Martha, and Kitty and Sender over for a late-night cup of tea.

"Helen and her family will be all right," said Sari, trying to assure herself as much as anyone. "They sent all their furniture from storage. And you know, Helen still has most of her dowry. They never did see fit to invest it in a business or a house."

"Speaking of dowries," said Kitty carefully, "whatever happened to mine?"

Sari and Martha gasped in unison.

"Go ahead and tell her," Joseph said gently to his wife. "She's a big girl now, a married woman. You can tell her."

Martha's eyes filled with tears. Sari assumed a stern look.

"Kitty and Sender would never hold it against you," said Joseph. Kitty nodded. "We love you both, and we always will."

"It's not us," said Martha, "but promise that no matter what you hear, you won't hate your...your other sisters."

"Of course not," said Kitty.

"Well then," said Sari, clearing her throat. "You'll remember that after that big mess, we finally arranged to have the two weddings. Your sister...R-Renee...was to marry Benny Fruchter, and then, a few weeks later, as was proper, Eva would marry Martin Blumenthal.

"All the arrangements had been made, the gowns sewn, the trousseaux packed up. And then we get a visit from Benny's parents.

"They said her dowry was not enough. They said Renee had turned Benny's head, but that they would prevail upon him with sense and reason to break the engagement. Their darling, only son was not to be had cheaply. On the open market he could get twice as much as the Lebows were offering.

"We were shocked. Ordinarily, we would not have hesitated to send the Fruchters packing with an earful. Imagine the nerve! Their little mama's boy getting the most desirable girl in the Zionist Club. They should have been offering *us* money!

"But there was the family honor to consider. It would be humiliating to have a boy break an engagement with our sister. And then, what of Eva and Martin? They couldn't get married before Renee did. And compounding the shame, everybody knew about Martin switching his affections from one sister to another. We couldn't let that happen to Renee.

"A lot of thanks we got for that," Sari said bitterly.

"What did you do?" asked Kitty calmly.

"Well, after the six of us consulted together—Joseph and I and Martha and Ignatz and Helen and Thomas..."

"Ignatz and I guaranteed everything," Martha broke in. "We wanted to pay for everything, but the factory..." she started to cry, "the factory needed all the liquid assets we...It was a mistake, we should have given the cash. What use is the factory now? What use are the Swiss accounts?"

"There, there," Kitty calmed Martha, just as she had seen Martha calm her own children a thousand times. "Please continue, Sari."

"We decided to sell the house and promised them the proceeds. But we made sure—Ignatz made sure—that the house would be sold only after both weddings. That way the Fruchters wouldn't try to extort anything more."

"Did they?"

"No. But that wasn't the end of our troubles.

"Shortly after we made the arrangements—secret, we thought—Eva came to us. She was tearing her hair and accusing us of terrible things. She said Martin and his family would throw her out in the street unless we matched her dowry to Renee's.

"We thought, what a nerve the young man has. Wasn't it enough to toy with one sister, then another? Did he mean to insult us further? Breaking off that engagement wouldn't be so terrible. No one else's marriage depended on it. If that's the kind of man he is, we told Eva, you're better off without him.

"But she screamed at us. 'I have to marry him, I *have* to.' You see, by then Martin had already..."

Sari stopped and took a sip of tea. "He, they, hadddd..."

Martha said, "He had already, already..." She put a hand to her mouth as if to stop the rest of the sentence from coming out.

Kitty, perplexed, looked to Joseph.

Joseph blushed magenta. "He had already seduced her."

Sari recovered. "So then, of course, we had to pay up."

"Temporarily," said Martha, "pending our withdrawals from the Swiss bank."

Kitty was composed. Somehow none of this surprised her. "But you'd already promised the money from the house, so you had to liquidate..."

"Your dowry."

"Please don't be angry with Eva," Sari begged. "She is your flesh and blood."

"And don't be angry with Martin, either," said Martha. "We got to know him so well. He never, ever spoke of this thing. I am sure that he repented of all his sins. He died a hero and a martyr, may the Lord avenge his blood."

Kitty dabbed at her eyes. "Of course I bear Martin no grudge.

"May he plead for us all before the Heavenly Throne."

CHAPTER NINETEEN

It was the middle of the day and the House of Study was packed with men studying Talmud in pairs and reciting Psalms in intense circles. Ordinarily during working hours one would have found, at most, a small group of elderly men or perhaps a visitor or two. But these were not ordinary times. The edicts against the Jews had come down from the new Slovak regime like a hammer.

No business concern could be owned by Jews. Jewish merchants now scurried to find Gentile partners to install as the titular owners. The figurehead "partners" did none of the work, put up none of the capital, and took whatever profits they pleased. If it weren't for the expertise of running the businesses, the original owners would have been kicked out too. Jews had no legal recourse.

First Sender's younger brother lost his job; others followed. Mr. Halter's employers begrudged even the few hours' work he'd had. Reuven came next. The loss of the grocery job was crushing; two families depended on Reuven's income, and the food packages he brought home had been especially valued.

Only Sender kept his position. Since Sender was the best mechanic at the shop, he was assured of being kept on by the Gentile owner. But his boss worried that the noose would tighten further. The order to fire all Jews was a growing possibility.

Sender no longer came to the House of Study at all. Neither did Joseph Wassermann. The authorities had imposed a five to eight curfew on all Jews and any man lucky enough to have work had to get it done and be back home by five sharp.

Joseph, who used to travel all over Slovakia, was forced to buy fruit from nearby farms only. His markets shrank as well. Most of the distilleries that bought the fruit had been owned by Jews and were now mismanaged by rapacious opportunists.

Joseph had always been liked and respected by both farmers and distillers. Now he was locked in a vicious cycle. The new owners offered him little for the fruit, and he, in turn, could pay the farmers less, so they punished him by selling him rotten produce. It was Joseph, of course, whom everyone resented for the consequences.

All Jews were ordered to wear the yellow star. It had to be sewn on both the front and back of all outerwear. A Jew could not be seen on his own porch or taking out the trash without the conspicuous badges.

That killed Martha's alteration business. Who cared about any dress that was defaced by the glaring brand? Malvine and Clara earned a few pennies, however. Once every middle-class household had had a stout peasant laundress to wash the linens. But since it was forbidden to employ non-Jews, Malvine and Clara did this heavy labor for the few Jewish housewives who could still afford the service. The delicately reared daughters of one of Czechoslovakia's richest men labored like dray horses.

Only Mrs. Halter's business increased. People could not afford to see a doctor for even the most excruciating pain. But the Halter coffers were not enriched. Few could pay the herbalist with anything but promises.

The load was unbearable. The slightest infraction of the anti-Semitic laws resulted in a crushing fine. No one could pay these fines, but they were not dismissed. The Jewish community as a whole was forced to pay them.

The poorest, such as the Meisels family, had no choice but to put their children in the orphanage. The Meisels did not get rid of Anschel, however. The gifts of food which the Halters continued to bring kept the couple from starving.

Fascist thugs roamed the streets night and day, looking for Jews to beat up for sport. A pregnant woman was caught digging potatoes in her back yard and was brutally abused. She died of her wounds a few days later.

This incident prompted the Rebbe to issue a stunning ruling. All couples who were already parents were to avoid another pregnancy. The community was astounded. Even those who could remember the cholera epidemic of the previous century had never heard of such an extreme measure.

One morning Kitty was hanging laundry. It was well before eight, but the wash had to be up or it would never dry before evening curfew.

"Psst, Kitty."

Kitty's whirled around. "Rachel-Leah! What a treat." They hadn't seen each other in quite a while. Who could afford to invite family and friends for lavish Sabbath dinners these days, and young wives no longer had the heart to linger and chat with one another. "Quick, come inside."

Kitty made some coffee. It was mostly chicory, but at least it was hot.

"Oooh, cookies. I haven't had those in ages," said Rachel-Leah.

"I'm afraid they're made with saccharin," Kitty apologized.

"Still," said Rachel-Leah, saying the blessing, then munching happily. "How's Chaim?"

"Fantastic."

"Really? Has he got work?"

"No. But we have something better."

"What?"

"Kitty, at long last, I'm pregnant."

Kitty put her coffee cup down carefully into its saucer. "Oh, God, Rachel-Leah. What will you do?"

"What do you mean, Kitty? You know we've prayed for this baby for ages."

"But the situation."

"I don't care." Rachel-Leah folded her arms over her stomach, both protectively and stubbornly.

"You know there are things that can be done," breathed Kitty.

"Kitty!"

"The peasant grannies. Our laundress back home got pregnant by her lover. Twice. Her husband would have killed her, so she had..."

"God help us! Even for a Christian that's a sin."

"But even the Rebbe..."

"Not for first-time parents."

"But you can deduce for yourself..."

"Stop it!" Rachel-Leah put her hands over her ears. "I don't want to hear any more. Nobody, not Jew or Gentile, is going to keep me from having this child."

While it had been a special pleasure to see her best friend, the conversation with Rachel-Leah upset Kitty all day. Maybe it was just the time of the month. She was expecting her period any minute now.

But it did not come any minute, or all that day, or the next, or that week. Kitty was in a panic. It was the first time in her life that she felt she had a secret to keep from every living soul. Yet to speak was to spread suffering wherever words could seed.

"Mother Halter, may I speak with you alone?"

"Of course, Daughter!"

"It's about my friend Rachel-Leah..."

When Kitty told her mother-in-law what was needed, the older woman's face turned as white as the cut end of a tap-root in the forest.

"I cannot make such a potion. It is immoral and against God's law."

"Doesn't the Torah say of the Laws, 'that you live in them?' The sages interpreted: 'that you live, and not die.' Today, a Jewish woman who has a child endangers her life, and dooms the baby. Even the Rebbe as much as says so."

"But I have never...It is too awful to contemplate. What little knowledge I have is for holding on to life, not bringing death."

"This *is* about holding on to life. Please, give Rachel-Leah a chance to survive."

As always, Kitty prevailed upon Sender's mother. Mrs. Halter handed over a packet of pungent-smelling leaves. She cried as she explained the directions to Kitty.

After dinner, when the household was asleep, Kitty brewed the tea and drank it. The following morning she experienced cramps so severe that she could not help groaning in agony.

"What's the matter? What's wrong?" asked Sender, his eyes round with fear.

"Oh, it's just diarrhea combined with a really bad menstrual period," said Kitty, figuring her husband would shy away from a discussion of "female" matters.

"Diarrhea?" He was more frightened than ever. As poverty, hunger, and sickness advanced relentlessly into the Jewish community of Janace, diarrhea went from comic unpleasantness to life-threatening terror. "I'll stay home from work today, I can't leave you by yourself."

"Sender! That's crazy. Your job is the only thing sustaining the family. And I'm not alone. Bayla is here."

His sister hustled Sender to the door. Then, faster than Kitty had ever seen her do anything, Bayla half-carried her to the privy.

Kitty could feel clots of *something* coming out of her body, but she did not dare to look down. With what seemed like the last ounce of her energy, she tied a menstrual cloth between her legs.

Bayla was waiting at the back door of the house and immediately came forward to help her. Again, she half-carried Kitty, this time up the stairs to her room.

Kitty slept all day. When she awoke, Sender was home, and the family getting ready for dinner.

Dinner!

She wanted to run, but couldn't. The best she could do was to get herself downstairs and to the table.

Bayla was at the stove, doling out soup. She had cooked dinner exactly the way Kitty did. No one noticed any difference.

"Kitty was feeling ill this morning," Sender announced.

Frightened faces looked up at him.

"But I'm fine now," Kitty hastened to assure the family. "All back to normal."

Afterwards Kitty tried to do penance for her sin, but she could not. She felt only relief, and not the least bit sorry. She tried to conjure up a vision of the baby; perhaps if she saw it, she would be able to feel remorse for its death. But she couldn't even imagine it. Couldn't even picture if it had been a boy or a girl.

Many women were attending Sabbath services now. There was a vain hope that in the synagogue they might hear some good tidings, or at least some useful information. But all the relief to be found was in the ancient prayers. The news was entirely evil.

Kitty stood with her mother-in-law as the latecomers passed by their pew in the middle of "Sanctification." Rachel-Leah came in and passed by them in silence, but with a radiant smile.

She was wearing a borrowed maternity gown, several sizes too big for her. Rachel-Leah walked with an exaggerated swayback, because she wanted it to look as if she had begun to show. The yellow Jewish star glared down on her smock.

"We will praise you and sanctify you in the secret words of the Seraphim," Kitty sang, but her mind was elsewhere. Her mother-in-law was very intelligent. She saw everything. What would she say about—or to—Rachel-Leah?

"From his place he will turn to face us in compassion. He will have mercy upon the nation that declares his One name night and day, the nation that says the 'Shma' twice daily, in love.

"Shma Yisrael! The Lord is our God, the Lord is One!

"He is our father, he is our king, he is our savior. And in his love he will betroth us again, in the sight of every living thing."

Kitty was crying softly now. *She had made this righteous woman kill her own grandchild.*

No one stared. There were many women crying during prayers these days even though it was a desecration of the holy Sabbath.

"The Lord reigns forever from Zion, hallelujah."

Tears were wiped away, and everyone felt a little comforted.

Sender's mother never mentioned Rachel-Leah.

The Slovak laws regulating Jewish life, a torturer's screw, tightened once again. The president of the Reform temple, a former banker, and his teenage son threw themselves into the river from the Old Bridge. The Jewish orphanage declared itself full to capacity. The Halter family, despite every effort, finally defaulted on its loans. Adults were no longer ashamed to stand on line for charity soup, rather than send their children to do the task.

The Rebbe of Janace ordered the ritual bath house closed. Jewish husbands and wives were no longer to sleep together.

CHAPTER TWENTY

In the old days, the end of the Sabbath-morning prayers was a time for friendly greetings and banter, but now the men packed up their prayer shawls in silence.

"Excuse me, pardon me..." A young man was coming through the crowd. "Alexander Halter? Reb Sender?"

"Yes," said Sender. He recognized the man as a secretary to the Rebbe.

Because of his extreme age and special mystical practices, the Rebbe did not pray in the main synagogue of Janace, but in a chapel attached to his house. There he was joined by a small group of fervent Hasidim. At least two secretaries attended the Rebbe at all times.

"Reb Sender, the Rebbe, may he live long good years, requests an audience with you and your wife, the revered Mrs. Halter. Tomorrow morning, after prayers. Please come nicely dressed. Good Shabbos."

Sender rushed out of the synagogue to tell Kitty what had happened, but by the time he got out she had already heard. The talk had spread through the synagogue and up to the women's balcony, quick as flame.

What a mystery. Since when did the Rebbe summon people to an audience? It was the Hasidim—hundreds of them in these desperate times—who asked for an audience with the Rebbe! And why Sender? The Halter family was not among the most ardent of the flock. And if the Rebbe had some reason to ask a Halter, why not his father, or his older brother?

And since when did the Rebbe receive ladies in audience, unless they had no husband or father? And why the bizarre request for nice clothing? Would anyone—much less the elegant young Halters—don second best for a meeting with the Rebbe?

Most serious of all, how could the Rebbe send his secretary to conduct weekday business on the Holy Sabbath? It was a public desecration of sacred law.

All day Saturday, Kitty and Sender tried not to think about the meeting with the Rebbe. "Let us enjoy the day of rest while we can," they kept telling each other, "there are few enough pleasures left to Jews."

But as soon as three stars were seen in the heavens and the men had said the evening service, and the women had said their own special prayer, Kitty rushed to the storage closet and took out their best suits and coats.

The clothing needed airing, they had not been worn since the hard times began. There had been no celebrations to which they could wear finery. Besides, the garments would be ruined by the horrible yellow stars.

Now she basted the stars on lightly with a single thread; the clothes would only be worn this once and then she would remove the offending badges and back into storage they would go.

Sender joined her. He polished their shoes to a deep shine. He put out his best white shirt, thankfully clean.

"This is my favorite tie, but it's kind of flamboyant for a visit with the Rebbe, don't you think?" He held it up for Kitty's inspection.

"Oh, I forgot what that one looked like. It's so pretty. Wear it, Sender. If anyone can pull off flamboyant, you can. Besides, look what I've got to wear." Kitty held up a satin turban festooned with veiling, silk flowers, and an attached scarf.

"That is a bit much. Don't you have anything else? A black suit shouldn't be that hard to match."

"Yes, but it's the Rebbe we're meeting with. I need something modest to cover every hair on my head. It's either this hat or your mother's wig."

"The hat," agreed Sender.

Sunday morning curfew had not yet lifted when Sari came running breathlessly to the Halters.

"Sari, are you suicidal, about in the streets at this hour?"

"It's not so dangerous. The uncircumcised ones are too busy for us now. They're either in church or nursing hangovers."

"But what can be so important that you would take the risk?"

"For your appointment with the Rebbe I wanted you to have this."

Sari reached into a soft cloth sack and withdrew her treasured leather handbag. It had been the anniversary gift of many anniversaries ago, but, like Sari herself, it was still majestic. Superbly crafted and rarely used, the bag looked new and fashionable.

"Oh Sari, it's much too special. My good bag will do for today."

"Go ahead, Kitty. Who knows how many more occasions there will be for carrying it."

"Don't be pessimistic, Sari. God always comes through for us, doesn't he? But the pocketbook is so beautiful, I can't resist borrowing it. Thank you." She kissed her sister on the cheek.

Sari and all the Halters stood at the doorway seeing Kitty and Sender off. They were so proud of the handsomely turned-out young couple. Not since the wedding had so many smiles been seen in the household.

"Kitty," Sari called after her.

Kitty turned around. "What is it?"

"I just wanted to tell you..."

"What, Sari?"

"That you look beautiful."

They walked as quickly as Kitty's high heels would allow. If there was anything sure to enrage the Gentiles it was a Jewish couple who looked as sharp as the Windsors.

The front door of the Rebbe's house opened before they got there. There were already a dozen worried people in the waiting room, but a young Hasid led Kitty and Sender straight into the Rebbe's office.

Greetings were perfunctory and they were asked to take a seat. Kitty hesitated, but one of the three secretaries indicated that, yes, she was to sit beside her husband right in front of the Rebbe.

The Rebbe was tiny, smaller than Kitty. The shriveled, ancient man was well into his nineties. The oldest part of him were his eyes, pinpricks of light in caverns of sorrow.

"Do you have your identity papers with you Reb Sender, Mrs. Halter?"

Sender took his out of his breast pocket, Kitty fished hers out of one of the silk-lined pockets of Sari's handbag. A secretary took them away and handed them two other documents. Sender and Kitty examined these with surprise.

"These are your new, Gentile identity papers. The forgeries are unfortunately poor, but they must do for now."

"Revered Rebbe," said Sender. Why do we need these?"

"Children, you are going to Hungary, with God's help."

"Hungary?"

"Yes. It is much safer there, for now. They are still one step ahead of

Germany, may its name be erased. Now listen carefully, we have much ground to cover."

"Begging the Rebbe's pardon," said Sender, "but we cannot do such a thing. My whole family depends on my earnings."

Kitty looked at Sender proudly. Not many men, much less Hasidim, would boldly contradict the Rebbe to his face. Of course, Sender had only said what had to be said. They were simply not free to attempt a madcap escape.

"You cannot return to work in the garage, Alexander."

"Why not?"

"Tomorrow morning all able-bodied Jewish men and boys are to be drafted into forced-labor brigades."

Their mouths dropped open.

"A death march," Kitty breathed. "My nephews...my brothers-in-law..."

The Rebbe glanced at the three secretaries and saw the fear in their faces.

"No. But slave-labor camps."

"So," the Rebbe said, drawing their attention to a scrap of paper on his desk. "This is the address of our loyal Hasid in Budapest. Both of you should memorize it. Reb Mordecai Fried will help you get settled. Remember, Hungarian Jews are safe for now, but if they are found harboring foreign Jews, they can be punished by death.

"You will be transported across the border by a peasant called Miklos."

"Is this Miklos trustworthy?" asked Kitty.

The Rebbe said, "He earns his pay, which is very dear indeed. Nowadays, greed is a virtue in a Gentile. But this journey is perilous. Very, very perilous. Only divine intervention will get you safely across. Never forget."

The Rebbe nodded at one of the secretaries, who took a wad of bills out of an envelope and handed it to Sender.

Sender took the money, as if he handled small fortunes in cash regularly. "American dollars and pounds sterling?"

"Yes," said the Rebbe. His voice was tired. "All the foreign currency in the holy community of Janace. By accepting this money you become their legal agents."

"Agents for what?" asked Kitty.

The Rebbe closed his eyes for a moment, as if in prayer. He nodded at Sender.

Sender looked at his wife. She blinked consent. He tucked the money into yet another pocket. Custom-made suits had all sorts of conveniences.

"Well," said Kitty. "We'd better get back and tell our families goodbye."

"No" said the Rebbe. "No goodbyes. Miklos is waiting for you."

"But we *have* to..."

"No! Your safety is the only farewell they require."

How could he be so heartless? What if she never saw...

"One more thing before you go," said the Rebbe. He took something from a chair next to his own.

"These are my trousers. Mrs. Halter, would you please put them on."

"What!"

"My trousers. An extra pair. I won't be needing them. You may use that room there for privacy.

Kitty hardly knew what to say. Pants? It was bizarre. What woman wore trousers? What was she, an American film star? And wasn't it forbidden by the Torah to wear the clothes of the opposite sex? Could it be that the Rebbe had become senile?

"Please, Mrs. Halter. Just put them on under your clothing. All but three laws of the Torah are nullified—must be nullified—to preserve life. Wearing men's clothing is neither murder, idolatry, or incest," said the Rebbe.

Kitty went into the indicated room. It was the Rebbe's bedchamber, and it was austere as a jail cell. She removed her shoes and pulled on the pants. They were knickers really, buttoning under the knees. She didn't button the bottoms, but folded them up instead, so they wouldn't show under her skirt.

The pants fit perfectly. She smoothed her clothes, touched her hat, and marched back into the office, feeling confident and adventurous.

CHAPTER TWENTY-ONE

The Rebbe's secretaries brought Kitty and Sender to a clearing near the Old Bridge. Once farmers and townspeople used to trade there, but now it was overgrown with weeds.

Four harnessed horses were pawing the ground impatiently, steam puffing from their nostrils. Miklos leaned casually on a wagon. His powerful build and the cigarette smoke he exhaled gave him a resemblance to the horses, but that stopped at the eyes. The horses' were soft and dreamy; Miklos' clever and alert.

The wagon's bed was covered with a layer of potatoes and there were additional crates of potatoes nearby. The secretaries smoothed the potatoes, while Kitty and Sender removed each other's stars.

"Lie down there," said Miklos.

Sender and Kitty looked at each other. Lie down on the filthy potatoes? In their best clothes?

"Please Reb Sender, Mrs. Halter," said one of the secretaries. "Do as the gentleman says."

They climbed up on the wagon and lay down, about six inches apart. Miklos and the secretaries emptied the crates over them.

"Make a noise if you have trouble breathing," said Miklos.

The potatoes were arranged so that nothing showed through.

One of the secretaries leaned down over the sides of the wagon and whispered to the potatoes, "'May you go out in joy, and come in to peace.'"

They were off. The ride was bumpy and rough. The dust and dirt fell from the potatoes and into their throats, but they didn't cough. There would be no coughing, sneezing, gasping or even loud breathing until Miklos gave the go-ahead.

They rode for hours. Potato dust got into Kitty's eyes and ears and mouth. Each potato was an enemy fist, punching her everywhere. Would they ever get out of this alive? Would she ever see her family again? What if she and Sender were parted?

Oh, if only she could lie in Sender's arms, or even hold hands beneath the potatoes. But it was forbidden. She had not been to the ritual bath after her last period—the postponed period—so they were forbidden to touch.

The wagon slowed down.

"Hey Gabor, how ya doin'?"

"Same as you, Miklos, same as you."

"Get a better price over in Hungary?"

"Nah, not really. Just that the Slovak money isn't worth shit."

The wagon stopped.

"What's holding it up there at the checkpost, Gabor?"

"They're looking for Jews."

The wagon inched up.

"Halt there!" came a gruff voice.

"Whatever you say, commander," Gabor said sarcastically.

"Wise guy, eh? You hiding any Jews back there?"

"Yeah, thousands of them. An old witch turned 'em all into beets."

"Get down off the wagon."

"Huh? Why?"

"'Cause I said so, moron."

There was a pause. Then there was an ear-splitting volley of gun fire. It went on and on.

Kitty was glad now for the potatoes. If it weren't for their weight holding her down she could not have stopped herself from jumping.

"Hey, what did you do?" screamed Gabor. "You ruined my beets."

"Oh, your beets. Your bewitched beets. Well then, that's just Jew-blood oozing out. Go to the synagogue and you'll find your beets nice and safe. Get outta here, you son-of-a-bitch."

Their wagon started up again and rolled for a few yards.

"Any Jews in there?" The border guard's voice was still very hostile.

"No sir. Would you like me to go through the potatoes, sir? It's no big trouble."

The guard muttered something.

"I really need to sell the potatoes, sir. There's a girl I'm hoping to marry and..."

"Yeah, yeah. Keep your pants on. You'll get back home before the priest sees her swollen tummy."

Miklos did not get off the wagon, but Kitty could feel someone else getting on.

Stop beating, heart. He can hear you!

Swish! Swish! Swish! Swish!

Something was coming down right next to her. A knife? No, bigger. A bayonet! Oh, God, Sender! Did he stab Sender? No, he couldn't have. Sender could not have avoided screaming; no human being could.

Swish! Swish!

The stabbing was vigorous and methodical, going down the center of the wagon. Where would he stab next? Almighty One, make the guard tired. Make him stop.

"Ha!" The guard laughed. "Look at this. I skewered four potatoes, all in a row. Now what are the odds of that happening?"

"Incredible," said Miklos. "Say, those spuds should make a fine dinner for you. And you could wash it down with this."

"Home brew?"

"Yeah. You know, the Jews don't make the good stuff anymore."

"No, it's not like it was in the old days."

Kitty listened to them indulge in maudlin nostalgia. Her fear was almost overcome by rage. Everything was the Jews' fault. If you kill them and they die, that's their fault too. Sue the corpses for loss of services!

"Well, any drink's better than thirst."

"You're right about that, pal. Thanks for the bottle, go right ahead."

Kitty exhaled so deeply that potatoes collapsed on her chest.

Much later the wagon stopped.

"All right," Miklos called out, but not too loudly. "It's safe to get out now."

The potatoes rumbled and Kitty and Sender emerged. Seeing each other well, they cried with relief.

"Blessed is the Shield of Abraham," said Sender.

"Amen," said Kitty. Then she burst into uncontrollable laughter.

"What is it?" asked Sender.

"You, my handsome, debonair husband, look like a giant potato."

They were at a rest stop and tram depot just north of Budapest. It was Sunday afternoon so they were pretty much on their own in a parking area behind a tavern. There were outhouses and a water pump, which they were about to use gratefully.

"I'm going in to wet my whistle," said Miklos, indicating the tavern. "The bus you folks need is across the way, over there. Good luck."

They both thanked him profusely. Kitty and Sender dusted themselves off.

"Let's go," said Kitty.

"No, let's wait for Miklos. He did a great job with that guard. Let's give him a tip."

"A tip? But he was paid very handsomely. You heard the Rebbe."

"Still, he deserves something extra."

"Sender! We don't have money to waste. Who knows how long it'll take 'till we find housing and work."

"God will provide; he has until now. But Miklos should have his tip."

Kitty sighed. There was no moving Sender when he got into a regal frame of mind. They didn't call him "Baron" for nothing.

"I just hope he isn't a major drinker, or we'll be here till nightfall."

He was not. Miklos came out soon after, quite alert and surprised to see them.

"I thought you'd gone."

"We wanted to show you our gratitude for your kindness and quick thinking," said Sender. He reached into his pocket and pulled out a one-hundred-dollar bill.

Miklos turned pale. "One hundred American dollars!"

Kitty turned pale too. Sender said, "It's the least we can do. You saved our lives."

Miklos examined the bill. "This is an American president?"

"No, it's Benjamin Franklin, a wise man."

Miklos nodded. "Wisdom leads to wealth and power."

"True wisdom," said Sender, "leads to goodness."

Miklos put the money inside his shirt as they walked toward the tram stop.

Suddenly, he grabbed them both by the elbows. "No, don't go there."

"Why not?" asked Kitty.

"The Arrow Cross. They're waiting to pick you up at your tram stop."

The Arrow Cross, Hungary's fascist guard, had a zeal for murdering Jews that would have done an SS division proud.

"How do they know?" whispered Sender.

"I told them. I informed." Miklos looked at his shoes and shrugged his shoulders. "They promised me a kilo of sugar a head," he explained. "But this," he patted his chest where he'd hidden the money, "will buy a whole lot more sugar."

Kitty's field of vision turned red. But Sender wasn't angry at all. He smiled at Miklos and shook hands. "Thanks," he said, "see you again some time."

Sender took Kitty's arm and led her to the street.

"Where are you going, Sender? We should take a tram in the opposite direction."

"And go where?"

"I don't know. Not to Mordecai Fried's though. Not tonight. Where *are* you going, Sender? There are no streetcars here."

Sender whistled sharply, and a taxi stopped before them. He hustled his startled wife into the back seat.

"What's the best hotel in Budapest, driver?"

The driver turned around. "Well, there are several good ones, but..."

"The best one, driver. Take us to the best."

Kitty opened her mouth, but thought better of what she was about to say and sank back in the seat in silence. No nagging about money now. Her husband was doing a great job handling the cash.

CHAPTER TWENTY-TWO

The concierge looked up at the eccentrically dressed couple. Anyone with money could dress well, he thought, but only a man of supreme confidence would wear that sort of tie. Even more to the point, a great beauty or a famed diva might sport a hat like that, but a plain, anonymous woman who wore it had to have *confidence*. The kind of confidence that came with very old money or noble blood.

"May I help you?" the concierge said, wiping his hands.

"Yes," the man said. "I'd like a room for the night."

The concierge did not ask about reservations. Whom would he be kidding? The hotel was all but vacant. Ever since the Munich Agreement tourists had disappeared.

"A single room?" The concierge lifted his eyebrow slightly. No luggage and the woman looked nervous. Good. An illicit affair meant hush money spread around.

"Yes. Or," he turned to the woman, "would you prefer a suite, my dear?"

"No, Baron," she answered tartly, "a room will do."

"If you would be so kind," the concierge said, turning the registry to the man and handing him a pen. "And the identity cards."

The man reached in his pocket and the woman into her purse. She was upset.

"Yours won't be necessary, Madam." There was nothing to be gained from invading her privacy.

The man signed in as the concierge opened his identity card.

"Ah, pardon me, young fellow," the gentleman said, disturbing the concierge's perusal. "Will you accept foreign currency?"

The concierge closed the card with a scowl. "The hotel does not accept the new Slovak money at this time."

The man continued to speak politely. Aristocrats didn't notice when they were insulted. "I meant English pounds," he said, reaching for the identity card with one hand, and into his breast pocket with the other.

"Oh, of course. Very sorry for the misunderstanding, er..." He looked at the registry. "Baron..." The rest was a scrawl. "Deepest apologies, Baron."

"Quite all right." He handed a bill to the concierge.

The concierge's eyes popped at the size of the British note.

"I take it that will cover any additional needs we may have?"

"Of course! I should be honored to serve those needs personally, Baron."

There was a lavish basket of fruit and a big box of chocolate in their room. Kitty and Sender polished them off, but they were more tired than hungry.

The big bed was inviting, but they couldn't sleep together in a state of ritual impurity.

"I'll take the sofa," Sender volunteered.

"No, I will. It's too short for you, darling."

"Are you sure?"

"Yes. And it's no sacrifice. Look, it's covered in satin. And there's an extra down comforter and plenty of pillows."

Sender yawned. "All right. If you insist." He was folding his clothes and laying them out on the armchair. He crept into the bed and was asleep before he could pull the comforter up to his chin.

Kitty covered him lovingly. She made up the sofa neatly. Then she folded her clothes so the wrinkles would relax, and put them on a little lacquered coffee table.

The rabbi's trousers. She'd forgotten she had those on.

Kitty took off the pants, folded them, and put them on the table with the other clothes. She went to the sofa and...

The trousers slid off the table and fell to the floor.

She got off the sofa and put the pants back on the table securely, next to her other clothes. Then she returned to bed.

But before she could even sit down, the trousers slid to the floor again.

How annoying. For ordinary wool gabardine, the pants were awfully slippery. Well, she couldn't go to sleep in a mess.

Kitty picked up the pants and looked for a closet. There was a beautiful carved armoire with gleaming brass doorknobs.

She opened the doors and removed a suit hanger of polished ebony.

She carefully draped the pants on the hanger, then replaced it on the rack.

The pants slid off the hanger and to the floor of the armoire.

Cursing under her breath, Kitty reached down for the trousers. Her hand touched leather.

What on earth?

She pulled out a black crocodile document portfolio, the sort rich people used for their personal papers. Who would have left this behind? People hung on to their documents with greater tenacity than they grasped their wallets. In these times, one's papers *were* one's identity.

She pulled out the official Hungarian identity card.

Name: Ficsorcsak, Julia

Date of Birth: September 20, 1920

Kitty laughed. Exactly one month before her own. Place of birth was some town, a hamlet probably, that she'd never heard of.

Height: 4'11"

Kitty gasped. She gasped again at Weight: 90 lbs.

After that she just held her breath as she read.

Eyes: brown

Complexion: olive

Hair: blond

Kitty let out her breath. Well she wasn't blond, that was a difference! It wasn't as if this were some sort of doppelganger.

Citizenship: Hungarian

Race: Magyar

Religion: Roman Catholic

Marital status: single

The photograph, distorted by stamps and seals, showed a small face, more saucy than pretty, artfully made-up, surrounded by carefully waved blond hair.

Well, it didn't look exactly like her. But then her own identity card photo didn't look exactly like her, either.

"Sender! Sender, get up."

Her husband hurled himself out of bed, ready to run.

"It's all right. Look at these papers I found in the closet. An identity card, baptismal records. All sorts of stuff."

Sender examined the identity card silently. He looked at Kitty, then at the photo in the card, then at Kitty. "It's a miracle," he breathed.

"I'll have to bleach my hair." She would look like one of the Lebow girls at last.

Sender studied the card, "Julia's color doesn't look natural, either."

"Who is she? What's this card doing here?" Kitty's face fell. "She'll be coming back for it."

Sender stroked the portfolio. "There's a layer of dust on it. It's been here for a while." He opened the card again and looked at the picture. "A young village girl, maybe a chambermaid. She probably dropped this while she was cleaning the room."

Kitty took the portfolio from him. "Crocodile? For a chambermaid? I don't think so. Do you know what I think?"

"Never," muttered Sender.

"I think she's a prostitute! Yes, that would explain how a village girl came to spend the night in the best hotel in Budapest. And how she could afford crocodile accessories. And why she couldn't come back for her papers."

"Kitty!" How could his innocent, devout Jewish wife think of such a thing? But it did make sense.

"It's been a day of miracles. God willing, there will be more tomorrow. Now let's get some sleep."

Kitty snuggled in between the satin and the down. This had been the most frightening day of her life. And the most exciting.

In the morning, Sender rang the concierge. "Is the perfumery open, young man?"

"Of course, of course. For his lordship, it's always open."

Sender gave him a list of toiletries to purchase, including peroxide and hair dye.

"And curlers," said Kitty.

"Would Madam wish for a hairdresser to attend to her?"

"That won't be necessary," said Kitty, before Sender could graciously agree.

As a young wife in Janace Kitty had covered most of her hair with a kerchief or hat. Not as pious as Sari or her mother-in-law, who clipped their hair to the skull and wore wigs and tight headdresses, she'd had her hair cut to the shortest length in vogue, and covered most of it with the most modish confection her discount could get at the hat store. Kitty had grown so used to a hair-covering that going bareheaded felt as wanton as exposing her breasts.

But all that would have to change. She was a Gentile now, and not a very modest one, either. Her hair was now her marker, the seal of her caste and religion and "race," broadcasting the type of woman she was.

It was afternoon when Kitty removed the curlers and brushed out her hair. How strange it felt to use a new hairbrush. She glanced in the gilt dresser mirror and her hands froze on the way up to her hair.

The look, platinum waves around her dusky face, was unnatural, yet satisfying. It fit better than her own hair. Kitty was reminded of Rachel-Leah before her marriage. Rachel-Leah's thick braids had seemed like a costume; her marriage wig looked organic.

Kitty moved closer to the mirror. With a blond frame her face seemed more open, more animated, her eyes dilated. Or was that just her excitement?

Anyway, nice. She needed a different shade of lipstick.

The British note Sender had peeled off his wad must have been a high denomination indeed, for they were presented with no further charges on their way out of the hotel. Half a dozen uniformed staff lined the lobby to see them off. They stood at attention with the sincere smiles of those who have been generously tipped.

Chief among them was the concierge. Bowing and scraping as he walked backwards, he said, "What an honor it was to have you grace our humble hotel, Baron. We beg your lordship think of us on your next visit to Budapest."

CHAPTER TWENTY-THREE

Before Sender's knuckles could touch it, the door to Mordecai Fried's apartment swung open. A gray-skinned man, who must have been looking out the peephole, cowered before them, his eyes darting everywhere but ahead. This couldn't be Fried.

"Where is..."

The man pushed his hand over Sender's mouth, then pulled them both inside the room, shutting the door silently. He scribbled briefly on a scrap of paper. "Food." Then he turned his back on them and resumed his watch at the peephole.

Mordecai Fried's home must have been gracious, even palatial, at one time. The rooms were large, with floor-to-ceiling windows. These windows were, in mid-morning, closely draped with heavy curtains. In the gloom they could make out fine carpets and exquisite parquet floors.

What made the apartment bizarre were the two hundred people in it.

There were whole families stuffed into every crevice, entire clans huddling in each corner. Young couples like themselves were perched on top of dressers; others bent under tables over their small children. There were ancient crones, compressed by age and worry. There were tiny babies with the raw look of recent birth.

There were people everywhere, and everyone had a bundle: shredded suitcases held together by twine and old belts, bursting pillowcases, four corners of a kerchief tied together to make a package.

But the most peculiar thing was that all these people were absolutely quiet. Babies silent as sculptures. Old people heaving with suffering, but not sounding sighs.

Kitty and Sender could find no place to sit. They leaned against a small bit of a wall, pressed between strangers, and waited for the return of Mordecai Fried.

After an endless hour, he arrived. The Halters were surprised to see a man of about sixty in full Hasidic dress. Kitty touched her hand to her exposed hair. A strand fell in her eyes. It was blond hair, foreign, almost like a wig.

Mordecai Fried had dancing eyes that belied his white hair and creased forehead. He was strong for his age too, because he carried four shopping baskets overflowing with food.

Fried put the baskets on the floor and his guests began an orderly—soundless—distribution of the food. He gestured to Sender and Kitty and they followed him into what was once a powder room.

The windowless lavatory smelled horrible, but it must have been pretty once, with flocked velvet wallpaper and gleaming brass faucet handles.

Speaking very softly, Mordecai Fried welcomed them as if they were paying a holiday call. It turned out that he had not been expecting them; he had received no communication from the Rebbe.

Fried told them that the people in the apartment had come from all over Europe, but mostly Poland. They were Jews who could not speak Hungarian, who had no false papers, who were more than desperate. But Mordecai Fried refused no one sanctuary.

They showed Fried their documents. His expert eye ascertained the legitimacy of "Julia"'s papers. "This is wonderful," he said. But he sighed as he glanced over Sender's. "I can get you something better than this, but not much better. I'm afraid all the best forgers have been..."

His face brightened. "But I can find work for you. A mechanic! Marvelous. And I can find work for you, too, Mrs. Halter, I'm sure of it."

"Not to boast, but I'm an excellent seamstress. And milliner."

Fried shook his head. "Those occupations would be dangerous for you, even with good papers. The sewing trades are top-heavy with Jewish women. They're the first places the Evil Ones raid."

"Something else, then. I want to work," said Kitty. "Sender too. We'll do anything to earn our own living."

Fried sighed. Every one of the refugees felt the same. "I'll get to it right away."

"May I ask you a question, Reb Mordecai," said Sender.

"Of course."

"Can you tell me where Budapest's red-light district is?"

Kitty went crimson. Had Sender lost his wits? Even if he had a reason for asking such a question, why would he ask it of Fried, obviously a very religious Jew?

Mordecai Fried didn't blink. "Yes, let me make a map, Reb Sender."

It was a sunny day, and Kitty and Sender, strolling the gorgeous streets of Hungary's capital, fit right in, although they had to fight their instinct to gape at the city's beauty. Like them, the people of Budapest were very fashionable, the "Parisians of the East." Even in turbulent times Budapest seemed light-hearted, hedonistic, and naughty. It was like a beautiful, spoiled woman who would not be daunted by any misfortune. Some man was sure to show up and provide her with luxuries! Kitty wondered if the red-light district could be any more ornamented than the respectable ones they had seen thus far.

"Why are we going to th...that place?"

"We need a place to sleep tonight."

"Well we can't afford another night at that fancy hotel. We'll just have to manage at Mordecai Fried's, for now."

"Don't be ridiculous," said Sender.

Kitty fumed. Perhaps the Baron would like to purchase an estate.

"This is no time to sulk," said Sender. "Keep your eyes open."

"For what?"

"For an apartment."

Kitty looked around purposefully. Within a few minutes she saw a "To Let" sign.

"Up there," she gestured to Sender.

Sender turned. Under the sign was a fat woman in her fifties wearing a red nightgown. As soon as she saw Sender looking at her, she grinned and picked up one of her breasts, an effort that took both hands. She pointed the breast at Sender as if showing off a prize heifer at a village fair.

"I don't think we want a roommate," said Sender.

Kitty blushed hard. Was that a real prostitute? Weren't they supposed to be ravishingly beautiful? Weren't they supposed to be young? It seemed a man could do better with almost any wife than with the woman in the window.

They trudged on. There were a few possibilities, but Sender rejected them. Kitty feared that they would have to return to Mordecai Fried's apartment after all.

Then they both saw the sign. "Furnished Flat for Rent." It was on top of a tavern, which was flanked on both sides by what looked like abandoned factories.

They went into the bar. Kitty had never been in one before. The few customers there must have been dedicated drunks as they were already slumped to the tables. They might have been in that position since the night before.

"You renting out the place upstairs?" Sender asked the bartender.

"Not me," said the serving man, rubbing at an invisible spot on the bar, although it was covered with the remains of spilled drinks and other large stains. "But you're in luck, the landlord's in town today. It's pretty rare that he honors us with a visit," he said with a laugh.

"Where can I find him?"

"Round the corner at Aggie's.

Finding the place was easy. The building with the cheap, ornate portal and the louts hanging around the entrance, was clearly "Aggie's."

Sender looked at the building, then at the youths, then at the building again. "You'd better stay here," he said to Kitty.

He came out of Aggie's a few minutes later, followed by the landlord. The gentleman's hat-brim was a little too wide and his shoes were too pointy. A cigarette dangled from his lower lip.

"It's a real nice flat," the landlord said, "despite the location. Fully furnished, too. I can let you have it cheap, considering."

He stated his price. Sender and Kitty said nothing.

"All right. Ten less a month. But I'll need first and last month's rent in advance."

Sender said, "Take another fifteen off and I'll pay you a year in advance. In American dollars.

"Deal," said the landlord, very quickly. He extended his hand to Sender. "Pleasure doing business with you, Mr...?"

"Sandor," said Sender, giving the Hungarian version of his real name, not the one in his papers.

"That's Sandor...?"

"Petofy," said Sender. Sandor Petofy was Hungary's national poet. "The rental will be under her name," he said, indicating Kitty.

The landlord winked at Sender. "Got it," he said. He smirked as Kitty handed him the crocodile document case for inspection. When Sender handed him the money, he smiled a genuine smile and jauntily tossed over the keys.

"Furnished" was a rather fanciful description of the apartment. There was a bare mattress in one room, a card table and a single chair in the other. On the positive side, there was a cooking ring and indoor plumbing. The flat wasn't clean, but it wasn't vile.

Sender made two trips to the market for cleaning supplies, bedding, and kitchen goods. By nightfall Kitty had the place in decent shape, and a simple supper going. They dined and went to sleep, as pleased as newlyweds with a handsome trousseau.

The next morning they bought a lot of food and although they ate a large breakfast, there were plenty of leftovers to take to Mordecai Fried's house. Fried accepted the food gratefully, but stopped Sender from telling him their new address.

"No. Don't tell anyone."

"But..."

"The Evil Ones have methods. They can get anyone to reveal anything."

"But what if our families try to contact us?" asked Kitty.

Mordecai Fried turned away in pain. After a while he cleared his throat. "Your good luck is holding, thank God. Reb Sender, I have a job for you at a garage. The owner is a God-fearing Jew and won't look too closely at your papers.

"Mrs. Halter, I found something for you, too. It's not exactly what I'd hoped for, but it's not that bad. Really. Just hear me out."

"It doesn't matter. Beggars can't be choosers..."

"The position is for a maid."

"No!" said Kitty and Sender simultaneously. Whoever heard of such a thing as a Jewish maid? The common Yiddish term for female servant was "shiksa," a disparaging word for Gentile woman.

Neither of them had ever seen a Jewish family so poor that it sent its daughters into servitude. The Meisels, even, had never reached that depth. As for a married woman—it was unthinkable.

"Please," said Fried. "It's not what you think. This woman who agreed to take you on is a pious Jewish widow. Her late husband was a dear friend. And it's very little work. A bit of cleaning, a little cooking, how much labor can one woman generate?"

"Well," said Kitty, "perhaps we've been hasty." She'd rather work as a maid than stay idle all day, even in their cozy apartment.

"There's one more thing," said Fried. "Mrs. Gordon, the widow, she would like you to stay over in the house."

"To sleep in?"

"Yes. But you get to go home every other Sunday. And it's safer, really, what with Sender's shaky papers."

Away from Sender. Away from her love.

But it was safer for him. Safer for her love.

Anyway, they couldn't sleep together now. It would be so painful if they were living otherwise as husband and wife.

"Whatever God wills, that is best," she said.

The woman who answered the doorbell was wearing a starched collar and cuffs. Kitty was surprised. She didn't know there was other help in the household.

"May I speak with Mrs. Gordon? I have an appointment."

"I am Mrs. Gordon."

Kitty was taken aback. This widow was about a year or two older than she was!

The woman indicated that Kitty was to follow her.

The apartment was as grand as Mordecai Fried's. It was empty of human beings but full of *things*. The ornamentation was stupefying. Fringes, crystals, knickknacks hung from every object. It made her aunt's home in Vienna seem like a hermit's cell.

They passed through the parlor, the dining room, a study and a sun-dappled morning room, but although each of the rooms had ample seating, Mrs. Gordon led on. Finally they came to the kitchen. It was large and modern, with an electric refrigerator and every convenience. At its center was a marble-topped table, perfect for making pastry. What a homey place to chat, thought Kitty.

But Mrs. Gordon kept walking. At the far end of the kitchen was a tiny pantry with only a splintered wood table and a matching chair. Mrs. Gordon indicated that Kitty was to sit. She pulled another chair away from the kitchen table and sat on that.

"Show me your papers," she said. "Mr. Fried said you had authentic papers. They better be. I can't jeopardize myself for a stranger."

Kitty handed over the crocodile wallet. Mrs. Gordon touched the case and looked at it as if she were about to eat it. She took out the documents and examined them for a long time.

"Well," she allowed, "these look almost real."

"They *are* real," said Kitty.

"I don't feel that I have a responsibility for refugees," whined Mrs. Gordon. "I am not a martyr. I'm taking you on solely as a favor to my late husband's business partner."

Aha, thought Kitty, and the executor of his estate?

Mrs. Gordon then stated flatly what she would be paying Kitty.

"But that's not even a living wage!"

"You have some nerve, Julia, chiseling for money. You'll be getting room and board from the fat of the land. Have you any idea how many of you little rats have come scurrying over the border to Hungary? Hundreds, thousands, would grab at my offer."

Kitty knew this was true. "I'm not rejecting the offer, Mrs. Gordon. I accept your terms. And, by the way, my real name is..."

"I don't want to hear it!" Mrs. Gordon clapped her hands over her ears. "As far as I'm concerned you're a Christian. If anyone finds out you're a Jew, that's your business. The risk will be entirely yours. Don't expect me to jump in and save you. I'll have nothing to do with it. In fact, you must buy a necklace with a crucifix, and wear it all the time. I want everyone to know I hired a Catholic."

Kitty was aghast. How could Mrs. Gordon, so religious that she wore an old-fashioned wig, ask her to do such a thing? It was forbidden, except to save one's life.

Mealy-mouthed hypocrite, thought Kitty. But she mustn't hate a fellow Jew. That was their people's great tragedy, that had been their downfall.

She would simply have to accept that she had a demanding employer. Many people did, in all places and times. And then, it was always best to hold one's tongue.

"Speaking of appearances," said Mrs. Gordon, "you can't wear that fancy clothing here. You'll need a maid's uniform. I can sell you some from my previous girls. One of them must have been your size."

"Thank you, but I'll sew my own."

"As you wish. There's a sewing room near your quarters. You can buy the material and notions, and I'll deduct the use of the sewing machine from your wages."

"Very well."

"That's 'very well, Mrs. Gordon,' or 'very well, ma'am.'"

Kitty closed her eyes and sought strength. "Yes, ma'am."

Sender had much better luck with his employer. The garage owner had sympathy for the Halters' plight, paid Sender a decent salary, and was grateful for his excellent skills. He even piled some old furniture on a truck, drove it to the apartment, and helped Sender carry it in.

"We too, were strangers in the Land of Egypt," the garage owner quoted. His wife pressed so much food on Sender, that he often brought the remainders to Mordecai Fried's hungry houseguests.

"Where is Reb Mordecai's family?" Sender asked one day when business was slow. "A man like that, so loving and devoted to strangers must be a dedicated husband and father."

"Oh, he is! He has a wife and daughter in Romania."

"Really? I thought he was born and bred here in Hungary."

"Oh, yes, and they were, too. But they're in Romania now.

"Fried and his wife were always beloved members of the community.

For years they had no children, and it seemed an especially terrible thing that such kind people would be denied by God. I tell you, everyone prayed for them.

"Then, late in life, they were blessed with a little girl, and she was the joy of their existence. She is the sweetest thing, pretty, good-natured like her parents, and of course, there is all that dowry money.

"No one could understand why, when the time came for her to marry, there were no suitors. You'd think they'd snap up a girl like that before she turned eighteen.

"After a year or two with no serious bites, they decided to go abroad to other communities. The mother and daughter went off to resorts, distant relatives, conventions, any opportunity to travel to a place where there are eligible men. But the girl is now in her late twenties, and nothing in sight. You'd think, with war and everything, someone would want her at least for the dowry. Not that Reb Mordecai would give away the apple of his eye to a gold digger, but if desperate enough...

"Anyway, after roaming around Europe, the mother and daughter found themselves in Romania. The way things were looking, Reb Mordecai told them to hang tight there. There aren't any anti-Semitic laws like there are here. Not yet, anyway."

That evening Sender got his pay and he spent most of it on groceries for the people at Mordecai Fried's.

"You shouldn't do this, Reb Sender," said Mordecai Fried, "it's dangerous for you, being a foreigner yourself."

"It's dangerous for you, too, Reb Mordecai."

Fried shrugged. "What else can a Jew do?"

Sender nodded.

"Reb Sender, may I walk you home part of the way? I'd like to talk privately."

They stopped in a darkened park and sat down on a bench. "I have a terrible problem, Reb Sender. A dilemma of faith. Please, help me."

Sender was surprised. An elderly, prosperous, respected Hasid seeking out his advice? "Whatever I could do for you, Mr. Fried, I would do with all my heart."

Fried's lip quivered and he looked down into his beard. "You see, I have a wife and daughter in Romania."

"Yes, I've heard."

"My wife wrote to say she bought three tickets on a ship to Lisbon."

"That's wonderful!" Lisbon was a free port.

"Yes. And even better, she has three tickets from Lisbon to...to America."

"America!"

"Yes. Passage. Visas. Everything."

"But that's nothing short of miraculous."

Fried smiled sadly. "With money miracles can happen. My wife had a lot of money with her, our daughter's dowry. That's what it cost to bribe the Americans."

"Even money can't always buy entrance to America. But your wife managed, God bless her. What's the problem?"

"The problem is there is no longer entrance to Romania. The noose is tightening, here, Romania, everywhere. I know a few people who tried to get over. Young men, strong men. None of them has been heard from again.

"I wrote to my wife. I begged her to take our daughter and go, but she won't. And my daughter won't. They refuse to leave without me. What should I do?

"Reb Sender, I am so afraid. I know a Jew should fear only God, but I am a bad Jew. I fear the fascists. I fear the Germans. I fear them more than God himself."

"Reb Mordecai, if you are a bad Jew, then what is a good one? You ask my advice, well I'll give it to you: you must go to Romania. *Now.* Leave tonight if you can. Do not be afraid, 'be strong and have courage,' as the Torah commands."

"But I *am* afraid."

"Reb Mordecai, let me speak frankly with you. We are both religious Jews, but we are also logical human beings. Religion aside, there are two—and only two—possibilities. Either there is a God, or there isn't.

"If there is a God, how can he not save you? What more can a Jew do than you have done for your brothers? If you are not a 'good' Jew, what does that mean? No question about it. *If* there is a God, you will reach Romania safely."

Fried looked up at him. In the park lights his eyes glinted with terror. He could hardly open his mouth. When he did speak, he almost choked on the words.

"And if there isn't?"

"If there is no God, Reb Mordecai, if this is a world without a God, well then, you and I don't want to live in it anyway."

CHAPTER TWENTY-FOUR

"Hey there, who are you?"

The maids and laundresses gathered around Kitty. They were in the courtyard of the apartment house, hanging laundry.

"I'm Julia. I do for Mrs. Gordon."

"We can see that," said a big-breasted peasant woman, pointing at Kitty's laundry basket. It had just a few items in it. Mrs. Gordon did not like the idea of the maid mixing her laundry with that of the lady of the house. She made Kitty dry her own things on a chair in her tiny room.

Kitty learned that Mrs. Gordon had been through dozens of maids. For obvious reasons, none stayed long.

"Slave driver," spat one servant.

"Jewish bitch," said another. And they all nodded. "Jew bitch. Jew bitch."

There were other Jews in the building, some of them well-liked. Mr. and Mrs. Weiss on the fourth floor had paid their Elizabeth's rent the whole time her husband was in jail. Dr. Kaplan, with offices as well as an apartment on the ground floor, never turned a patient away and never dunned them for money. His wife was a saint too. When the sick woke her at ungodly hours, instead of being irritated or angry, she greeted them with a smile and a cup of tea.

Yet none of the others was called "Jew." Only Mrs. Gordon was considered representative of the religion. And with her pious exterior, Kitty knew, Mrs. Gordon also represented religious Jews to their freethinking brethren.

Her face burned with shame.

"Don't feel stupid," said a laundress, stroking Kitty's arm with a rough red hand. "It isn't your fault. How were you supposed to know? We country folk always get taken. But you're a hard-working girl, I can see. You're sure to find another position soon."

"Not too soon," said the big-breasted woman with a snort. "In these times who can afford servants—except war profiteers and Jews."

The work itself should have been easy. As Mordecai Fried had said, how much labor could one woman generate? And Mrs. Gordon never had guests.

In cosmopolitan Kosice as in small-town Janace, well-to-do widows were the mainstay of every Jewish charity. But Mrs. Gordon participated neither in the outfitting of poor brides nor in visiting the sick, neither packing food for the Sabbath nor sewing shrouds for the poor.

Mrs. Gordon never visited friends or relatives, and none visited her. She never attended the cinema or the theater. She was indifferent to fashion, to gardens, to cuisine. She owned no gramophone and no radio, and never whistled a tune. She read neither the newspapers, nor romances, nor books of Jewish wisdom.

Her one genuine interest was astrology. Horoscope books were the sum total of her secular library (her late husband had left the usual bookcases full of sacred works, which lay untouched since his death). On Fridays Mrs. Gordon would often purchase gossip magazines of the most mindless sort, and save their astrology sections for her Sabbath treat.

What was it her mistress saw in the stars? Certainly not the truth, a static life, boring, and mean-spirited. Or was she waiting for some predicted comet to come blazing into her dreary and selfish existence?

Kitty wanted to cry out, *There is no luck in Israel.*

"What do you think you're doing, Julia?"

"Taking out the vacuum cleaner."

"What?"

"Ma'am."

"Not that. Who told you to take out the machine? Do you even know how to work a vacuum cleaner?"

"I can figure it out. Ma'am."

"No! You're to take the rugs out on the balcony and beat them manually."

Actually Kitty enjoyed beating the rugs. She got out all her anger at her mistress, all her fear for her family in Slovakia, all her frustrated desire for Sender, on the poor, pretty carpets. In return they did nothing but cough up little puffs of dust, the sad residue of the sad little lives lived upon them.

Most of the day Kitty dusted. The apartment was full of knickknacks and figurines, incoherent collections united by neither theme nor quality. Once in a while Mrs. Gordon would go out and buy a new curio, place it on an overcrowded shelf, and never look at it again. Of course, Kitty would have to dust it every day.

Otherwise, Mrs. Gordon filled her days and evenings with needlework. She embroidered dozens of cloths with identical cross-stitch patterns, and filled the rooms with so many badly crocheted doilies that it seemed as if a patchy snow had fallen inside her home. Kitty was expected to wash and iron the doilies regularly and return them to their precisely appointed places.

Kitty also cooked, under Mrs. Gordon's hawkish eye. She had done the shopping only once. On that occasion Mrs. Gordon had cursed her roundly, claiming that Kitty had either stolen the change or been cheated by a shopkeeper.

So Mrs. Gordon did all the shopping, withholding from Kitty even that bit of fresh air and human intercourse. At the kosher butcher she complained loudly that her new Gentile maid could not be trusted to shop for a Jewish woman; she'd likely buy non-kosher meat and pocket the difference in price.

When Mrs. Gordon bought potatoes, she would get large, fresh "American bakers" for herself. For Kitty she bought cheap, cellar-stored little spuds bristling with eyes. After Kitty cut away the green-tinged peels there was hardly any food left. Going hungry from the first such meal, Kitty took to saving the peelings of Mrs. Gordon's potatoes. They were very tasty when baked and salted, but Kitty could never eat them without crying tears of humiliation. Even the Halters had never been brought so low as to eat vegetable peelings.

But the worst time of all was the Sabbath. Kitty had hoped that in a Jewish home she would find peace on the holy day, if only vicariously. But Mrs. Gordon would allow Kitty not even the shadow of the Sabbath.

On Friday nights the mistress of the house lit the Sabbath candles in a curtain-shrouded dining room, but she was furious at the suggestion that Kitty light two more, or even mouth the blessings over the lit candles. On that evening, Mrs. Gordon would not let Kitty enter the dining room except to serve dinner.

"I won't have you risk my life, Julia!"

It was almost three weeks before Kitty got to see Sender. They fell into each other's arms and cried tears of relief.

Kitty finally gathered herself. "Have you heard any news from Janace?"

"You don't know?"

"I hardly know what the weather is outside the window, living with that witch."

"The Slovaks made a deal with the Germans. They've paid them to get rid of the Jews."

"The Germans are paying the Slovaks to do their evil?"

"No, no. The *Slovaks* are paying the *Germans*."

"Oh, my God! But didn't the Slovaks take the Jews for labor? Didn't they steal all the wealth? What more could they want from us?"

"They want us dead."

Kitty nodded. "Yes, the Slovaks and the Germans. And the Hungarians, too, I think. The whole world wants us dead. Oh, Sender. What are we going to do?"

"We have no choice but to do as we always have. Trust in God. Obey his word."

"How can you say that? Look at the Polish Jews. They were the most devout of all, yet God let them be struck down as if they were so many baptized German Jews, or godless communists."

Sender cleared his throat. "That brings me to more bad news. The Ukraine has fallen to the Germans."

"Helen!" Kitty gasped.

For several minutes they sat in silence. Terror blurred the air between them.

"My darling," Sender said at last, "let's eat."

"Yes," said Kitty, sighing. She looked over the fine meal that Sender had prepared in her honor. "Who knows what tomorrow will bring."

Thinking of her sisters, scattered over the carnivorous planet, Kitty dropped a figurine. It was a little dog, and its ear broke off.

Mrs. Gordon went into a frenzy. She would deduct the cost of the china dog from Kitty's salary. But even so she went on and on, raging for an hour.

"Enough," cried Kitty at last. "I'm paying for the dog, aren't I? Do you want interest, too? It's forbidden by the Torah."

"You insolent wretch! I'll throw you out on the street." Her eyes narrowed and she smiled. "You can go back to Slovakia. See how your people are keeping the Torah there these days."

So! Mrs. Gordon had had information, about her and about her homeland all along. She'd probably picked up news at the kosher butcher. But she had never shared a word of it with Kitty.

It is a cardinal commandment of the Torah: "You shall not despise your brother in your heart." Kitty had struggled to keep this precept. But now she let herself succumb to hatred. She churned it as she worked, she dreamed of it at night, she rolled her tongue around it as if it were a candy.

The shrine to her hatred was the single photograph in the Gordon apartment. Framed in heavy silver that required daily polishing, the wedding picture of Mr. and Mrs. Gordon was like something taken at the turn of the century rather than the late thirties. It was a studio shot against a fake-bucolic backdrop. The bridegroom was seated, the bride stood respectfully at his side.

Mr. Gordon was then a man in his seventies. He had a pleased and pleasing face, framed by the full beard and square cap of the traditional Jew. His arthritic hands were folded over a cane.

The bride was dressed in a very beautiful lace gown and matching veil. Hothouse flowers crowned her head and also formed a huge bouquet that she wielded like a shield. Diamond earrings, a diamond necklace, two diamond bracelets and a pearl-and-diamond brooch completed the ensemble.

"They are in a safe in the bank," Mrs. Gordon informed Kitty the first time she cleaned the picture, "just in case you get any ideas."

In the photograph, Mrs. Gordon's teenage face radiated sheer fury.

Mrs. Gordon's face was always hostile; even in repose it was pinched. But never, not even during her angriest tantrums, did she look as livid as she did in the photograph. She had learned to mask her true, ugliest feelings since the marriage.

How long did it take Mrs. Gordon to drive her elderly husband to the grave? He must have had a first wife. Were there children? If so, they never visited or wrote their stepmother. What about her family, parents, siblings, in-laws? Either Mrs. Gordon was the loneliest person on earth, or the most loathed. Either way, Kitty had her revenge.

Whenever Kitty cleaned around the photograph, she cheered in her heart. For Mrs. Gordon, devoted to making her servant miserable, would never succeed in making anyone half as miserable as she was herself.

The next time Kitty visited with Sender there was good news—and bad. The watchman at Fried's apartment had reported a cryptic postcard from Lisbon. Reb Mordecai and his family were safely reunited and on their way to America! The bad news was that, now that Reb Mordecai was out of the country, it was unclear who the apartment belonged to. Sender's boss was of the opinion that it was owned by Reb Mordecai's business, and hence would fall to the partner's heir—Mrs. Gordon.

"Oh, no!" Kitty cried. "She'll turn the refugees in."

"Come now, Kitty. You're exaggerating. She may be a cruel mistress but she is still a believing Jew. Surely, she would not permit those innocent people to be killed."

"She might. For heaven's sake, Sender, you've got to get those people out of that house. Mrs. Gordon has sold her soul. There's no telling what she's capable of."

"All right, I'll tell them. But it's going to be hell trying to find shelter for all those refugees."

"Not like the hell that awaits them if that demon informs to the Arrow Cross."

"I don't understand. How could a Jewish woman come to this?"

Kitty told him about the photograph.

"So," said Sender, "she sold herself to the old man and lived to regret it."

"Maybe her family forced her," said Kitty, defending Mrs. Gordon in the name of fairness. "Maybe they were in desperate circumstances."

"But then why don't they visit her?"

Kitty had no answer to that. "You know, Joseph once taught me that when a man marries his daughter to an older man, it's as if he sold her to a brothel."

"So it's no wonder that she is bitter and vindictive."

"If, in fact, that's the case. But we'll never know. Nowadays everything's a mystery."

The confusion escalated when new anti-Semitic laws were enacted in Hungary. Non-Jews were not to be employed in any Jewish home.

The Weiss' Elizabeth went to the police station to beg for an exemption.

"It's for your own good," she was told. "You don't want your boss' hairy hands all over your boobs, do you? We've got to protect our pure Magyar stock from defilement."

Elizabeth thought, if Mr. Weiss ever touched her breasts she would faint with pleasure. Pure Magyar stock! Hah! She came from a village and she knew what she knew. Father did it with daughter, brother did it with sister, and no one was ever sure where they came from. These city folks, for all their shouting and newspapers, were a bunch of idiots.

Kitty prepared herself for dismissal, but Mrs. Gordon was not about to let go such cheap and efficient help. "You're not to hang laundry in the courtyard anymore. After a while, people will forget you are here."

"Where then should I hang the clothes to dry?" Kitty no longer said ma'am. If Mrs. Gordon kept her on despite a serious risk, she wasn't about to be fired.

"Put them up in your room with your things."

Mrs. Gordon wasn't about to fire her, but neither was she going to ease up.

"Go beat the carpets Julia!"

Kitty opened the French windows onto the balcony. "I'd better use the vacuum cleaner. Mrs. Kaplan, the doctor's wife, is hanging laundry."

"It's not wash day," Mrs. Gordon said petulantly.

"They had to let go their maid and their laundress. With all the bandages and sheets from her husband's office, she needs to wash several times a week."

"Well, that's not my problem. Go beat the carpets, like I told you."

Kitty hauled the rugs out onto the balcony railing. She was going to barely tap them with the beater, so the dirt wouldn't get on Mrs. Kaplan's wash.

Kitty wasn't the only one who noticed Mrs. Kaplan. One of the Gentile families' maids, one who swore that Dr. Kaplan had saved the life of her little boy, ran downstairs.

"You go on in, Mrs. Doctor. I'll hang up the rest of this."

No wonder she pitied Mrs. Kaplan, thought Kitty. Even from the balcony she could see that the gentlewoman's hands were rubbed bright red.

"But it's forbidden by law, dear."

"The devil take the law. Law!" she spat. "Look up there, that bitch Gordon gets to keep a Christian maid just to wipe her wicked ass, while a lady like you has to rub the blood and puss off those sheets with your pretty hands. That's the law for you."

Kitty retreated from the balcony immediately but it was too late. News of her presence spread like a dry flame through the apartment house. Within the hour, the fascist guards came calling.

"*Madame* Gordon?" The Arrow Cross man said sarcastically.

"Yes, I'm Mrs. Gordon. Good morning, officer. What can I do for you?"

Kitty was awestruck. Mrs. Gordon was as cool and slick as a pond in February. She, on the other hand, could barely stand. The insides of her body had turned to liquid.

The guardsmen were not pleased. "We have a report on good

authority that, contrary to the law, you are keeping a racial superior as a servant in this household."

"Oh, no, Excellency. Not at all. My maid is a Jewish girl."

Everyone stared at Kitty. Kitty stared, open-mouthed, at Mrs. Gordon.

"But Julia's a Christian girl," said one of the servants in the hallway.

"That's what I thought, too," said Mrs. Gordon, "when I hired her. But take a look in her room. Under her pillow, stuffed in her mattress, there are Jewish books. I ask you, Captain, what sort of Christian girl reads Hebrew?"

That snake! She had been foolish to take the risk. It was just that she had read the astrology books over and over until she knew them by heart, and she was going crazy with no stimulation at all. So she had sneaked a few books out of Mr. Gordon's bookcases, where Mrs. Gordon never even looked.

There was a rush into the maid's room. The books were found, and the room ransacked. The guards found nothing to excite them, but the maids came out pleased with their booty of damp underwear and tiny, high-heeled shoes.

"Look what I found," exulted one servant girl, holding up Sari's pocketbook and the crocodile document case. Kitty closed her eyes in pain. Still, the loss was not as great as it might have been. Since the law was passed she had been keeping her money and her papers in her bra, wearing it day and night.

Having exhausted the loot, the crowd moved toward the front door. But the head guard wasn't through with Mrs. Gordon. "Why would a Jewish girl work as a maid? And why would she pretend to be a Christian, when the employer is herself a Jewess?"

"I've wondered about that myself, Excellency."

"I'll tell you why, she's a foreigner. You're harboring an alien, Jew-woman."

"Oh, no, Excellency. I would never do that. Of course she's Hungarian. She speaks the language perfectly, and it's not one that's easily picked up by foreigners."

"The Slovak Jews defile the Mother Tongue. They speak Hungarian."

"Oh," said Mrs. Gordon, as if this was a revelation. "That certainly explains things to me. But you must understand, sir, that I acted correctly throughout."

The head guard grunted unhappily. He would have liked to take the rich Jewess in, would have liked to have looted the whole apartment. But there were too many witnesses, too many people in the hallway.

Who knew which ones were her friends, other rich people with powerful connections. He let it go.

They handcuffed Kitty and drove her out the door with blows and kicks.

"Time to go home, Sarah Goldstein."

"Haven't you always wanted to see the world? Now you'll see Poland."

"And the Ukraine."

"And some other vacation spots, courtesy of Uncle Adolf."

"Mrs. Gordon!" Kitty screamed.

But the door had slammed shut.

CHAPTER TWENTY-FIVE

The Ukraine

Erich Muller was stationed on the top balcony of the luxury apartment building overlooking the synagogue. The area had been decorated with potted plants by the former residents. Some of the plants had died of neglect, but most of them flourished even without human care, craning their necks toward the spring sun and gentle rains. Living things, given half a chance, continue to live.

The penthouse was completely empty. There were gouged-out places in the floors and walls where there must have been fancy tiles. Only the balcony recalled the grace of what must have been one of the handsomest flats in the city.

All the residents of the building had been communist party bigwigs. In the other apartments wives and children still huddled, but the family in the penthouse had been Jewish. The orders called for eliminating all top communists, but not their families. There was no need to antagonize civilians unnecessarily. It was a policy that paid off. Most Ukrainians backed the Germans. Women smiled at Erich in the streets.

It was different with Jews, of course. There they had to take the man of the house and the rest too. It didn't matter if they were communists or not. For the same money, thought Erich, they might as well be communists.

It was pleasant up on the balcony. His whole military service had been suspiciously easy, so far. He was a member of the Einzatzgruppen, the special division responsible for eliminating the "Jewish enemy." He'd wondered how he had landed such a lucky spot. The other guys in the unit were all rich kids, or sons of Nazi Party officials.

He'd found out the answer when he received a letter from his older brother, Walter. Walter said that there was another fellow fighting with him called Erich Muller. This Erich was the son of the famous Field Marshall Muller from the Great War. Apparently they'd gotten the two Erich Mullers mixed up. So the farm boy got to sunbathe on a patio and the general's son went to fight in Russia's frozen hell.

It was hell, he knew, no matter what crap the officers told them. He could read between the lines of Walter's letters. His parents knew, too. Already they wrote things like, "Keep in mind that when you come back you will be the leader to your little brothers." He was only second oldest, not supposed to be the leader. No one said anything about Walter coming back.

The synagogue was a beautiful building. It looked exotically oriental, with a dome and pillars and lattice decorations. Erich admired the way the top, where no one would ordinarily look, was smoothly finished. The Reds had built the apartment house to be grand and modern, but under the surface it was so badly constructed as to be dangerous. It looked especially shabby compared to the building next door.

The synagogue had been built a long time ago, before Stalin. When the communists took over and closed all religious establishments, it had been turned into a commercial laundry. Now the big industrial washing machines had been moved out and the Jews moved back in. "We'll clean up those dirty Yids," Erich's commander quipped.

The beauty of the building was now marred by wood boards that had been nailed across the doors and windows after the Jews had been crammed in. Erich thought it looked like Marlene Dietrich gagged and blindfolded in some movie.

Now Klaus, Peter, and the guy from Hesse who had been a professor, were unloading jerrycans of gasoline and pouring them all around on the synagogue walls.

A soapy taste rose in Erich's mouth. Look at how they threw the gasoline around as if it were water. He couldn't help thinking of the tractor back home, and how it stood idle for lack of fuel.

He and Walter had left school early, although they were both good students. If they worked hard, Papa promised, they would be able to buy a tractor. The younger boys could finish school, while the machine brought easy prosperity. Well now they had their tractor, but the younger boys were leaving school even earlier than he had. With the tractor stilled and him and Walter in the army, someone had to do the work.

His father took these events without complaining. He had the forbearance and pessimism of all farmers. Erich wondered why he hadn't inherited any of that. Of course Papa was a religious man, which kept him quiet and uncomplaining.

Mother had been religious too, but not anymore. Instead of church, she now went to meetings of the German Women's League. She and the other farm wives sat around sewing and composing crush notes to Hitler, and gossiping viciously about any neighbor who wore makeup. The League gave Mother a brooch with seven golden swastikas on it. This was for her seven sons, each of whom was either serving the Fuhrer or would do so in the future.

Erich also had a sister, but there was no golden swastika for her. There was something mentally wrong with his sister, and she had been in an institution for so long that Erich could hardly remember her. He and Walter were forbidden to mention her name to the younger children, so they were unaware of their sister's existence.

Nevertheless when, several years ago the government began a program of "liquidating" cripples and mental defectives, his parents took to arms. Mother wrote stiff letters to Party headquarters on League stationery. Papa got the local pastor to bring the matter to the bishop, who gave a scathing and well-publicized sermon about it.

Because of people like his parents the policy was eventually lifted, despite the insistence by the Party chiefs (even Hitler himself!) and the medical establishment, that the designated victims had "lives not worth living."

Erich leaned carefully against the railing. It seemed solid enough, but it was best to be careful with cheap Russky ironwork.

In this action, he was assigned sniper duty. If anyone escaped the synagogue—a highly unlikely event—Erich was supposed to shoot him. It was an easy job. They were all easy jobs; Jews had no guns. And a safe job, too. The only Einsatzgruppen casualty he'd ever heard of was of one fellow who'd gotten drunk in a Polish whorehouse and shot himself in the balls. His buddies had laughed so hard, he almost bled to death before they got around to calling for a medic.

Before his assignment Erich had never laid eyes on a Jew, nor ever met anyone who had. But the notion that they were not really human beings was too much to swallow. In the same position, Erich told the others, Germans would behave exactly the way they did.

"No we wouldn't!" they shouted.

Twice, there were requests that Erich's racial background be checked, but search as they would, he always came up as the purest of Aryans.

The commander liked to say that he did his best to make the work efficient, that there was no element of sadism in the way they executed their orders. Erich knew this wasn't true. For example, they always had to kill the children first, before the mother. This made the mothers go crazy. Had they killed the mothers first, the kids wouldn't know what hit them, and it wouldn't make the business any less efficient.

The commander had come up with the original idea of a circular walkway to the slaughtering centers, so the Jews didn't know what lay up ahead. They heard explosions and shooting and screaming, but they couldn't imagine what it came from. Their minds could not conceive of where the path ended. But the commander was no humanitarian. If Jews could see the killing grounds straight ahead there would be stampedes. Although the Yids would be finished off just the same, panic and confusion could not be tolerated by a German military unit.

It was all out of control anyway, the commander complained. The job was just too big. Word from Berlin was that there were new methods being tested, scientific, orderly systems for disposing of the Jews neatly.

Meanwhile they had operations like this one today. Tidy, if primitive. Lock them in their prayer-house and burn it down. Get rid of Jews, books, synagogue and all. And with minimum contact, so that no soldier would be distracted by a gorgeous girl or see some old lady who reminded him of his grandmother.

Klaus and the professor lit torches and circled the building slowly, lighting the gasoline at intervals. The flames spread slowly, then picked up speed.

Inside the synagogue Helen, Thomas, and their two children huddled together. There wasn't much shouting, just quiet whimpering. The town's Jewish life had been dormant for decades. The people didn't know each other. For most, it was the first time they had entered the building.

"Comrades, lend me your ears."

A man had climbed up on the lectern and waved his arms for attention. It was the former tenant of the penthouse next door.

"Do not fear, comrades, and be of good cheer. This offense against the workers will never be forgotten. All over the world, wherever laborers break the chains of their oppressors, our sacrifice will be remembered. Take heart! Germany is the last gasp of the capitalist system."

"Shut up, you idiot."

The heckler was a man who a week before, would not have dared raise his voice to a Party boss. But now many others joined him, booing and throwing boxes of washing powder until the former leader was forced off his pedestal.

"It's all shit," whispered Helen to her husband. "It was always all shit, wasn't it?"

Thomas looked at her blue eyes, huge with disillusion. He amazed himself once again by how beautiful she was, and this time he did not reprove himself mentally for the incorrect thought.

Two men went up to the Ark of the Law. This had been the place where the biggest washing machines had been placed, and it was scratched and dusty. The doors of the ark opened with a creak.

One of the men paused, remembering something. He took a handkerchief from his pocket and twisted its four ends, making a cap that he placed on his head. Then he and his friend each lifted a Torah scroll from the ark.

Thomas glanced guiltily at his son, who was bareheaded. The boy didn't even know that you were supposed to cover your head in a house of God. He had not kept his promise to Sari and Joseph. His son had never had the bar-mitzvah. It was enough, he and Helen thought, for the children to be good human beings. They hadn't taught either child how to be a decent Jew. Now the children were going like dumb animals to the altar of the Temple in Jerusalem.

The people in the synagogue were quiet, watching the procession of the scrolls.

"All, all shit," said Helen. Though she spoke quietly, everyone heard. The bitterness of her words mingled with the acrid smell of burning gasoline.

Someone, at some time had secretly taught the man with the handkerchief-cap the Sabbath service, because he raised a rich baritone in the traditional melody.

"And it was when the Ark passed that Moses declared: 'Rise, O Lord, and disperse your enemies, let those who hate you flee from your face.'"

Suddenly there was a deafening sound, then a series of thunderbolts, then a horrendous cracking.

No one in the synagogue could have understood what happened, but from his vantage point Erich Muller could see. The pillars of the synagogue had exploded.

The columns were made of porous stone that had thirstily absorbed the spring rains. The flames set by the soldiers had heated the water in the stone to a steam of such tremendous pressure that the stone itself exploded.

The pillars were not just decorative but actually supported the central dome of the building. Erich watched, plaster dust rising into his open mouth, as the dome split cleanly in half, then crumbled.

It was as if the manhole cover of the pit of hell had been removed so that he could look into it. People on fire, people crushed by stone. People pierced through by chunks of metal, choking on crumbled masonry, decapitated by flying glass. And over it all a new roof, a dome of sound. Screams and horror and confusion.

Erich used the scope of his rifle for a better look. He saw a man rise from a pile of bodies. The man examined the other bodies—a woman, a boy, a girl—then dropped them and ran, clambering over the ruins.

Through the crosshairs he could see the man was not young, but muscular. He ran over the rubble and chaos, over the collapsed walls, and away.

Erich had no intention of shooting him, though that was specifically his assignment. He followed the man with great excitement, as if he were a horse that Erich had bet a lot of money on.

"Go, Jew, go!"

The man leaped like a gazelle over every obstacle, and with him Erich's heart leaped too. Funny, he hadn't felt for any of the pretty girls or the tow-headed boys who reminded him of his little brothers. He hadn't felt for them the way he felt for this middle-aged, un-lovely man.

Peter, two buildings away, caught sight of the running man. He raised his rifle, but before his finger touched the trigger, Erich shot Peter dead. Peter had been a decent fellow, thought Erich, sharing the contents of his generous packages from home. But shooting him felt no different from shooting Jews.

Let the Jew run, Erich thought, annoyed with his dead comrade. What did it matter, one Jew escaping, one out of so many?

He turned the scope back to the demolished synagogue. The horror seemed to be going on for hours, though Erich knew it was only seconds. Then he had a thought of such clarity, that he wondered that it never occurred to him before.

A few seconds, just a few more seconds, and it would all be over for the Jews. But as for him, this was his destiny. This was going to be his reality for all eternity. For them, death was the end of it. For him it would be the beginning.

A man with a silly handkerchief-hat got up. His jacket was on fire, but he didn't seem to notice. He looked around and found what he had dropped, the scroll.

Erich had seen lots of those scrolls. The Jews always took the scrolls with them, as if they were children. He had even looked at the scrolls close up, at the little Jewish letters with their tiny peaks, like candle-flames.

The man was entirely on fire now, and the scroll cover beginning to smolder. Some others of the doomed congregation saw him and reached for him, for the scroll, as if it offered help.

Erich looked harder, screwing the scope into his eye socket. He could swear that the letters of the scroll were rising up, ahead of the flames, escaping upwards. And something else was going up with them. Something...the souls. The souls of the burning man and the people who clung to him, and the people who grabbed at the scroll, and the people who reached out, and those too weak and wounded even to reach out.

Erich could clearly see their souls flying up and away, cool and light and free. Suddenly he was overcome by a yearning, a passion that he had never felt before.

He dropped the rifle to the terrace floor. He climbed up on the balcony railing, balancing delicately, and for once the lousy Russian railing held.

Klaus and the university professor looked up and beheld the strangest of all the strange sights they had seen in the war. Erich Muller, balanced on the railing, gave a shout of triumph. Then he positioned himself in the classic diver's pose and, graceful as an athlete in a Leni Riefenstahl film, dove into the center of the synagogue.

Reichsminister Goebbels squinted in the unaccustomed sunlight of the farm. Smiling into the newsreel cameras he pinned a gold-toned eagle grasping a swastika onto the ample bosom of Frau Muller. He gave a little speech about how young Erich had fallen to the Jews. The Jews, whose pernicious cunning was such that every last one of them had to be removed from the face of Germany.

His first choice, of course, had been the noble boy, Peter von whatever. It was good to show that the aristocracy was serving—and dying—right along with the rubes. But when the camera crew showed up at the boy's ancestral castle they were dismissed by the butler! The dowager countess was in deep mourning and not receiving.

Those people had their nerve, Goebbels thought bitterly. Aristocrats. They thought they were better than him, him, the Propaganda Minister! He'd show them.

He smiled benignly at the camera, and let it impart its blessings on the ox-like farm family. This story—shorn of the unpleasant details—made good news. It was safe to point out an Einsatzgruppen casualty. No one would be reminded of another. On the other hand, you didn't want to mention any of the Army fallen—too many comrades in the same boat.

Frau Muller made a little speech that she had prepared herself. About how she had six sons more, and proudly offered them to the Fuhrer to do with as he wished. In her heart she thought: now they won't take the others. And actually, Erich had been the least favorite of her children. Always thinking, always questioning, almost disobedient. A stranger to her.

After the speech Goebbels smiled at her, but his smile twisted involuntarily. The old cow was grotesque, with overhanging blond brows and bleached eyelashes, her dirndl billowing over massive thighs. It was the ideal image he had created for the German masses, but he found it repulsive himself. His own taste ran to quick-mouthed women with elegant bones and wicked smiles.

He let his mouth do whatever it wanted as he parted curtly from the stupid sow.

He'd simply have them cut the last part from the film before it was sent to the theaters of the Reich.

CHAPTER TWENTY-SIX

Outskirts of Budapest

Kitty lucked out. The beating she received from the guards left her with a bloody nose and a stomachache so bad that she couldn't stand up straight for a week, but there were no broken bones or teeth. Most important of all, she hadn't been raped. Her priceless identity papers, and some money, remained safe in her bra.

This particular patrol of the Arrow Cross favored boys. She watched as young yeshiva students were sodomized, crying like girls with pain and humiliation.

She was sent with others—thousands of others—to a holding compound for foreign Jews. They were herded into an open field, without reason, without food, without information. Children were lost, lovers were separated, possessions, valuable or sentimental, vanished. And somewhere, Kitty lost her shoes.

They were house slippers, really, without backs, and they might have fallen off at any point. She tried looking for them on her hands and knees. At ground level all she saw was a myriad of legs milling like night insects.

Legs ran into other legs, changed directions, ran back again in the same futile direction, tried another direction, equally futile. It was *confusion*.

A passage from the Book of Esther popped into Kitty's head and wouldn't let go. The book was read twice on the happy holiday of Purim, and the frivolity of the day imprinted many passages in her mind.

"And the letters were sent by post to all the king's provinces, to destroy, to kill, and to cause to perish: all Jews, both young and old, little children and women, in one day...The posts went out, speeded by the

171

king's command, and the law was decreed in Shushan the capital. And the Jews of Shushan were *confused.*"

But that passage was from the middle of the tale, with the threats underscored to heighten dramatic tension. In the end it turned out to be a jolly story. The villains were caught in their own wicked trap and punished. As for the Jews, they lived on in triumph, joy, honor, and prosperity.

Was that going to happen here? Was there, even now, a master plan at work to save them in the nick of time? Maybe Eva Braun was secretly a brilliant Jew, instead of the Aryan pumpkin-brain she appeared. Maybe the Americans and the British were already planning the Jews' salvation. Maybe the Messiah was around the corner. Meanwhile, there was *confusion.*

"Please, folks, does anyone have an extra pair of shoes? I have money, I'll pay well. Any kind of shoes."

She tried saying this in several languages, but everyone just stared at her, stupefied, annoyed.

"Money," a woman said. "I need money." But she had no shoes to sell. Most people had been robbed of their valuables. Those who had managed to bring a satchel had packed critical things, not extra shoes.

At leg level, Kitty saw that there were now people lying dead. Dead people with shoes. She shook her head. Was she mad? Was she about to despoil corpses?

But it wasn't her fault. She had offered to pay. She would gladly have paid the living, or the survivors. And dead people didn't need shoes.

Stop that! She almost slapped herself with self-disgust. Looting the dead? What was she becoming?

But she *really* needed shoes. It was one of life's necessities. Necessary for the living; irrelevant to the dead.

Kitty stooped over a dead woman. She was old, like most of the dead. Kitty tried to unlace the ugly, old-lady brogues, but the corpse's feet had swollen, and the shoes wouldn't come off. Kitty got up from the ground and moved on.

Then she spotted the girl. Young, in her late teens. It was hard to tell exactly, as the girl had pitched forward and her thick, curly hair hid the sides of her face.

Who was she, Kitty wondered, and how could her mother let her out of the house in an outfit like that? Her suit was so tight, and of such cheap, skimpy material, that the hooks of her brassiere and her garters showed through. Her white cotton gloves were soiled and a hat with more veiling than cap had fallen away from her head.

Most glaring of all were her shoes. They were red patent leather with high, thin heels. Two black bows winked seductively at the ankles.

Kitty looked around. No one else approached the body. Could the girl have died of a contagious disease? It didn't matter, she was desperate for the shoes.

The red pumps came easily off the dead girl's feet. Kitty put them on. They almost fit. A half-size too big perhaps, but that was better than too small. Kitty's stockings had long since shredded. She thought about taking the girl's stockings too, but it seemed too great an assault on the dead girl's modesty.

As soon as Kitty was steady on her feet the crowd began to heave and move. No one seemed to know where they were going, or why, but they were grateful for direction. The mob picked up speed. More bodies fell to the ground.

A cry went up. "The menfolk! The men!"

Kitty had seen right away that there were mostly women, children, and old men in the compound. They wouldn't include the strong and capable young men among the disposable Jews. Everybody knew men were valuable, men were useful, men *produced*. Rumors flew that the prisoners in the compound would be sent to Slovakia, to Ukraine, to Poland, but surely the men were to remain here to enrich the Hungarians.

She thought: Sender is safe. He is tucked into our little bed in our little apartment above the sleepy little bar. He is safe, my heart is safe.

And even if he had been caught, rounded up in this action, which seemed to have found every foreign Jew in hiding, he'd still be safe, because he was a man. A wonderfully skilled, and clever, and handy man. A man!

A convoy of trucks appeared. "The men are in there!" someone shouted. "They're being transported to labor camps." Kitty's heart sank. The men were being taken away. For work, or for the fate of the Rosen men?

Almighty, please don't let Sender be in there!

The vehicles rolled by, boarded up, anonymous, and sealed tight. There was no way to tell who was on them, or even if the passengers were dead or alive. A keening went up from the crowd of women and children and old men.

The last truck moved. The crowd began to disperse. Kitty refused to leave her spot. She kept staring at the back of the truck as if her gaze would cut through the doors like an ironworker's torch, and the prisoners would tumble out.

A tiny crack appeared in the back door of the last truck, growing slightly wider while Kitty watched. She walked closer toward the truck, her heart suspecting. Something snaked from the crack, forcing its way out to freedom. It was thin, it was long, it trailed behind like the standard on a knight's lance.

It was a brilliantly patterned—some would say flamboyant—silk tie.

"Sender!" She began to run.

The tie unfurled.

"Sender, Sender, I will come for you." She got closer to the truck, despite growing breathless. But the convoy began to pick up speed.

The tie was now pushed out to its full extent. It caught in a splintered bit of fencing and was pulled entirely from the truck.

Kitty couldn't run any faster, and the truck was getting away from her.

"Sender, don't lose hope! I swear by the One God, I will come. I will find you."

The voice was low and hoarse, the background a steady din, but one's own name is unnaturally audible.

"Kitty, Kitty Halter."

"Who is it? Who are you?"

"Don't you recognize me, dear? Aranka Wassermann. Rachel-Leah's mother. Joseph's sister-in-law."

While Kitty struggled to reconcile this identity with the woman before her, Mrs. Wassermann collapsed, felled by a paroxysm of coughing. She wiped her mouth. The handkerchief came away a gummy wad of bright red.

"Mrs. Wassermann?" It was impossible. How could this shrunken ghost be the woman she knew, the hearty, jolly mother of thirteen who had wielded her wooden cooking spoon over three generations, like a conductor's baton over a symphony orchestra?

Mrs. Wassermann indicated that Kitty sit down on the ground next to her.

"Kitty. When I saw you, I knew God had answered me. Blessed is he, and blessed is his name."

"But Mrs. Wassermann..."

"My Judith is there. Do you see her? There, with the carpetbag. You will save her."

Mrs. Wassermann's eyes went blank, like electric lamps snapped off. Kitty had never seen anyone die before but she was certain that that was what Mrs. Wassermann had done.

Kitty stood up, looking for the daughter. Young Judith was trading something for a salami.

With the woman's shawl Kitty covered as much of Mrs. Wassermann as was possible. She let the crowd close in over the body, like the soil around a grave. Kitty approached Judith from a different direction.

"Kitty Halter, oh wow!"

Like many young girls in Janace, Judith Wassermann had idolized Kitty for her style—and her handsome husband.

"Hello Judith. Your mother had to leave. She says you're to come with me and do exactly as I say. Do you understand?"

"Sure thing, Kitty. Wow! What fabulous shoes."

Kitty had no idea where she was going, but she headed for the edge of the field. Away from the center. The further away the better.

As they walked through the crowd Kitty inspected Judith. She was as homely as her sisters and, as the youngest, slightly spoiled. But she was also a very shrewd child.

"You mustn't call me Kitty anymore. I have a new identity, Julia Ficsorcsak, a Christian woman."

"Excellent. And I can be your kid sister, uh, Christina."

"Lots of Christian girls are called Judith," said Kitty reprovingly.

"Better safe than sorry," said Judith.

"It's enough that they want our bodies," said Kitty. "We shouldn't give our souls."

Judith snorted. "They don't want our souls. They don't even want their own."

"Don't be flip. You're only a child, you can't imagine the danger we're in."

Judith thrust out her pointy little chin. "I'm going to be fine. After the war I'm going to Eretz Yisrael and marrying a Hasid. A Hasid who is also a pioneer. And handsome, like your Sender, or even more handsome. And I'm going to run a dress shop. A fancy store, like Alma's, on the grandest street in Tel Aviv."

Kitty stared at the girl. All around them thousands upon thousands of Jews were crying, moaning, screaming, cursing God for their fate.

Judith put her hands on her hips. "See if I don't!"

Kitty blinked. "Do you have any identification papers?"

"I threw them away."

"How could you do such a thing? How can anyone walk around without papers?"

"They were terrible fakes. They said 'Jew' as much as my real papers. Even nothing is better."

This was true. "Here, you might as well have this." Kitty took off the crucifix necklace that Mrs. Gordon had made her wear. She felt a sense of relief, as if the pendant had been made of lead.

Judith put it on without a qualm. She inspected it carefully, then positioned it neatly over the collar of her blouse.

Kitty looked her over and sighed. With frizzy hair and a big nose, Judith was a Nazi caricaturist's idea of a Jew. But Kitty had promised to save her.

"Do you know how to make the sign of the cross?"

"Not exactly. Do you?"

Kitty showed her. She also told her as much as she remembered of what Sari had related about Catholic practice and theology from her school days. Judith had a thousand questions and comments. The one topic she avoided was her mother.

A ring of fascist guards surrounded the field. In some places the Jews approached the guards, trying to bribe, cajole, or wheedle information from them. Kitty noticed one guard who had quite an empty margin around his station. Whenever a Jew approached he lifted his truncheon, smiling in anticipation.

"Hey handsome," called Kitty. She walked fearlessly, exaggerating the swing of her hips caused by the high heels. The guard blinked in surprise, his club at the ready.

"To coin a phrase," drawled Kitty, "what the hell is a nice girl like me doing in a place like this? I've never seen a jail like this. The whole shithole is full of Jews!"

"Yeah, all foreign Jew-pigs, just like you, bitch."

"Me? You've got to be kidding. I've got nothing to do with Jews. And if I do, I charge them double."

The big guard knitted his brows. "This place is supposed to be just for Jews."

"Well, I sure don't belong here, then." Kitty removed her identity papers from her bra, showing the top of her breast.

The guard looked over the papers. Evidently his superior Aryan brain had a bit of trouble with reading. "Well, shit. You shouldn't be here."

"No, not my kid sister, either."

Judith made the sign of the cross.

The guard thought hard. "Why *are* you here?"

"Beats me. I was just picked up on a morals charge."

"Oh. Well, stand over by the guard house." He turned toward the milling compound and shouted. "Anybody else? Anybody who isn't a

Jew? All regular criminals, stand over there with those two girls."

Kitty closed her eyes. Please, please Jews. Come over here. Take a chance. Any risk is better than going where the Jews are going.

But no one came forward.

A car was called, and it took Kitty and Judith to a police station.

In a courtroom within the station house justice was being meted out. Kitty and Judith sat among the women, all of whom were prostitutes, waiting for their turn before the magistrate.

Finally Kitty was called to the bench. Her sexy high heels clicked on the stone floor. Judith was right behind her.

"Name?"

"Julia Ficsorscak." She reached into her bra to retrieve the papers. The magistrate looked at her exposed chest with distaste.

"Address?"

She gave the address of the apartment, in the heart of the red-light district. The magistrate's scowl deepened.

"Charge?"

"I lost my card, your honor." Prostitution was legal in Hungary, but every working girl needed a medical card that was regularly stamped after an examination for venereal disease. When a whore "lost" her card, it was likely she hadn't passed her last exam and was barred from working.

"And who is that behind you?"

"My sister, sir."

Judith stepped out and curtsied adorably. "Christina Ficsorcsak, your honor."

"And where are your papers, little miss?"

Kitty froze. They'd never be able to explain away a young girl's lost papers.

Judith began to cry. "Julia sold them, your honor. To some Jews."

The magistrate glared at Kitty. His gaze softened when it returned to Judith. "And how old are you, Christina?"

"Eleven, sir."

Kitty stared. The kid was at least fourteen.

"And where do you attend school, my dear?"

Judith's tears flowed rapidly. "I don't go to school anymore, your honor. Julia says I have to start working soon."

"What's us poor girls to do?" said Kitty. "I started working when I was no older."

"Disgusting," said the magistrate. He turned to Judith once more. "And do you want to do what your sister does, Christina?"

"No, sir. All I ever wanted," she sniffled, "was to serve Jesus Christ. I've prayed that he would let me become a nun."

Kitty almost choked.

The magistrate called the bailiff. "Get Mother Immaculata on the telephone."

"But your honor, she said specifically that you were not to send her any more girls. She says they're not a charity order and they can't just take any poor urchin in."

"Oh, they'll take this one. She's a precious Christian soul who must not be lost to the church.

"Go along with the bailiff now, Christina."

Judith crossed herself. "Thank you, your honor, thank you."

"As for you," the magistrate looked at Kitty with slit eyes, "one hundred and twenty days."

CHAPTER TWENTY-SEVEN

Kitty was glad to be in jail. Here there was no fear of round-ups and actions and deportations. There was no fear of hunger or cold, either. The prison provisions were spartan but the prostitutes' boyfriends and pimps brought them all sorts of luxuries.

The prison uniform was better than Kitty's bedraggled maid's outfit, and she happily changed into it. But the rule of uniforms was not at all enforced and Kitty parted with some of her cash to buy a dress and some underwear from an enterprising pimp.

For a bit more money she purchased sewing tools and trimmings and turned the simple dress into a chic confection. The other prisoners admired it and paid her to spruce up their own clothes. Kitty's wad of bills grew.

The problem with prison life was boredom. The prostitutes were uneducated and their conversation was mostly rehashing articles from gossip sheets. They all seemed to have a great capacity for sleep. Their lives outside of prison kept them up nights, and many saw jail time as an opportunity to rest. The old-fashioned Hungarian jailers did not expect women to work, not even prisoners.

But Kitty was not sleepy. As she sewed in silence her mind roiled with the fate of Sender and of her family. She avidly joined in even the silliest conversation to keep away her own fearful imaginings.

She was now grateful for the lessons learned at Mrs. Gordon's. One really should bless God for the evil, as well as the good. At that detested job she had developed a high tolerance for dullness, and she had learned to keep her thoughts to herself. She had learned to hide every element of Jewishness in her speech and behavior. She had learned to obscure the education and wit that would have placed her under suspicion. But the most valuable thing she'd learned was astrology.

One day a fellow prisoner woke from an afternoon nap babbling about a lurid dream. To Kitty it seemed like a divine invitation. Hadn't dream interpretation been the salvation of Joseph in the prisons of Pharaoh's Egypt.

"What your dream clearly foretells," said Kitty, "is that you will soon become the top girl in your pimp's stable."

"Really?" said the prostitute, eyes wide open now. She had imagined herself top girl for a while, but it was good to be vindicated by an authority. "What else?"

"Oh, a great deal. But I'd need to know the exact time and date and place of your birth, and..."

"March 16th 1921, at eight in the evening! Right here in Budapest!"

"*And...*"

"And?"

"And it will cost you, honey."

From then on Kitty regularly cast the horoscope for everyone in the jail who could afford it, including the guards. It was more lucrative than sewing. The girls teased Kitty about how much she liked money, how hard she worked.

"What are you knocking yourself out for, Julia? When you get out you'll be able to make plenty just lying on your back."

"Those days are over for me. I've got a little sister in the convent. Besides, this infection of mine keeps coming back and I'm tired of dodging the doctors and the cops. Anyway, how long can I stay in the life? All of us have to think of another way to make a living eventually."

"Not me. My man's going to marry me."

"Me too."

"Yeah, me too," said a third whore, oblivious to the fact that her lover/ pimp was the same as that of the first girl. "Your problem Julia, is that you think money can buy everything. But it can't. It can't buy love. Someday you'll find a man to love, then you won't be running after every penny like some Jew."

Kitty flinched and saw that they saw.

"I had a man once," she segued gracefully, letting the tears fill her eyes. "But he left me, and I'll never love another."

All the girls gathered round to hear the colorful details of "Julia's heartbreak"—amazingly similar to a story that had appeared in one of Mrs. Gordon's magazines—and indulge happily in the vicarious misery of another woman's star-crossed romance.

"Which of you lazy cows wants to make some money?"

The screw looked morose. Experience had taught him that few if any volunteers would come forward. If they did, they would laugh at the pathetic wages. If one of them actually took the job, she'd likely quit after the first day.

Generally, they had a peasant woman from outside come and clean the captain's offices. But each time the charwoman quit the captain tried to save money by trying to recruit a non-violent prisoner—a whore—to do the work.

"*She* does. Julia Ficsorcsak always wants to make money."

"Who, the Gypsy?"

"She's a fortuneteller, but she's no Gypsy. A real refined lady, Julia is."

Kitty licked her lips. She had not really mastered the coarse speech and mannerisms of her fellow prisoners. On the other hand, it was not quite safe to be suspected a Gypsy either, so it was all for the best. Thank God, again.

"Such a fancy dame won't want to do housework, I'll bet."

"Oh, I don't mind. Let's see what you got."

However comfortable and safe the jail was, freedom felt better. It was wonderful to get out from behind bars, even if no farther than the halls and offices of police headquarters. The work was very easy. A quick dusting, a swabbing of the floor, emptying the trash, more than satisfied the captain.

In the beginning, Kitty found large amounts of money lying around the captain's office. It occurred to her only later that she was being tested for honesty. The money was paid by pimps and madams who wanted their employees released before their sentences ended.

Kitty's skill at predicting the future grew. She now had the uncanny ability of foreseeing which girls would be sprung early. Her fees went up.

Once she was trusted by the captain, Kitty was left on her own for hours. She learned that records were haphazardly kept for most criminals, even the more serious offenders. Only the offenses of Jews were meticulously recorded, with duplicates of everything sent to the Germans. Any time Jews were rounded up for deportation, or accused of harboring foreigners, or informed on for other offenses, everything was written up exhaustively and neatly filed.

Somewhere, somewhere in this very office, she was certain, was a record of Sender's arrest—and of his destination.

Every day Kitty's feather duster seemed to catch in another file cabinet. She opened it carefully, ever so carefully, to remove the stray feather.

And then one day, she found it, the file for the day the truck convoy was dispatched!

It contained information about the thousands of Jews with whom she had been herded in the compound on that terrible day. In accordance with Reich directives the women, children, and elderly were termed "useless Jews," and sent by railway to Oswiecim, Poland, 55 kilometers west of Cracow, for "special treatment."

The captain had signed the sheet that indicated the Hungarian Arrow Cross had properly concluded its role in the operation. Another man's signature indicated that the trains had been officially signed over to the Germans, without incident, at the Hungarian border. There were cordial notes with Germans and Hungarians congratulating each other for exemplary cooperation.

Kitty swallowed. What did that mean, "special treatment?" What person was actually "useless?" Why were they sent to this town in Poland? How could so many people be sent to a small town and not overwhelm the population?

But she couldn't consider these things now. She had to find out where the men in the trucks had been sent. The information had to be in this file.

The last page in the folder listed the number of trucks, and the number of men in each truck. Kitty's eyes popped. How could they fit all those men in one truck?

Her eyes moved on voraciously. Where were they taken? Please, God, not to this Oswiecim. She had a bad, bad feeling about that place.

The page had endless details that meant nothing to her, but finally, she got to what she wanted, the destination.

A labor camp. Labor, labor, labor. Her eye rested lovingly on the word. Not the "special treatment" of the useless, but blessed labor, the heart of usefulness.

The camp was called Neuhedwigburg. She frowned. Something about the name seemed familiar. Neuhedwigburg. In Poland? In their arrogance the Nazis Germanized everything. Neuhedwigburg was Nowy Jadwigatow! Kitty literally leaped up, throwing the feather duster high in the air.

She didn't know much about Poland. The big cities, of course, and the smaller ones that were centers of Jewish scholarship or Yiddish culture. But Nowy Jadwigatow wasn't any of these, it was a small town. Yet entirely by chance, she knew where it was.

The town—now a hamlet, probably—was nestled in Subcarpathian Ruthenia. It had developed about a hundred years before, due to the nearby quarries which yielded a valuable form of granite. Jewish merchants had gravitated to the town and enjoyed some prosperity there.

Kitty had heard all about it from Mrs. Kandinsky, the milliner, who had been born in the Polish town. She often spoke of the pretty little place in the enchanted forest. Of course, Mrs. Kandinsky had left Poland as a little girl, so perhaps her memories were a bit rosy, still it was a comfort to think of Sender working in a lush and lovely setting.

The surface supply of the precious granite eventually became exhausted, and the town's prosperity ebbed. Dynamite blasting was needed to get at more granite, but that was prohibitively expensive at the beginning of the century.

The townspeople, as always, blamed the Jews for their decline, and rioted in a series of bloody pogroms. That was when Mrs. Kandinsky's family fled south to Janace.

But it was wartime now, and dynamite blasting was feasible to get at a necessary material. Dynamite blasts were frightening, but at least it was legitimate work in the healthy outdoors. Mrs. Kandinsky had often spoken of the region's flower-dappled meadows, of the forests that yielded up luscious berries and delicious mushrooms and cool streams of pure water. She was certain that Sender would be worked hard, but at least he could be comforted by generous Mother Nature.

Kitty replaced the file carefully. She whistled as she finished cleaning the office.

"Ah, there you are, Julia. Such a ray of sunshine."

It was the captain. Had he seen her snooping through the files?

"Oh, I like to get at every nook and cranny, sir. And sometimes the feathers get stuck..."

He came very close. "You really don't have to call me sir, Julia. My Christian name is Imre."

He drew her waist close to him with a hand, her head with the other.

Kitty froze. She would never, ever, ever be with another man!

And *this* man, this butcher? She'd never forget his insolent signature on the "bill of lading" that had been sent with the thousands of doomed and helpless Jews.

She grabbed his head close to hers and started kissing his face wildly.

"Heh, heh, quite the wildcat, eh Julia? I like that in a woman."

"I'm the best, Imre, the best. Do you hear? Listen to what I say, not to what those bitches tell you."

"Bitches? What do you mean? No one told me anything."

"Oh, sure! I know how jealous those whores are. They told you lies. Lies!"

"What do you mean?"

"I mean those sores don't indicate anything. Everybody gets a pimple now and then. Just because they're down there on the privates and oozing a little bit, doesn't mean..."

"Ugh, get away from me!" He pushed Kitty so that she fell against the desk.

"But Imre, darling..."

"It's 'Captain' to you."

Kitty looked hurt. The captain reconsidered. She was an awfully good cleaner, and for next to nothing.

"Just carry on with your work, Julia. You're doing a fine job, a fine job. And we all appreciate it." He shut the door behind him, and Kitty knew he would be taking pains to avoid her from now on.

CHAPTER TWENTY-EIGHT

Janace, March 1942

Rachel-Leah was delivered of an undersized but healthy boy. The birth was quick—as if the infant were apologizing for the difficulty of his conception—and the delivery almost painless—as if reluctant to add to the great troubles into which he was born.

Rachel-Leah was living with one of her sisters-in-law. In the last few months the Jews had been ordered into an ever-smaller sector of the town, a progressively shrinking ghetto. Those who had lived outside the strict borders were forced to find shelter within.

The circumcision feast was to take place in the house, which, cramped as it was, felt lonely and distraught. All of Rachel-Leah's brothers and brothers-in-law had been drafted into forced labor. The absence of men was haunting.

The religious ceremony was illegal, and the penalty for conducting or attending it was death. But on the eighth day after birth old men and anxious women packed the house. Because of the danger of discovery by the Nazis, no children were present. It was just as well. There were no festive cakes, nor candies to stuff into their pockets.

A few months before the women of the household would have been mortified to offer their guests a meal of "wine" made of boiled raisins and a few skinny loaves of barley bread, but shame had long ago disappeared in overwhelming hunger.

Rachel-Leah's father was to serve as godfather and Joseph and Sari as godparents. The role of godparents was usually given to a young, childless couple, as the honor was said to confer a blessing of fertility. Rachel-Leah had expected to give this honor to Kitty and Sender. Now she was glad that they were not here. That was the biggest blessing of all.

Sari took the baby from the mother and carried him to her husband. Joseph took the baby and laid it upon the lap of his venerable brother. They were smooth and practiced in the ceremony. In their youth Sari and Joseph had been honored as godparents dozens of times, but somehow the blessing never materialized.

Sari had unraveled two pairs of old gloves and crocheted a tiny sweater and matching cap for Rachel-Leah's baby. The child lay cozily in the outfit until the circumciser came and removed his diaper. Even then, exposed to the cold air, he whimpered very softly.

The ancient *mohel* had long since retired and handed over his sacred calling to a younger man. But the current mohel had been force-marched out of town with the others, so the old circumciser retrieved his instruments and once more performed the ceremony he had done thousands of times before.

The old mohel squinted behind his thick glasses and his hands shook so much that the knife flashed. But he was so skilled and experienced that the cut was made, clean and perfect, in the blink of an eye. The baby uttered no sound, he had even stopped whimpering. By the time he could express surprise, he was bandaged and diapered and at his mother's breast.

The next blessing was made by Rachel-Leah's father, whose obligation it was, in the absence of the father, to bring the boy into the Covenant of Abraham.

He recited the words in a cold voice lacking emotion. He had run out of emotion, out of sentiment, out of hope for all that was left of his family.

He had raised thirteen children. Wasn't he supposed to spend his old age basking in the love of dozens of grandchildren and great-grandchildren? He and his wife had toiled and sacrificed and suffered for that. But God had other plans.

And now here was a new grandchild, but he could not summon any excitement for it. He was tired, tired of the exhilaration that grew naturally from birth, tired of the traditional welcoming speech that segued into eulogy. There was only one warm spot left in his heart—for his wife and their angel, their Judith. His wife was the cleverest woman in the universe. She had said she would save Judith and he believed her utterly.

People had said he was crazy to allow his wife and youngest daughter to go down to Hungary by themselves, but he never doubted or questioned his wife's plan. Now he realized, that had been the best "plan" he had made in his life, the only one that would matter.

The assembly responded to his blessing with the rote words. "Just as this child has entered into the Covenant of Abraham, so may he enter into the study of Torah, so may he enter under the wedding canopy, so may he enter into a life of good deeds."

They all said the formula, but their throats were dry with disbelief.

It was the quietest circumcision feast anyone could remember. Absent were the clever Torah bon-mots that young men served up at such occasions. Absent also was the joking advice of experienced mothers, the squealing gossip of impending engagements, the tidbits of news about family and neighbors.

Utterly absent was the usual speculation about what the baby was to be named. Traditionally, the child was named for a deceased grandfather or great-grandfather or other relative, whose lovingly recalled virtues would be the child's inheritance. But this baby's legacy was all too clear.

"And his name shall be called in Israel: Chaim ben Chaim."

One woman burst into tears, and the entire assembly joined her.

The first labor conscription had been on the day after Kitty and Sender escaped. It turned out to be less fearful than expected. There were exemptions and loopholes in the call-up, and many found that they could bribe the officials in charge to leave their families alone.

Those who left were never heard from again, except for one man who returned from a labor camp. He reported that conditions were harsh and food scarce, but that life there was bearable. They certainly hadn't taken the men to be annihilated, as everyone had feared. He himself had run away only because he had had rheumatic fever and was weak in the heart and wouldn't have been able to stand exertion.

The community sighed in relief. They even chided Joseph for his cries of warning about the labor marches.

"But I heard from the refugee, Zlotnik, that..."

"Zlotnik! He was a madman. You could tell just by looking at him. Why would they want to kill strong young men?"

But by the second conscription no one was mocking or reassuring anyone else. The draft was airtight and shockingly broad. Boys of thirteen were required to go and healthy men as old as fifty. Joseph himself might have been drafted, except for a ten-year error on his birth certificate that had been made by the careless registrars of the decaying Austro-Hungarian Empire.

This conscription was relentless and precise. This time it was conducted by the Germans themselves, not the Slovak fascists. The men were lined up at the old brick factory outside of town. The day was cold, a vinegary wind was blowing, but sweat dripped from every brow.

"I've got to appeal to the officer," Chaim said to his neighbor.

"Don't be an idiot. These Germans are looking for an excuse to shoot. Look how itchy their hands are on the guns."

"I'll appeal to reason. I'll do it with humor. Who could take offense?"

"Chaim, don't..."

But Chaim stepped forward. He spoke to the man in charge. Not an officer. Just a regular guy, a fellow like himself.

Chaim explained how his wife was pregnant and due any day. He recounted what a struggle it had been to conceive the child, how long they had waited, what a once-in-a-lifetime event the birth would be.

Chaim used his most ingratiating tone of voice, he made a little joke, he pointed out that he only needed a few days, just till the birth. Then he would be delighted to go with his brethren and, in gratitude, work harder than ever for the Reich.

But the German soldier heard nothing of what Chaim said. All he could think of was *how* Chaim was saying it. Chaim didn't really know German, he just spoke Yiddish with a barking little accent and hoped it would do.

The soldier's milky skin went red all the way up to his peaked cap. How dare he! How dare this Jew soil the sacred German tongue.

The German shot Chaim in the chest at point-blank range, and Chaim crumpled instantly to the ground. The soldier was so enraged he kept shooting, squandering bullets, until one of his colleagues stopped him.

That night, long after the labor detail had left, six white-bearded ancients of the Men's Burial Society came to gather Chaim's body. They also dug up the cobblestones that were stained with his blood and took them along for internment.

There was no need to prepare Chaim's body in the ancient rituals of washing and shrouding. A murder victim is buried in his clothes, every drop of his spilled blood a screaming witness from the earth.

Jewish custom frowns on burial at night, but a sense of extreme urgency guided the six old men. They did not have the strength or the time to dig a new grave, so they buried Chaim in the crypt of the holy Rebbe, who had died the month before.

The Rebbe had been old, but never ill. One night he awoke screaming, "Do not make me go with them. I refuse! This much I cannot do!" In the morning the leader of the community was dead.

The earth in the crypt was still soft but the bent spines of the ancient gravediggers ached as they dug. They had to perform this last act of kindness for Chaim. Since he could never repay them, God himself would be in their debt.

It was a lucky thing that they did bury Chaim that night because the next day a long list of new laws was enacted, including one forbidding burial of the Jewish dead. Corpses of Jews were to be laid out on the sidewalk each day, to be collected with other rubbish by the regular sanitation detail, which would dispose of them in the town's garbage dump. Like other refuse, the order stated, Jewish carcasses were to be burned. Chaim was the last Jew buried in the cemetery in Janace.

Finally, universal Jewish deportation was ordered. Women, children, the aged, the crippled. All, all were to leave the land of their birth.

The community reacted with heated debates.

"They say there are retirement homes for the Jewish elderly there, in Poland."

"*They*? How can you believe what *they* say? The evil ones do nothing but lie. Think, you fool, have they ever done us any good at all. God knows what horrors they have waiting for us in Poland."

"Oy, always such a pessimist. A Jew can't live like that, without hope."

"They say the retirement homes are cheek-by-jowl with schools for the children."

Everyone moved closer to the last speaker. Schools. They had suffered most of all from the closing of the schools. If only they could have their schools back they could revive everything!

"We'll have to leave information for the menfolk, for when they come back, so they know to go to Poland to find us."

"Idiot!" said the pessimist, "They're never coming back."

"That's not true. They *will* come back. Some already came back. They come back all the time."

"One. One man. And did it ever occur to you that he lied?"

"No, no. I knew him, knew his family. A good boy. An honest boy, rheumatic fever and all."

"Yes, good. So good that he wanted to spare your feelings. Notice how he left town as fast as he could?" And another thing. That first conscription was the damn Slovaks. This one was under the Germans, may their name be erased. This last one you'll never hear of again."

"Evil ones, evil ones, to be sure. But still, the Germans are human beings too, aren't they?"

"I for one am glad we're going. I can't go on like this. The hunger, the crowding, the sickness. Anything has to be better than this."

Joseph was in a bind. The orders were that the Jews bring no more than a single bag for each adult. In their household they would all be filling their bags with food. Some—including the strangers from the other side of town whom they had put up for pity's sake—said that there would be plenty to eat at their destination, but he didn't believe it, and neither did Sari or Martha. They would be filling their satchels with the dried fruit leather and nuts that the women had rolled into tight, nutritious tubes.

After his truck had been confiscated, and before they were banned from leaving the Jewish sector during the day, Joseph had tried to eke out a living by walking to the farms of his nearest customers and buying a sack at a time of bruised fruit. This Sari, Martha, and the girls turned into the preserved product.

You never knew about people's true selves. Some of his best customers, farmers he'd helped enrich, turned vicious. They threw stones at him and cursed him and laughed about what the Germans would be doing to all the Jews.

There were others, a few, who behaved decently. Some, he could tell, were even ashamed of what their fellow Christians were doing. There was one farm wife who, after all his cash ran out, told him he could come and take all the fallen fruit he wanted. She refused to accept Sari's wedding band in payment.

The food saved them. It had seen the entire family through the winter, and made for the best barter. So the house guests might fill their permitted luggage with family photographs and sentimental treasures, but they would be packing theirs with food. It was their wealth—their life.

Sari was already in her nightgown. Her hand reached across the modest expanse between their two beds.

"Come to me my love. Come this one last time."

She mustn't talk that way. They were healthy, vigorous people, thank God, with many years ahead of them, surely. But he said nothing. It was a husband's duty to do his wife's bidding in such matters.

Sari had experienced the woman's change and had attended the ritual bath for the last time. Now they were permitted each other forever.

"Our last night in this house," she whispered. "I have been so happy in this house, so happy with you."

"I will always be with you, my Sari. We don't need a house to make us happy."

Sari sighed. "It won't be the same."

"Sh....Go to sleep now, my love. We'll need all our strength tomorrow."

Malvine and Clara indicated to the adults that they had something to say. Little Vera would speak for them.

"There is a secret hiding place in the house."

"Nonsense," said Sari.

"Look." Vera pointed to the grate above the dining room.

"That's just ventilation..."

"It's a tunnel of sorts. Aunt Kitty showed me. Malvine and Clara want to hide in there. They don't want to go to Poland."

The two older girls nodded their heads vigorously.

Joseph and Sari investigated the hiding place.

"I can't believe that I never knew..." said Sari.

"If we didn't know after all these years in the house," said Joseph, "surely no one else could find it."

They decided to let the girls stay. After all, the most important thing would be to keep quiet in the hiding place, and Malvine and Clara would be forever silent.

It was hard to believe that a mother like Martha could be so cool in saying goodbye to her daughters, thought Sari. Didn't Martha understand what was happening? Poor simple thing, her mind has been addled by the grief of losing her husband and boys.

After everyone else had hugged the girls, Joseph pushed four large jugs of water and all the rest of the food in the house around Malvine and Clara, whose faces were pressed to the grate for air and for the vital view.

Joseph made them promise not to come out until at least three days had passed after the last looter had gone. Just before leaving, they replaced the hiding place's false cover.

After deportation, standard procedure was to send SS teams through the former ghetto to look for any Jews in hiding. Each team consisted of four men and a German shepherd. It was said that if a Jew was found by the team, his best hope was to throw himself at the mercy of the dog.

This team's dog was called Keks—cracker. To Keks all Jews were dog biscuits. He could shear off a man's genitals in a single bite, he could rip out the throat of a four-foot tall child. Keks earned his keep.

The SS men treated Keks well. Even in wartime when everyone, including upright citizens, were deprived of delicacies, Keks always had meat. Fresh meat.

The beast was talented, but by now even the least experienced member of the team had developed the sixth sense that told him when someone was hiding in a house.

When the team entered the former Wassermann home, the men of the team were disappointed. All the Jewish homes in this town were disappointing. Where were the fabled riches that the Jews had sucked parasitically from the world?

The damn Jews, fiendishly clever even now, had already sold everything of value. The silver candlesticks, the ritual objects, the musical instruments, the good furniture, all were bartered as soon as the Hebrews got the tiniest bit hungry. The junk that was left was hardly worth the attention of those primitives, the Slovaks.

As soon as they walked through the door Keks began to bark meaningfully and wag his tail with intent. They let the dog off his leash so that he could go directly to his prey, but Keks stayed in the nexus of the little house, the area between the dining and living rooms. The animal turned around and around in a circle, jumping up and yelping.

One of the men took Keks by the collar, holding him down, quieting him. This man had a keen sense of hearing. He closed his eyes and concentrated, but all he could hear was the panting of the dog.

Another of the men pulled a revolver and shot into the air. Usually, the sudden report of a bullet elicited a sharp intake of breath, at least, but they heard nothing.

It was annoying. There was someone in the house, Keks could sense it and so could they. The man with the revolver shot into the air again. Then again and again.

"Losing your temper and wasting bullets is not going to help," the officer holding Keks admonished the shooter.

"I don't care," said the shooter, reloading his revolver and discharging it into the air again. "What lousy luck. How am I going to explain this to my wife? We were supposed to come home with all kinds of Jewish treasure, but what do we have to show for our work? Nothing. Not a damn thing."

He reloaded once more and emptied the revolver. The walls and ceilings of the parlor and dining room were riddled with holes.

Finally the team gave up and left the house. "There never was such bad luck as we Germans have," said the shooter. The others nodded. They'd had this conversation before, about cruel fate, the tragic destiny of their nation. It always left them in tears.

Inside the house blood seeped from the grate and dripped to the floor below.

CHAPTER TWENTY-NINE

Martha had always loved trains. Trains meant adventure, celebration, love. Czechoslovakia was a landlocked country, and it was trains she had taken on annual "honeymoons" with Ignatz, trains to weddings and circumcision parties, trains to shopping sprees in the great cities of Europe.

Martha understood that they would not be traveling as she had been accustomed, in first-class compartments, they would have to go in third-class, with its over-crowded benches and dirty toilets. But once the train got going, the exhilarating rush of freedom, the comforting rhythm of the wheels, would return. They would look out the windows and see spring's first stirring and be reminded that, while God had turned away from his people, he still had pity upon the earth.

The official order, in German, was for all the remaining Jews of Janace to gather at the train station at exactly six in the morning. Everyone would be prompt—they knew how the Germans punished tardiness.

But what rumbled into the station wasn't a train at all. It was—boxes. A string of boxes on wheels. People around her breathed "cattle cars," but Martha had never seen cattle transported in such vehicles.

The train squealed to a stop, as if the cars were screaming in protest at the engine. The masses at the station, on the other hand, were sickly quiet.

The sides of the cars rumbled open. The crowd cringed backward instinctively.

Slovak and German officers walked purposefully among the Jews. They were dressed in sharply pressed uniforms and brilliant white gloves.

The first thing the Nazis did was spill the milk. Martha's two boys had each brought along a thermos of milk (they had illegally traded fruit rolls with a peasant woman) and mothers of the luckiest families brought along jugs of milk for their smallest children. For babies, milk was life.

The Nazis walked among the Jews, calmly and methodically pouring milk on the ground in front of the mothers and children.

Then they confiscated suitcases and satchels, arbitrarily deciding that one was too large, another so small it surely held cash or jewels. They took Vera's valise, saying she was not an adult, and therefore not allowed baggage.

"In you go, you lazy Jew-dogs!" said a hugely fat Slovak officer.

Nobody moved.

He let forth a stream of obscenities. The Germans laughed at the buffoonish officer, and laughed harder still at the Slovak guards, who were now in a frenzy, whipping and kicking the Jews to get them into the cattle cars.

Lack of food and lack of sleep and the sight of grandmothers bloodied and toddlers knocked unconscious, led to a stampede.

The noise became deafening. The senior German officer raised a revolver and fired off a round. Everyone stopped and whirled toward him.

"We will have *order* here," he said with icy calm. "This is a German action, and it will be conducted in the appropriate, German, manner." He directed a contemptuous look at the Slovak officer.

The boarding resumed. It was much calmer now. The Jews were resigned.

"Joseph," Sari whispered to her husband.

"What is it, my love?"

"Joseph, you must run away now."

"No, I go with you, my heart."

"No, no! 'Make a thousand separations between the living and the dead.'"

Joseph froze. It was a well-known Jewish principle. "What do you mean, Sari?"

"You are fated to live, the rest of us to die."

He struggled against her piercing words. "No. I won't leave you. Our fates were soldered together under the wedding canopy."

Old Rabbi Axelrod was the only teacher left from the boys' school. It had long been illegal to teach Torah, but the Rabbi was a widower, alone in his house within the Jewish sector, and he took in all the older boys who were displaced or orphaned, continuing to teach secretly, and, somehow, to feed them.

They had all arrived in a group now, the last of the Jews. Rabbi Axelrod took one look at the situation, and shouted, "Now, boys, now. Run! Into the woods!"

The boys scattered. Immediately the Nazis opened fire on them. When the fusillade was over, all but two of the boys lay dead on the patch of ground between the train station and the woods.

Old Rabbi Axelrod's eyes were closed, a look of perfect concentration on his face. "Blessed are you, O Lord, our God, king of the universe, who has sanctified us in his commandments..."

The Slovak officer ran up and screamed filthy things directly in his face, but Rabbi Axelrod's expression didn't change. "...and commanded us..."

The fat officer ripped the wispy white beard right out of the rabbi's face, but still there was no change in the old man's tone of voice. "...to sanctify his Name..."

Finally, the Slovak pistol-whipped him until the rabbi fell to the ground, silent at last, his face flashing the shocking color of blood, but its expression blank. The German soldiers tittered.

The German officer called out again. "I will not have this," he said gravely, "One more infraction against order and I will have all Jews present liquidated."

He looked over the crowd. "Ah, Frau Doctor Bloch. How good to see you! I know I can depend on you and your children to set a good example."

"Jawohl, Herr Kommandant!" said the director of the Jewish orphanage.

Dr. Bloch's words and tone dripped scornful irony to the ears of the Jews. But the Germans, like simpletons who couldn't get a joke, heard only her precise obedience, fastidious control, and total lack of emotion. She was a German.

"Ach, Frau Doctor," sighed the officer, "If only all the Jews were like you then perhaps we wouldn't have to be doing what we must do."

Dr. Bloch paused for a moment thinking maybe she could make one last-ditch appeal for the lives of her charges. She opened her mouth to speak, then closed it. She knew what the answer was. She knew the Germans.

Fredricka Bloch had been raised to believe that German culture, scholarship, and social order were the greatest achievements of mankind. If Mama and Papa could see them now.

Her orphanage was closed, her children dead or dying. The end was coming, in horror and tears. Yet Fredricka felt that, contrary to all predictions, her life work had had real worth.

"Will there be anything else, sir?"

The officer smiled benignly, as if bestowing a kindness. "You may bring the children into the train now."

Dr. Bloch turned to the pathetic gaggle of gaunt children. Their cheeks were sunken, like those of toothless old people. Despite matchstick limbs the children's hard round bellies were so swollen that they protruded from their clothing.

"Forward, with energy!" the Director cheered enthusiastically.

Holding hands, the half-dead orphans proceeded. Dr. Bloch led them in a rousing Zionist song, which they sang as loudly as their weak throats could manage.

We ascended to the Land,
We ascended to the Land,
We have plowed and sown
And the harvest is at hand

The Director helped each child board the train, then got on herself.

The conscription of the men had been the first blow to the Jewish families of Janace. It could have been worse. In the nearby town of Michalovce the Nazis surprised the Jews by drafting the *women*. They took young girls and wives and mothers of babies. The community was felled as if by an ax-blow to the head.

The situation in Janace had been more predictable. Families, composed solely of women, old men, children, and the physically or mentally frail, learned to cope.

But the ghetto period eventually destroyed even the most tightly-bound of clans. After the Nazis cut off the water supply to the choked ghetto, the Jews, desperate for drinking water, dug wells. But no well could be far from latrines. Typhus and dysentery raged, carrying off many children and old people.

Their families shattered, many Jews regrouped themselves with the members of charitable and religious organizations. The surviving members of the Committee for Visiting the Sick were at the station together, and those of the Ritual Bath Association, and the Sabbath Supporters League. The dormant Burial Society, men's and women's, came, dragging grandchildren with them.

The simple, devout folk who made up the Fellowship for Reciting Psalms were pressed into a corner of a car, cheek-by-jowl with the learned old men devoted to the daily study of the Talmud.

These sages had filled their retirement days with the study of a single intricately printed folio page of the great set of books each calendar day, and were now half-way through the seven-and-a-half year cycle. The Talmud had been burned in the streets, and its possession made a capital crime, but the men of the Daily Page did not despair, not as long as they had Mr. Trebitz. Trebitz knew the entire Talmud by heart.

The most poignant group was the Society for Honoring the Bride. There was no trace left of the beauty of these, the loveliest and most stylish young women of the town. Hunger and disease had ravaged their faces, and made a mockery of their lithe bodies. They scrambled into the cattle car as if in shame.

Hewing close to her mother and little brothers, Vera Rosen led the remains of the Kindness Club. Membership had dwindled to one seventh-grader, two fifth-graders, and one each from the fourth and third grades. Incredibly, there were two kindergartners, who had been members-in-training. The relatives of all the girls except Vera had died or disappeared. The older girls helped the little ones board the train.

Other Jews came by themselves, with a partner, or with a business associate. Old Mr. Hochberg, after so many years of emphysema, was still alive. Coughing horribly, he boarded the train with a suitcase full of tobacco and snuff.

The Minsky triplets and their sister got on together, their glories gone, quadruplicate copies of despair. Sender Halter's nieces had also lost their beauty, except for the glorious black braids weighing down their heads.

Although their shops had been closed long, long before, Mrs. Kandinsky the milliner, and Mr. Schneider the tailor came with their staffs, skilled hands clutching satchels of rags, and the illusion that they would practice their crafts again.

A dapper man approached the Slovak officer.

"There's been a terrible mistake! I'm not a Jew. I don't see how such a mistake could have been made!" He waved his papers under the officer's nose.

The Slovak took the papers and perused them with difficulty.

"What do you mean you're not a Jew?"

It had been a long time since any of the women had gone shopping for clothes, but the man's identity was unmistakable. It was young Mr. Nagy, the owner of Alma's dress shop. Of course he wasn't a Jew.

"Here. Here are my baptismal records. Besides, ask any priest in town. Everyone knows us. We're the Nagys. The best Catholics you can find. None of us ever miss Mass. Never."

"Says here your mother's name was Gross," the officer said loudly, making a point of his literary acumen.

"But she was Catholic!"

"Gross. Was she German?" interrupted the German officer.

"Well, no, but..."

"Then you are a half-Jew," the German said icily.

"No, no! Entirely Christian. A Catholic. I swear by the Holy Trinity."

"Unbutton your pants," said the Slovak officer, smiling broadly.

"What?"

"Unbutton your pants. Let's see if you're circumcised, Mr. Christian."

The Slovak winked at the Germans, as if he had come up with a clever test.

Nagy didn't stand on modesty and hurriedly undid the shell buttons of his fine wool pants.

The soldiers peered at his tiny shriveled penis; the Jews looked away.

"There, you see. A foreskin, just like your own." Nagy laughed nervously.

"Ah," said the German officer, "so it's your bottom half that's Christian. Very good. It can stay here in town. We'll just send the top half to Poland."

The soldiers guffawed, but Nagy screamed. "No! For the love of Christ and your eternal soul," he said to the Slovak soldier, "you've got to get me out of here."

The fat officer frowned. "All right," he said, "take him to police headquarters."

Nagy sighed with relief, but the Jews winced. Many people had been taken to police headquarters. Few, if any, returned.

The Jews kept boarding the train in their odd groupings and splintered families. Wealth and poverty, luck and misfortune, no longer meant anything. Sender's rich Uncle Mechel climbed in, the last living member of his great household. Luckless Pollack came in, accompanied by his crippled and feebleminded son, who had inexplicably managed to survive.

Finally, the last of the Jews were crammed into the train. The sides of the cars were rolled shut, muffling the screams of the crushed. Outside, heavy iron bars locked shut and the signal was given for the train to leave the station.

More than half of the Jews would be dead before they reached Poland.

CHAPTER THIRTY

No one talked inside the car; it was hard enough to breathe. Infants and toddlers, weak with hunger, fell asleep easily. Older children had no energy to cry.

There was a sudden swerving of the train. Mechel Halter fell on his back and could not right himself. Try as he might, he couldn't get his feet to touch the floor.

"Have mercy, Jews," he called. "Move your bags so a man can stand up."

A minute or two passed before Mechel realized that he was lying on a pile of people who had suffocated.

He was about to scream in horror when something caught his eye and stopped his mouth. There was a tiny, ragged beam of light piercing the ceiling of the cattle car.

"Look," he pointed his hand upwards. "Look," he called again, righting himself, standing on a corpse.

Joseph Wassermann, the tallest man in the car, looked up. So did Luckless Pollack, who was in the habit of blindly following every word of his benefactor.

"It's a hole," said Pollack.

"The whole roof is rotten," Joseph said. "If you can boost me up there, I think I can punch it out."

"And what, fly away?" someone laughed bitterly.

"At least we'd get some air," said Mechel.

A few people did try to lift Joseph, but it was no use. Even together, standing on a pile of the dead, they didn't have the strength.

All eyes glazed over once again. But Mechel couldn't get his mind off the hole.

His eyes fell on the son of Luckless Pollack. Surprisingly, the boy—

he was a middle-aged man, really—was standing quite upright. How odd. Young Pollack's right leg was withered and his spine bent like a question mark. Then Mechel saw that the boy was leaning on a crutch.

Amazing. The Nazis had confiscating all crutches, canes, and prosthetic devices. They threw the disabled from their wheel chairs, forcing relatives to give up their suitcases in order to carry them.

But this strange lad, crippled and crazy, had slipped his crutch down the leg of his pants and under his jacket.

"Give me the crutch," said Mechel.

The crippled man shook his head violently.

"Give me the crutch and your father will live," said Mechel.

Immediately, he wriggled the crutch up out of his clothes and handed it over to Mechel. Without support, Pollack's son collapsed and came to rest upon a woman who was cooing softly to her dead baby.

Mechel poked the tip of the crutch into the tiny hole. The rotten wood crumbled, and a fist-sized gap appeared. A plume of clean, cold air curled into the car.

But his outstretched arm shook too much to widen the hole further. He was an old man, and hungry.

"Joseph, here, you take this."

Joseph Wassermann took the crutch and punched at the hole. Soon it was large enough for a fat man to pass through, and none of them was fat.

Excitement passed through the car. Adults wakened and became alert. An unknown strength came into exhausted arms. This time the people had no trouble in hoisting Mechel Halter up, up, until he disappeared.

Then his head appeared in the hole. "Pollack! Shmuel Pollack. Come up here."

Pollack hesitated. "But my son..." The son was lying on the keening woman, exhausted, and he had never been able to express himself in speech. Yet his eyes spoke vividly. "Go Father. Go."

The hands rose again and hoisted Luckless Pollack through the roof.

"Now," said Sari to her husband. "Now you."

"Only if you come with me, Sari."

"No."

Joseph hesitated, but men and women were exhausting themselves lifting him as high as they could. He pulled himself the rest of the way to the top.

From the roof, he wiggled back part way, hanging upside down through the hole like a bat. "There's room for more. There are shrubs near the tracks. We can jump. Come on, Jews!"

No one came up.

"Come on," said Joseph. "Don't worry. I can pull you up."

But no one stretched out their arms to his dangling ones.

"Ladies," he called desperately. "You could do it, ladies. Girls!"

No women pushed forward.

Joseph's hand fell on the head of Bayla Halter. He tugged at the thick tangle of black hair. "Come on, Bayla, you're young. You have a chance."

"No!" she shrieked, ducking so sharply that Joseph was left with strands of hair in his fingers.

"They've spotted us," cried Mechel Halter, pulling Joseph to the train top. "We've got to jump now."

"Now!"

The three men jumped.

Outside the train a tattoo of bullets sounded.

Joseph's suitcase lay at Sari's feet. She opened the latches and pulled out the fruit and nut rolls. "Time to eat, children." She passed the food over to Dr. Bloch's orphans. It was a tightly packed suitcase and there was enough to feed all of them.

Sari saw the hunger in the eyes of the adults. She opened her own suitcase. "Eat, everyone. Bless God and eat."

The adults thought Sari had gone crazy, but they took the food. They crammed it into their mouths, some without blessing God, to Sari's chagrin.

There was a peaceful quiet now, broken only by the sucking sounds of babies and toothless old crones.

"Ehh, ehh," said Sender's twin Anschel to his caretaker, Reb Meisels.

"Oh, no," said Meisels, under his breath. This always happened after Anschel ate. He had to move his bowels.

But there was nowhere to go, not even a corner of the train.

"Ehh, ehh," Anschel insisted.

Meisels didn't know what to do. They were near the door of the car and were particularly tightly packed in. He couldn't move his arms, much less undo Anschel's pants and seat him on the floor.

A dreadful stench went up from Anschel. He was sick with some intestinal parasite, but Meisels had not brought along the healing herbs from Mrs. Halter.

Standing immediately next to Anschel was young Mrs. Adler, the dentist's wife. She was holding her red-headed son. Her arms trembled with hatred.

At the train station, her son had thrown a screaming fit. When the German officer demanded order, the people around them had insisted she pick the child up to quiet him. The boy scratched and kicked and in the end she had no choice but to carry him on—leaving her suitcase, which contained her husband's million-dollar insurance policy, and the strand of pearls from her dowry—in the station.

Now she was on the train, crazy with rage. Her traveling suit was torn and stinking, her hair a ruin. The little demon in her arms amused himself by kicking and scratching her. Having wolfed down the Hasidic lady's fruit roll, he grabbed at hers and stuffed it all into his mouth.

Her eyes bulged. What if she killed him now? What if she did. Who would care? All the people on the train had more grief of their own than they could handle. They probably wouldn't do anything to her.

A Jewish mother killing her own child? They might turn on her. There were some lines that couldn't be crossed. Mrs. Adler took a deep breath. The cold air seeping in from the hole in the roof shook her back to sanity.

Then she felt it, the warm, wet feces oozing out of the retard's pant leg and onto her feet. And it was too much. Her shoes—her genuine crocodile shoes—were the only thing of value she had left. And that *vegetable* was destroying it.

The dentist's wife held up her son and brought him down hard, with all her strength, on the head of poor, addled Anschel Halter. Reb Meisels jumped to intervene, and the madwoman struck him with the child too. Meisels went down on the body of his life-long charge, tripping the woman, who suffocated in the mess. Anschel, Mrs. Adler, the child, and Meisels lay dead together.

At long last Meisels' terrible debt was discharged

In another part of the car Mrs. Halter gripped her suitcase until a blister rose on her finger. She was not aware that her son had died only a few feet away from her. She did not know whether any of her sons were alive or dead. That was the good thing about girls. Her two oldest daughters were right here with her, and their girls, too, and Bayla, of course. While Bayla was often far away in spirit, she was always nearby in fact. When Joseph had reached out for her, she knew Bayla would not go. She knew Bayla would stay with the family.

But Mrs. Halter's mind was not at rest. The contents of her suitcase left her in terrible limbo. Until the water to the Jewish quarter was shut off, and the siege around the ghetto became impenetrable, Mrs. Halter had risked her life nightly, sneaking out to the woods for herbs and roots and mysterious mushrooms.

Only food was more precious than Mrs. Halter's potions. In the last weeks it was the doctors—the doctors who had always spurned her—who begged her for the contents of her satchels. She did not begrudge them but gave them everything she could. After all, didn't they serve the sick as selflessly as she did?

When their morphine ran out, she gave them pain-killers almost as powerful. Alongside the doctors she fought typhus with antiseptic washes and astringent teas. At the very end, she gave them strange herbs to administer to the dying, herbs that made the starving nauseated, herbs that made the fevered hallucinate paradise.

But she would not give her medical partners their ultimate request. She knew the doctors were not pious people. They wanted poison not for their patients but for themselves.

Afterwards, after what happened in the Jewish hospital, she wondered if she had done the right thing. When the hospital had been burned with the patients inside, and the doctors and nurses forced to watch, many had martyred themselves trying to save the sick. So when it came time to pack her suitcase, she filled it with the plump berries that could freeze the heart in mid-beat, and with the beautiful toadstools that turned lungs into concrete.

Mrs. Halter looked at the heavenly face of Sari Wassermann, her *machateniste*. Her children's in-laws were as close to her as blood-kin, and none of these was as revered as Sari. What Sari had just done was typical. Feeding the hungry with the last of one's food, was this not the highest and most saintly act? What would Sari do in my shoes, she wondered. Would she open this suitcase, too, and pass around the ultimate relief? Or would she stick to the letter of the Holy Law, and choose life.

The latter, Mrs. Halter decided. Tears stung her eyes, but she kept her suitcase pressed tightly to her thin coat.

When Joseph regained consciousness, he thought he was at work and that an entire truckload of crated fruit had fallen on him. A few minutes later, however, he realized that he had jumped off the train and landed in a ditch near the tracks.

Slowly he rose. He had never hurt so much in his life, yet he was alive, and not seriously injured. He began to recite prayers of thanksgiving, then stopped with a jolt.

Mechel Halter and Shmuel Pollack! Hadn't they jumped too?

He looked around. There was no sign of anyone. There was not even a puff of smoke to indicate that a train had been there. He was exposed on an empty plain. Joseph jumped back into the ditch.

Cowering, he started to walk. Back to Janace. That didn't make any sense, he knew. There were no Jews left in Janace, and the Gentiles had shown the extent of their hospitality. But where else could he go? His parents and grandparents had been born in Janace. It was his only home.

A few yards away he found the body of Mechel Halter. The old man had a bullet-hole in his neck. He gently straightened the body in the ditch. Then he saw the body of Luckless Pollack in the shrubbery between the ditch and the tracks.

The Nazis' bullets missed Pollack, but he had fallen on his head and broken his neck. Groaning with pain, Joseph moved the body down into the ditch, next to that of Mechel Halter.

He ought to bury them, he thought. It was his obligation as a Jew to bury them. The Torah said even a Gentile criminal deserved a proper grave. He had no tool so he tried to dig with his hands.

Joseph sighed in frustration. It couldn't be done. He hurt too much and it was taking too long. And he was very exposed out here. What if a Nazi, or even a farmer came by? They would surely kill him or report him to someone who would.

He arranged the bodies next to each other, like brothers. He took the dirt he had scraped up and sprinkled it on them. He added a few coarse bushes from the side. They were covered naturally, as if the wind had blown the grasses into the ditch.

Joseph said the prayer for the dead, "Lord full of mercy..." He tried to memorize the location of the ersatz graves. Maybe someday he could find them and give both men a decent burial.

Pollack's son would die, but Mechel Halter had so many sons and grandsons. All so strong and smart and resourceful. Surely some of them would survive even the most brutal forced labor. Then they would bury the patriarch properly. And they would bury Shmuel Pollack, too, because, in death as in life, the two were entwined.

Joseph entered a more wooded area but kept an eye on the tracks. He wasn't much of a woodsman, and couldn't find his way in the wild. He was very thirsty, but he had no idea how to find water.

It was near dusk when he saw the outer buildings of Janace. What would he do now? He was obviously a Jew, a Hasid with the yellow star on the front and back of his jacket. It was forbidden for a Jew to be outside the ghetto. But all Jews were supposed to be out of the city entirely. Besides, there was no "inside" to the ghetto now.

Joseph shook his aching head. Anyway, before the sun set he had to say his afternoon prayers. He turned east, to Jerusalem, and prayed. Afterwards, he felt a bit relieved.

It was dark now and he stood in a doorway until he found an even darker doorway. He kept moving until he could move no more. He was faint with pain and overwhelming thirst.

Joseph sat down on the threshold of a house, and his eyes started to close.

Someone tapped his shoulder.

Joseph turned and gasped.

He had chosen the worst possible place to stop. This was the house of the former mayor of Janace—and the founder of its Anti-Semitic League.

CHAPTER THIRTY-ONE

Auschwitz

Dr. Mengele would be in seventh heaven.

The cargo from eastern Slovakia contained a bumper crop of twins, a dwarf, three congenital cripples, and, miracle of miracles, a set of adult quadruplets.

The previous shipment had come from the west, Belgium, France, and Holland, and the very young, the twisted, the sick, had not survived the long journey. Only the hardiest and healthiest had made it to the end of the transport. That load contributed no new subjects for Dr. Mengele's experiments

The officer at the unloading dock did the recruiting for Mengele. "Twins, twins. Special housing and hot meals are available for all identical twins. Bring them forward, please. Hospital treatment available for all dwarfs and sufferers of birth defects. Kind Jewish people, help them out, please."

His words made Mrs. Halter loosen her grip on her case full of poisons. The lying German presented an immediate danger. She had to separate the twins!

She pulled the turban off her head. For a Hasidic woman it was as shocking as tearing her skirt off. She jammed the hat on the head of one of her granddaughters and stuffed the child's glorious black braids into it.

Then she grabbed the hand of the other twin and ran as far to the other side of the car as she could. It was easier to move in the car now. There were so many dead, and others had begun to get out of the train in a rush for relief. Working quickly, she unbraided the little girl's hair and fluffed it out in a fan, as if the child was a bride.

"Hold onto Aunt Bayla's hand," she commanded. "If anyone asks, she's your mother. Do you understand?"

"Yes, Granny," the child whispered.

She was so beautiful, so perfect, so sweet. Mrs. Halter's hand ached to open the valise and keep her babies from the horrors ahead. But she did not. She could not.

"Ladies and gentlemen, please leave your suitcases at the tracks. You will receive a receipt for each piece of baggage, so you can claim it later. Please hold on to your receipts! Do not misplace your receipts. Without them we cannot guarantee the return of luggage."

The German's voice was so business-like that some of the western Jews who had arrived that morning had given the baggage handlers *tips*. The skeletal porters had looked at them in fatigued pity. Could they really not know?

The officer moved things along at a steady clip. Men were separated from the women and children. Lines were formed. Everything had to be just so for when Dr. Mengele appeared, which he certainly would. They processed about nine thousand Jews daily, and Mengele never skipped a single day for sickness or vacation.

The Minsky sisters jostled their way to the front of the line. Each of them flipped her hair back over the same ear and put the same foot forward in a model's stance. They stood with their arms around each other's waists to emphasize their resemblance.

The officer suspected that the women were triplets and a singleton, despite their best efforts. But what did it matter, the experiments were a farce anyway. All the subjects always died, and all the controls always died. What did that prove? But the scientific institutes in Berlin couldn't get enough of his pointless studies. They, and their corporate sponsors, gave Mengele a huge budget to continue.

Mengele came out, a crisp lab coat buttoned over his equally crisp officer's uniform. He smiled at the assembled Jews—the mass reached to the horizon. He smiled hardest at the "quadruplets" who, birds mesmerized by a snake, smiled back.

The officer wondered how long their smiles would last. That depended on what Mengele did with them. Sometimes he sewed twins to each other, creating Siamese twins. Perhaps he'd sew the four together in a Siamese box.

The twins would get double rations, 1500 calories. What they would not get was anesthesia or treatment for gangrene. They'd lose their appetites quickly enough.

Speaking of appetites, the German considered the dinner menu posted at the officers' mess: baked pike, tomato soup, roast half of chicken with potatoes and red cabbage, and vanilla ice cream. And coffee and beer. The brew and the coffee served in camp were excellent. You could have as much as you wanted of anything at dinner, and if you didn't like the menu, there were always sandwiches.

The very thought was refreshing and the officer resumed his duties with vigor. He checked his clipboard. The previous cargo produced 981 Jews from the camp at Drancy, France. Sixteen men and 38 women were admitted as prisoners to the camp. The rest, of course, were gassed.

Dr. Mengele sent the Slovak shipment's experiment subjects to the "hospital" and then began to deal with the women. There were no workers in the first batch. Almost all the women were either accompanying children or too old to be productive. Mengele kept nodding them briskly to the left, to the "Path to Heaven."

Sari watched carefully as the line of women inched forward. Her eyes moved with the few women who went to the right, to life.

She looked at Rachel-Leah, standing next to her. She knew her niece was starving and exhausted, but Rachel-Leah's shapeless torso and thick legs gave the illusion of solidity.

Rachel-Leah was trying to nurse her baby. Her milk had completely dried up, so she had cut her nipple with her fingernails and tried to coax little Chaim to drink the blood. But the baby was too weak to suck.

"Rachel-Leah," said Sari, "would you do me one last act of loving-kindness?"

Rachel-Leah turned. An act of kindness? To agree was almost an instinct. "How can I, Aunt Sari? Has God granted me the means to fulfill any more commandments on this earth?"

"Rachel-Leah, you know that my whole life I wanted only one thing, to have a baby. Now it's all over and I will never realize my dream. Please, just for a few minutes, can I hold little Chaim?"

"Of course, Auntie, of course."

Sari took the baby carefully. He did not cry or even fuss. His eyes were filmed by something unhealthy.

The line was moving faster, with all the women and their children sent to the left. They were almost at the head now, almost facing the Nazi doctors.

"I'll just hold him a little while longer, if you don't mind. And if you should become separated from us, dear niece, rest assured that I will take care of him as if he were my own, with all my heart."

"Thank you, Aunt Sari."

They were facing Dr. Mengele now. He paused, and the women's breaths held, as he lifted his index finger.

"You," he pointed at Rachel-Leah and then to the right.

Sari wrapped herself around the baby and ran up the Path to Heaven.

The baby's nose twitched. Sari stroked his cheek to soothe him. It was the stink. She had smelled it as soon as they opened the sides of the car. Burning meat.

She'd certainly had experience with burned meat. How many times had dinner gone up in smoke as she sat absorbed in a book? But this wasn't chicken or beef or any other food she'd ever cooked. Perhaps it was pork or rabbit, something Gentiles ate? But why would they burn it? Why would they waste so many animals?

The humming became louder, an insistent buzz, like a giant swarm of bees. She identified the sound of thousands and thousands of women screaming in the distance.

Chaim shifted slightly in her arms, and Sari's shoulders tightened protectively. Babies, even quiet ones, needed so much attention!

Sari stopped running and turned around. Her sister Martha was coming with her two boys. Vera was right behind them with all that remained of the Kindness Club, a single kindergardener. Mrs. Halter was coming too, her head bare but held high. There was a married daughter with her and the single daughter and the ex-daughter-in-law and the grandchildren.

A whip slashed across Sari's back. She almost dropped the baby. While she steadied herself, the others ran ahead of her. Guards had come out to hurry the women. They ran alongside the Jews, whipping, kicking, trouncing.

"Move it, you sows!"

The guards were big and ugly. They had close-cropped, bullet-shaped heads and their eyes were flat and colorless. But the guards weren't German. Germans always smiled at the Jews.

A whip caught Bayla Halter on the buttocks and a bloody red line formed on the back of her skirt. It looked like a heavy period had seeped through, but all the women had stopped menstruating months before.

They jammed into a big building that was colder inside than it was out in the open. Here the women and children were to have their heads shaved. Barbers sat on tall stools, wielding huge shears and clippers, their arms aching with the unending work.

One after another the Jews knelt before the barbers: young women with thick shining hair, toddlers with wisps fine as corn silk, old ladies with yellowed buns. All the hair went on a great pile, which workers periodically removed for sanitizing and stuffing into mattress ticking. What fine bedding, so soft yet so springy, for the ladies and gentlemen back in Germany.

Hasidic matrons like Sari and Mrs. Halter, who had worn their hair closely cropped under their wigs and kerchiefs, had nothing for the barbers to cut. Ironically, they alone walked with that inch of dignity intact.

One particular barber was working in a daze. That morning he had snipped the brown ponytail from the head of his own three-year-old daughter. Since then he had been concentrating his efforts on not plunging the shears into his own chest.

He did notice, though, as he cut the magnificent manes of two little girls, that they were identical twins. Somehow they had eluded Dr. Mengele. The barber took a little comfort in that.

The little girls cried. Not for their hair, but for the pair of watered silk ribbons that flew onto the pile with one girl's braids. The ribbons shimmered blue and green, like a peacock's tail, and were the last of the rainbow that their Uncle Sender had bought them in the wonderful times of the past.

Vera managed not to cry when the man shaved her head. The procedure didn't hurt at all. It had been much worse for her sister Malvine, who'd had her hair ripped out, and even in Malvine's case, it eventually grew back, just as nice as before. The kindergartener took her cue from Vera and didn't cry either.

Something basic had changed in the universe. In all the world, no mother, no father, would ever again be able to say, "Hush little one, there is no bogeyman hiding in the closet. There are no such things as ghouls that lurk in the dark.

"Why would anyone hurt you if you eat your vegetables and don't fight with your little brother?

"There are no monsters who come, for no reason, to do unspeakable things to good little boys and girls.

"Go to sleep, little one, we will keep you from all harm."

The Germans had made liars out of all the parents in the world.

CHAPTER THIRTY-TWO

"Take your clothes off, you dirty bitches," the guards screamed, "you're going to take a shower.

"Put your clothes on the hooks. Remember the numbers on the hooks, bitches, so you can find them later."

Only the children were fooled. The adults saw that shoes, eyeglasses, and toys were being thrown onto mountainous heaps by skeletal Jewish men.

Sari lay Chaim down gently while she took off her clothes. Her eyes didn't leave him for a moment. Once she was naked she undressed him. She was relieved to find that Chaim's diaper was clean and dry. Although this was not a good sign, so far into the day, Sari had no idea what she would have done otherwise. Her mother had always dealt with her little sisters' diapers. Mother said the girls would have enough of the chore when they grew up.

"Look!" whispered Martha to Sari as she pulled a small bottle from the pocket of her discarded dress.

"What is it?"

"Joy de Jean Patou." Martha said with a flourish, pulling out the crystal stopper. "I traded it for a single roll of fruit leather!"

"That's great," said Sari, carefully humoring Martha, who had apparently and at long last, gone mad. "Such expensive perfume. And the bottle's almost full."

Martha beamed with the triumph of the bargain. She laughed as she poured the entire contents over her body. The scent of a million jasmine flowers overpowered the stink of desperation and of burning flesh.

"Forgive me for taking it all, sister, but I must prepare myself. I will be with my Ignatz tonight."

The whipping and beating started again, driving the women and children towards their final destination. The buzzing Sari had heard from far away had become ear-splitting.

Even those who had borne in silence the shaving of their heads, could not endure nakedness. They wept and screamed as they struggled to cover their shame and hold onto their children at the same time.

A big Ukrainian came through, shoving bare flesh aside.

"You, you, you, and you," he said, pointing to Sari last. "Come with me."

The chosen women all carried babies in their arms. One of the mothers was about to hand her infant to an older woman, but the Ukrainian stopped her. "No, bring the little bastard with you."

He led them to a small room. Sari managed to get herself to the back of the line of women, but it didn't matter. Another guard slammed a door, locking them all in.

The room was lined with concrete, but the lower half looked like an old brick wall. That part was discolored by dried blood and the mortar-like gray of brain.

The best minds of German science and the shrewdest heads of German industry had worked together to perfect the killing machines. The fruit of their research was Zyklon B, prussic acid in crystalline form.

When Jews were packed in really, really tightly, they could be eliminated for a fraction of a penny per head. Since Zyklon B cartridges killed everything in the chamber, economy demanded a maximum number of victims per load.

They soon found that infants took up too much room in the gas chambers. A babe in arms, studies showed, actually took up more room than an adult. The camp planners came up with a frugal solution: the room into which the Ukrainian had herded Sari and the other women with babies.

Until the age of about a year, when the bones of the infant head grow together to form the mature skull, the heads of babies are very soft. Sari stroked Chaim's head and felt the tender spot where the pulsing measured the beat of his tiny heart.

At this age, the studies proved, the head could be crushed like a ripe tomato.

The Ukrainian took the baby from the first woman. He was practiced in the movement and easily deflected the nails and teeth of the naked mother. He took the baby's two feet in one hand, and with the other hand on his hip, like a folk dancer, he whirled around in a full circle.

The baby's head smashed almost flat against the wall. The Ukrainian was strong, but this gesture required little effort. Centrifugal force, though he could not say it in so many words, did all the work.

The mother of the baby went completely berserk. So did all the other women in the room, except Sari. She watched, frozen, as the women careened about the room, breaking their fingers trying to pry open the door, trying to climb the walls with a baby in one arm.

The Ukrainian ignored everything and chose another baby, plucking it effortlessly from its mother's crushing embrace, and repeating his graceful dance step. Sari couldn't bear to look anymore. She shut her eyes tightly, then opened them to the sight of a mother who had smothered her own baby in the madness.

An eternity later, there remained only one other woman holding a child, besides Sari. The Ukrainian took the other baby and did his twirl. This time the head did not explode against the cement, but the infant screamed as loudly as its mother. Again the Ukrainian whirled, now putting more effort into it. The blow was so powerful it left downy hair embedded in the wall, but it failed to crack the skull or silence the baby.

The Ukrainian cursed loudly in his native language but the screams of the mothers and that one child drowned out his words.

This was happening more and more now, he thought dully. The women were bringing in older children who had failed to thrive in the ghettoes. He had mistaken this one for an infant, when in fact it was more like two or three years old, its body stunted but its skull bones fused.

He was stuck with it now. The Ukrainian got down on his hands and knees and had to hit the kid's head on the floor repeatedly before it would die.

Finally only Chaim was left. The Ukrainian looked at Sari quizzically. She did not scream or clutch the baby or hurl herself onto him. Dry-eyed, she handed him the child. It really was an infant, he could see. There would be no more trouble.

Sari turned away from the Ukrainian, to face the door. She wondered briefly if Chaim would whimper just once as he was hurled through the air. But no. In death as in life, little Chaim was silent.

She heard the splat of his dear little head, then, only the screams of the insane women. The screams of real mothers.

The door was opened and Sari was the first one out. The others had to be pulled and whipped and prodded to clear them out of the room and let the clean-up crew in.

Outside, Sari wiped her brow with her palm. She was sweating, although she was naked and cold.

She had done a terrible, terrible thing. All these years she had secretly raged at God for making her infertile. Now she knew the truth. Fool that she was! She had thought God had cursed her, when really he had *blessed* her.

All those years of praying and pleading. How stupid, how blind! God had blessed her above every woman here. She, who was so undeserving, so ungrateful, so obtuse. Could he ever forgive her? Was there still time?

Sari slipped but righted herself quickly. The floor of the room was unspeakable. Auschwitz was built on a malarial swamp, and the mud beneath it never dried completely. The mess was compounded with urine and feces from bodies loosened by vicious beatings, and the sphincter-paralyzing fear of death. She stubbed her toes and cut her heels on dentures, dolls, and baby pacifiers.

But wait! If the horror of losing a baby was so great, the loss so unbearable, what of the loss of an older child? Of adult children? Of *seven* children?

Martha. Her sister, her beloved sister! The sister she had patronized all these years. Martha had never said a word of protest, much less blasphemy. She had not denied the Architect of her fate. *Martha* was the righteous one.

But it was too late to tell her sister how sorry she was. The Nazis had already driven the women from Janace to their deaths; the madwomen were to go with the strangers from the next shipment.

She mustn't waste these last precious minutes as she had wasted all her life, Sari admonished herself. She must ask God for forgiveness for her failings as a Jew, for ignoring his compassion, and for her great sins against her sisters.

Against Renee. Oh, oh, how she had sinned against Renee. *Thank you God for giving her the spirit to go to your Holy Land. Protect her from all evil.*

And her sins against Eva. *Forgive me, for I never could feel sisterly warmth for her. Forgive me for making no attempt to bring her home from the Germans. Forgive me for not taking her baby.*

And Helen. They had never again heard from Helen. She had done her best for Helen, but Helen had made up her own mind. But she should have done more for Helen's children. They deserved to choose for themselves, between God and Marx. She had not done her best for them.

Kitty.

No, there could be no guilty thoughts about Kitty. It was like thinking about Joseph. Flesh of my flesh, soul of my soul. The child had always found grace in her eyes, in the eyes of all. *Creator of the universe, let her find grace with you. Let her live, let her live, let her live.*

She exhaled. She had confessed her sins in the nick of time. Still, her heart was heavy for her sins against Martha. Even God could not forgive that.

And then, the women were stopped. The guards, instead of beating them forwards, slashed them to a halt. The group ahead of them was being beaten backwards. From her height, Sari could make out the women and children of Janace: Bayla Halter, the twin nieces...Vera!

And, unmistakably, Martha. Martha's back looked soft, her rear and thighs rounded. She had long ago stopped being anything like plump, but she still had a womanly fleshiness. And her smell. The odor of Joy fanned out from her body.

Sari pushed her way through the stagnant crowd. The Halter women recognized her and squeezed over to let her pass, although one of the guards raised his truncheon.

"Martha," Sari called out, holding out her arms.

Martha turned and smiled broadly, her face radiant.

"Martha," Sari cried above the din, "*mechilla.*"

The word was Hebrew for forgiveness. It was the plea from one Jew to another for unconditional forgiveness.

Martha heard, but she misunderstood. She thought it was a demand for an apology. "Oh, please, Sari. Grant me *mechilla* for all the sins I have sinned against you. Please, please."

Sari wept softly. Her sister was such a saint that she hadn't suspected that she had been sinned *against*. So holy, Sari thought. Perhaps God would overlook her own record and bless her in death as he had in life. Maybe she would be bound with her sister, also, in the next world.

The sound in the area ahead of them changed in tone and texture. It stopped being noise and turned, unmistakably, to music.

The *Hatikvah*. The national anthem of the Zionists. The Hope.

They stood transfixed as the sweet, familiar song washed over them.

"As long as the heart longs,
As long as the Jewish soul yearns
As long as the face turns eastward
As long as the eye turns to Zion.

Our hope is not yet lost
The hope of two thousand years,
To be a free people in our own land
The Land of Zion and Jerusalem.

It seemed as if they had all been still and silent during the song, but in fact information was passing quickly through the crowd.

A revolt had erupted at gas chamber #2. When the gas pellet had been dropped one of the women smashed her hand through the thick glass peephole used by the supervising doctor. She had broken both hands doing so, but other women took her place and tore away at the rubber sealant. They had died anyway, but not before gas had leaked out, felling one of the guards.

The women outside formed a phalanx of the strongest among them and began to batter the door of the gas chamber with their bodies. It was solid and did not give at all, but the guards panicked. They had never had to deal with anything more than individual resistance. Suddenly, they were afraid.

That was when the Hatikvah started. The guards were familiar with the "Shma," the affirmation of the One God, and the "Ani Maamin," the declaration of faith in the coming of the Messiah. The guards knew the words to those prayers by heart. But they had never heard this one.

They cowered, revolvers drawn, into a corner.

The SS command was alerted. The women heard the whine of an ambulance siren. They had seen the ambulance on the way up the Path to Heaven, modern, spotlessly white, with cleanly painted red crosses on its sides.

Doctors wearing gas masks came running in. They administered antidote to the fallen guard and carried him away. The doctors were followed by SS men, also wearing gas masks, who soldered a steel plate across the broken peephole. They did the same to the peepholes of the other gas chambers.

Shamed by the presence of their peers, the guards on duty holstered their revolvers and took out their whips and truncheons again. Anyway, they weren't supposed to shoot Jews right outside the gas chambers. Besides the expense of bullets, it was almost impossible to remove bodies from the tightly packed area.

The incident had caused a back-up. There would be a delay of half an hour.

"Mama," cried one of Martha's little boys. "I'm hungry."

"Oh, my darling," said Martha, with a confident laugh. "We can't eat today. You see it is Yom Kippur. The Sabbath of Sabbaths, the holy fast."

His older brother frowned. That couldn't be right. The Day of Atonement was in the fall and this was springtime. Besides, he and his brother were too young to fast.

His mother sensed his doubts and peered into the older boy's eyes.

"Now boys, it being the holiest day of the year, we must say our prayers with all our hearts."

"What do you mean, Mama?" said the little one.

"Just as the prayer says: to love God with all your heart and all your soul and all your ability.

"Now let us say the 'Shma.'"

Everybody, *everybody* joined in. Even the guards mouthed the words.

"HEAR O ISRAEL, THE LORD IS OUR GOD, THE LORD IS ONE."

The next line of the prayer was always said in silence. At morning, afternoon, and evening services. At bedtime. On weekdays and on the Sabbath and on holidays.

Except for the Day of Atonement. And because it *was* Yom Kippur, they shouted at the top of their voices.

"BLESSED IS THE NAME OF HIS GLORIOUS KINGDOM FOREVER AND EVER!"

"That's all I know Mama," said the little boy. "I don't know the rest of the prayer."

"Very well," said Martha, her voice as melodious and projecting as an actress in a theater. "We will sing the 'Ani Maamin.'"

All sang together. Again, the guards mouthed along to the melody.

"I believe, I believe, I believe
In complete faith
In the coming of the Messiah, I believe.
He delays, but even so,
I believe."

"Mama," said the older boy suddenly. "I'm afraid of dying."

"Why, my little angel, what is there to fear? Before this day is done we will be together again with Papa. Soon you two will be on the laps of your big brothers and they will teach you Torah. This very night we will be in Jerusalem."

"But I'm afraid of Jerusalem. There are Arabs there and they will kill us."

"Oh, no, no. After today, no one will kill us.

"Now then, my dearest, honored sister, Sari. You are the most learned among us. Will you lead us in prayer?"

Sari concentrated. The final hours of the Day of Atonement, the Sealing service, was her favorite of the whole year. By that time, she had gone a full day without food and drink, and felt light and high—higher, higher—sure of God's forgiveness.

"Next year in Jerusalem," she whooped.

"Next year in Jerusalem," the crowd echoed. "Now, now, now," they sang in Yiddish, "in Jerusalem the rebuilt."

The gas chambers had been emptied, and the group from Janace was being moved in. Fear and silence gripped the women.

Suddenly, the words rang out in Martha's rich, motherly voice.

"THE LORD IS GOD."

The women and children all responded. "THE LORD IS GOD."

Sari looked at her sister. "THE LORD IS GOD."

Martha was chanting joyfully as she led her two little boys. Vera looked up into her mother's encouraging face.

"THE LORD IS GOD."

Sari beamed at her niece, Vera. She would have grown up to be just like her mother, the ideal Jewish woman. "THE LORD IS GOD."

They were being crammed into the gas chamber, pressed like a swollen foot into a shoe several sizes too small. The two little boys were wedged against Martha's legs, Vera was pressed against her breast and Sari squeezed against Vera.

THE LORD IS GOD! THE LORD IS GOD!

At this point, Sari didn't know if she was actually still saying the words. On Yom Kippur, at nightfall, the congregation said it seven times. But it was the men who kept count, the men whose duty was the precise letter of the law.

They were women, they could be free, free to forget the count, to become one with the words.

"THE LORD IS GOD."

This time, Sari was sure, someone did say the words. She opened her eyes and saw the joyful face of her sister.

Sari struggled to free her arms and raise them over her head. Martha did the same, and there, over the head of Vera, their hands touched and held.

God blessed me, thought Sari, and honored me.

The door of the gas chamber was shut and sealed. The bolts were slammed into place, the iron screws turned until they stopped.

A floor above them, the guards and the supervising physician donned gas masks. They dropped the cartridge of Zyklon B into the chute.

An invisible cloud of poison rose in the chamber, searing noses and mouths and tracheas and lungs. Even the most faithful stopped their prayers and screamed in pain, but it took less than half an hour until all the screaming had stopped.

Yet Sari didn't scream, she never felt the pain. By the time the gas wafted up to where she was locked with her sister, she was already dead. Her heart had burst with pride.

CHAPTER THIRTY-THREE

Dr. Adler realized with a start that the woman he was working on had been one of his patients *before*. This stack of bodies was from Janace.

His heart beat hard. Not fast—his whole metabolism had slowed as an adjustment to the severe restriction in calories—but hard. None of his relatives were here, he assured himself. Certainly his wife wasn't here. She would have gotten out with the boy. She was probably in Budapest right now, sitting in a cafe, eating pureed chestnuts with rum sauce and whipped cream.

He couldn't think very clearly any more. He was too hungry. When had he last seen his family? Months ago. It was hard to tell exactly. There was the conscription and the march and labor camps and more marches. Then they found out he was a dentist and sent him to Auschwitz.

Must keep mind on job. His job wasn't dentistry any more. He held a big set of pliers and pulled out a gold crown from the head of...old Mrs. Halter, it looked like. The witch woman. Well, no more spells, or even prayers here. This was Auschwitz.

He put the tooth in a vat of muriatic acid, which ate away the scraps of muscle tissue and bone that clung to the crown. Finally, he gouged the anus and the vagina of the body for hidden jewels.

The next corpse seemed familiar, although he couldn't quite identify it. Not that he himself could be identified. Adler's hair, which had been red, had turned pure white on the first march. Afterwards, when they shaved his head, the hair didn't grow back, so it looked as if he had a white film over his freckled pate. He hadn't shaved since he'd left Janace, yet there was barely a five-o'clock shadow on his chin. The starving body doesn't waste itself on non-vital functions.

The next cadaver was just a little girl. No earrings, certainly no ring, and he doubted that she would have any gold teeth. Why were the Muselmanns, the Jews who cleared the gas chambers, wasting his time?

The girl was warm to the touch.

Not so unusual, he reminded himself. Most of the bodies were still warm, unless there was a backlog. He pried her mouth with his left hand, the pliers ready in his right.

On his fingers, he felt a breath.

He dropped the head and looked around quickly. Dentists were valuable, but if he was going crazy, they'd bundle him right off to the crematoria.

The girl's eyes fluttered. It wasn't craziness this time.

"Guard!" he called out. "My lord guard."

The guard was right there. No place in the camp was better policed. Not that any Jewish dentist would dare to steal gold. The guards were present to watch each other, to keep a limit on the theft. Berlin demanded at least five thousand pounds of valuables per month from Auschwitz.

Finally, thought the guard, diamonds. Or maybe American dollars rolled tight and stuffed into the kid's asshole. It was about time he made some profit off this job.

He tried to move nonchalantly towards the dentist and his prize. But as he approached, he cried out in amazement, catching everyone's attention.

The corpse had opened its eyes and stared right at him. The pupils contracted in the light, so he could see these huge blue things glaring at him.

The guard came from a secluded village in a part of Europe awash in tales of werewolves and the living dead.

"A vampire!" he wailed.

The others snickered. But when they approached and saw what he had seen, they crossed themselves fervently.

Finally, their divisional commander was summoned. He inspected the girl from a safe distance. Still, he was not satisfied that she was, indeed, alive.

She coughed. He jumped back.

"Who brought this body in?" he asked gruffly, trying to hide his momentary lapse.

"That one, sir," said the dentist instantly, pointing to the Muselmann.

What little color there was, drained from the prisoner's face. He snatched the cap off his head, stepped forward smartly, and pronounced his number.

"And you got her where, off a train?"

"No sir, begging pardon, sir. From Gas Chamber #2, like the rest of this batch."

"Impossible. No one has ever survived a gassing. Tell the truth, dog, or it's the standing cell for you."

The Muselmann began to weep helplessly. No one survived the standing cell. No one survived it sane.

"No sir. He's telling the truth."

Everyone gasped at the rasping sound of the voice. The guards who had dispersed gathered round again.

She gained a little strength. "My mother and aunt—they're both tall—embraced on top of me. I guess they made a little tent. That's the last thing I remember."

"All right!" shouted the commander with unconvincing assurance, "I've decided what to do. Muselmann! Take her to the office of the Camp Commandant!"

Just get her out of here, he thought. Maybe she *was* a vampire.

As light as Vera was, the Muselmann was too weak to carry her in his arms, so he hoisted her on his back, and, bent over double, he carried her to the headquarters of Rudolf Franz Ferdinand Hoss, the commander-in-chief of Auschwitz.

There was a cluster of German officers waiting with Hoss. The Muselmann laid Vera down on the polished top of the Commandant's desk, as instructed.

"Amazing."

"Incredible."

One of the officers was a doctor. He placed a stethoscope on Vera's chest and listened intently. The others stood in silent respect.

"Slight damage to the lungs. But very slight. And it might be the result of previous injury, or a lingering illness. Altogether good condition, though."

Commandant Hoss stroked Vera's shorn head tenderly and caressed her cheek.

He loved children. And animals and plants and nature in general. The Commandant had a large family and they were housed right there in Auschwitz in a charming little cottage. The house was surrounded by gorgeous flower gardens and its grounds included a small petting zoo for the children. Inmates assigned to the Commandant's children and home took excellent care of everything. Only once he'd had to "send away" a worker who had eaten the animals' food.

Rudolf Hoss considered himself a sensitive man. He appreciated the beauty of the child, her fine-textured skin and delicate features. He admired her resilience. No one had ever before survived gassing.

There was no hint of lust in his adoration of the lovely girl. She might have been one of his own daughters. She was just at the very cusp of adolescence, her breasts beginning to bud, the nipples rosy as her cupid's-bow mouth. The faintest, blondest swansdown had begun to grow between her legs.

In respect to the child's modesty, and to shield her from the cold, Hoss took one of his own blankets and wrapped it around her. Very gently, the camp commandant lifted Vera from the table and cradled her in his arms. She was as light as eiderdown.

Vera nestled against Hoss' warm uniform and was soon asleep. Her breaths whistled slightly, just like his own children's when they slept. How he loved that sound, the music of innocence.

He carried her across the camp, officers following him as if in a religious procession. They came to the building, the familiar building, and the Muselmann slipped away, taking the opportunity to go back to his job before anyone would notice him.

Rudolf Hoss unwrapped the blanket very gently, so as not to awaken the sleeping girl. Tenderly, he kissed her forehead.

And then he put her into the oven and latched the door.

CHAPTER THIRTY-FOUR

Janace

Joseph recoiled into the shadow of the doorway.

He'd always pictured the Mayor as fearsome, spouting the poison of the Anti-Semitic League from the heights of Janace's city hall. In reality he was short and slight.

Exhausted as he was, Joseph realized he was much stronger than the old man. Why, he could put his hands around the little Mayor's neck and...

What was he thinking? Was he really planning to murder an innocent man? Was he turning into one of *them*?

The Mayor put a finger to his lips and opened the door quickly. He waved Joseph in.

"Lie down."

Joseph dropped to the floor. The Mayor double-shuttered the windows and turned on the light.

"All right, then. No one can see in now."

Joseph put his hand to his mouth.

"Nothing to worry about. I always talk to myself," he chuckled. "Loud too."

He looked Joseph over. "So you're a Jew."

Joseph nodded carefully. Whom could he fool, with the star still on his jacket?

"You were on that train this morning?"

Joseph nodded again. He wanted to cry.

"You must be hungry. I'm just about to have supper myself."

The Mayor busied himself with pots and plates.

Joseph lay low, watching. He remembered the day of the inauguration of the New Bridge when the Mayor had slapped the face of the Jewish community. The Mayor had declared himself an enemy of the Jews. But when election time came around, he was re-elected in a landslide that included the Jewish vote. He was a scrupulously honest administrator, and, as a bachelor with no family, he kept Janace free of nepotism.

Long after retirement age, the Mayor kept getting re-elected and would have been in office still, had he not quit in disgust when Monsignor Tiso's corrupt goons took power. The man, despite his antipathy to Jews, was not without decency.

Joseph looked around the simple, one-room house. It was clean, and as comfortable as a house could be that had never known a woman's touch.

The old man called Joseph to the table. Joseph mouthed the blessing on a plate of boiled potatoes.

"So you're one of the religious ones. Don't mind if I eat all the meat, do you?"

"What? Eat in good health, Mr. Mayor."

Joseph ate the potatoes with a bowl of sour cream. It was the most delicious dish he had ever tasted. If only he could share it with Sari. Tears flowed down his face.

After the meal the Mayor said, "You're welcome to stay here as long as you need to, until the Slovaks overthrow that red-sashed bandit.

"Now about that train. What about the others? Did anyone else manage…"

Joseph closed his eyes and shook his head slowly.

"Are you sure? We can go out there in the morning..."

"No." The truth bubbled up out of Joseph. "They are all dead. Everyone, men, women, children."

"Jesus Christ."

Joseph wanted to say, *exactly*. Look at what Christianity had done to Europe.

The Mayor fixed up a cozy little corner with bedding. Joseph blinked. Would the man go out for "a little visit" and turn him over to the Nazis for a few crowns—or just the pleasure of it? But the old man got into pajamas and settled by the stove with a book and a pipe.

"Mr. Mayor, sir" Joseph ventured.

"Yes?"

"Why are you doing this?"

"Doing what?"

"Saving my life."

The Mayor snorted. "For heaven's sake, Wassermann. Any minimally human being would do the same."

"But you always said you were an anti-Semite."

"I am," said the Mayor defiantly.

"But..."

"I was always against the Jews in this town. They took over everything. Everything good in Janace, the Jews had to have a hand in. It was an outrage. You wanted to buy a suit? You had to go to a Jewish store. You needed a doctor or a lawyer or a dentist? You had to go to a Jew—at least if you wanted a decent one. It wasn't right!"

"But it's not as if..."

"What was left for us Slovaks? Practically nothing. Why didn't you Jews go to your own country? Why did you have to take charge of everything of ours?"

The Mayor took a furious puff of his pipe. "So of course I'm an anti-Semite." He puffed again, peering at Joseph through the smoke. "But this, what the Germans are doing, this..." He searched for the right words, but there weren't any. "This, this...is not...human."

The Mayor kept to his daily schedule, his walks, his meetings with old cronies at the cafe, his shopping. He increased his purchases of food very gradually. No one suspected a thing.

In the evenings he brought home newspapers. They were slanted propaganda sheets, but you could read between the lines. The Mayor also had a small library of classic books, particularly about government. Translations of the Federalist Papers, the speeches of Lincoln, the writings of the English suffragists. Oh, how Sari would have loved those!

Weeks passed. Joseph learned to sleep through the night. He confessed to himself that, not only had the Mayor saved his life, he was very congenial company.

To avoid suspicion, Joseph and the Mayor regulated the flushing of the toilet. One day Joseph notice blood in the commode.

"Mr. Mayor, you must consult a doctor."

"Bah, the only doctors left in town are quacks."

"No, no. There's Dr. Kemeny. He's excellent. The grand rabbi used to consult with him."

The Mayor raised an eyebrow. "Your rabbi went to a Gentile doctor?"

"Our law says to go to the best doctor, whatever his religion."

On the day of the appointment, Joseph fidgeted. He could not concentrate on reading. He wished he could have gone along with the Mayor. It wasn't good to visit the doctor by yourself. He and Sari had always accompanied each other.

As soon as the Mayor came in, Joseph could tell the news was bad.

"It's cancer."

Joseph gasped, not only because of the diagnosis but because the Mayor had said the word out loud. Everyone he knew referred to the disease by euphemism.

"Did Kemeny recommend treatment?"

"He's scheduled me for surgery next week."

"Then he has hopes for a cure."

"He can hope all he wants. I'm not coming back from that hospital."

"Don't say that, Mr. Mayor. God will be merciful to a just man like yourself."

The Mayor laughed. "You're quite a Jew, Wassermann. But you'd better grab whatever help your God is offering for yourself and your own people."

"His power and goodness are infinite. He can save all the Jews and all the Gentiles too, with no extra trouble," Joseph said earnestly.

The Mayor waved his hand. "Well, he needn't waste any on me. I've led a good life, and for long enough. I'm ready to go. Heaven, hell, oblivion—it doesn't matter. I'm ready. But we need to figure out where you will go."

The Mayor carefully sounded out his friends but knew Joseph would be safe with none of them.

"I'm afraid you'll have to leave town. Maybe one of your farmers..."

"No. I've already exhausted their kindness. They—some of them—gave me food. But they won't do more."

"There is no place for you anywhere," said the Mayor, ashamed.

"I have kinfolk—a sister-in-law and her husband—in Hungary. But there is no way to get there."

"Listen, Joseph. In the bottom kitchen drawer is some money. My savings. You are welcome to all of it. I won't be needing it."

"But what if you..."

"No. Come on, wrap up this cheese too. There's a night train to Budapest. We'll get you on it."

They walked together on the streets. Joseph had his collar pulled up and his hat pulled down over his eyes. The Mayor diverted attention by cheerfully returning the greetings of those they passed as they strolled.

At the train station the ticket seller asked, "One way, Mr. Mayor?"

He smiled sardonically. "My round-trip days are over."

On the platform the Mayor handed Joseph the ticket and another document. "Here, take this, too. I won't be needing it."

It was his identity card/ passport. A special one for senior public servants. Unfortunately, the photograph and description in no way portrayed Joseph. But it was better than nothing.

The Mayor extended his hand in farewell. Joseph said, "Thank you, thank you, Mr. Mayor. May God repay my debt to you."

"Goodbye," the Mayor said simply, "Goodbye, my friend."

The train was a local that made stops in many anonymous villages and would arrive in Budapest before daybreak. It was mostly empty and Joseph had a choice of compartments all to himself.

He examined the passport. It was quite hopeless. He took out the money that the Mayor had given him. It was not much of a nest egg for someone who had spent a lifetime serving the public. But at least it was hard cash, not Slovak money. He put the bills in his breast pocket, and the change in his pants.

A large family of Gypsies boarded the train and came directly to his compartment. Joseph was annoyed. Why did they have to come to this compartment, there was plenty of room elsewhere. To steal from him? He placed a hand on the breast of his jacket above the pocket with the money.

No. How terrible to assume they would steal just because they were Gypsies.

The father opened a bag and distributed food to the children. They ate with gusto, and threw trash on the floor. The children laughed a lot. Joseph couldn't help laughing with them, although he didn't understand their language, and suspected they were making fun of him.

Joseph remembered that it was Friday night. The Gypsy family reminded him of the nephews and nieces who gathered at the Sabbath table. He wondered if he would ever bless the wine again.

At every stop the conductor came into the compartment and demanded to see the Gypsies' tickets, but never Joseph's. Once the conductor said that the tickets were "wrong," and they would have to get off. The father looked dejected. He couldn't read. Joseph took the tickets and assured him that they were indeed for the city of Miskolc. "Oh, Miskolc," the conductor replied disingenuously, "I thought he said Budapest."

Why did the Christians hate the Gypsies? They were content with the very bottom rung of society. Yet the Jews, who were ambitious, were even more hated.

There were rumors that the Germans were picking up Gypsies and deporting them. But it wasn't like the Jews. The Nazis only went after Gypsies who lived in nomadic caravans. Those with permanent homes, jobs, and money—like this family, with the means to buy so many tickets—were safe.

The train halted at the border between Slovakia and Hungary. A young Hungarian official boarded, his strut and haircut showing him a fascist. His mouth curling at the sight of the Gypsy family, and he demanded passports. Ignoring the papers offered by the father, he took Joseph's document.

Suddenly the core of a green pepper flew through the air and landed against the official's starched shirt. He dropped the passport and fell upon one of the older boys. All the children jumped to the aid of their brother, flailing the Hungarian with their dirty fists.

It took a while for the official to free himself. He cursed the Gypsies with profanity so blue that Joseph's ears stung.

"Oh," he said to Joseph, "begging your pardon, sir," as if there was no woman in the compartment. "Be careful, mister, they steal like the devil."

"Our Lord gave us the right to steal," the Gypsy father said. "They were supposed to hit another nail into him, in the groin, but a Gypsy stole the nail, so now we can steal whatever we want."

Sure, thought Joseph, the Christians will fall for that. We gave Jesus *life*. See how grateful they are.

The official demanded the family's passports, muttering as he inspected them carefully. When he was done, he noticed Joseph's still on the floor.

He kicked one of the boys. "You! Pick that up and give it to the gentleman."

The boy did, and the Hungarian left.

Joseph looked up at the Gypsy father sitting across from him. The man grinned broadly, showing a mouthful of teeth rotten down to the gums.

It was still dark when the train reached Budapest. The train station roiled between the night world of clandestine commerce and the opening of the legitimate shops. Joseph didn't want to risk trading on the black market, though the rate was likely to be better. He waited until the official moneychangers opened to exchange his bills.

Joseph waited patiently on line. He reached into his jacket pocket. There was nothing in it.

He must be mistaken. Fighting to keep calm, he checked the pocket on the other side. Empty. The mist of sweat on his body turned to streaming rivulets as he checked every pocket in his suit, then rechecked them. The only one with anything in it was the right one in his pants. It contained nothing but the coins.

All day he wandered, sick and dazed. But the train station was a busy hub so he did not stand out. Toward evening the crowds began to thin. He was getting suspicious glances now. If only he knew where to go. But he'd only been to Budapest a few times in his life and didn't know the way to the Jewish neighborhoods.

Even if he did, he would endanger anyone who took him in. Even if he could find Kitty and Sender, he'd be nothing but a burden to them! He would rather die.

Night came. The last train left the station. A cleaning woman gave him a dirty look, until he rose from the bench he'd been sitting on, weak with fear and hunger.

He shuffled to the information booth and read and re-read the timetables. There was just enough money in his pocket to buy a ticket good for a single stop on the local. It would get him only to a suburb of Budapest.

The next one would be leaving in the morning. At least he had an excuse to spend the night at the station. He squeezed his eyes shut to stop the tears from forming. What good did time do? Buy him a few more hours of desperation?

Stop it. Joseph reminded himself of the Yiddish saying, "an hour of life can be a lifetime." Hadn't God been merciful to him all his years? Hadn't the Almighty performed miracles for his lowly and unworthy servant? He would keep it up, for sure.

Joseph sat on another bench, drifting between troubled sleep and wide-eyed anxiety. He was acutely aware of how strange he looked, unshaved, unshorn, and, alone among the travelers, without baggage.

Well past midnight two policemen began an inspection of the train station. They went about rousting sleeping Gypsies with blows and kicks, and making long, careful examinations of everyone's papers.

Joseph was suddenly alert. He had better make a run for it! The cops wouldn't want to cause a panic by shooting in the middle of the station. He would take his chances and make a break for the nearest exit.

But when he tried to get up, Joseph found that his feet were frozen to the floor, his thighs plastered to the bench. He could not move so much as an eyelash. He tried but he was as paralyzed as if he'd suffered a stroke.

The policemen were ten feet away. Five. Now they were staring him in the face.

And they moved on.

Joseph stayed in the same position all night long. Only when dawn broke and the train rolled in, did he get up to go to the men's room. He washed his face and looked at himself in the mirror. Dear God! He might as well wear a placard reading "Jew."

The train was old, and it ran a line so quaint that there was only one class designation for seating. Few passengers boarded.

Joseph shuffled from car to car until he passed two empty ones. In the third vacant car, he took a window seat. Outside the window, a station clock indicated that they were forty-five minutes from scheduled departure. His stomach turned. Forty-five minutes, then another ten. And then what?

It was morning, he would do what he did every morning, say his prayers. Because he was all alone, he allowed himself the luxury of moving his lips.

"Whether asleep or awake, I leave my soul in his hands. And, as with my soul, so with my body. God is with me, I shall not fear..."

He was beginning to feel a little better, but as the morning service went on, the sour taste of hypocrisy flavored the words.

"Blessed are you, O Lord, our God, King of the Universe, who gave the rooster the knowledge to distinguish day from night." But what good does morning bring for a Jew? Doesn't he suffer equally, day or night?

The second blessing was even worse. Bile filled his mouth as he said, "Blessed are you, O Lord, our God, King of the Universe, who has not made me a Gentile."

The door to the car opened. A Catholic priest entered, bearing two heavy, expensive-looking bags. Behind him came a porter, overburdened with three suitcases.

"Over here," the priest told the porter. "This car will do."

Why me? A whole empty train, why does he have to choose this car?

The porter stored the baggage overhead and the priest tipped him. "Oh, Father, thank you. Thanks so much. You needn't have..."

"That's all right..." The priest spoke in an undertone.

231

After the porter left, the priest stood hesitating in the aisle, then pointed at the seat next to Joseph. "Excuse me, is this seat taken?"

Joseph shook his head, not daring to speak. What did this man suspect? Please God, don't put me in the hands of an anti-Semitic priest! In Czechoslovakia there had been some who outdid the Germans at Jew-hating.

The priest sat down, smoothing his cassock. He looked sadly down into his lap.

Joseph tried to clear his mind of panic. Where was he? Oh, yes. "Blessed...who has not made me a Gentile." He almost laughed out loud at the irony. The priest was young, good-looking, and blooming with health. He was fair-haired, and his complexion was rosy from the morning's fresh shave. He was as tall as Joseph, and the cassock fell handsomely from his broad shoulders.

Joseph resumed his prayers, keeping his lips still. "Blessed are you...who has not made me a slave." A slave? Hah! It must be paradise to be a slave! A slave was valued for his labor. A master wouldn't let a hard-working slave die.

"Going far?" asked the priest.

Now Joseph had to answer, but he covered his mouth with his hand. He knew his breath stank with the night—and with dread. He stated the name of the suburb.

"Ah," said the priest, "a wonderful, wonderful place. Such charming architecture. And so close to town." His voice dropped. "I'm going to Kisvar. You've probably never heard of it. Nobody has. No one ever will. It's as far as you can go and still be in Hungary." His voice dropped even lower. "It might as well be off the edge of the earth."

Joseph resumed praying. A sound from the priest interrupted his thoughts. He moved his head the slightest bit, so as not to seem obtrusive, or even curious.

The priest was crying!

It was a terrible thing to see such a youthful, handsome face marred by tears.

"Don't do that, mister, uh, Father. At your age, nothing can be that bad."

"Oh, yes it can," sobbed the priest. "It's so bad, I think I...I may end it all."

"You mustn't say such a thing. What you're thinking of is the greatest sin before God." He was pretty sure the Christians thought so too.

"Don't talk to me of God. It's all his fault!"

"'God created all the cures before he created the diseases,'" said

Joseph, before realizing that this was a Hebrew saying. He hoped the priest wasn't too educated.

"What is his cure for a broken heart?"

"A forbidden woman. Ah, they are a snare."

"Jolie's no snare. She's the kindest, sweetest, most beautiful girl in the world." His voice got hard. "It's all my parents' fault. I never did want to be a priest. But, you know, being a third son...

"Jolie and I were childhood friends. When I entered the seminary, I thought I would forget all about her. But last year, I was posted to our old parish—my parents' doing—and, well...

"We love each other. Our love is pure, holy. But they don't understand that. I mean my parents do, but the bishop doesn't understand. He's exiled me to this Kisvar. He's insured I will never see my beloved again."

The priest grabbed Joseph by the lapels. "Our love is clean, I tell you. All we want in the world is to marry and raise a family. Is that such a terrible thing?"

"No," said Joseph, "it is not a terrible thing. It's the best thing in the world."

"It's the only thing. If I can't have it, if I can't have Jolie, life is not worth living."

They sat in silence, but not for too long. There was no time to lose. "This will sound crazy," said Joseph, "but I have an idea."

By the time the train pulled out of the station, the former mayor of Janace, Slovakia—Catholic and a bachelor, according to his documents—stood clutching his ticket, ready to leave the train at the next stop. He was so handsome that he made the old jacket and cap he wore look dashing instead of shabby.

"Father Istvan Szep," sat by the window, preparing for a very long journey.

"Aren't you frightened, young man? Your papers say you are sixty years old."

Istvan brushed the thought away as if it were a fly. "My parents will get that fixed soon enough. And then, maybe we'll go abroad to get married, lay low for a while.

"But what about you, sir? Are you really ready to be a priest? Do you want money for doing this?"

"No, no. I am happy to help young lovers. But I don't know what a priest does. I...I've never even been inside a church."

"That's no problem," said Istvan, with the insouciance of youth.

"The black suitcase is full of books. You'll find all the information you'll need. Besides, the folks in Kisvar are not exactly on top of the latest directives from the Vatican."

The train stopped briefly, and Istvan jumped from the top step, running jubilantly to a taxi stand. Joseph watched him recede, as the train moved away. He gathered the black robes around him and continued with the morning service.

"Blessed are you, O God...who gives sight to the blind...who gives strength to the weary."

CHAPTER THIRTY-FIVE

Budapest

The evening before Kitty's release from jail the "girls" threw a going-away party. There was wine, beer, and cake, courtesy of the men outside. Her fellow prisoners presented Julia with a new suitcase filled with stockings, lingerie, and costume jewelry.

The official time of release was noon but Kitty was up and dressed well before dawn. She was very anxious. Where had Sender been arrested? At work? At Mordecai Fried's? Or at their apartment? If the latter, was it safe for her to go back there, or had the landlord discovered her real identity?

Even if no one knew of her, would the apartment still be vacant, or had the owner rented it out to someone else? Would the key still be under the mat?

But no matter what, freedom was a good thing. Freedom meant she could start working at finding Sender and bringing him back.

One of the guards opened the cell door. "Hey Julia, how about cleaning the captain's office one last time?"

Kitty was already dressed in high heels and hat and was about to refuse. But then she thought, nothing is coincidence; all is God's will.

"Sure thing, handsome."

There was nothing much to be found in the office. The captain's desk was clean, and she had been through all the files. But in the wastepaper basket she found something interesting—a used piece of carbon paper. Kitty held it up against the light. She couldn't see anything. She turned the carbon over. She had to read backwards, but at least she could make out words.

Reported Rats' Nests: Foreign Jews.

The carbon listed no names, only addresses. The middle of the page, where the carbon paper had been reused was blurred. But she could make out two addresses at the top, and six at the bottom.

There was no time to look for the originals in the files, and she didn't dare try to take the carbon with her. Memorize, memorize. It was so hard with the words and numbers backwards. But Joseph had taught her tricks, that last year in high school.

Kitty was released an hour early, with friendly farewells from the staff. She walked casually down the block, until the policemen were out of sight. Then she ran.

It took fifteen minute to reach the first address. The targeted apartment was all too obvious. A stream of debris led to an open door. Shreds of clothing, a child's shoe, a slice of bread that had been trod into the ground. Out of the door came a teenage girl with two light bulbs in her hands. "You're too late," she told Kitty. "Everything is gone."

The second address on the list was in Buda, on the other side of the Danube. It would be foolish to waste precious time traveling. Mentally, Kitty went down the sheet of carbon paper. The next address was only two blocks from Mrs. Gordon's house. Dare she risk it? There was no choice. If Jews didn't help one another, who would?

She was pained to find that it was the meat store where Mrs. Gordon shopped. The butcher had hidden a family in the storage area. A mob had gathered. Kitty could see the thugs of the Arrow Cross shoving people and tearing at pieces of meat.

A woman near Kitty said "Poor things. I used to shop there, when I had the money. The Jewish meat is expensive, but so clean and fresh. I heard the family were relatives of hers, the butcher's wife."

Another woman snorted. "Relatives! They're all related, the Jews. Aren't all vermin kin? I say get rid of the lot of them, the sooner the better."

Kitty walked away. She'd head for the last address on the list. Maybe the police and their fascist friends hadn't gotten there yet.

When Kitty got to that apartment there was a sign on the mailbox, "For Rent." She sighed heavily and put down her suitcase. She was tired and her feet were killing her. The shoes she had asked a pimp to buy for her fit better than the ones she'd taken off the dead girl, but they were still whore's shoes.

A woman came out of the adjoining apartment. She looked Kitty up and down with distaste. "Sorry, miss, I don't think this would be the right apartment for you. Besides, the previous tenants might come back. Lovely people. Don't know why they had to leave in such a rush.

Probably an illness in the family. They were from Prague. Very refined. Lovely, lovely people."

The next-to-last address on the list was not too far away, also in the same tony neighborhood. There was both a knocker and a bell on the door. Kitty tried one and then the other, but no one answered. She paused. Not a sound came from the place but Kitty had the distinct feeling that the flat was occupied.

She tried again. Still no answer. The apartment was on the ground floor. She walked around the building, through a small garden. A window was open and a gentle breeze blew an organdy curtain through it.

Somehow she knew, she absolutely *knew* that there were Jews in the apartment. But how to get them out?

Kitty whistled a tune. It was a lively melody, a lot like a drinking song, but in fact it had been a popular religious hymn just a few years ago. Kitty's lips quivered as she whistled. To think there was a time when Jews did things like write songs.

"Light is cast before the righteous,

And joy for the good-of-heart."

The song continued in Yiddish. "Come in come in, Little Consolation,

Come in come in, little Jewish soul."

The song referred to coming in instead of going out, which is what she wanted the people in the apartment to do.

Kitty waited. Well, she couldn't spend any more time here. She'd done her best, and now it was getting dangerous for her to be loitering.

Suddenly a woman emerged. She was about Sari's age and with Sari's bearing, only shorter. She even dressed like Sari. Her gray skirt and white blouse were impeccably clean. Simple as the outfit was, Kitty's expert eye saw it was expensive.

The woman looked at Kitty, and Kitty at the woman, and they both knew that the other was a Jew, a Slovak Jew.

"You've got to leave," Kitty whispered in the woman's ear.

"Today?"

"Right now. This minute. The evil ones are already on their way."

"Please, wait here. Don't leave us."

"Us?"

"My son and daughter."

"Hurry! There's no time to pack anything."

In a minute the woman had emerged with her two children, both in their late teens. Everyone was wearing overcoats and both women

237

carried large handbags, nothing else.

"Here," said Kitty, handing the girl her suitcase. "The two of you keep a bit of distance behind me and your brother."

Kitty took the boy's arm and cozied up to him with more familiarity than was proper, leading him purposefully forward. He blushed, looking like a young man who'd hired a streetwalker for the first time. That was what she hoped.

They had not gone more than a few yards toward the tram stop when they met a troop of Arrow Cross marching down the middle of the street

The fascist hoodlums were already quite drunk, singing obscene and anti-Semitic songs at the top of their lungs. Kitty froze and she felt the young man freeze. But their legs kept going in unison, their lower bodies working on an independent muscle system.

"Hey, comrade!" one of the Arrow Cross thugs called to Kitty's companion, "come join us. We've got us a bunch of Jews to flush out. Rich Jews! Loot enough for everyone. Come fight for Hungary's glory!"

"Never mind that, can't you see he's got plenty of glory right there."

"I'll say. Bet the flagpole is sticking right up already!"

The whole troop guffawed, breaking rank. Some lurched to the side, fighting the urge to vomit.

Kitty and the boy kept going. They did not dare look back.

They boarded the tram heading towards Kitty's apartment. The mother and daughter boarded too, but neither pair acknowledged the other.

Kitty wondered if she was endangering herself, bringing these strangers to her own safe haven. Or was she endangering them, leading them out of the frying pan of their old hideaway into the fire of a trap set for her?

Kitty rose at her stop, pulling the boy up with her. Mother and daughter followed wordlessly. Finally, they reached the apartment. Kitty entered the inner courtyard.

She faced the older woman. "Look up there," she said under her breath, "that's my place. If I open the window it's safe to come up. If anyone asks what you're doing here, tell them you're selling door-to-door. The stuff in my suitcase is mostly new." She took the boy's arm again.

"Wait," said the mother, "you can't take my son. God knows what's waiting up there. Besides, how do we know you aren't springing a trap."

Kitty's jaw clenched. She had a religious obligation to save the woman's life, but no obligation to coddle an ingrate.

"Fine. I'll take my suitcase now, since you feel it's rigged. It's true that there might be a trap up there, but I'll take my chances. Chances are all I have right now, and I was willing to share them with you. But if you don't want to, you're welcome to stay down here until the Americans arrive."

"No, I'm sorry. I didn't mean that, the stress..."

"This is no place for conversation," said Kitty. She turned to the boy. "Coming?"

"Yes, I am."

She liked his confident tone of voice, so different from his mother's.

They went up carefully. The key was under the mat. She opened the door slowly. It creaked.

The boy motioned her to stay outside, while he gallantly went in. He came out a minute later.

"It's fine. There's no one in there."

Kitty entered. It was musty, having been locked up for months, but everything was in order. The apartment had not been raided.

Kitty relaxed. How the apartment reminded her of Sender! She bent over a mattress and picked up his pillow. His delicious scent was still embedded in it. She remembered those long-ago mornings when Sender rose early for morning prayers, and she would turn over onto his perfumed bedding and luxuriate in sleep a little longer.

She buried her head in the pillow and wept until the pillowcase was soggy.

"Miss," said the boy. "Miss?"

Kitty picked up her head.

"Can I open the window now, for my mother and sister?"

"Oh, I'm sorry." She ran there herself, and opened it wide.

Their name was Solomon—the mother was Hannah, the children, Edward and Rose—and Kitty had heard of them before. The family had owned a brewery in Hummene, a town near Janace. Experts said it was the equal of any brew in the nation. The family was famous, besides, for philanthropy. The Solomon name, along with scales of justice, formed the brewery logo. It was emblazoned on synagogues, Torah mantles, and ritual bathhouses throughout the region.

Long before the troubles began, Hannah's husband had taken a trustworthy and talented Gentile into the business. When the anti-Semitic edicts went into effect, the brewery passed to the non-Jewish partner, and operations continued seamlessly. The family enterprise remained safely insulated from major damage.

Mr. Solomon had been prescient about many things. He had seen to it that master artists forged identity papers for each of them. This was long before the documents had become a life-and-death issue for which thousands scrambled hysterically, before forgers exhausted their talents on their own escapes.

Hannah handed Kitty the papers. They were excellent facsimiles, as far as Kitty could tell, but there was a problem. The documents were Slovak, not Hungarian. If the documents were checked, they would be deported, even as Gentiles. And the fact that someone had informed on them to the police was proof that they had already been found out.

"You'd have been better off staying home," said Kitty, wringing her hands.

"God forbid," whispered Edward.

"But your papers would have passed muster there."

"You don't understand, Miss Ficsorcsak," said Rose "there are no Jews left in Eastern Slovakia."

Kitty wondered why the mother didn't contradict this silly girl. Of course there were Jews left there. Even with the most horrible pogroms, how could you eliminate so many people? Why, Jews made up more than half of Janace, large proportions of the surrounding towns, at least twenty percent of the city of Kosice. They couldn't be eliminated. The whole country would grind to a halt.

Her own family had always managed, even in the toughest times. And the Halters, the Wassermann clan, all those tough, resilient people, they couldn't have vanished into thin air.

What about the rich people, the politically connected, the journalists and newspaper editors. What an uproar there would be if they left the cities and towns.

Oppression, yes. Terror and fear and impoverishment and misery, yes. But to *completely disappear?*

Kitty frowned at the mother.

"What happened to your friend who ran the brewery for you?" asked Kitty. "Couldn't he take care of you?"

The three Solomons sighed.

"He is a good man," Hannah said. "What happened was not his fault."

"It was the Germans," said Rose. "They took it away from our partner. They paid him a pittance and took the brewery away from him."

"Only a German can make beer, you see," said Edward. "Not Slovaks, not Hungarians—to say nothing of Jews. Only a German can make..."

"Piss," said Mrs. Solomon, unabashed. "They produced piss, undiluted urine, under the Libra name." Tears welled in her eyes. "My husband's family had made Libra for five generations. Edward was to be the sixth. And they...those barbarians...dared to change it! All those years—centuries—of building up our good name ruined. Ruined."

"And your husband?"

"He was called to the police station..." said Mrs. Solomon. There was no need to elaborate.

An odd woman, thought Kitty. She was more upset about the loss of the beer's reputation than the loss of her husband.

But she mustn't judge the Solomons. She must love and protect all Jews with the single-minded ferocity with which the Nazis hated and killed them.

For several days Kitty and the Solomons canvassed the building and the neighborhood. They were lucky. The apartments in the house were either empty or rented by shady individuals eager to keep to themselves.

They busied themselves cleaning, shopping, and cooking. The Solomons had been in hiding for a long time and had developed many little games to keep themselves quietly amused.

But Kitty was paralyzed with frustration and fear. There was nothing she could do for Sender or her sisters.

"I think we should go out for a bit," Hannah said.

"We were already out today," Kitty answered lethargically, "for onions."

"No, not to shop. Just for a bit of fresh air."

It was risky but Kitty felt better just getting out. Her spirits rose again as soon as they stepped outside. They strolled along in silence but companionably, arm in arm, as if they were mother and daughter. Or sisters.

Kitty stopped, her face brightening. "I've got an idea. Let's go to a cafe."

Mrs. Solomon looked skeptical. "A cafe? What cafe?"

Kitty beamed. Sender would be so proud of her. "Why, the best cafe in Budapest, of course."

No violinist circulated in mid-day, but otherwise the cafe was as festive as it was at night. Ladies' laughter tinkled like the chandeliers overhead. Gentleman blew circles of cigar smoke. Clouds of whipped cream hovered over every cup and platter.

The cafe was a preserved tableau of ancient empire. Age had

burnished the Art Nouveau fixtures and lent a rich patina to the marble tile floors. Kitty and Hannah floated in like two aristocratic ladies entering a ballroom in belle époque Vienna. They were a bit down at the heels, but, in these hard times, hardly the shabbiest women in the room.

They were seated, at their request, in the farthest corner of the cafe. A waiter handed them leather-bound, gilt-edged menus.

"Oh my," said Mrs. Solomon, "the prices are so dear." She leaned conspiratorially towards Kitty, as if she were about to speak in Yiddish. "We—the children and I—don't have any money, I'm afraid."

Kitty pretended fascination with her menu. The apartment from which she had brought the Solomons must have rented for ten times the one in the red-light district. And the two large bags that Hannah and Rose had carried were as heavy as if they were filled with iron. She'd bet wise Mr. Solomon had made financial provisions for his family's future.

"That's all right. It's my treat."

They ate in silence, all the better to savor every bite of luscious, cream-oozing torte, every sip of sweet, cinnamon-dusted coffee. Finally, they had to rise from their satin-upholstered chairs, had to push aside the three layers of lace tablecloth, had to return to a more modern and infinitely crueler world.

As they walked past the cloakroom Kitty noticed a small board pinned with discreet little notices. Most were requests for employment, but there were a few help-wanted ads as well.

She looked longingly at the notices. How she would love to work again. But she couldn't risk the exposure of a shop, she hadn't the skills to work in an office, and she was not about to be a domestic again.

Then, a card with ornate, old-fashioned script caught Kitty's eye.

Required: Progressive young lady of intelligence and culture, as companion to a disabled gentlewoman.

The address given for inquiries was on the most soignée of Budapest's sumptuous boulevards, Stefania Street.

CHAPTER THIRTY-SIX

A uniformed butler answered the door.

"What do you want?" he demanded with a scowl.

"About the companion's position, is it still..."

He waved her in with a white-gloved hand. "Of course it's still open. All the positions in this household are always open. I've given notice for the end of the month myself. Miss Pallfey is impossible to work for."

"Oh."

Since no one asked her to sit anywhere, Kitty remained standing in the foyer. The room was as large as any home she had ever been in, and furnished like a movie set. But the marble mantle on which she leaned was thick with dust, and cigarette butts mulched the six-foot palms in their porcelain planters.

The butler sat down, stretching his legs and yawning. Soon a maid came down and joined him. They gossiped viciously without the least concern for Kitty's ears.

Yet another contemptuous servant came to fetch Kitty. They climbed up a staircase the width of a city street and entered a rococo library. There, enthroned on a wheelchair, sat the mistress of the house, Therese Pallfey.

Applicant and doyenne sized each other up. Miss Pallfey was a big woman with a large square head set on man-sized shoulders. Bracelets squeezed her plump wrists and rings strangled her fingers. The jewels, along with strings of plump pearls, looked real to Kitty.

Miss Pallfey's hands sat idly in her expansive lap but her head moved up and down, like a shrewd housewife inspecting overpriced fillet. Having anticipated such scrutiny, Kitty had prepared by trading jailhouse treasure, a candy-pink sweater, for Rose's fine white batiste blouse.

"Awfully plain, aren't you?" snapped Miss Pallfey.

Kitty was flabbergasted. Pretty enough for the handsomest man in Europe. And who ever loved you, you mean old witch—mansion, jewels, and all?

But she wanted this job. "Excuse me?"

"I love beauty. Art. Literature. The life of the mind. I choose to surround myself with what is highest in human achievement! I won't have anything less!"

Kitty could sense that she would get this job if she played along. "Oh, yes, the world is so full of wonders, why not delight in them all?"

"Hmmm," said Miss Pallfey, and Kitty could tell this was a high mark of approval.

"Can you read?"

Kitty wanted to burst out laughing. Did this silly woman think illiterates answered want ads for ladies' companions posted in elegant cafes?

"Only in five languages, I'm afraid."

"Hmmm," said Miss Pallfey again. "I need someone to read to me. I can no longer read for myself," she said, sniffling for effect. "Where do you come from?"

Kitty froze. Julia was a country girl/ prostitute. Where would she have picked up foreign languages? But the only possible answer was the village on Julia's papers.

"Hah!" cried Miss Pallfey with satisfaction. "I've never heard of it, so it might as well not exist."

"Yes, Ma'am," said Kitty.

"As long as you've got that straight," she said, suspecting sarcasm.

"Yes, Ma'am," Kitty said, as sincerely as she could.

"In fact, there is not one city in Hungary worthy of the name, except Budapest."

"Oh, yes, Ma'am," Kitty agreed.

"And my house, you will find, is at the epicenter of Budapest life, of its intellect, culture, and science."

Kitty smiled and nodded.

"Speaking of science, I brook no superstition, miss. I won't have my people running off to masses on working days. If you want to trade your freedom to some fool priest, do it on your days off, and make sure I don't hear about it."

Kitty tried to look self-sacrificing. "Very well, Miss Pallfey."

Suddenly Miss Pallfey's face lit up. "Oh, there you are my angel. Where have you been? Mummy has missed you so!"

Kitty turned. Miss Pallfey had a child?

A blur of white flitted across the Persian carpet.

"Mitzi, my angel"

It was a dog. A little ball of fur, yet Miss Pallfey was transformed by the creature.

Ah, the power of love, thought Kitty. The dog *was* terribly cute.

"Do you like animals, Miss, eh, Julia is it?"

Kitty hesitated. She'd never had a pet. But country folk would have a dog to guard the hen house or a cat to chase vermin from the barn.

"Of course I like animals."

"Good. Because you'll have to take Mitzi out for a nice long walk every day, and I would hate for her to go with an unsympathetic person. She'd die of boredom!"

Miss Pallfey buried her face sensuously in the dog's fur. "Oh what times we had on our walks together, back when I had my health."

Miss Pallfey closed her eyes as she cuddled the dog for a long time. When she opened them she looked irritated at finding Kitty still in the room.

"Well, what else do you want?" she asked, as if Kitty had been pestering her.

"Er, the wages, Ma'am?" Kitty hoped she wasn't jumping to conclusions. She *did* have the job, didn't she?

Miss Pallfey stated the amount, dismissing her with a wave of bejeweled hand.

"So what did she offer you?" asked the butler, who was still lounging at the bottom of the staircase.

"Not very much," said Kitty, stating the amount.

"Hey, that's more than the last companion got. You must have impressed her."

"Heavens. She practically called me ugly."

"The old bat. Lots of girls tell her to shove it when she does that, job or no job."

Those girls are not on the run from hell, thought Kitty.

"Illness and disability do put people in bad humor," she said charitably.

"Illness? You and I should be as healthy as Terrible Therese. It's all a show. Her last-ditch effort to win some attention."

"So she hasn't much company?" That would be best. When many people were around, someone was likely to know, or suspect, something.

"Nobody can stand her. Nobody but her brother, Count Pallfey, ever visits. Even the Countess can't bear her."

"I suppose it's the privilege of the rich and high-born to be a bit eccentric." Eccentric was good. It meant the spotlight would be drawn away from a companion.

"Not for these wages," snorted the butler. "Aristocrats!" He spat into a gilded urn. "They think you should pay *them* for the honor of serving."

What the butler said was true, but Kitty found her situation ideal. Her cozy room in Ms. Pallfey's mansion was far better than the apartment shared with the Solomons, which was filled with heartbreaking reminders of Sender. She wasn't making much money, but she could add every penny of her salary to her funds. The opportunity to save Sender, when it came—and it would come—was sure to cost money.

The work was easy. Every day she read to Miss Pallfey, educating herself at the same time. Despite the lady's annoying mannerisms, Kitty came to enjoy her company. Miss Pallfey was spoiled, willfully ignorant of real life, but full of the wisdom of books.

Several times a week they attended the theater, the ballet, the opera. If only Sender could have been there.

Miss Pallfey's personal maid left even before the butler, and Kitty volunteered to take on her duties. The thrift of this arrangement pleased the mistress and further elevated Kitty's position in the household.

There was little additional work. Miss Pallfey was no fashion plate. Mostly, Kitty piled up the old lady's hair, which she had worn in the same style since her heyday in the Hapsburg court. Kitty also dosed her with a startling number of pills, which Miss Pallfey had browbeaten her doctors into prescribing.

Miss Pallfey rose at noon. Kitty, who habitually woke early, filled the mornings with long walks in the company of Mitzi. How beautiful Budapest was! She bought a pair of comfortable shoes, and could have walked forever.

Time weighed more heavily on her heart than on her hands. There was no new information about Sender. Although Hungary was officially part of the Axis, Miss Pallfey had no trouble getting publications from England and elsewhere. Even the local papers reported frankly on conditions throughout Europe, and the waning fortunes of Germany were widely discussed.

Only the Jews was never mentioned, as if theirs was a separate war. She could only guess at Sender's condition in Poland, and she had even less to go on about the fate of her sisters and their families, scattered over Slovakia, Sudetenland, the Ukraine, and Palestine.

"Psst."

Kitty stopped. Mitzi gamboled on her hand-tooled leash, her toenails scratching softly on the pavement.

"Psst, lady."

Yiddish.

Kitty turned, holding her breath.

"Do you remember me?" whispered a voice from deep shadow.

Kitty peered into the doorway. Yes, she did. It was not so much that she recognized the face, as the furtive movements. It was the man who had guarded the door at Mordecai Fried's apartment.

"Speak Hungarian at least!"

"I can't," he said miserably. "All I know is Polish and the Mother Tongue."

"What do you want?" Mitzi was pulling at her leash and Kitty desperately wanted to follow her.

"Please, help me."

"What can I do?"

"I...I don't know. I haven't slept in three days, or eaten in two..."

The man looked about to faint.

It was madness, but she had no choice. "All right. I have a place. But it's far from here and we can't take the tram...because of the dog." *Because you look like a Jewish fugitive.* "Do you think, you can walk?"

"God will help me."`

That is how the first man came to live at the apartment. Soon afterwards there would be others. Men, women. Families.

Hannah Solomon complained to Kitty. "It is getting dangerous. So many people. And the kinds of Jews who've come here! The retarded boy, for example. What would happen if he should blurt something out somewhere?"

Kitty glared at her. If she didn't like the apartment she could go someplace else.

"The retarded boy hardly speaks at all. He's the least likely to make a mistake."

"It isn't for my sake," Hannah whined. "I'm concerned only with my children's fate. My children are cooped up here like chickens waiting for the slaughterer."

Kitty looked at Edward and Rose. Their pallor was unhealthy. Confinement was especially hard for young people—though not as hard as being found by the fascists.

"I have an idea. My employer is looking for a new butler and a new maid. I'm sure I can get her to take Edward and Rose."

"What? My children, servants?"

"Oh, please Mama. It would be a welcome break."

"Yes, and we could earn some money to repay Miss Ficsorcsak."

Despite Mrs. Solomon's protests they did join the Pallfey staff. Having grown up with servants of their own they knew the duties and demeanor expected in their positions. Later, Kitty got a woman—a widow whose children were butchered in pogroms, but who always maintained a cheerful disposition—hired as a cook. There were now no security cracks in the Pallfey household.

As the former butler had said, no one but her brother visited Miss Pallfey, occasionally bringing along one of his children. The count, conscious of intricate class distinctions, joked charmingly with his sister's companion, but politely ignored the other servants. Still, his visits caused anxiety.

One day Kitty brought Miss Pallfey back from a constitutional in the park. The count and his eight-year-old son had arrived and were waiting in one of the parlors. As Edward ushered them in, Miss Pallfey exclaimed, "Lord Jesus Christ! Stop that immediately! Stop that!"

Everyone looked in horror at the atheist, then at the direction of her pointing finger. The little nephew's dachshund was copulating vigorously with beloved Mitzi.

"This is not to be believed," screamed Miss Pallfey. She jumped up from her wheelchair and ran toward the offending canine.

"Take that, you dirty, dirty dog," she said, swatting it with a Dresden milkmaid.

The nephew ran to his pup's defense. Miss Pallfey raised the statue as if to bring it down on the child's head, but the count was already behind her. Thanks to his height and military training, he managed to avert murder.

Miss Pallfey was furious at being thwarted. "You, all of you, get out of my house. And never darken this doorway again."

"Therese, please..." the count pleaded.

"Out! I said out."

The count gathered his hat, cane, and little boy, who was cradling a whimpering dachshund. "If you change your mind, dearest, we are always..."

"Never!"

Kitty and the staff were relieved at the household being sealed off from all outside eyes. Miss Palffy took to her bed and spent the rest of the day trying to comfort Mitzi after her ravishment.

She never did let her brother back in the house, but her anger cooled sufficiently so that a few weeks later, she accepted an invitation to visit him in the country. Naturally, Kitty would be accompanying her.

The occasion was a hunting party attended by a score of Hungary's aristocrats. There would be a non-stop string of entertainments, hunting and balls.

By the second day, Miss Pallfey had managed to offend or be offended by almost everyone there, so she refused to attend the gala ball that night. Kitty was just as glad. She went to bed early and rose refreshed.

After a long night of revelry only the count and a handful of fanatical hunters made it to breakfast. Kitty ate quietly while the others spoke of the nobility of the stag, the courage of the boar.

Gentiles loved animals so much that they killed them for pleasure. They must really love us Jews a lot, she thought.

"Some more bacon, Miss Julia?"

"No, thank you, m'lord."

"Can't have more if she hasn't had any," guffawed a baron. He was so obese that a special horse had to be brought for him to ride.

"I can't bear anything for breakfast besides coffee and fruit," said Kitty with a bit of hauteur. She had noticed how much the upper classes respected willfulness.

"Will you be hunting with us today, Miss Julia?" the baron asked.

Kitty laughed. Few of the women hunted.

"Well, why not? You can ride, can't you?"

She would not pretend to be above her class. "No. And I can't shoot, either."

"You can't?" said the count. "Well, we'll have to remedy that. Come meet us at the shooting range after lunch, Miss Julia."

Kitty raised the rifle to her shoulder. At the center of the target she imagined the spot where the German helmet cornered. She squeezed. The bullet hit dead center.

"Incredible!" cried the count. "You aren't fooling Julia? You've never shot before?"

"Never." She lifted the weapon again. The recoil would hurt her shoulder, but she didn't care. She squeezed again, at the phantom German's vulnerable spot.

"Perfect." "Bravo." "Magnificent."

You had to stop, she learned, when the bullets ran out.

"Jolly good sporting," the fat baron congratulated his host. "But where do you get bullets? I haven't been able to get any, or any service either, since the war started."

"You can have all the arms you want, Baron, if you pay for them. Come meet my supplier. Miklos!"

The sweat froze on Kitty's skin. It was Miklos, *that* Miklos. The same man who had driven her and Sender over the border in his potato wagon.

Miklos' cunning eyes recognized her immediately, and just as quickly diverted to greet the count. When the nobles were done and on their way back to the house, Kitty said shyly, "Miklos, Miklos, don't you remember me?"

Miklos pretended confusion.

"It's me, Julia. From the village."

"Of course, of course. My, you look so different, Julia. How have you been?"

"Ah," said the count, "an old beau. Well, you two carry on. I won't tell Therese."

Kitty walked Miklos over to his truck. "My husband's in Poland, in the camp at Neuhedwigburg. Nowy Jadwigatow. Do you know it?"

"Yes."

"Can you get him out?"

"You ask the impossible, lady."

"It's not such a bad place, not like that Auschwitz."

"Every place they take you people is a bad place. And your man didn't look all that tough. He's probably dead."

"He's alive." Her voice was iron.

Miklos shrugged.

"All right," Kitty persisted, "You can't get him out. But you could get me in."

"What good would that do? Germans aren't targets in a Hungarian meadow. If I wanted you dead—and me, as well—I wouldn't need to drag you all the way to Neuhedwigburg."

Kitty wouldn't give up. "But you could get something in to him. You could do that. I know you can do that."

Miklos slammed the doors of the truck shut. "Yes, I could do that. For a price."

"I understand that," said Kitty. Of course it would cost money. But she had savings. From her fortune-telling career, and from cleaning the captain's office, and from her current job. True, some of it had been spent to feed the new families in the apartment. But they would pay her back when they could, she knew. "How much?"

"Three thousand dollars."

She hiccupped with shock. It was an astounding sum. She could not even picture it. She must have misheard him. "Three thousand dollars?"

"American. Or its equivalent."

CHAPTER THIRTY-SEVEN

Ruhigbad

"I said I wanted it crispy, moron!"

Odilo's wife, Dagmar, jumped back from the sizzling pan, but it was too late. As Elsa threw the offending bacon into it, a spray of hot grease hit Dagmar's hand, raising an ugly red welt.

The pain was intense, but Dagmar stifled her cries. Tears only egged Elsa on. Nor did Dagmar look to her husband for help. He might add a stinging slap to the burn.

Once the bacon was done to her taste, Elsa served herself. Some of the fat fell on the stove grate, where it would bake on hard as a turtle's shell. Dagmar would have a devil of a time scrubbing it off.

Too bad for her. Some people were just born to serve and to suffer. That much, everyone in the Konrad household agreed upon.

Dagmar straightened her husband's tie and brushed some dandruff from his uniform. He left for work without kissing either his wife or his mistress goodbye.

Elsa lingered with her coffee as Dagmar cleaned up the kitchen. Elsa was bored. She noticed her nail polish was chipped. The hell with it, she thought, manicures were expensive. Men didn't look at your nails anyhow.

"Dagmar!"

Dagmar jumped. "Yes, Elsa," she said timidly.

"Come here."

Dagmar limped over to the kitchen table. It was the only table in the house; Odilo had never earned enough or stolen enough to afford dining-room furniture.

"Look at this!"

"You need more coffee?"

"No, cretin. The tablecloth is dirty."

Dagmar looked, careful not to venture within reach of Elsa's hands. "I'll turn it over when you've finished breakfast."

Elsa snorted in disgust. German housewifery, another oxymoron. The Germans were meticulously neat—on the surface. Below, all was filth and stench. Bedspreads were pulled tight enough to skate on, but the linens beneath were stiff with the smearings of unwashed bodies. Boots were polished to a blinding shine, but the socks worn inside festered like sewage.

Elsa smirked, relishing the irony. Filthy Jews. Wasn't that their very favorite epithet? But she'd yet to see a Jew—man, woman, or child—who didn't bathe for the Sabbath. Germans, on the other hand, could go for months without washing the parts of their bodies hidden by clothing.

Elsa shrugged to herself. What did it matter if the Jews were clean. They were dead. It was said that there was a Jewish museum now in Prague, the Museum of an Extinct People. She'd talk Odilo into taking her there one of these days. It would be amusing to see if the curators got things right.

If she could still recall it herself. She had just about forgotten all of that stuff. The rituals, the laws, the funny language, all of it was beginning to slip away. She could hardly remember her name. Eva. Chava, the first woman. And maybe the last.

Elsa brushed back her uncombed hair. Who cared? All that mattered was the present. Like the business with Dagmar and Odilo. Dagmar was the wife and Odilo would never divorce her. Odilo remained a Catholic at heart, despite external obedience to Party policy. Just as well, concluded Elsa. She would hate to have to marry him. She had other plans for moving onward and upward.

Dagmar had always done all the housework, so Elsa let her continue doing it. She also forced Dagmar to do many other tasks, the more humiliating and back-breaking, the better. If Dagmar demurred—and sometimes even if she didn't—Elsa would punish her. Odilo had made it clear that the women were to handle their own affairs, and not disturb his peace.

Officially, Dagmar was Mrs. Konrad and that was just fine with Elsa, as long as it was she who accompanied Odilo to Party functions and State festivities. It was at these evenings that she cast out her nets in the sea of opportunity.

She flirted with the top officers. Odilo, the self-absorbed fool, thought attention to her was a compliment from his superiors. In fact he was playing the pimp.

Meanwhile Dagmar the cripple stayed home, in a reversal of the Cinderella story. As a mother of two sons in military academy, sons she might never see again, she was given a great deal of lip-service honor. But, with her obvious, disgusting disability she was lucky not to be taken out and gassed, much less whirled around a dance floor.

For partying, everyone much preferred pretty, vivacious, *healthy* young Elsa. Today's German was no slave to foolish bourgeois convention. Why even the Fuhrer sported a mistress socially, not a wife.

On those rare occasions when Elsa felt herself drifting into pity for Dagmar, she quickly reminded herself that Dagmar had no business being out in public. Odilo himself pointed this out regularly, although, by beating her once too often and always too hard, it was he who had turned Dagmar into a gimp.

Elsa stretched her legs out under the table and took another sip of coffee. There was another party tonight, a reception for an official of the Slovak Hlinka organization.

Elsa's eyes narrowed. She had practically nothing to wear, just one or two evening things, which she kept re-doing. Thank goodness she could sew brilliantly.

Her eyes filled with tears of self-pity, then dried from the heat of rage. Why did Odilo have to be such a failure! Why couldn't he be posted to the occupying forces in Paris? Had he been the least bit ambitious they could be sitting now in some fine apartment in a fashionable *arrondissement*. She would be choosing among dozens of chic confections. She'd have her choice of dresses, accessories, perfume— anything from the top couturiers who collaborated. Dagmar would have been happy left behind in sleepy old Sudetenland.

Elsa sighed. Perhaps tonight she'd find another man, a man who would be her springboard from this backwater penal colony. The guest of honor maybe, the Hlinka Party man. No, that wouldn't do. The Slovaks weren't going anywhere. All the talk about their Aryan blood was for the boobs who watched the newsreels. They weren't Germans and would never be treated as such in the new world order.

The party that night was in a magnificent chateau, a confiscated summer residence of one of the French Rothschilds. Elsa shivered in her low-cut gown. With its high ceilings, the house was too expensive to heat.

She clung to Odilo for warmth, although she yearned to be free of him so that she might appear available to other men. But before she could do that she saw something that made her stop dead. Without thinking she dug her fingers into Odilo's arm.

"What are you doing, you bitch?"

She ignored his complaint, digging deeper. "That woman. Who is she?"

"Ow!" Odilo said, with far less bluster. Like most bullies, he retreated at a show of force. "What woman?"

She indicated a matron with the sunburned, prematurely aged skin of a peasant.

"Oh, that one. She's the wife of the district commander. You've met him."

Elsa nodded, bug-eyed.

Around the woman's wattled neck, and hanging from her bat-wing earlobes, was *Martha's ruby parure*.

Elsa wandered in a daze. There was French champagne, and she drank two glasses of it, but it might as well have been sulfur water from the Ruhigbad springs.

Then she saw *him*, his back. He was surrounded by the Gestapo chief and the district commander and two other heavy hitters. Whatever the talk was about, it must have been engrossing, because the men used their glasses mostly to gesture and none of them seemed drunk.

Even in the strange uniform, even from the back, Elsa knew who it was: her brother-in-law, Thomas Gantz.

They found a tiny closet off a dark and freezing hallway. It was a good foil. Everyone at the party would think they were screwing.

"Eva, little Eva. To see you here, alive and well! It's almost enough to make me believe in God again."

Religion, thought Elsa. Opiate of the masses? More like arsenic.

"What are you doing here, Thomas?"

"I'll tell you in a minute, little sister. But first tell me, how is the baby?"

"Baby?"

"Your son."

"Oh." Christ! She'd forgotten. "He's hardly a baby anymore. Quite the big boy."

"Thank heaven." Thomas seemed ready to weep. "You are wise not to ask about Helen and the children. They are dead, all dead."

"Dead?" Too bad about Helen, who, except for her politics, had been the only one of her sisters with enough sense to get rid of the religious gibberish. Her children had not been very attractive, though.

"Yes. Dead. But what they died for will live forever," said Thomas.

"What's that?"

"The rights of the workers and the equality of man. World peace."

The man was a total idiot.

Thomas must have seen the look in her eye, because he took one of her hands and pressed it between both of his. "Helen always said that you gave the impression of being cold because of how much you suffered as a child, with your mother ill.

"But your strength and resilience was something we both admired. And we also felt you were bright, really sharp. That is why I am going to ask you for a favor. A terrible favor that will put you and your child in jeopardy."

Elsa put her other hand over Thomas'. "You know you can rely on me.

"I always knew it, Eva." His voice went even lower. "I am a member of the Slovak partisans. For months we have been organizing the workers and the peasants and gathering weapons. It's very difficult, but the people are with us, almost everyone. The Hlinka party is rotten to the core. Even some of the priests have come over to us. There is going to be an uprising. Soon."

"A revolt against the German-backed regime?" Elsa asked skeptically.

"Yes. And it will succeed. There is no question of that."

Elsa raised her eyebrows. "The Slovaks are just as anti-Semitic as the Germans. *And* they're fanatical Catholics."

"We aren't speaking of the Jews anymore. There are no Jews left in Slovakia. Our goals now are universal ones."

If universalism is such a great idea, thought Elsa, how come the Gentiles don't buy it? "If your victory is certain, Thomas, what are you doing here?"

"Victory *is* certain. But the cost is not. This is where I need your help, Eva. We need to know whether the Sudetens will intervene to defend the Hlinkas. As a 'German' and a woman, perhaps you'd hear more honest remarks. Such information would save lives, Eva. Hundreds, perhaps thousands of lives."

And cost me mine, thought Eva. Not much of a bargain.

"We've been away from the gathering for too long. Let's speak later, Thomas."

All eyes turned as Elsa sashayed past the semi-circle of men. She walked over to the white, concert-sized piano. The piano had been silent since the Rothschilds had gone, because no one present could play it. But she knew it flattered her figure to lean against its undulating curves.

The secret she possessed was of inestimable value. She had to be sure that it was revealed to the man who could give her the best reward.

Elsa walked slowly back towards the men, her hips swaying hypnotically in the tight gown. She stopped before the district commander.

"Herr Kommandant," she purred, "could I see you in private?"

The district commander blushed above his tight uniform collar, grinning happily. "Why, certainly Fraulein." A few feet away, Odilo beamed with pride.

The walls of the room they entered were covered in silk moire. Elsa wondered if she could somehow tear some of it off for a dress. There was also a large chandelier, and a white marble fireplace large enough to roast a horse in. Other than that, there was only a small settee. The other furniture had been stolen.

The district commander seated himself, indicating the narrow space next to him. Elsa sat down even closer than he expected, pressing her thigh into his.

"Karl...you don't mind if I call you Karl, do you Herr Kommandant?"

"Of course not, of course not. I wouldn't have it any other way."

"Good," she said, moving even closer. "I have just found out some shocking information, Karl. I felt it was my duty as a German patriot to report it to you."

"You have done the right thing and come to the right person, Fraulein."

"I know," she said, giving his hand a tight little squeeze. "And I know that you will reward my loyalty to the Fatherland with an appropriate token." She touched her throat, making a necklace of her hand, then pulled on the lobe of her ear.

"Absolutely. Every dedicated person deserves to be generously compensated by a grateful Volk. Now, what is this information you have, my dear."

She smiled sweetly. "You know our guest of honor, the Hlinka Party official?"

"Yes, yes. I noticed you, er, spent some time with him earlier."

"Oh, yes. And I found out some *very* interesting things. Karl, the man is an imposter! He's a communist."

"Yes."

The district commander was nodding. He was not at all surprised. He knew! Oh, no. Could Thomas have led her into a trap?

"Yes, yes. Go on."

"A communist! A communist and a Jew."

"Yes, yes."

"You knew that?"

"Yes we did, Fraulein Elsa."

"But how?"

"We had an anonymous tip. A fellow Red ratted on him. Those Bolshies, they hate the Jews worse than they hate us. And with good reason."

"So you know who he is." She had nothing for him. She saw the rubies crumbling like dust. Elsa fought to keep down panic. "But do you know *why* he is here?"

"I expect our Gestapo will find out tomorrow," he said with a chuckle.

"I can save them the trouble." Her mind was calculating fast now, retrieving the fallen stones. "In fact, this is surely better. Once the Gestapo was done with him, he'd be of no further use to us. But—listen to me—you can pretend nothing has happened and send this spy back to Slovakia with deadly misinformation!"

The district commander could sit no closer. But he tilted his head over with new interest. "Go on, Fraulein."

So she told him all about the rebellion. She told him about the partisans' desperate need to know how the Sudeten would react. She told him all.

"Excellent work, Fraulein. The Fatherland will not forget your courage and sacrifice, you may be sure."

On her way to Gestapo headquarters, Dagmar Konrad was so nervous that she tripped and fell flat on her face. She banged her forehead viciously on the pavement, tore the knees of both cotton stockings, and broke the clasp on her imitation leather pocketbook, sending her few possessions flying. No one stopped to help her up.

Because of the accident Dagmar was almost late for her appointment with the Gestapo chief. That, and the rather serious injury to her head, made her feel faint.

The officer tried to calm her down. It was not unheard of for one of his interview subjects to pass out or even have a heart attack, and the abrasion to her head was rather nasty. He was a connoisseur of bruises.

"Shall I have the sergeant bring you some iodine and a plaster, Frau

Konrad?"

"No, no. Please don't trouble yourself." She took a handkerchief from her bag and dabbed at her forehead with the clean side.

"A coffee then, or some tea?"

She refused that too but relaxed. How bad could the man be. So polite.

He leaned across the desk, like a woman leaning over the washline. "May I ask you something in confidence, Frau Konrad?"

"Of course."

"It's about Elsa Kreutzer."

"Oh!" She jerked back as if she'd touched something hot.

"Now please tell me truthfully, Madam, does Miss Kreutzer fulfill all your expectations as a German worker?"

"Absolutely."

"Don't be afraid to tell the truth. No harm will come to you or to her. I swear it."

"But it is the truth. She's a wonderful Aryan girl any mother would be proud of."

"You mean you have never heard her express any inappropriate thoughts? Sympathy for the lesser races? Discouragement at the progress of the war?"

"Never. Never."

"You've seen no incorrect emotions? Religious interests? Humanist tendencies? The softness that comes naturally to the maternal sex?"

"Softness? Oh, sir, she's just like the Fuhrer exhorts us to be: hard as frozen iron."

Elsa was early for her summoned meeting with the district commander. Even so, he welcomed her into his office immediately, with the greatest warmth.

"I am delighted to report, Elsa, that all our inquiries into your background have fully supported our expectations of your exquisite racial breeding and robust political commitment. We have received authorization from Berlin to award you with the highest honor that can be bestowed upon a woman."

"Really, Karl. There was no need for all that. I'm just a simple girl at heart. All I really want is a little token of appreciation. Something pretty perhaps?"

"What nonsense, my dear. The Fatherland owes you much more than trinkets. Germany owes you blood and glory. If you were a man you would demand as much. And on my honor, you shall have it!

"Tomorrow morning, at eight hundred hours, you will report to Gestapo headquarters for transportation to an induction center."

Elsa went pale. "Induction?" Oh, God. They had found out! She was being deported for Jewish "resettlement."

The commander's smile was radiant. "Heartiest congratulations! You have been chosen for membership in the Women's Division of the Waffen SS.

"Heil Hitler!"

CHAPTER THIRTY-EIGHT

Neuhedwigburg Labor Camp, Poland

Sender was dying.

He dropped the stone he was carrying and didn't pick it up. The last of his strength was gone.

He knew he was at the hour of death because of the cold. He had been cold since the day he was brought to the camp, but this cold was different. He could feel the soul leaking out of his body like water from a punctured radiator.

Alexander Halter was no longer a handsome man. He weighed less than ninety pounds. Much of his body was covered with the nipple-shaped pustules of typhus. All his teeth had been loosened by malnutrition, and several on the left side of his mouth had been knocked out by a guard, leaving him with a lopsided expression. His thick hair had been shaved when he'd gotten to the camp and had grown back as a filthy fuzz.

The interior of Sender's body was as ravaged as the outside. A diamond-like headache split his brain and blurred his vision, while a 104-degree fever raged.

Only his eyes remained beautiful. They were still as blue as violets. The violet, an inedible plant, continued to grow at Neuhedwigburg.

In recent weeks Sender's mind had begun to slow down, to drift in the symptom common to late-stage starvation. He no longer kept himself alert by mentally reviewing passages of Talmud, or reciting the psalms he knew by heart. The idea of Kitty still kept him company, like a warm blanket, but specific memories were now impossible to recall.

He was accepting of death. It was God's will, and the end of his suffering. The only thing that still bothered him was that there was no one to recite Kaddish, the prayer for the dead, for him. He was quite certain now that his brothers were dead, so Sender decided to recite it for himself. But he needed the presence of ten adult Jews, and he was all alone in this part of the quarry. The others had all managed to carry their stones over to the mound on the other side of the camp.

All day they hauled chunks of granite from one end of the camp to the other, then back again. At the beginning of the war the quarries had supplied the grandiose impulses of Hitler's favorite architect, Albert Speer. Dynamite being precious, the rock was carved out by hand. But the days of giant temples to the gods of war and sport were over. Even Speer could not divert so much material and manpower from the failing military forces. Now the men's labor was completely pointless.

Sender decided that since he was flouting the letter of the law by reciting the Kaddish for himself, he might as well go ahead without the quorum of ten.

Exalted and sanctified is the Great Name of God, throughout the world...

In the corner of his eye a figure appeared, but Sender ignored it. His power of concentration was limited, and all of it was now devoted to the Kaddish.

May he reign in your lifetimes and in your days, and in the lifetime of the entire House of Israel, swiftly and soon. Now respond: Amen.

Someone had responded, but it wasn't "Amen."

In fact it sounded like "Hey, you! Jew!" In German.

Sender did not move. He knew he was going to die, and he chose to die like a Jew, not like a dog who goes running to a cruel master.

May his great Name be blessed forever and ever.

"I said you, Jew."

Get lost, blood-eater. *Blessed, praised, glorified, exalted, raised-high, adored, magnified, celebrated, is the Name of the Holy One, blessed is he. He is beyond all blessing, song, praise, and comfort that can be uttered in this world. Now say: Amen.*

If you won't say amen, shut up.

Sender took three steps back, bowed to the left, *May he who makes peace in his heavens...* He bowed to the right, *Make peace upon us...* He bowed forward, *and upon all Israel.*

Sender paused in final communion, then stepped forward three steps and said, *Now respond: Amen.*

It was deliciously quiet, as if he had passed into the next world already. But then he opened his eyes and saw The Tenderizer.

The German's name was Eugene Milch, but even his fellow guards declined to call him by such a prissy and inappropriate name. The Jews had only one nickname for him: The Tenderizer. He would beat a Jew as thoroughly as a chef pounding a veal fillet until it was paper-thin.

Good, thought Sender. A single blow by The Tenderizer, applied to any part of his body, would finish him off so quickly that he would feel nothing.

"Come here, Jew."

Sender moved forward faster than he thought he could. He was anticipating Paradise. The divine light was warming him already, and he could smell the perfume of the heavenly fruit. In the Next World the righteous studied Torah all day long. He wondered what Tractate they were up to.

"I've been watching you, Jew, and I've come to a conclusion."

Sender blinked. Get on with it. Do your job. Just as a Jew's work is to praise the Almighty, the Amalekite's is to shed blood.

"I've decided that, of all the Jews in this camp, you're the most likely to survive."

Sender blinked again. What did he say?

"So I have a message for you, for your children. Do you understand?"

Understand? What children? All Jewish children had been murdered.

"The message—and don't forget it, Jew—the message is: it isn't over until the last one of us is dead."

"Right. The last one of us is dead," mumbled Sender.

"No! The last one of *us*. Us. Do you understand?"

Sender nodded, but he didn't.

The response satisfied The Tenderizer, though. "All right, come with me."

Sender followed the guard to a lean-to. Inside a picnic was laid, two large sandwiches and a container of beer.

"Here," said The Tenderizer, handing Sender one of the sandwiches. Sender put it into his shirt, which hung so loosely from his frame that it could have concealed a whole breadbox.

"You can rest here until the group comes back to this side of the quarry."

Sender lay down and, despite great confusion, fell immediately asleep. He awoke to the sound of thudding boulders. The men had returned.

He looked around. There was no sign of The Tenderizer but the sandwich was still snug in his shirt.

He re-joined the group, curiously refreshed. His fever seemed to have cooled and he was able to pick up and carry a regulation-sized stone. It was as if he had eaten the sandwich already, though he hadn't taken a single bite.

The rest of the day's routine was unbearable. It was an average afternoon and evening—a showcase of horrors. Three men had died in the quarry. The others had to carry them back to the camp, then to the burning lime pits. Previously, they had simply thrown corpses into a quick-flowing creek, but the local Poles had complained about body parts bobbing up downstream. Any change meant more work for the prisoners.

At roll-call two men collapsed, and were dragged away to the lime pits, even though one was breathing. And at the dinner line a man showed too much eagerness at the soup cauldron so a guard punished him by holding his head in the pot until he drowned. Worse, half the soup was spilled, so the men got even less to eat than usual.

Finally, they lay down in their bunks for the night. There were only four men on the narrow wooden plank that made up Sender's bunk. The ones who had died had not been replaced. There had been no new prisoners at Labor Camp Neuhedwigburg for more than a month. Rumor had it that as soon as all the inmates were dead—which wouldn't be long—the camp would be evacuated.

The Jew on the far side of the bunk had no name. He had never shared it or any other information with the others. Any attempt to engage him in conversation, particularly of a religious nature, resulted in a stream of bitter invective.

Sender lay between two men, Bentzi and Vlad. Sender and Bentzi were actually acquainted. Bentzi was Polish, but his father had been a Hasid of the Janace Rebbe. On major holidays Bentzi and his father came to the town to commune with the Master.

Sender would never have recognized Bentzi. The young man had been a monster. He had been covered, scalp to sole, with the most hideous manifestation of the disease psoriasis. When he blinked a shower of skin flakes fell into his eyes. He left a trail like a molting snake, and any place he rested showed a powdery residue of human dust.

There had been a constant sickly-sweet smell about him, whether from the disease or from the many unguents he applied to treat it, even he couldn't tell. And Bentzi had been enormously fat. He had gone as far as America to reducing spas and special doctors, but nothing helped.

Despite wealth, intelligence, and a gentle nature, no match could be found for Bentzi. A marriage proposal had been extended to Sender's sister Bayla, but his parents wouldn't hear of it. On several occasions desperately poor girls willing to sacrifice themselves for their families' welfare had agreed to marry Bentzi, but each time the parents broke the engagement at the last minute. Nobody could bear to send a daughter to such a fate.

In the camps a remarkable thing happened. Like everyone, Bentzi lost weight at an alarming rate, but unlike everyone else on the rations designed to kill by starvation, he stabilized. Bentzi was very skinny, but not cadaverous. And his body, sensing there was no flesh to spare, stopped producing extra skin. He was now a normal, if very slim, human being with smooth, supple flesh. He was almost handsome.

Vlad, on Sender's other side, was also from Poland and had also been heir to a fortune, but there all similarities to Bentzi ended. His family had been completely assimilated. Although Vlad had been circumcised, his little brother, born after their grandparents were dead, had not been given the most basic Jewish rite.

Being uncircumcised hadn't helped his brother. He'd been killed, along with their mother, just days after the German invasion. She had come to police headquarters with her younger son and a gigantic bribe. "There must be some mistake," she said.

There must be some mistake. Those were the words by which secular Jews perished as surely as the Shma, "Hear O Israel, the Lord is our God, the Lord is One," marked the martyrdom of the faithful.

Vlad was determined to right the mistake. He would find out what it was to be a Jew, although, most likely, it would be the last thing he would ever do. He latched on to Sender and Bentzi like a baby to its mother's milk-heavy breasts. Every moment that they could spare, he begged them to teach him of Judaism.

But this night there was no talk of Torah.

"I have...food," Sender whispered.

"Real food?" asked Bentzi. They discussed food fantasies constantly.

"Yes. Look." Sender withdrew the sandwich. The tight space between the men and the bunk above them was instantly filled with the intoxicating odor of bread. Carefully, as if he were dismantling a grenade, Sender opened the sandwich.

"Look! Margarine."

"Margarine nothing. It's butter."

"And what's that, meat?"

"Pork," said Vlad.

Sender could not think of eating the huge sandwich himself. He decided to split it in three parts, enough for a real meal for him, Vlad, and Bentzi.

"I'm not going to eat the meat," said Sender. "The bread and butter is enough to keep me alive, so my life doesn't depend on eating it."

"I won't eat it either," said Bentzi.

"Nor I," said Vlad proudly.

"You idiots, give it to me, then," whispered the man with no name.

The four men fell asleep right after their feast, unlike every other night, when hunger pangs kept them drifting between exhaustion and consciousness.

But an hour later they were awakened by horrible screaming. The man with no name was writhing, his hands clutching his abdomen as if to tear out his guts.

"Quick, let's get him to the latrines before the kapo hears him." It was forbidden to use the latrines at night, but better to take the risk than let the kapo—the Jewish overseer—come storming in, dealing death-blows with his truncheon.

The three of them tried carrying the nameless man, who was beyond walking, but it was no use. His bowels exploded, spraying the room with liquid feces. As the others groaned in disgust, the man with no name sank to the ground dead.

The following afternoon Sender found himself lagging behind again at the quarry. Once again, he felt near death, as if he had never eaten of the sandwich the night before. But once again The Tenderizer called to him. The German repeated the same bizarre speech, gave him a large sandwich, and let him rest in the lean-to.

That night, two men from the bunk above fought for the meat in the sandwich. One of the men grabbed the meat, then his bunkmate tore it from his grasp. In the end, they stuffed the food in their mouths, each tearing as much as he could from the other. Not much later, both men woke screaming, dying the same horrible way as the man with no name.

On the third day Sender felt stronger, but he waited for The Tenderizer. If the sandwiches stopped coming, he would die.

The German was true to form. Everything happened exactly as before.

That night there was a loud clamoring from many men who wanted the meat. Sender, Vlad, and Bentzi were reluctant to hand it out. "There's something wrong with the meat. Three men have died. What if it's poisoned."

"What if it is, I'm dying anyway."

"You saw what happened. It's a terrible way to go."

"It's just a coincidence. Prisoners die all the time."

"No, it's not a coincidence," said the Russian Doctor. The speaker was neither Russian nor a doctor. He had been born in Warsaw, where his parents fled after the Revolution. He had been in the last year of medical school when the Germans invaded.

"The digestion of meat is complicated. Our systems have had to adapt to diets without any protein. We can't do it anymore. For us, all meat is poisonous."

None of the men were interested in explanations. "I don't care, give it here."

"No, here."

A fistfight broke out. The men were in no condition for boxing; every blow extracted loud gasps of pain.

It was inevitable. The kapo bounded in, his truncheon flying, furious at having been wakened.

The kapo was given extra food for keeping order among the inmates. Kapos were chosen from the most brutal men, and their jobs made them more brutal still. It didn't take long for a kapo to think of himself as a German, and to act like one.

Sender saved the men from a general bloodbath by offering the meat to the kapo. It was an inspired solution. The kapo's diet was rich enough to support digestion, and he held his hand back from Sender and his friends—the source of the bounty.

Sender kept producing food. Every day, with meticulous attention to detail, The Tenderizer gave the same incomprehensible speech, provided the break from killing labor, and handed Sender the life-saving sandwich.

One night the kapo called Sender over to the empty latrines.

"You've been good to me, Jew-boy, and I'm going to return the favor. Here's the scoop: they're going to liquidate the camp."

"I know that. They've stopped sending new prisoners a long time ago. There's no real work here."

"Nah, not that, not just letting it fade out. They're going to destroy the camp."

"When?"

"I don't know for sure. Maybe two weeks."

"What about the surviving inmates?"

"They'll send you out to a death march. Or straight to the lime pits to be shot."

Sender looked at the kapo. A man who would beat and kill Jews, even to save his life, was no Jew. But he still cared about the man.

"What are you going to do?"

"Me?" The kapo laughed, incredulous. "Don't worry about me." He held up two fingers tightly. "Me and the Germans, we're like that."

Sender went back to his place on the plank between Bentzi and Vlad. He repeated nothing of his conversation. What was the use of plunging everyone into deeper despair. The last time there was talk of liquidation, two men killed themselves. This news was even worse. God forbid, others might do similar terrible things. He didn't want it on his conscience. Let the Nazis do their own dirty work.

With only three now, there was room to twist and turn in the bunk. The other two slept deeply; that was another way the food helped revive them.

But Sender could not sleep. All night he fought despair, like Jacob fighting the angel. His memory was sharper now, and he chanted the series of ten Psalms that, according to Hasidic teaching, could break down the very gates of heaven.

CHAPTER THIRTY-NINE

Stefania Street, Budapest

It was early morning and the day promised to be lovely. Rose Solomon hummed as she dusted the Pallfey mansion.

She loved her work, handling so many beautiful objects. It didn't matter that she didn't own them. They gave her more enjoyment than they ever gave the mistress. In this house she was well fed, and warm, and usefully occupied, and as safe as a Jew anywhere in Europe could be. She was almost happy.

So she was shocked to find Julia in the front foyer, lying on a chaise, dressed in her coat and hat, crying her heart out. Little Mitzi, the dog, was rubbing herself against Kitty's leg, trying in her canine way to console.

"Julia! What on earth is the matter?" Rose had come to see Julia as the very symbol of strength and optimism.

"I don't know what to do. I think and think, but I come up with nothing."

"What are you talking about?"

"My husband."

"You have a husband?" It seemed so improbable. Julia was the most independent young woman she'd ever met.

"Oh, yes. The most wonderful husband in the world."

"Where is he?" Rose asked.

"He was taken to a slave labor camp in Poland."

Rose blanched. "Miss Julia," she said, as tenderly as she could, "So few survive those camps..." Rose let the words drift off.

"Oh, no," said Kitty, drawing herself upright. "I'm absolutely sure he's still alive. I even know the location of the camp.

"And," she added, eyes blazing, "I've found a way to get him out."

"The thing is," she pounded her fist into the sofa cushion, "it costs a fortune—three thousand American dollars."

Rose smiled. "Oh, it's just money. My father, of blessed memory, used to say, 'money is not a problem, it's just an expense.'"

"No offense to the memory of your dear father, may the Lord avenge his blood, but those were different times. Today a Jew with money is almost as rare as one with freedom. I've tried and tried, but I can't figure out how to raise anything like that sum. All the people I know are lucky to own the flesh on their bones."

Kitty sank back into the cushions and covered her face with her hands. Mitzi whimpered in sympathy.

Rose leaned down and whispered in Kitty's ear. "Julia, what about this house?"

Kitty looked up at her, raising an eyebrow.

"You know what I mean. There's a fortune here—jewels, art, silver—and Miss Pallfey doesn't pay attention."

"I thought about that," Kitty said. "I wouldn't hesitate for a minute to steal, cheat, and bite the hand that feeds me, if it meant bringing my Sender back. But it wouldn't work. Sooner or later Miss Pallfey, or her relatives, would suspect something. And the police would be called in to investigate."

Rose shrank back. If the police came in they would all be interrogated. Julia, with her priceless papers, would be all right. The worst they could do would be to throw her in jail, and she'd already survived that.

But the rest of them, the rest of the staff with their inadequate documents, would be sent to the Germans...

Rose took a deep breath. It felt like she was inhaling shards of ice. Julia must be a saint. She was willing to give up something she valued more than her own life—the life of her husband—to spare her, Rose, and her brother, and the cook.

"Julia," she whispered, "I know where you can get the money."

Since starting her job Kitty had rarely been back to the flat, and the only thing she had taken from it was the pillow that still smelled of Sender—all piney and sweet, like the forest edge bordered in violets.

The apartment, now stuffed with haunted adults and unnaturally silent children, resembled that of Mordecai Fried. People and wretched belongings hung from the walls like lichen. Unlike Fried's apartment, this one had never been either beautiful or spacious. It was gloomy even at midday, and it stank of fear.

The denizens were glad to see Kitty. All but Mrs. Solomon. She always acted as if Kitty's invitations to the fugitives was a personal imposition on her.

"What now, Julia? Refugees from Turkey?"

"You're free to leave any time," Kitty said spitefully. She could live with Hannah's ingratitude, but she couldn't stand the woman's claim that she alone deserved a haven, while others ought to be left to the mercies of the Nazis.

"You can't do anything more to me than you already have," Hannah sniffled.

"What's that?" asked Kitty. What harm had she ever done to Mrs. Solomon?

"You've taken away my children!"

"Taken them away? They live in safety and...and *luxury*."

"But not with me!"

"I would have taken you along, too, for their sakes. But you refuse to work."

"Work as a servant. Why, do you know who I am, what sort of position I have?" she said, puffing herself up.

"Of course I do. I know you are a very rich woman."

Hannah Solomon blanched and backtracked. "Was. I *used* to be, that is."

"No. Are. For the next few minutes, that is."

"Whatever do you mean, Julia? I have nothing. Everyone knows that. The Nazis took everything we had."

Kitty went to her bed, which had been commandeered by Hannah while everyone else in the apartment, including the old and the sick, slept on the bare floor. Kitty pulled off the linens and pushed the mattress aside. There was clothing there, and a purse.

Mrs. Solomon's handbag was made of ostrich leather and it was very heavy. The brass clasp was solid as an ingot in a bank vault. It opened with a satisfying sigh, but the bag was empty.

Kitty ran her hand around the calf lining and inner pockets. All was smooth duchess satin, and bare. The purse was formidably constructed, but still, it was so heavy. There had to be something in it.

"Anyone here have a sharp knife or scissors?" Kitty asked.

Someone produced a pair of dressmaker shears.

"Oh, no," Hannah Solomon fell to her knees, "please don't destroy my handbag. It's the one good thing I have left in this world, the only thing."

"Really? I thought you had both a son and a daughter."

Hannah didn't seem to hear. She was sobbing now, as if she'd been caught by the Germans. "Oh, please, Julia. You don't know, you just couldn't know what it's like to lose such a beautiful handbag."

"Don't I?" Kitty was scaring herself. She had never felt so pitiless.

She ripped the lining out of the handbag viciously, then turned it upside down. Out of the purse fell—flowed—diamonds.

Streams, rivers, cascades of diamonds.

"They're fake!" screamed Hannah.

"Then it's no big deal for me to take them."

"No, please, Julia, no!" Hannah was on the floor, groveling.

"Get up, Mrs. Solomon. Jews don't kneel."

"Please, for God's sake, Miss Ficsorcsak. It's my daughter's dowry."

"Dowry." Kitty's voice was a dangerous whisper. As if the whole idea of dowries wasn't poisonous enough in the best of times! She was so angry, she could have killed the woman. But something greater than anger swept over her. Sheer, undiluted joy. She had everything she needed to bring Sender back into her arms.

"You've got the money?" Miklos was incredulous.

"Yes," said Kitty.

"In full?"

"That and more."

"That's good," Miklos couldn't help smiling. Then his voice grew stern. "But you better understand, I can't guarantee anything. Springing a Jew loose from a camp, that's like Jesus raising the dead. And speaking of the dead, your man may be dead already. Almost certainly is."

"He's not dead," Kitty said evenly.

"Whether he is or not, no refunds. You got that straight?"

"Yes."

"All right. Let's see the cash."

"Or its equivalent, that's what you said."

"Come on. If I have to wait any longer I just may ditch the whole deal."

"No! You promised."

"Come on, come on." Miklos reached greedily for the knotted handkerchief. He opened it deftly and the diamonds poured out.

He gasped involuntarily. "Are they real?"

"Let's take them to a jeweler, if you don't believe me."

"No, I believe you. Besides, no more Jewish jewelers around, and I don't trust the other kind."

"On behalf of my people, I'm flattered."

"All right. I'm satisfied with the merchandise. But do you really trust me? Getting into a Polish camp, that's no picnic. And getting out with a Jew...What's to prevent me with just walking away with these?"

Kitty pointed to the necklace. "Touch the ends."

Miklos held the diamonds up and caressed the two ends. "Ouch," he yelped. He had cut his finger on one end, where the platinum had been crudely chopped.

"Bring Alexander Halter back to me, and you get the other half."

The Slovak Army truck rolled up to the gates of the Neuhedwigburg camp. Miklos, in a major's uniform, came to a careful stop. The uniform was his—he'd bought it outright—but the truck was on loan. He had the resources now to bribe an officer for anything, but why waste money? It was cheaper to engineer a "loan" than a "keeper."

The Slovaks were so demoralized now that they were giving the farm away for a pittance. The cost of the entire operation was less than he'd thought possible. The uniform, the truck, the telephone call from Bratislava High Command to the camp quartermaster, the sum he was asked for was small change. He could have hired a couple of tanks for escort and still not used up the cash he got for the first diamond.

The Slovak Fascist-Catholic regime was about to go under. After this job, he'd figure out how to profit from that too.

A German guard came out of the checkpoint and saluted smartly. No sign of rot with those guys.

"I've had a bit of trouble with the truck, soldier. You got a smart boy here can give it a look?" That Halter was supposed to be an expert mechanic.

"We certainly do," said the guard. "We've a fellow here whose father is high up in Mercedes-Benz."

Say what you will about the Master Race, they had no head for business. Why did they waste the cream of the Wehrmacht on jobs Jews could do for free? Why did they waste the Jews, for that matter? Didn't they realize that the Yids were worth more alive then dead.

"Never mind," said Miklos. "We need to start loading up."

A number of officers came out to watch the operation. It was extremely unusual, a paid order for granite chunks. They couldn't remember the last one.

A dozen Jews were marched out, quickly, to load the truck. The overseers were hard on the workers, and two of them collapsed, presumably dead. Miklos checked out their faces, and the faces of the so-called living Jews. None of them was Halter. He'd recognize Halter.

"Hey," he complained to the Germans, "these Jews are nothing but corpses. Get me workers with some flesh on their bones. Otherwise, I'll be here till the war is over." If he had the big-spending operator figured right, Halter would have gotten himself some food, even in a place dedicated to starving the inmates.

The ten workers were marched off.

"Shoot them," the head guard said casually. "Their work was not up to snuff."

Another dozen Jews were marched in. As Miklos had guessed, Sender Halter was among them. Miklos would have recognized those pretty purple eyes anywhere. They were even more prominent now, staring from the skull-like head.

Overseeing this detail was The Tenderizer. He didn't like the idea that *his* Jew had been called out here. Even beefed up, his Jew was too weak to hoist granite. The Slovak major insisted that he wanted Halter to do something up on the truck.

Sender climbed up, breathing hard from the effort. Suddenly, he recognized Miklos. A miracle had happened! Kitty had arranged to have him freed!

"Quick, lie down," Miklos whispered.

Sender dropped.

"You're going home," said Miklos, glancing at Sender's body. "Guess your girlfriend needs servicing bad."

"My friends," whispered Sender, "you've got to get them in here too."

"Are you crazy? No!"

Sender wasn't listening. "The two fat guys."

"I said no. The deal's just for you."

Sender stood up. "I'm not going without them."

Miklos was enraged. This faggot was not going to keep him from his money!

"The hell you're not," he said, pulling a tiny ladies' revolver.

"You're going to shoot me with that?"

Miklos grinned. "Actually, that's a present from your girl. Here, she sent this, too." Miklos tossed something small and shiny at Sender. He caught it without identifying it, and put it in his shirt with the sandwich.

"But I will shoot you if I have to," said Miklos, pulling a much more serious Slovak-Army issue pistol, "so do what I say."

Just then The Tenderizer appeared in the truck's opening. He took one look at the man threatening his Jew with two guns, and shot.

Miklos fell to the rocks. For once his tightly grasping fists relaxed and opened.

Outside, the men—both laborers and guards—continued without pause. They assumed that the shot they'd heard had simply hit one more Jew.

CHAPTER FORTY

Neither Bentzi nor Vlad asked about the events in the truck that afternoon and Sender didn't volunteer anything.

The three friends ate their bread, and whispered the grace after meals. Later, Sender slipped out to the latrines to give the kapo his meat.

"Bad news," said the kapo ominously.

Was there any other kind, wondered Sender.

"There was a shipment of five hundred yesterday. Healthy young bucks, survivors of a long march. They took them out by the creek, made them dig a ditch..."

Sender understood. The men had been shot. None had been assigned to labor because the camp was being liquidated. Soon. Very soon.

The kapo shrugged. "Not that there's anything anyone can do about it. But you and the other two being religious, I figured you'd want to pray."

Sender looked at the kapo. Could this debased creature still believe in God?

"We'll pray for you too."

The kapo didn't snicker or hit him. Sender decided to press his luck.

"Is it all right to take a leak, sir?"

The kapo turned his back and walked away.

The latrines were out in the open. A full moon was blazing.

Carefully, Sender took the shiny little tube out of his shirt. He caressed it. Kitty, his Kitty, had sent it. Miklos had slipped it to him without anyone noticing.

He weighed the heavy little cylinder in his hand with satisfaction. It was proof. Proof that Kitty was alive and knew he was too.

276

But what was it? He turned the metal tube over in the moonlight. A bullet? No. He considered the object, then almost laughed when he recognized it. A lipstick.

A letter! Kitty must have sent a note, tightly wound and tucked into the case.

It was almost too exciting to open the tube. But maybe it wasn't a letter, he thought, hopes plunging. Very, very slowly he pulled the top from the lipstick. Inside, where the red paint should have been, was a white powder.

Poison? No, Kitty could have no idea what conditions were like in the camp. Besides, she would never succumb to despair, and never let him either. As he returned to the barracks, he pondered what the powder was, and how he could use it.

The next day at their usual midday meeting in the lean-to, The Tenderizer said to Sender, "Don't come here tomorrow. Just stay with me through the morning detail."

Sender nodded. "Yes, sir."

"You know I'll protect you. You'll be all right."

"Thank you, sir."

"But nobody else. You're the only one I want."

Sender said nothing.

After The Tenderizer left the lean-to, Sender uncapped the lipstick and poured the contents into the Nazi's beer.

That afternoon, when Sender rejoined the labor detail in the quarry, he wondered if he had just signed his own death sentence. If the powder was poison, there would be no one to protect him from the liquidation tomorrow.

But, he reproved himself, it was God, and God alone, who protected him, not some German sadist with a bizarre obsession. There was only one real choice he had: to save his hide and forget about the others, or try to rescue as many Jews as he could.

As the men worked, The Tenderizer beat and cursed them as usual. But within half an hour his truncheon began to miss its mark and his curses started to slur. Breathing hard, The Tenderizer sat down on a ledge gouged from the rock. The truncheon tumbled from his grasp.

"He's dead," cried one of the men.

All looked up in alarm. A dead German bode no good to the Jews he oversaw.

"Let's get his gun," said Sender.

But as they approached him, The Tenderizer snored. The men jumped back.

The Tenderizer shifted against the sharp crags, but didn't waken.

"I've drugged him. We've all got to make a run for it. Tomorrow the camp will be liquidated. We're finished."

To Sender's disbelief the men started arguing.

"We can't do that!"

"They'll find us for sure. And kill us."

"Yes, and we're in big trouble already because you drugged The Tenderizer."

"Who told you about the liquidation? There are always stupid rumors around."

"Even if there is a liquidation, maybe they'll take us to a different camp."

"A better camp."

"Besides, they'll need to dismantle the buildings first. That'll take days."

"We can't waste any more time," said Sender. "Who's coming with me?"

Only Vlad and Bentzi came to his side.

"I'd go," said one man, "but I'm too weak. I'd only slow you guys down."

"May God be with you," said Sender. The words seemed hypocritical and bare. Sender took the sandwich out from his shirt and threw it to the man.

He ran with Bentzi and Vlad to the barbed-wire fence, but there they hesitated. Was the electricity on?

Hesitation was death. With both hands and gritted teeth, he grasped the wire.

He opened his eyes. His palms stung with the cuts from the barbs, but he was otherwise unharmed. He gestured for the men to follow.

Emaciated, they managed to squeeze through the fence, but they were cut by the barbed wire. Still, the wounds acted as spurs, and they moved even faster.

Into the underbrush they ran, flailing against the brambles, which were almost as vicious as the barbed wire. They ran straight ahead, they thought, with no goal other than to get as far from the camp as possible. Each paused only long enough to make sure that the others stayed in sight.

It wasn't a very long time after their escape when they collapsed, utterly exhausted. Bentzi and Vlad stared at Sender. He knew what they were thinking.

You fool, why did you throw our sandwich to the dead man? We're too hungry to go another step. And there won't be any camp dinner tonight. As poor as the meal of a slice of bread and bowl of dishwater was, it was more than they were going to get today.

"Get up," said Sender.

"Why?" said Bentzi, "we don't even know where we're going."

"Maybe we'll find some berries. Or at least a stream to drink from."

"Maybe we'll find roast chickens and carrots stewed in honey," Bentzi snapped.

"If God wills it," Vlad said earnestly.

Sender nodded his approval. "You're right, Vlad. It's said 'if God wills it, even a broom can shoot.'"

Bentzi got up. "But if God decides to knock us out right here, who's to know or care? We're nothing but splinters and ashes to him."

"Don't say that," Vlad said. "Let's give him a chance to help us. Let's get going."

They began to trudge again, but soon stopped. They had come to a clearing.

It was the main road from Neuhedwigburg, half a mile from the camp. They had been walking in a circle.

"No! No, no, no."

Sender seemed to take it harder than the other men.

Sender ran out of the woods and into the middle of the road.

"Sender, have you lost your mind?"

"Get back, Sender. You're visible for a half a mile out there."

Sender just stood in the middle of the road, shaking his fist at the heavens.

"I've had enough of this. Enough! No more games, do you understand, God? Enough. You want me to die? Fine. You want me to live? I'll live as you command. But no more games!"

Sender put his hands on his hips. His eyes narrowed. "I want an answer, Master of the Universe, and I want it right now! Do you hear? I won't move from this spot until you answer me."

"The poor fellow's lost his mind," said Bentzi to Vlad. "Someone will see him or hear him. We should get out of here."

"We can't just abandon him," said Vlad, "not after all he's done for us."

Bentzi nodded in sad agreement. They stood still, watching Sender rant.

Sender crossed his arms across his chest. "Nu," he taunted Heaven, "I'm waiting."

A small figure appeared on the horizon, then grew larger. A car? No, a truck winding erratically down the road from the camp.

"Please, Sender, please. Get out of the road. If you won't do it for yourself, do it for us. You're throwing away all our lives."

"Sorry, friends, but I've made up my mind. I'm at the end of my rope."

He stood his ground at the road's center.

As the vehicle approached, they recognized it as the Slovak Army truck, its sides freshly painted over with Wehrmacht insignia.

The truck wasn't going very fast, but neither did it slow down when the driver spotted Sender. Bentzi and Vlad cringed behind the trees. Sender's legs were spread solidly across the road divider. He waved his arms at the truck.

The truck stopped. A German soldier looked out the driver's side window.

"What's the matter?" he said, quite amiably. Then he hiccupped loudly.

"Motor pool," said Sender. "We need to check the truck."

"Good," said the driver pleasantly. "Who's 'we?'"

"My assistants." Sender whistled towards the roadside. Vlad and Bentzi were forced to come out.

Sender lifted the hood. The three of them huddled beneath it.

"You have to get us all killed, don't you," snarled Bentzi.

"'I shall not die, but I shall live, and tell of God's works,'" quoted Sender.

"Oh, Sender," said Vlad, wringing his hands, "if only your German accent didn't sound so Yiddish."

Sender slammed the hood shut. "She's smooth as a polished apple, boys." Although he could see only the driver, he felt there were other men in the cab.

"Thank you, fellas," said the driver. "Can we give you a lift?"

Bentzi and Vlad looked at each other. It had to be a trick. They were shaven-headed stick figures in camp pajamas. How could the Germans mistake them for anything but Jews? But they had no choice. They had to go along now.

"That would be great," said Sender. "Where are you headed?"

"To the Russian front. We're supposed to deliver warm winter clothing to the fighting forces."

"Any chance of going to Hungary?" Sender asked.

His two friends stared with eyes wide as saucers. Halter was very, very far gone.

The driver consulted his comrades. "No problem we can see."

Bentzi and Vlad were beyond shock now. Hungary was hundreds of miles in the wrong direction!

The three Jews scrambled into the back of the truck. It was piled high with pants, shirts, coats, shoes. Sender swallowed. The worldly goods of the five hundred men who had been murdered at the creek.

They climbed over the clothes, towards the back of the truck. It started moving, in the same lurching way it had come down the road.

The three soldiers in the cab, sang lustily. They hiccupped and belched. They emptied bottles at a remarkable pace, and threw them to the back of the truck.

Sender poked his head into the opening to the cab. "Say, guys, you got anything to eat?"

"Sure," said the soldier sitting in the middle. He turned his shoulder to indicate the direction, and Sender saw a pile of bread. "Hearty appetite," said the soldier.

It was coarse brown bread, going stale. Not like the fresh white loaves of The Tenderizer's sandwiches, but not like the wormy, sawdust-filled bread of the inmates' dinner, either. This bread had not been baked in the camp.

They ate until they were full. Sender silently led the grace, and Bentzi and Vlad mouthed the responses.

The truck picked up speed. They were heading south, towards Hungary.

Sender stuck his head into the cab again. "Sorry to bother you folks again, but is it all right if we take some of these clothes?"

The third German soldier said, "Help yourselves to anything you like."

The Jews shed their prison clothes and dressed in garments from the piles. Sender took much longer than the other men, who put on the first clothes they found. He tried on an overcoat, then discarded it. Chose another, tried it on, rejected that too.

"You're really crazy," said Vlad, "but your luck is simply unbelievable."

"Luck has nothing to do with it," said Sender.

The other two gaped at him. "Keep your voice down," said Bentzi, indicating the front of the truck.

"There's nothing to be afraid of," Sender laughed.

They stared at him. A lunatic.

"Don't you understand, they're *angels*."

They stared harder than ever.

"Look at them. They're identical, they look like triplets."

Bentzi and Vlad pulled away from him.

"And there are three of them," said Sender, "because each angel can perform only one task. There's one to drive us, one to feed us, and one to clothe us."

Vlad and Bentzi were pressing themselves to the walls of the truck now.

"Look," said Sender. "Look at the bottles. Smell them."

Bentzi and Vlad picked up a few of the liquor bottles that the soldiers had thrown back. They sniffed. Then they picked up other bottles and inspected those too.

The bottles were bone dry, and had no odor.

Sender found a coat he liked. It was pure cashmere.

Vlad kept sniffing bottles. "I don't understand."

Bentzi stared into space. "He's right. Sender's crazy, but he's right."

"Right about what?" Vlad asked, confused.

"Angels." Bentzi picked up a bottle but he didn't bother to smell it. "Angels don't eat or drink."

CHAPTER FORTY-ONE

Germany, March 18, 1944

Admiral Horthy, the Regent of Hungary, looked around expectantly. The main hall of Hitler's fabulous retreat, Klessheim, was filled with German officials in uniform and in diplomatic dress.

Adolf Hitler had just delivered himself of more than an hour of tirade, and he wasn't anywhere near finished. His shrieks made the chandeliers' crystal pendants strike each other. Spittle flew. At times his voice descended to the low growl of a rabid dog. Hitler was as crazy as a beetle on gasoline. Horty looked around, expecting someone to wink, nod or smirk knowingly, but every face was gazing upon the Fuhrer in adoration.

"Traitor!" screamed Hitler, pounding the table with such force that the medals bounced on the chests of field marshals. Horthy was so enthralled by the spectacle that it took him a moment to realize that Hitler had been addressing *him*.

"Hungary has been a staunch supporter of the Axis in men and materiel," he mumbled quickly. He didn't care if his statement sounded weak. The war was as good as over; Germany had lost. The sooner they surrendered, the better. There was no point in sacrificing more young boys for nothing. Maybe Hungary could still keep some of the territories that the Germans had dished out at the beginning of the war. If they waited too long, the Russians would gobble them up like chocolate truffles.

"Staunch supporter, indeed!" Hitler was foaming at the mouth. "Half a million Jews in Budapest alone. Half a m-m-m-million! Everyone a p-p-poisoned arrow in the German heart." He struck himself in the chest with a closed fist.

Horthy pressed his lips together. He was no lover of Jews, but he had expropriated their property, had locked them out of the schools and squeezed them out of the professions. He'd drafted tens of thousands into forced labor. He turned his head when the Arrow Cross had their fun. But enough was enough. The Jews made up a substantial part of the population. This was wartime, there were more urgent matters than hunting down the last of the Jews.

Finally Hitler's temper tantrum was over. Horthy was informed that he was now to meet with two senior officers, Veesenmayer and Eichmann.

The meeting was in a different room, where he was invited to take a comfortable seat and served coffee and cake. He was relieved to find that at least Veesenmayer and Eichmann looked and acted like perfectly normal people.

Horthy took a bite of cake. The Master Race had yet to create a really decent hazelnut torte. He pushed his plate away and indicated that the Germans proceed.

Quietly, modestly, the two men described a plan. For the purpose of concentrating Jews, Hungary was to be divided into six zones. Within thirteen weeks, the Jews were to be systematically funneled into the Polish resettlement area. By July seventh Hungary would be Judenrein, "cleansed" of Jews.

"Ridiculous," said Horthy, spilling coffee. "My cabinet will not allow that."

"I'm afraid they have no choice, Admiral," said Veesenmayer politely.

"Of course they do," Horthy sputtered. "Ours is an independent government."

"No," said Eichmann, eyes downcast, "they are not. They are no longer a government at all."

"What?" said Horthy, rising. Demitasse cups and spoons clattered to the floor.

"Hungary is to be occupied by German forces."

"What! When?"

"Today."

For unknown reasons, the truck driver refused to take Sender and his companions to Budapest and dumped the three in the middle of the forest.

It was long past dark but the night was balmy and the men were warmed by their new clothes and the food in their stomachs. They found a spot between some bushes and slept deeply for a few hours.

The morning was as brilliant as their new hopes. Bentzi got up and stretched.

"Aaargh," he yawned, the yawn extending into a wild roar, his arms reaching up through the trees as if he could touch the new sun.

A loud, sharp sound reverberated through the forest, as if someone had broken a large branch.

Bentzi, arms still extended, legs wide apart, fell forward and lay still.

He had been shot in the back.

Sender and Vlad remained upright, stone still. Horror overcame even the fear for their own lives.

Bentzi was dead. Bentzi who had, only hours ago, miraculously escaped the kingdom of death, had run right into death in a beautiful forest bursting with spring.

Three men came into sight, then four and five.

"Oh, shit," said the last. "Look what you've done, Erno."

Sender and Vlad jumped back. The men weren't Germans, and they didn't look like fascists. But they were Gentiles and their hands were bloody.

Sender stepped forward. "Who are you? Why did you kill this man?"

The man who'd spoken before removed his cap. "Begging m'lordship's pardon," he said in florid Hungarian, "it was all a mistake. We're partisans. We thought you were some Germans we've been tracking all night. That man..." he indicated Erno, slouched against a tree picking his teeth, "that man's tired. We all are."

"Partisans?" said Sender, "in Hungary?"

"Yessir. We're going to fight until we've driven every last German out of the sweet motherland. Hungary for the Magyars!"

"Germans in Hungary," Sender translated for Vlad. He turned back to the Hungarian. "Please, officer. Do you know? Are the Germans in Budapest, too?"

"I'm afraid so, your grace. And it's real bad for you people. They've herded them all into these 'ghettoes.'"

Vlad jumped at the word. There was no need to translate. He put his hands over his face.

"Sorry about that. But say, if you fellows can shoot, you're welcome to join us."

Erno and two other partisans scowled.

"Thanks, but we can't shoot," Sender lied. He'd served in the army, and he knew that Vlad, back when he lived like a Gentile, had gone hunting for sport. But he figured the officer's invitation was hypocritical Hungarian courtesy. And he suspected that Erno's shooting of Bentzi was not entirely accidental. "But we'd be obliged if you could lend us a shovel, so that we can bury our dead."

Sender and Vlad tried to make it on their own. They did not succeed. Soon they were hungrier than they had ever been in the camp.

They were forced to inch to the borders of the forest. They began to pilfer from the fields and barns at the edge of settled land, but only tiny bits, only enough to keep from starving.

One of the farmers caught on to their scheme. Each time they came around his field there appeared to be more food, left around invitingly.

"Maybe the farmer's a man of compassion," said Vlad.

"I don't like it," said Sender. "I think it's a trap."

But Vlad couldn't stand any more. "I'm going to give myself up to him."

"You don't even speak Hungarian."

"I speak many other languages. Besides, the language of mercy is universal."

"Throw yourself at the mercy of a Gentile?" Sender asked skeptically. But he could not dissuade Vlad.

As Sender watched from a distance, Vlad walked into the clearing before the farmhouse. His arms were raised in the air, and he called out in German and Polish and French and Russian and English.

"For the love of Almighty God, will you help a starving man?"

The door opened and Vlad disappeared into the house.

Every few hours Sender ventured near the farmhouse looking for some sign of Vlad. For a whole day he saw and heard nothing. On the second day he saw two men leave the house, carrying something wrapped in a filthy blanket. They dumped it in the forest. As soon as the men were gone, Sender leaped out from behind the trees to inspect it.

Vlad's hand, crushed, protruded from a hole in the threadbare wrapping. Even in the fading light Sender could see that the whole blanket was crawling with maggots.

He limped away but could get no more than a few yards. Hungrier than he had ever been in his life, he fell down among the brambles. Too tired to pick himself up, he wrapped himself more tightly in the cashmere coat.

It was still early evening, but if he slept, maybe death would be painless. Faint and exhausted, Sender still could not sleep.

He started to cry.

It was not the hunger or the fatigue or the terrible loneliness that led him to tears. It was not the fear of what had happened to the woman he loved, and all the Jews of Budapest. He wept for *shame*.

He was ashamed for God. Ashamed of how God had desecrated his own Name in the face of those who feared him, and those who despised him, and those who denied the very idea of him. Why had God dishonored himself?

Sender woke with a start. A man was shaking him.

"Friend, friend, don't die. We need you." The man was speaking Yiddish.

"Do you have any food?" rasped Sender.

"Very little, but you are welcome to share it with us."

"Who are you?"

"Partisans. Jewish partisans. By the way, do you know how to shoot?"

Like a sick old vulture the airplane buzzed low over the wooded terrain. It passed over northern Yugoslavia and into southern Hungary.

The Englishman gave his signal. Prepare to jump, he indicated to the paratroopers.

There were five men and a woman, packed like mules with the maximum amount of ordinance a person could carry. The woman carried as much as the men.

Renee Lebow scrutinized the RAF officer from under her lashes. She did not trust him; she trusted none of the British. Even so, she would put her life in his hands. When he said "jump," she would fling herself from the plane without a second's hesitation. Please, God, let it not be a jump to death. Not that it was death she feared, but it would be a tragic waste of her precious load—weapons for the Jewish partisans.

The officer sent off the first two paratroopers in his clipped British way. As a trained fighter Renee valued precision, yet she knew it had its limits. Jewish soldiers needed a lot more—ingenuity, flexibility, a genius for second-guessing. The British had reluctantly taught them the basics, but the Jewish teachers at the field school taught them the most important skills.

The big man Zlotnik, the one who had met practically all of her family during his daring escape, was one such teacher. There was nothing theoretical about his lessons; he taught his young charges what he had learned clawing his way through hell. He had walked out of the maw of Nazi Germany and all the way to Palestine, dodging every trap that the anti-Semites could devise.

The enemy was legion. Renee looked at the British officer and pursed her lips. She would never forget September 2, 1939, the day England declared war on Germany. The first shots England fired, the very first of the war, were not aimed at Germany at all, but at a boatload of desperate Jewish refugees trying to land in Palestine.

"Wouldn't do to boil up the wogs…er…Arabs, would it?" she'd heard one British lady say. No matter how much contempt the English had for the Arabs, no matter how boldly the Arabs supported Germany, no matter how outrageous the Arab claims, England still preferred them to the Jews.

But the Jews swallowed every insult and injury and backed the British with everything, including their lives. England, after all, gave them the one opportunity to fight their common enemy with arms. The British were false friends, but they were the only friends they had.

The RAF man gave the signal, and Renee jumped.

CHAPTER FORTY-TWO

Auschwitz

Corporal Elsa Kreutzer twisted and turned under the coverlet until all the eiderdown traveled down to the foot of the bed, leaving her with nothing but a wrinkled duvet cover to press around her shoulders.

What a horrible nightmare! She had dreamt that she was a Jew.

It was indigestion that did it. Rich food upset her. She had to stop this gorging so close to bedtime.

Besides, she was getting fat. If she kept this up, she'd look just like the other girls, with huge breasts straining at their uniform blouses like the overstuffed suitcases from the incoming trains. Already she was hiding her unbuttoned skirts under the peplum of the jackets.

Elsa made a mental note to have her skirts let out by Sonia. Sonia was a genius with a needle, better, Elsa had to admit, than she herself. Still, sewing tricks were no substitute for losing the extra weight. She could do it. She was a *German soldier* and certainly had the self-discipline.

But by lunchtime Elsa's resolve had vanished. There was pork with dumplings and applesauce, and like the others, she dug into the serving platters with gusto. Conversation did not even begin until the women had taken second helpings.

"Fried eggs would be delicious with these," Heide said wistfully. The local chickens, alas, were poor producers because of the bad air.

"Y'know," said Johanna, "this doesn't taste like pork."

Elsa had thought the same thing. It didn't taste like any meat she'd had before. But then, she hadn't had such long experience with pork dishes. There might have been parts of the pig, or pigs from some regions, that she hadn't tasted, so she kept her mouth shut. As the Talmud says, where a word is silver, silence is gold.

"You're right," said Heide, "it doesn't taste like pork. It's good, but it isn't pork."

"Don't be ridiculous," said Barbara. "What else could it be?" The meat on the plates was firm and smooth-textured, pale gray-pink, like fine marble.

Magda, the ranking woman officer, cleared her throat. "It's true, it isn't pork."

"What is it then?" asked Johanna, chewing.

"It's...well, it's Jew-flesh."

Elsa thought she would throw up, but she didn't.

"Chef said the men had had a big reception and used up the camp's entire provisions for the week," Lieutenant Magda said petulantly, "and here's all this fresh meat lying around." She stabbed deliberately at a slice on the serving platter.

The women stared at their plates in silence.

"The doctors posted a certificate in the kitchen. It's perfectly healthy."

One woman picked up her fork, looked at the meat, dipped it in applesauce, and carefully put it in her mouth. She chewed slowly, swallowed, then took another bite.

Eventually, all the women resumed eating.

Sonia, the talented seamstress, had been sent from Cracow to Paris as a young girl. At one of the major couture houses she rose from the lowest assistant to the trusted right hand of the master. Colleagues, clients, and even the couturier himself declared that she would one day rank among the great female designers of the century, with Vionnet and Schiaparelli and Chanel.

But when the first sign of trouble came, Sonia was promptly turned in. "I'm not an anti-Semite," insisted the master, "I'm a patriot. Sonia is not really French. She was born in Poland. France should be for the French."

The Paris couture had been Sonia's universe. With parents left behind in Poland, the artists and craftsmen had become her entire family. Once betrayed, she was lost.

Sonia was pushed onto one of the earliest western transports and landed in Auschwitz. An able-bodied young woman, she was sent to the work camp. There she might have died quickly, but as she was changing into the camp uniform Lieutenant Magda noticed her stunning, if ragged, outfit. Magda tested Sonia's skills by having her construct a secret pocket in her officer's uniform, where jewels could be hidden.

Sonia did the job with speed and finesse. She was elevated to the position of seamstress to the guards and officers.

But Sonia was too demoralized to exploit her role. The only extra food she received were the scraps that her "clientele" left thoughtlessly in the fitting room.

"These waistbands are bad," said Elsa, throwing her skirts at Sonia.

"And when you're done with those, I want you to work on my summer gown," said Lieutenant Magda.

Sonia nodded. Her neck was so thin it looked like her head might snap right off.

Johanna was standing next to the sewing machine. She had no clothes to alter; she was just taking a cigarette break. "Stop sneering, you sow," she barked at Sonia.

Sonia was not sneering. Her facial muscles were rigid with starvation. She tried to rearrange her mouth, but failed.

Johanna smacked the Jewish woman. When she pulled away her hand the cigarette was flat as a coin. Sonia fell over the sewing machine, and stayed down.

"All right, that's enough lying around. Get to work on those skirts," said Elsa.

Sonia didn't move.

Johanna was incensed. "Did you hear Corporal Kreutzer? Get up!" She pulled Sonia up from the machine by her hair. One look at the face, and the practiced eyes in the room could see that the young woman was dead.

"Look what you've done, Tiedemann" fumed the lieutenant. "And that summer gown not half done."

"Some of these Jew-bitches think they're so special," Johanna said defensively, although her slap couldn't have killed the woman by itself. "They need to be taught that they're all replaceable."

No one pointed out that Sonia was not replaceable. Elsa pushed Sonia's body away from the sewing machine and got to work on her skirts.

On her induction to the SS, Elsa had been given a battery of tests and declared a perfect example of Aryan health. Her high physical and racial profile put her in a position to choose a specialty. What she wanted most of all was stationing to a Lebensborn home, a spa-like breeding center for Aryans, but the program had been discontinued with the diminishing fortunes of the Reich.

Bouncing back from disappointment, Elsa shrewdly reviewed her other prospects in the SS. Whatever the respect for the uniform, the vast majority of Germans felt that the only proper place for a woman was in the home. A woman in the military was scorned. She had gone down several rungs, even from her position as a "maid."

Then she found out about the opportunities that awaited female guards in the concentration camps. She was accepted in the service, completed a whirlwind training course, and was warmly welcomed at the system's flagship: Auschwitz.

Conditions in the camp turned her stomach. Half the officers were lesbians, and the other half were fat pigs unworthy of any man's attention!

Elsa steadied herself. With her looks and clever mind she could surely turn this set of circumstances to advantage.

It wasn't easy to stay optimistic. Of the men in the camp, most were non-Germans, who were beneath consideration. Of the Germans, most were married. Ordinarily that meant nothing to her. Except for the privileged few who housed their families at the camp itself, the men were far away from their wives, which should have left her with a wide-open field. But the sexual order was twisted at Auschwitz.

In the beginning there had been the "Doll's House," a special barracks for the youngest and most beautiful Jewish girls brought to the camp. In this place the needs of the camp's male staff was serviced. But the ideological fanatics seethed at the idea of sex between SS supermen and Jewesses. Finally, the Doll's House was shut down.

The women guards thought the men would flock to them for some good, clean National Socialist fun. But, to their fury, the men found comfort instead among the Polish slatterns in the towns outside the camp. Imagine! While the Poles were not contaminated subhumans like the Jews, they were a slave-race, unfit for the precious semen of Aryans. The appeal to racial decency fell on deaf ears. Men!

Yet there were exceptions to the perfidy of the males. Elsa set her sights on one of the camp's political purists, a man so dedicated that he never left the grounds of Auschwitz except on official business. He did have a wife, but he so seldom took leave that one had to assume the marriage was more a matter of duty than of romance.

Dr. Mengele was darkly handsome (she had always been a sucker for dark men) and had the most lovely manners. He was of the gentry and had resources of his own. It was rumored that despite his fanatical loyalty to the Fuhrer he had managed to fill the family coffers. Elsa sighed happily. It was time she got her rich man at last.

Another thing she liked about Mengele was that, despite his rigid devotion to Nazi ideals, he seemed to have a flexibility that mirrored her own. Not for them a fiery sunset of the gods, an end with Hitler and his mindless minions. After the war, she and Josef would go on to bigger and better things.

The war was going to end, and not with victory for Germany. Another year—two at most—and it would be finished. The truly superior among them would rise in whatever conditions prevailed. Rise and thrive. Elsa decided that Dr. Mengele would be her partner in that new world.

The next time they dined with the men, Elsa dressed with care. She did her hair in a thick roll, emphasizing the pure blondness of it, the platinum roots. Makeup was frowned upon, but she slicked her lips with red. Her message had to be unmistakable.

Choosing the perfect moment, oozing allure, she approached the doctor. He was seated at the table, eating his careful portion of dinner, a model of self-control.

Elsa brushed against the back of his chair. Too subtle. She went by again, this time running a finger up the nape of his neck, scratching him.

He rose to his feet, turned, and surveyed her icily. "What can I do for you, corporal?"

She licked her puffed and reddened lips. His coldness was unbearably exciting. She crooked her finger.

He bent down stiffly, and she whispered in his ear. "What you can do for me, Dr. Mengele, is give me a baby.

He jerked back up, stung. "Excuse me!"

"Yes," she said, "a little gift. From you to me. From us to the Fuhrer."

His eyes narrowed. He looked at Elsa as if she were a newly discovered species of insect that it was his onerous duty as a scientist to type and classify.

"Corporal," he said, his voice flat. "Your appearance and behavior are treasonous acts against the ancestors, against the race."

Elsa ran from the dining room. As a sure sign of the depth of her humiliation, she left dinner behind. She cried in her room until her comrades returned, but they could not comfort her.

"Oh, Mengele is such a stiff," said Johanna, "he's got an iron rod up his ass."

"But that's what our men *should* be like," wailed Elsa. "He's a war hero, and the most dedicated man in the camp. I don't measure up, that's why he despises me."

"Bullshit," said Barbara, "he's a faggot, like the rest of them."

"No, no," said Elsa, "he doesn't take little boys, like some of them."

"That's true," said Heide. "He doesn't seem to have sex, or want sex, with anyone. There's a few like that. Downright odd."

"It's not odd, it's tragic. My fate is tragic," said Elsa.

Everyone agreed that her fate, their fate, and that of all Germany, was tragic.

Later the lieutenant came to see Elsa, who was still sobbing into her pillow.

"There, there," said the officer, stroking her hair, letting the strokes lengthen until her hand slid down Elsa's spine to its root.

Massive transports were coming in now from Hungary. Elsa, with the rare ability to speak that quirkiest of languages, was much in demand. Many talents were needed to keep order because the Hungarian Jews were in relatively good physical condition. They had been in the ghetto for a short time, so they weren't half-dead on arrival, like Jews from other countries. The girls joked, "These Jews will have to be gassed twice."

Elsa sniffed in contempt at the strange Jewish women put in her charge. They were so ridiculously optimistic. The stupid bitches had it coming. Each of them thought: yes, terrible things were happening to Jews. But other kinds of Jews. Not people like us.

Each of them thought, *it could never happen to me.*

CHAPTER FORTY-THREE

Budapest

From the front parlor window, Kitty looked out to see the sad parade. The elegant people of Stefania Street left their gracious homes in taxis and hired limousines. They wore silk and lambswool, but they bore the bright yellow badges all the same.

Since the Germans marched in, there had been no end to the shocks. In the neighborhood where she kept the apartment, cheap whores could be seen, garishly dyed hair competing with the glare of their badges. They rushed around pulling the hands of tiny, fatherless children, also bearing the ghastly mark. Rich or poor, brilliant or simple, noble or tawdry, Hasidic or baptized, the Jews were in terrible trouble.

Kitty had to force herself to eat these days. Miklos had gone on his mission, but he had not returned. She had maneuvered Miss Pallfey into a visit to her brother in the country, but the estate staff had no information about Miklos. Finally, she asked the count about the man who provided the hunting weapons. He acknowledged that Miklos had disappeared.

The count looked at Julia's crestfallen face. "Why? Did he get you pregnant?"

She blushed furiously at his presumption. "Of course not."

"In that case," the count shrugged, "what difference does it make? With the Germans about there won't be much sport anyway." The count sneered. "Those parvenus. They think they're aristocrats, like that Goering. Hah! Rings on four of his fingers. Well, it's just a matter of time 'till they get their comeuppance."

Kitty returned to Budapest haggard with worry and fear. Sometimes she thought about telling all to Miss Pallfey. Her employer was an odd bird, but Therese was a formidably intelligent woman, and had nothing but contempt for superstition, ideology and politics. Maybe she'd have some helpful advice. Kitty was about to reveal her true identity, but hesitated at the last moment.

In her room, she and Mitzi buried their heads in the pillow that still smelled of Sender. Kitty rose at dawn, hours before Miss Pallfey woke. She'd take Mitzi out and bring some food up to the "tenants" of her apartment, who were now trapped like mice.

Auschwitz

The camp was changing dramatically. With the war drawing to a close, the Nazis had to act very quickly and very efficiently to kill the maximum number of Jews in the little time remaining. They considered themselves lucky to get Hungary at this time—with more than a million head, a sizable proportion of the Jews left in the world.

The giant transports ran day and night. Freight cars that could have brought warm clothing to the troops on the Russian front, were deployed to carry Jews instead. When the deportation traffic peaked, even ammunition had to wait at the side of the tracks. There were some things, as the Fuhrer saw it, that were more important than the lives of German boys.

Investments were made to make Auschwitz more efficient. Automatic elevators now brought the gassed corpses up to the crematoria. Excess heat from the high-speed, self-fueling ovens dried the washed hair of the Jews so quickly that they were processing seven tons of human hair at a time.

Germany's major corporations clamored for more workers, and Auschwitz churned out slave labor. Munitions factories had to maximize production now; once the war was over, there would be no more easy profits. So the camps sent out tens of thousands of healthy women to be worked to death. Women were preferred to men because they were more profitable. A man, lasting only a few months, would garner the factories only a few hundred dollars. A woman, with an average nine-month life span, yielded $745 in profit, not including her bones and other physical residue.

Southern Hungary

Inside the cave that was deep in the heart of the Hungarian forest, the sounds of shovels and picks and human voices were magnified.

"And after that," said Renee, her voice dripping irony, "you can always find another fish."

"Fish?" said the Jew from Sighet, "what are you talking about?"

Sender chuckled to himself. Those Lebow women! Weren't they the sharpest, most learned girls in the world?

Sender dug the spade in deeper and scooped up a huge chunk of earth. The work was going quickly. Renee's presence, literally dropped from the sky, was a divine sign that Kitty was alive. All he had to do was imagine he was digging a tunnel, and that Kitty was at the end of it, and the hours flew by.

A cloud of dust surrounded Renee. The young woman worked as hard as any man, and accomplished more. Renee had been sent from Palestine to help organize the Jewish resistance. Right now they were a disheveled, dazed, ragtag group of refugees, almost all men, who had escaped from ghettos and slave labor camps.

Although Renee had come bearing only the munitions strapped to her body, she carried greater gifts from the Jews of Palestine. She had knowledge of how to create weapons from next to nothing. She had a strategy for underground bunkers—one of which they were digging now. She had detailed plans for stealth missions into occupied territories, and for the detour of trains heading to Polish "resettlement."

Renee had information. She confirmed what they all suspected about the Germans dividing up Jewish Hungary for annihilation. Most of all, she had an abundance of what the Land of Israel provided its sons and daughters from its very soil: confidence.

Excavating the bunker at breakneck speed, Renee still managed to have ideological conversations with the men. The remark about the fish came during the discussion she kept up throughout the furious digging. They had been talking about what they would do *After*. It was just a matter of time now. The Soviets were already at the Carpathians, and the Americans were moving in from the west, unstoppable.

Left unsaid were the thousand "sure things" to end the horror that had turned to dust. There was the pope who hated fascism who had died suddenly, mysteriously, and been replaced by one who smiled at Germany. There had been deals to exchange Jews for trucks that had been scuttled by the Allies as counterproductive to the war effort. The list was endless.

One day, some day, God's anger would pass. If only they could hold out until then.

The man from Sighet said that he had a cousin in Canada. With all his family in Europe dead, he would go to Canada.

Renee explained her reference to a story from the Talmud. "Travelers on a ship come upon what looks like an idyllic little island. It's covered with lush vegetation and seems hospitable. Looking closer, they see that the place is no island, but the back of a gigantic fish. Still, they get off their ship and settle on the 'land.'

"A heat wave strikes, and the fish, seeking relief, turns over, destroying the entire 'island.' Some of the people manage to escape and board their old, trustworthy ship. As they sail, they come upon another, even more perfect island. Alas, this one too is the back of a fish. Even so..."

Sender shook his head. The guy from Sighet disdained the Talmud and refused to accept its bitter lesson about the Diaspora.

The Gestapo interrogator was at the point of giving up. He paused for a moment to consider what method of killing Renee would give him some satisfaction, a little return for his hard work.

Despite the pain that fogged her consciousness, Renee realized that this was the end. She had to seize the moment.

"All right," she wheezed, "I'll tell you."

The Gestapo interrogator was surprised, but he repeated mechanically, "You'll tell us where your fellow rats are, and the pain will stop."

Renee almost laughed. The hell she would. And, anyway, she knew there was only one way the pain would stop.

"I'll tell you where the arms are," she croaked.

"Arms?" he moved closer.

She thought quickly. Her mind was suddenly clear. The Germans knew full well how pathetic their cache was. That wasn't enough of a draw.

"Arms, yes. And...and...treasure."

"Treasure," he repeated, his eyes widening, and Renee knew she'd hooked him.

The idea that the Jews, after everything that had been done to them, were still incredibly wealthy, refused to die. No matter what experience had proved to the anti-Semites—that the Jews now had about as many treasures as they had friends who cared whether they lived or died—the myth persisted, immortal.

A string of staff cars packed with officers followed the one in which Renee sat. She directed the convoy to a clearing in the forest. Once on their feet, Renee hobbled and limped, but strode forward. She made as much noise as she could. Please God, she prayed, let no one be there. Let no one try to pull off a rescue.

After about a mile's hike, they came to the entrance of the cave, and she breathed a sigh of relief.

"There," she said, pointing a finger that had no nail. The Germans drew their weapons and directing their flashlights to every side, entering excitedly behind her.

Inside the cave, dozens of SS men illuminated the walls and were thrilled to find evidence of recent excavation. They put their weapons down and, holding the flashlights in their mouths, began digging furiously at the soft earth with their hands.

Renee lifted the weapon nearest her. It was an MP-40 submachine gun, a recent addition to the Wehrmacht's arsenal, but one she knew well. Had she tried to shoot the men, others would have overcome her. But she turned her back on them, hiding the weapon with her body.

What happened next, happened with blinding speed. Only to Renee did the time seem deliciously languid.

Happy. She was happier than she had ever been before. This was the greatest day of her life. She would be leaving this earth now, and she had produced no children. Still, the Jewish people lived, and would live forever, and she in them.

She had tilled no soil, planted no seeds, but her Land would bloom, would burst with flowers. Eretz Yisrael would become more and more beautiful, and she with it.

Renee held the submachine gun parallel to her ravaged body. Flame burst from it, splintering two overhead beams. Its support gone, the natural roof of the cave fell in, along with a hundred tons of rock, soil, and decayed wood.

The man from Sighet was no Zionist, and no Torah scholar. But he was a damn good engineer.

CHAPTER FORTY-FOUR

July 24, 1944, Auschwitz

In deepest summer, dawn comes early, but the train from Greece preceded the first rays of sun. It had been racing for days, stopping only to change crews.

Ordinarily, the stationmaster enjoyed making up lies to cajole new arrivals. "Will diabetics who are not permitted sugar *please* report to the staff after bathing," he might say, brow furrowed in concern. But it was hot already, and he was in a foul mood.

"Get your asses out of there, you lazy Jewish dogs!" he screamed.

There was no response.

He shot into the first cars that were opened. Still, silence.

Every single passenger on the train was dead.

That first train was an omen. Before nightfall, 24,000 Jews would be killed, not including the Greeks or any of the others who arrived dead. In all the history of mankind, it was the greatest number of people ever murdered in a single place in a single day.

Rachel-Leah trudged to the warehouse area to begin the day's work. It was general policy to let the women keep the shoes they came with, but hers had worn out an eternity ago. Every morning she put on a pair of the camp-issue wooden clogs to get through the mud, which even on a day of scalding sun, would not dry up.

The clogs were crude and splintered and came in only one size. However, she only had to get to the warehouses in them. Once there, she could choose another pair.

Nothing was as plentiful in the warehouses as shoes. There were literally mountains of them. Every day, she would pick a comfortable pair to work in. Then, just before leaving, she would change into another, very large pair. She would stuff these with food and medicine and wear them back to the barracks.

Rachel-Leah shuffled deftly on the swampy ground in the unwieldy clogs. She was bent nearly double, so that she looked like a gnarled old woman. But there was a sharpness to her eye and authority in her step. Of the 30,000 women in her barracks, Rachel-Leah was almost unique. She had been at Auschwitz for more than two years.

It was forbidden for Jews to speak to SS officers, but Ursula, the guard, gave her a flicker of a smile. Rachel-Leah had made Ursula very rich.

Rachel-Leah got immediately to work. Her specialty was theft, precision larceny for her select patrons. Besides Ursula and Ursula's male supervisor, Rachel-Leah procured for no less a dignitary than the wife of the camp commandant. Thanks to "her" Slovak Jewess, Mrs. Hoss was able to send her relatives regular packages of the most exotic luxuries, which they sold for huge profits.

About an hour into the workday Corporal Kreutzer appeared in the doorway.

"Come with me, Ursula."

"I'm busy, Elsa."

"Too bad. All hell is breaking loose at processing. We've never seen so many incoming trains, and it's going to get worse. We need every hand."

Ursula reluctantly left. Rachel-Leah was pleased. She would have just as much work as with Ursula hovering, but now she could talk to her "pupil" as she worked.

Goldie was her "ward." The girl had come recently from northern Romania, where most of the Jews spoke Hungarian, so they had that in common. Goldie had confided to Rachel-Leah that she was only twelve years old. She had passed selection because of her size and development. Goldie said that her mother used to wring her hands, wondering how she would marry off such a big hunk of a girl.

Goldie pulled silk underwear out of a suitcase. "Mrs. Hoss?" she asked.

Rachel-Leah gave a quick glance. "Not good enough. Put it aside for Ursula."

Next they came upon some long woolen underwear. "We'll put these on under our clothes and bring them back to the barracks," said Rachel-Leah.

"But it's so hot," complained Goldie.

"The starving ones are always cold."

Goldie did as she was told. When prisoners were that cold they were near death, but Rachel-Leah never accepted any excuse for abandoning them. You did what you could to relieve the suffering of your fellow Jews. Life and death were God's business.

They worked in silence for a while, then Rachel-Leah said, "You know that Elsa who came to pick up the boss?"

"Sure. May her name be erased." The erasure of a name was the ultimate Jewish curse. The women wished it regularly upon Germany and all things German.

"I know her from somewhere."

"Come on!"

"Really."

"Your town had Germans?"

"No, no. But I know her from *somewhere*. I'm sure of it."

They dropped back into silence. It was really too hot to talk. The temperature kept climbing, but there were no special water rations for the slave workers.

"I can't take this," said Goldie, choking on the stifling, ash-filled air. "I'm thinking, maybe I should volunteer to work in the factory tomorrow."

"God forbid!" The idea was so alarming that Rachel-Leah's busy hands stopped.

"Why? It's got to be better than this. Any place is better than the camp."

"You fool. The factory is like a gas chamber, only slower."

I.G. Farben had a synthetic rubber plant outside the camp. Hardly any of the workers there lasted as much as four months.

"But they don't have the SS over them, with the whips and the selections."

"Listen girl, the civilians who run the place are so sadistic that I've heard there were times when the *SS* has intervened on the prisoners' behalf."

"I don't believe it," said Goldie. She said that all the time.

By noon Elsa's head ached and the lower half of her belly cramped ominously. She could hardly wait for lunch. But when she got to the women's dining room they announced that, due to the crush of incoming Jews from Hungary, the full-course dinner would not be served. Staff were invited to help themselves to sandwiches and beer.

She gulped a few aspirin and ate a sandwich and a pickle. The beer was cool and refreshing, so she had two large glasses of it. Then of course she had to pee. Elsa cursed under her breath. This day should have been cut out of the calendar.

She went back to the dining room. "Anybody got a menstrual pad?" she asked loudly. A year ago she would never have been so crude. But look at her company. The women were snuffling at the buffet table like pigs at a trough. They were completely disheveled, and not one of them had bothered to button or belt her jacket. It didn't make matters any better that she hadn't, either.

Nobody had a rag for her. "Damn. Now I have to go back to quarters. I hate getting the curse."

"Yes," said Heide, her mouth full, "it's such a pain. The Jew-women are lucky. They never get it."

Elsa went back to her room. She cleaned herself up, then washed her face. It was puffy and tender and showed the beginning of an unsightly sunburn. She was getting old. She felt old.

She brushed back the white-blond hair. With that color it would be impossible to tell when the gray arrived. Old blondes just faded away. The luster, she thought, the luster is already gone.

Ugly. No wonder Mengele had rejected her.

"That's enough preening, Corporal." Magda Schmidt shoved her aside to use the mirror. The lieutenant was all dressed up in civilian clothes. She looked sharp in the summer dress that had been designed and cut by the much-missed Sonia. She also sported chic crocodile shoes and a crocodile handbag. Elsa noted with sour pleasure that Magda's hat and gloves were cheap and didn't match the rest of the outfit. Probably bought those herself. The cattle-car ride inevitably crushed hats and dirtied gloves.

Where the hell was Magda going? All leaves had been cancelled. But Elsa couldn't say anything. A German soldier never questions a superior.

The lieutenant finished off with some jewelry. She cocked her head as she clipped on earrings. Elsa glared enviously at a large pair of sapphires set in enamel.

She felt the bile rise up like mercury in a thermometer. Her head throbbed with rage. It was always someone else who got the jewels. That insipid Martha and her rubies. The ugly old political wife who got them next. And now this shirker, this lousy excuse for a soldier, was getting *her sapphires*.

The lieutenant sensed Elsa's eyes drilling. "Cute, aren't they?" she said, arranging her hair to better display the earrings.

"Sapphires that size can hardly be called 'cute.'"

"Sapphires!" Magda snorted. She removed an earring and handed it to Elsa.

Elsa examined the piece. It was not a stone at all. The earring was set with an eyeball. The iris was the dreamy blue of a baby whose eyes had not yet turned. In six months or so it might have become brown, or a clarified, vivid blue.

"You can have a pair cheap, if you like," said the lieutenant. "Heide makes them. She's so good at crafts."

It was after eight when the order came to stop work. Goldie and Rachel-Leah were exhausted and dehydrated, but glad that Ursula had not returned, so they could load up with booty. They left in shoes as big as clowns'.

Goldie's feet were small for her body size. Her large shoes contained bread and cheese. Rachel-Leah walked on a king's ransom of walnut meats and raisins.

They lined up for roll call, their faces in the uniform misery of the thousands of prisoners, but their hearts full of hope for the evening. After the supper of watery soup, they would feast. There was enough to pay off the kapo, and for the sick woman in the bunk, too. Real food might control her fever, and save her from the camp hospital.

Elsa was beside herself with rage. Her nerves felt as if they were sticking up out of her skin. Would this day never end?

Where was Lieutenant Schmidt? Where the hell was that sow? She was supposed to do roll-call. If she didn't show up, Elsa would have to do it.

But she didn't know how. Male guards were watching, smirks on their faces, waiting for her to make a fool of herself. Their guns were slung loosely. They were tired after a long day of brutalizing Jews. Now they expected entertainment.

Elsa was so on edge she thought: if anyone touches me I will burst into flames.

She strutted before one long row of Jewesses and then another, playing for time. Still, Magda did not appear. It was the second time that Elsa walked past that Rachel-Leah suddenly realized where she knew her from.

"Eva," she breathed. "Eva Lebow."

"What?" Elsa's word was quiet as a feather landing.

Rachel-Leah's voice was just a hush louder. "It's me, Rachel-Leah. Sari's niece. Kitty's best friend. Remember?"

The last word was stifled by Goldie's hand. She was so desperate to quiet her mentor, that she had broken rank.

Maybe if Goldie had stayed still, nothing would have happened. The whole exchange had been so quiet. Besides the three of them, only the prisoner on the other side of Rachel-Leah had heard. But Goldie was a child, didn't know the protocol.

Elsa felt a moment of relief. She didn't have to improvise now. Prisoners who broke rank had to be punished. It was a law written in stone. In blood. The male guards moved closer for the view.

Elsa relaxed the knot of fear in her neck. There was nothing to worry about. No one had heard the stupid sow from Janace. Even if they did, her words meant nothing. It was hardly unusual for prisoners to go raving mad. There was no record anywhere of Elsa's past. Nothing but the death certificate in Ruhigbad, and in six years neither the Gestapo nor the Party not the SS had bothered looking it up.

Punishment for roll-call violation was routine. Goldie and Rachel-Leah were called out in the center of the yard, where everyone could see them. They were ordered to raise their thin skirts and kneel on the gravel. Each of them was handed a large stone and made to hold it out with straight arms, parallel to the ground. To lower, much less drop, the stone, was to earn a severe beating.

Goldie tired very soon. She shifted her weight on her tortured knees. It caused one shoe to come off her foot, and the precious store of food spilled out.

"Look at that," Elsa said to Ursula, who had just arrived.

Ursula pretended to be shocked. She had always looked the other way when her girls stole food. She wanted them to stay nice and healthy, so they could continue scavenging for her. But now the sweet deal was over. Damn those Jew-girls.

Ursula hit Goldie over the head with a truncheon. "Jew-shit! How dare you steal from the Reich!" she roared.

Goldie dropped her stone. Ursula had no choice but to hit her again. And again. Goldie's last words were, "Mommy, Mommy." She sounded just like a twelve-year-old.

Rachel-Leah kept her feet still, her arms straight, and her eyes lowered. She was mistaken about Kreutzer. It wasn't that a masquerade as an SS woman was beyond a Lebow. They were so smart and fast on their feet. But, while Eva had always been stuck-up, and maybe mean, Elsa Kreutzer was a sadistic killer.

It was true that the Nazis had little trouble recruiting kapos from the Jewish girls. There were some Jews who agreed to torment the others for a little extra food. Kapos merely proved what everyone knew, that there were bad Jews. But Kreutzer crossed the last line. Her acts were impossible for "the merciful children of the merciful."

Rachel-Leah dared not raise her eyes to prove her hypothesis. Kreutzer walked by again. And again. She had beautiful legs. Slim ankles, gently curving calves. Rachel-Leah had seen those legs a hundred times. Shopping with Kitty for shoes and hose. Bending down to pin Sari's hem. Kreutzer *was* Eva Lebow Blumenthal.

Elsa trembled with rage. What should she do now? The lieutenant had still not arrived. She'd never seen anyone hold the rock as long as this Hasidic idiot. Why wouldn't she just call out "Hear O Israel" and get it over with, for Christ's sake.

It was getting dark. "No one gets supper until this piece of dirt has learned her lesson," Elsa cried out impulsively.

There was no groan. All sounds were prohibited. But the thought of it passed over the prisoners like wind over grass, bending each blade.

"Hurry up and die," Rachel-Leah could feel them saying in their heads.

I won't. I won't die for anyone. No one has the right to demand that of me. I am sorry for my sisters, for their hunger. But I will not die for anyone's sake.

The pain in her knees and her arm and her back made Rachel-Leah's eyes swim in her head. But she refused to shut her eyes, to ease the loss of consciousness.

It was fully dark now. The moon was a narrow crescent, because it was only the fourth day of the month. Of the evil month of Av. No, with night, it became the fifth. Just four more days until the blackest day of all, the Ninth of Av. But what difference did it make? With God's face in shadow, all days were equally evil. The Ninth of Av or the Rejoicing of the Law were all the same now.

The Rejoicing of the Law, the merriest holiday of all. The great synagogue of Janace is so packed, you can hardly breathe. She's saved a front-row seat for Kitty, but Kitty hasn't shown up yet.

Below, in the men's section, Chaim, her Chaim, is dancing around the bima with the other men. His back is to her—the prayer shawl soft ivory now—but soon he will come around and look up to the balcony, and meet her gaze, and smile. The blazing lights of the synagogue are dim compared to the smile on her darling's homely face.

Chaim is so happy. He has been honored with carrying a Torah scroll. It's the big one, with the maroon-velvet cover and the silver crown.

But wait! In his other arm, Chaim carries their son, little Chaim. He reaches out to her. "Mommy, Mommy, look at me!"

"What a darling child," exclaims the head of the women's burial society, who isn't at all cranky on this fine evening. "May no evil eye befall him."

No evil eye will, she's sure, for she's tied a red ribbon around little Chaim's pony tail. His hair is long and a bit wild, now that he's past two. On his third birthday he will get his first haircut at a large celebration, in the mystical Hasidic tradition.

She'd better hurry with the party plans, there are just a few months to go. Luckily, she has her mother and her sisters and sisters-in-law to help with the cooking.

Chaim comes around the bima again, with the Torah and the baby. It's such a heavy Torah, the biggest in the synagogue's Holy Ark, and little Chaim is fooling around mischievously in his father's grasp. Her arms tighten on the balcony rail, her knees push against the decorative grill-work. She's nervous about the possibility that, God forbid, he might drop the child or the Torah or both. The idea of giving a man his size, and with a kid to carry, such a large scroll! After services she will give the sexton what for.

"What a darling outfit on your son," says one of the Minsky girls, she can't tell which. They're all clothes horses, so it's quite a compliment. "Thank you," she says off-handedly, as if she dresses little Chaim in Belgian lace and velvet shorts every day.

Aunt Sari has made the outfit. She glances around and, sure enough, there's Aunt Sari with her nose in a holy book. But her expression isn't the usual anxious one. She's serene and prettier than ever. Next to her is her sister Martha, laughing at something one of her daughters said. They're such fine girls, she thinks, not at all conceited despite being rich.

Laughing with them—laughing?—is Bayla Halter. What's this? She must be engaged. Bayla reminds her that Kitty is still not here. Neither is Sender. Those two lovebirds, she can just imagine what they're up to. She feels herself blush.

At that very moment Chaim comes 'round the bima again. He catches her blush and knows exactly what she's thinking and blushes too. She thinks she will die of embarrassment and love at the same time.

Little Chaim waves his special Rejoicing of the Law flag, of which he's awfully proud. It's got a picture of happy children with a Torah scroll on it. She's made the flag even fancier by gluing on extra glitter and sequins. She's impaled a jelly apple on the flagstaff, too, and little Chaim has been taking bites of it all evening, so that his plump little cheeks are smeared bright red with the candy. She presses harder, harder against the balcony, for fear he will stain the lace shirt.

Uncle Joseph is also missing. Oh, he's likely to go to the special service in the Rebbe's chambers. That's probably where Sender is too. That explains everything. How awful of her to have thought ill of her friends.

Lieutenant Schmidt finally showed up. "What's this?" she asked, looking at the rows of rigid women, and those who had collapsed of thirst and hunger, doomed to be dragged away for incineration.

Elsa said nothing, only stared at Rachel-Leah's stiff form. Magda dismissed the prisoners, who could not scramble away fast enough.

"You've had a long day," the lieutenant said, but Elsa just stood silently, as still as the kneeling prisoner.

"Why don't you just shoot her?" said Magda. Elsa still didn't move. Her superior took the gun from Elsa's holster, cocked it and handed it back to her.

Elsa stood like a statue, the gun immobile in her hand.

Magda shrugged "Fine, do as you like. *I'm* not about to miss supper."

The yard was eerily lit, like the Walpurgis night ceremony. The crematoria had been working beyond capacity all day, and the chimneys glowed red in the sky, threatening to explode. In the distance, gigantic pyres of bodies continued to burn, their hellish illumination reaching up to meet the fiery sky.

Elsa wasn't hungry. She didn't feel irritable anymore either.

It was just the two of them in the big yard now, with the scattering of bodies.

Kitty still hasn't arrived. Everyone is invited over for late-night supper after services. There is a ton of food, she'd hate for it to go to waste.

Her house, not Sari's or Kitty's, because they were trying to teach little Chaim to sleep in a bed, not his crib. She and big Chaim had decided it was time little Chaim had a brother or sister...

Where is Kitty? Her sisters are here. The communist one, Helen, looks a bit ill at ease. Her daughter is enjoying herself, though. All kids love Rejoicing of the Law.

Renee is here, sitting next to Sari. It's so good that they've reconciled. She's a knockout, Renee, even in the severe Zionist outfit of white shirt and navy skirt. She'll find a good man in the Holy Land, for sure.

Who's this? That obnoxious sister, Eva. Ugh.

The rabbi's wife picks herself up, in all her dignity, and is confronting the loathsome Eva. "You have a lot of nerve, coming into a house of worship in that outfit. On a holiday, yet!"

It is an outrage. Eva is dressed in a Nazi uniform. Can you imagine?

Eva says, "All this is nothing but crap."

"Nobody's forcing you to stay here," says the rabbi's wife.

"Fine. I can't wait to leave."

Eva takes the long way out, and deliberately bumps Rachel-Leah, whose hands and knees are rigid against the balcony railing. Rachel-Leah loses her balance.

Elsa laughed as Rachel-Leah fell. All around her the red light blazed. It was hell. But she didn't believe in hell.

The gun was in her hand. She hit Rachel-Leah on the head with it. Because the woman was sprawled on the ground, Elsa had to kneel to finish her off.

"Jewish girls don't kneel," her mother's voice lectured softly.

She gave the splintered head one last blow.

"But I'm not Jewish, Mother," she said, getting to her feet.

Her left hand, the hand without the gun, swept gracefully around, indicating all of Auschwitz, as if she were showing off a newly-decorated home.

"See? There's nothing. No God. Nothing. Nothing at all."

She picked up her right hand. In the insufferable heat of the night, the gun was cool. The barrel tasted tart.

CHAPTER FORTY-FIVE

Kisvar, Hungary

"Father, come quick."

"What is it? What's the problem?" Joseph's heart sank. Was he found out?

"There's a man caught red-handed over on the Andras farm."

"A man? What sort of a man? A stranger? What did he do?" A Jew. Please God, a Jew. A Jew to be with me.

"A thief, Father! Geza and Lajos caught him right in the field."

A Jew. A hungry Jew.

Joseph ran, the cassock flying behind him like black wings.

The hamlet of Kisvar lay in an indentation of the great Hungarian plain. The land around the simple wooden church and handful of shops had been blessed with a combination of gentle air currents, bright sunshine and soft rains. Summer and winter were milder, so that the farmers could grow produce not seen elsewhere in Hungary. The climate, and the land's bounty, made it seem like a magic village.

The people of Kisvar had looked forward to a new priest who would be young and joyful and as breezy as their land. Old Father Janos had been a cold, strict drunkard. The villagers had been unhappy under his harsh rule, and they had hoped the bishop would reward their forbearance by sending them a gentle young man this time.

The entire community had gathered at the train station to meet the new priest. To greet him in style, they had brought along a cart and horse decorated with flowers and colored fringe. When the grizzled Father Istvan got off the train, they were disappointed. But they were hospitable and mannerly, so they accompanied him to his new home dancing and singing holy songs.

The villagers soon found that despite his years, Father Istvan was a man to their spirit. He had an easy way with ritual, and a calming way at the confessional. Where Father Janos's absolution was bought dearly, with long rosaries and arduous pilgrimages, Father Istvan was more likely to prescribe charity and reconciliation.

The new priest gave the most wonderful homilies. In a tiny village with nothing else to do, church attendance had always been universal (with the exception of one odd farmer, a Protestant or an atheist, no one knew which). But Father Istvan's entertaining tales of St. Mark and St. Aloysius and St. Istvan, tales with the sort of lessons ordinary folks understood, had the congregation begging for weeknight services.

People wondered why the bishop had sent such a talented man to the tiny parish. Father Istvan was no drunk; he didn't touch a drop, not even of their famous local wine. It was possible that the priest had been "indiscreet" in his former parish, but you couldn't tell from his behavior with the women—or boys—in Kisvar.

There were a few oddities. For the first week, Father Istvan said the word "plus" instead of making the sign of the cross. The sharper fellows thought his explanation—that that was how it was done in Budapest— sounded unlikely. But they wouldn't dare criticize the priest out loud. All in all, they considered themselves lucky in the new appointee.

"And where is the alleged wrongdoer?" Joseph asked the Andras brothers.

Geza and Lajos were stout, hard-working bachelors whose farm was the pearl of the county. "Where he belongs," said Geza, pointing to the ground.

Joseph blanched. "What do you mean? He's dead?"

"Sure is," Lajos nodded proudly.

"How could you do such a thing! You killed an innocent man."

"He wasn't innocent. I seen him do the stealing with my own eyes."

"You don't kill a man for stealing."

"Sure you do. Jesus said you should."

"He most certainly did not!" Joseph had read the New Testament rather hurriedly, but he was quite certain on this point.

"He didn't?" Lajos looked sheepish.

"No. Quite the contrary."

Lajos now looked worried. Then he brightened. "Maybe he isn't really dead."

"What? Hurry, take me to him."

The man—who was certainly dead—was lying in a vineyard. Joseph turned him over gently. His face was swarthy and handsome, his black hair glistened with youth.

"A terrible sin has been done today," Joseph declared to the men. "Our community, all of Kisvar, bears a grievous weight."

"Not me, I didn't have anything to do with it," a farmer burst out.

"Yes you. And I. We are responsible for our community. Every one of us is responsible for all our brothers and sisters."

The men were silenced. They turned the brims of their hats over in their hands.

Lajos Andras finally spoke. "What can we do to make up for it, Father?"

"There is no penance for murder. Not unless you can bring a man back from death." The men had never seen their priest so angry, so sad.

"The least we can do now, and it's little enough, is to give him a decent funeral. We will bury him in the churchyard."

A murmur went up from the assembled men. They had a perfectly good cemetery. The churchyard was small, and reserved for the most notable of citizens. The only person buried there in living memory had been Father Janos.

"Yes, the churchyard," the priest insisted. Where he could walk by every day and recite the kaddish, the prayer for the dead, in his heart.

The body was brought to the church. The village carpenter prepared a coffin, and women brought a shroud.

Joseph watched them remove the stranger's torn, filthy clothing. The man was not circumcised. A Gypsy.

He breathed a sigh of relief, then quickly repented. It was tragedy, unmitigated tragedy, that anyone had to die like this. For nothing. Outside Kisvar's bubble, tens of thousands (or even more?) were dying, and they were his own people. But it didn't make this one Gypsy's murder any easier to bear.

After the funeral, Lajos Andras approached him. "Father, Geza and me, we feel real bad about this. So bad we can't wait for confession. Can you see your way to absolve us? At least so we're like the rest of the village?"

Joseph frowned. "You and your brother must realize that you will have to spend the rest of your lives in penitence, prayer, and good deeds. But there is something you can do now to show your determination to do right."

"Anything, anything."

"You're to bring in the widow Kovacs' harvest."

The two brothers staggered in shock. Geza recovered himself first. "Of course, of course Father. Just as soon as we've brought in our own."

"No. Before. The work you do for God comes first."

"She has sons," Lajos pleaded.

"They're just little boys," said Joseph, "poor orphans without a father's care."

"Some of our crops may rot," said Geza.

"Yes they might."

"The widow Kovacs has such a lot of land," said Lajos.

"Yes she does," said Joseph. And still a good-looking woman. Either of the brothers could do worse.

The evening was soft as a mother. The last of the honeybees, swollen with nectar, were winding their way home from the fields, and the people of Kisvar, tired from a full summer's day of work, made their way to the little church.

Every pew was full and the young men had brought in fruit crates to sit on. Joseph decided to ignore the events of the day in his talk. He told them a story from the Talmud, with a message of repentance and forgiveness. All he changed were the names, so that Rabbi Meir became St. Mark, Rabbi Akiva, St. Aloysius.

The congregation sighed with pleasure.

"Now tell us the one about St. Aloysius and the water-smoothed rocks, Father."

"Not now, Bela. It is time for everyone to go home and have supper. Remember, there is no faith without bread, and no bread without faith."

The church emptied. Joseph was left all alone.

Alone in all the world. All day he dealt with people, yet he was lonelier than he had been hiding in the Mayor's house. There was no radio in all of Kisvar, no way to know what was happening in the world. Maybe all the Jews were dead by now, and he was the only one left.

Was he right in what he was doing, in teaching Torah to the Gentiles? The stricter rabbis would rule no. But what if there were no rabbis left? With no rabbis, and no Jews, what would become of the Torah? If God had regretted choosing the Jews, he'd need another people to give the Torah to.

The Hungarians? They were good, simple people, for the most part. But they were also capable of murder. Who then? If God had sentenced the Jews to obliteration, who could replace them? Which nation had showed itself more just or kind?

Sari. If only Sari were alive, she would be able to ease his mind. Oh, how he missed her. Everything she had ever done was a blessing to him. Even the casual talk with which she had amused him, the stories of the Catholics in the convent school, were life-saving now. She had taught him more about what the Christians were really like than all the books in the real Istvan's suitcases.

If only he hadn't jumped from the train, it would have been better. At least he could have died together with his soul, his Sari. They could have died in each other's arms. What good was life to him, now?

Joseph passed by the large crucifix at the center of the church. It was the only statue in the place, thank God.

A naive wooden piece, made by a village artisan, it couldn't have been very old. The paint was still very bright and Jesus' lips were as red as his wounds.

Lucky you, thought Joseph. In your day, all they did was crucify Jews. Look what they do to us now. Look what they do to the ones we love. Could you have stood it, could you have kept faith, if the Nazis came for your mother? He thought of that last train from Janace, of the mothers and the babies, and he sobbed and sobbed.

It was then that the housekeeper came into the church to see what was keeping Father Istvan from his supper. By breakfast time, everyone in Kisvar had heard of how their priest had stood crying at Christ's feet for the sins of the village. It proved what they'd suspected all along: Father Istvan was a saint.

CHAPTER FORTY-SIX

Budapest

Miss Pallfey smacked her lips. "Why is dinner taking so long?" she complained. Cook was making some special dishes tonight with the treasures they had received that afternoon. The smells of roast goose and apple strudel wafted through the house.

Miss Pallfey's latest freeze with her brother had been thawed with a wagon-load of presents from the country. Bags of beet sugar, flats of eggs, freshly killed partridges, live geese. There was even a new leash for Mitzi.

The gifts of food, could not have been more welcome. Hungary had begun to feel the real sting of war the past spring, when the Germans invaded, and conditions were getting worse, despite official devotion to the Fuhrer.

Stalin's troops were moving westward. Already they were bombing Buda. Over the Danube, in Pest, the sound was more beautiful to Kitty than a thousand choirs.

Miss Pallfey sat in her chair, her knees snug under a Scottish blanket, happily bossing her staff. "Not the Rosenthal china, you primitive boobs, the ones in that box, there. Yes, that's right, Julia. And you, girl, whatever your name is..."

"Rose, ma'am."

"Indeed. Fetch me some apples before I starve to death."

Outside, Stefania Street was dark and cold. The streetlights were shut off, and every window was blackened against bombing. But it was cozy inside the gracious mansion. The warmth and perfume of cooking filled every corner.

A knock on the door. Kitty's hands froze on a serving platter. Who could it be? The count would not press his luck and try for another visit with his sister.

"Answer that, Julia."

She opened the door, her other hand still frozen on the platter. "Good evening," she said, with a forced smile.

The fascists ignored her and went into the parlor.

"How dare you enter my home, you, you *barbarians*."

It was Miss Pallfey's most withering expletive. But the fascists took it lightly.

"Yes, it's sad to be away from one's family on a winter night," said the leader of the gang, "but we must all make sacrifices."

Kitty found her voice. "How can we help you gentlemen? Do you wish to dine with her ladyship?"

"Dine!" exploded Miss Pallfey. "Do you think these swine would know how to use a knife and fork? Cook will give them some bread and lard. Then they will go."

"We wouldn't dream of straining your pantry, Miss Pallfey," said the leader, to the disappointment of the sniffing gang. "Our mission is simply to protect you, madam, and all law-abiding citizens."

"Very well, then you may go and patrol the streets for your fellow hoodlums," Miss Pallfey snapped. "I am alone in this house, which is how I prefer it."

The Arrow Cross leader looked hard at Kitty.

"And the servants, of course," added Miss Pallfey. As if they counted.

"Your papers," he said to Kitty. He did not say please or address her as "miss."

Kitty took her identification out of the pocket of her cardigan. She always carried them on her person. Always.

The brute looked at the photograph, then at Kitty. She held still, her chin up.

Like husband and wife, master and dog, Kitty and the photograph of Julia Ficsorcsak resembled each other more as time passed.

Grudgingly, the Arrow Cross man returned the identity card.

"Where are the others?"

"Oh, Miss Pallfey is a bachelor-lady," Kitty chirped.

"The other *servants*, you stupid bitch."

Kitty tried to communicate telepathically. *Run, jump out the kitchen window, go, go, escape for your lives.*

"Oh, the servants. Yes, well, they're very comfortably off here. Would you like me to show you the quarters? There's something there you might find of interest. Great interest," she said, raising her eyebrows.

There was something there of interest. Diamonds. Half a necklace, a fortune in diamonds. His, if he leaves the house without the servants.

But he didn't get, or take, the hint.

"She said there's a cook. Where's the cook?"

"Where do you imagine a cook would be?" said Miss Pallfey. "In the library? What a soup-neck you are." Everyone looked at the sharp-tongued mistress. How would a titled lady know such an earthy Hungarian insult, a chicken's neck worthy of nothing but the soup pot. Kitty thought: the gnarled old walnut is smart; she's figured out who the servants are. She knows and she's not afraid. She will help.

But the thugs fanned out through the house, and returned after just a few minutes. They marched the cook, Rose, and Edward into the parlor.

The leader made short shrift of their papers. "What is this Slovak shit?" he said, throwing the papers on the floor. "Hands behind your heads. Get into the truck."

"Wait," said Kitty. "Let them get their things." She'd slip the servants the diamonds, and the rest of her money.

"They'll come back for their things," the leader said. The other men laughed.

"At least their coats," Kitty pleaded.

"It's warm where they're going."

The older woman and the young brother and sister left without looking at Kitty.

After they were gone, Miss Pallfey said, "Did you see that last one, Julia? The one with the moustache?"

Kitty leaned forward. "Yes, yes! You know him?"

"Know him? Really Julia, how would I know such trash?"

Kitty sank back. "Oh."

"No. But I did see him steal an ashtray. Imagine."

The bombing intensified. Miss Pallfey refused to let Kitty take Mitzi out, lest the dog get hurt. For exercise, she had Kitty walk Mitzi round and round the ballroom.

A shell hit near the house and plaster fell from the top-floor ceilings. Since Kitty was unable to maintain that floor by herself, they closed it off. Miss Pallfey used an old-fashioned cage elevator to get to her rooms on the second floor. But when the electricity flickered the elevator stalled. In a panic, Miss Pallfey had Kitty close off the second floor as well.

Only the telephone stayed in good working order. Several times a day Miss Pallfey called her brother at his Budapest pied-a-terre. She complained bitterly about her plight. Stuck in a crumbling house, the servants gone, and no one but good-for-nothing Julia who could hardly cook, and who was too lazy to clean the ballroom up properly after Mitzi did what she must. On the other hand, Miss Pallfey had little sympathy for the count, who had fled the country estate just ahead of the Russians.

Finally, he agreed to send her two servants, a peasant couple he had brought with him from the estate. The woman would cook, the man would do repairs.

Kitty thought the new help would give her the opportunity to leave the house. She had not been to the apartment in the red-light district since the bombing began. Even the bounteous stores of food at the mansion were running low; she could imagine how desperate the hidden Jews were.

The Russians had almost completely surrounded Budapest, yet Kitty witnessed one more action against the Jews. A family, hidden somewhere on the street, was brought out. In driving snow, with rubble falling around them, the Arrow Cross forced out the Jews. From her window, Kitty could see a little boy, still in short pants, following his parents, all of them with hands behind their heads.

Would it never end?

It was noon on one of those days when the sun reflects off brittle ice, deceiving with an impression of warmth. There was a knock at the door, but a soft one.

The peasant wife went to answer and found a woman who, despite a certain dishevelment, and with eyes and nose running from the cold, was of her mistress' class.

"A lady to see your highness, ma'am."

Kitty gasped. It was Mrs. Solomon.

Hannah was unsteady on her feet. Slowly she raised her arm up, as if to give the Hitler salute, but the gesture stopped midway, and her finger pointed. At Kitty.

"You! You, what have you done with my jewels?"

"Jewels," said Miss Pallfey. "You lent my companion jewelry?"

Mrs. Solomon ignored Miss Pallfey. She stared at Julia with crazy, blood-shot eyes. "Where are my jewels?"

Julia curtsied to Miss Pallfey. "I'll take care of this lady, Miss Pallfey."

Kitty took the woman firmly in hand and led her to her room.

"Please, Mrs. Solomon, be quiet. I'll give you what's left of the diamonds, but you must leave now."

Mrs. Solomon looked glazed, but said nothing more. Kitty undid her secret drawer and pulled out the second half of the diamond necklace. She didn't care. All the diamonds in the crust of the earth couldn't lure Miklos back with her Sender.

"Where are my jewels?" Mrs. Solomon repeated.

"I swear, this is all I have left. I'm sorry."

Mrs. Solomon took the necklace with disinterest and thrust it inside her coat.

"Where are my jewels?"

Kitty swallowed. The woman was not right in the head. She had just given a lunatic a fortune! But it was her own fortune. "Please, Mrs. Solomon..."

Suddenly the woman jumped on Kitty, her hands on her neck. "Where are my jewels, you wicked whore?" she screamed in Yiddish. "Where is my son, my kaddish-sayer? Where is my angel to take to the bridal canopy? Talk, you kidnapper!"

"Mrs. Solomon, steady yourself," Kitty whispered fiercely. "Edward and Rose may well be alive. They're young and healthy, and they've been well fed. For sure they were taken to work camps." She wished she were as certain as her words.

Mrs. Solomon dropped her hands from Kitty's neck, but reason hadn't swayed her. "Where are my jewels?" she repeated monotonously.

Kitty hustled Mrs. Solomon out of the house, quietly, she thought.

She returned to the parlor, ready to answer Miss Pallfey's questions.

But Miss Pallfey wasn't interested in the visitor.

"So, you're a Jew, Julia."

It was a relief to say it at last. "Yes, Miss Pallfey. I am."

"Get out."

"What?" She must have misheard. Miss Pallfey didn't look angry.

"Get out. I'll have no Jews in my house."

"Miss Pallfey, this isn't like you! Surely, you are above illogical prejudice. And there's nothing to fear from the authorities. They've already passed my papers."

"I'm not afraid of any stupid Arrow Cross. But I don't want any Jews in my house. Not now and not ever. Get your things and go."

There was nothing else to say. "Yes, ma'am."

Kitty packed her bags quickly. She put on boots, several sweaters, gloves. It was very cold out. She put on her coat and pinned her hat on securely. Then she opened her secret drawer.

The money was gone.

All of it, her savings, her jailhouse earnings. All gone.

She had seen it just minutes ago, when she gave the diamonds to Mrs. Solomon. Had the distraught woman taken the money? No, she had been too addled.

In the parlor Miss Pallfey said, "Hurry, get out. You've been here long enough."

Kitty was eager to leave. Miss Pallfey might call the police, might already have done so.

"I...I must ask you for my wages."

Miss Pallfey gestured in irritation for Kitty to wheel her over to a sideboard. She extracted a wallet and handed Kitty the exact amount owed, not counting payment for the day. A ballet of sneers played upon her face.

"Money. That's all you people care about, isn't it?"

Kitty didn't say thank you or goodbye, but headed straight for the front hall. Mitzi was waiting. Seeing Kitty dressed in a coat, she wagged her tail in excitement.

"Don't fuss, little darling," said Miss Pallfey. "The Jewess is clearing out."

Mitzi scurried out of the room then returned, her new leash in her mouth.

"No Mitzi," called Miss Pallfey, "come to Mother. Come sit in my lap."

But Mitzi followed Kitty without pause.

The peasant woman stood idly by the door. The look on her face solved the mystery of who took the money. "Stupid peasant, am I?" it said. "Look who's outsmarted those clever Jews. And there isn't a thing you can do about it."

Kitty put down her bags, and opened the front door. She did not bother to shut the door or look behind her as she walked out into the snow-covered street. But she could hear Miss Pallfey calling until her voice faded.

"Come back, my darling! Do you hear me? Where's that stupid peasant? Go get the dog. Do you hear me? Do you hear me?"

Even Mitzi knew the way to the apartment. Despite the snowy ground and the icy wind, they got there soon enough. Outside, Kitty paused. What other damage could the deranged Mrs. Solomon have done? Had she betrayed the other Jews in the apartment? Would it be a trap?

Kitty circled the building, her hands freezing on the suitcases, Mitzi following her every step. She stopped and looked up at the apartment window. A lace curtain (she had put it up herself) blew out of the window.

Why was the window open? It was January, and heating fuel was very dear.

There were so many people, and inadequate toilet facilities, and no opportunity for washing. Still, the open window was unnerving.

God of Israel, give me wisdom.

"Let's get out of here," she whispered to Mitzi.

There was no place in the world for her to go, nor any money to rent a room. "Oh, Mitzi, if only Sender were here," she cried illogically. "He'd see to it that we were warm and safe in a fancy hotel."

They had gotten only half a block away, in no particular direction, when they heard the song of a giant bird coming in their direction. The bird passed over them and dropped its egg.

The apartment house and two neighboring buildings disintegrated. Chaos and dust rose up, as neat structures and ordered lives went down. A white powder, soft as snow, fell onto Kitty's coat.

Central Hungary

Sender ran over the white landscape, swift as a rabbit. His flight was desperate and the snow covered a thousand traps.

Although most of Hungary was now in anti-fascist hands, and Budapest was under Soviet siege, the deportation of the Jews to the Polish camps continued unabated. Both Germans and Arrow Cross kept up anti-Jewish "actions" as if there was no war going on, as if there were no defeat to be reckoned with, as if their lives depended on it.

The Jewish partisans had long run out of weapons. But Sender had food. He was carrying a sack full to a band of refugees who needed the strength to escape.

"Halt! Hands up!"

Sender stopped, but he didn't raise his hands. The order had been given in German, but bad German, in a thick Russian accent.

"I'm friend, not foe, comrade," he said in Russian. His Russian wasn't that good, but a sight better than the other man's German.

The fellow came from the snowy brush. He was as blond and blue-eyed as any German, but his uniform was a comfort. A red star glinted on his military cap.

"I gave you an order," the soldier said in Russian. "Hands up."

Sender smiled. The boy was sixteen at most. The Soviets had suffered terrible losses, and been forced to draft youngsters.

Sender raised his hands. They were clothed in dove-gray kidskin gloves that he had found in a pocket of the cashmere coat. Despite their supple delicacy, they had worn well. Sender kept smiling.

"What are you laughing at?" The soldier jabbed Sender in the ribs with his rifle.

"I'm not laughing. Just being friendly."

"Friendly! I don't need the friendship of any damned fascist."

"Fascist? Hah. You're wrong about that, brother. Wrong as can be."

"Yeah, yeah, sure. I know you sons of bitches. As soon as you see a Red soldier, you're all partisans."

"I've been a partisan since before you were drafted, son. And before that, I was as far from being a fascist as it's possible to be."

"You were a Marxist?" the boy asked, lowering his rifle slightly.

I could tell him yes, thought Sender. But after all that I've been through—after all he's been through—why can't I just tell the truth? Why can't I be who I am?

"Never knew too much about politics, comrade. But I've always been a Jew."

"A Jew?" The young soldier's eyes widened, as if he'd found a striped tiger right in the forests of Hungary.

"Yes. Can I lower my hands now?"

A guttural tone came into the boy's voice, a tone too old for his face. "Just raise them higher, kike."

Involuntarily, a sigh escaped Sender. He was so *tired* of this crap.

"Come on, kid. Neither of us has the time for this nonsense."

"Time? What's your big rush, Zhid? Time is money, huh?"

"We're supposed to be fighting the Germans, aren't we, Vanya?"

"I don't see any guns on you. You Jews don't fight. You get out of serving in the army, one way or another."

"Tell you what. You lend me one of your guns, we find us some Germans, and we'll see who shoots more of them. Loser buys the drinks. All right?"

"Not all right, dirty Jew. You figure I'll get drunk and you'll take advantage of me. But I'm wise to your kind. Always out to chisel the worker. Jews! Every one a capitalist. Capitalist pigs from the cradle. And another thing..." He paused, trying to remember.

"Yes," muttered Sender, "also Commies. Straight from the cradle."

The Soviet soldier suddenly remembered. Color crept up his fair neck. "And another thing, *you killed Christ.*"

Sender looked up at his gloved hands. Between them, the skies had a slate veneer. It would snow again before nightfall. What did the God up there make of this bizarre conversation conducted in bad Russian? Did he catch the irony of a young atheist accusing him of deicide?

Sender had grappled with the big questions for so many years now. Why do the righteous suffer? Why do the wicked flourish? What had God proved with the blood and suffering of so many innocents?

"...and that's why I'm going to kill you, Jew."

"No you're not."

"I say I am!"

"No you're not. God's gone to a lot of trouble to get me this far, and the war is almost over, and you're not even a German or a fascist, so why the hell should he pick *you* to finish me off, at this stage of the game?"

"You think I'm not serious? That I'm a fool?" The boy's face was red as borscht.

"I'm sick of thinking. But I do declare: it's all in God's hands. Life, death, everything. Whatever he commands you to do, do it and get it over with. Because comrade, my arms—and everything else—are tired."

Shaking with fury, the soldier transferred his rifle to his left hand. With his right he pulled out a pistol.

He pressed the gun to Sender's head. It was still warm from his body, but cooling fast. "Say your prayers, Jew."

"I've already said them."

Rage poured through the soldier like lava. "I said I'm going to kill you, and I will!"

"Fine, fine. Do it."

The soldier couldn't believe it. Wasn't this the ultimate power he was exercising? And the Jew was mocking it. Mocking him. He had to fight to steady his hand.

The Soviet soldier dropped the rifle and braced his right hand with his left. He pressed the gun hard into Sender's temple.

And he squeezed the trigger.

The report cracked the forest air.

CHAPTER FORTY-SEVEN

Kisvar

For Christmas, the town carpenter had bought his family a repaired radio. The whole village gathered around it. They heard that the Soviets were marching across Hungary like fire across stubble. Most of the country—as well as Slovakia—was already liberated from Nazi rule.

While the radio did not mention Jews in so many words—no one but the fascists ever did—it announced that "partisans" and "others" were coming out of hiding.

Under his breath Joseph marked the news. "Blessed is the Lord, our God, king of the universe, who has sustained us, and kept us, and brought us to this day."

That night Joseph packed a small bag and laid out some clothes. He planned to rise before dawn, slip out of Kisvar, and get to the station in time for the first train.

He lay down on his soft downy bed, but could not sleep. The war was over. A remnant had survived, as God had promised. The Children of Israel were still alive.

It was very late when he finally fell asleep. He woke with a start. There was already light outside. He'd have to hurry to make the train.

"Father Istvan!" The housekeeper was aghast at the priest's clothing. "Where are you going? It's time for mass."

"I...I..."

The little village street started filling with curious people. Joseph licked his lips. He couldn't think of anything plausible to say. It was one thing to have a costume thrust upon him and to play a role, but now he stood naked before the entire parish.

"I have something terrible to confess to you, dear people."

"Bah," said a farmwife. "How bad can it be? It isn't even Lent yet."

"It's bad, really bad. An act of deception. Promise me that you won't kill me!"

The villagers looked at each other. A woman? A boy? Who could it be?

"We're disappointed in you, Father," said the blacksmith, "but a man's a man, subject to his flesh. Just tell us who it is, so we can punish the guilty party."

"Oh, no. It's nothing like that. Not at all." Joseph rubbed his chin nervously. They hadn't promised, as he'd asked. "You see...I...am...not...a...priest."

Every jaw dropped. A full minute later Geza Andras said, "You do a good job of it, though. We don't care what you did at the seminary to get thrown out."

Everyone nodded in agreement.

"And if you act like a good priest, then you are a good priest."

The idea won approval from the villagers.

Joseph shook his head. "No, you don't understand. It's not just a matter of credentials. I'm really no priest at all."

"What were you, then, if not a priest?" asked a farmer.

"Ummm...I bought and sold bruised fruit."

"See, didn't I tell you?" Lajos Andras said to his brother. "He's a working man, like us. Not one of those snooty types."

A thought occurred to the widow Kovacs, who had not hit it off with either of the Andras brothers. "So, if you're not a priest, you're free to marry, aren't you?"

Joseph shook his head. There was nothing to do but tell the truth.

"I am a Jew."

The shocked silence was even longer this time. I've missed the train now, Joseph thought, for good.

"But you don't have any horns," whispered the widow Kovacs.

"Don't be a fool, Maria," said the carpenter, "that's an old wives' tale." But several of the villagers looked hard, just the same.

"We need to discuss this, uh, Father, amongst ourselves," said the blacksmith.

The villagers gathered in a tight circle just out of Joseph's hearing. They gesticulated and shrugged and made wild motions with their hands. Oy, thought Joseph, I've taught them to argue like Jews. But will they have mercy like Jews?

Finally, the villagers came to an agreement and hurried back to Joseph. "It's unanimous," said the carpenter. "We've decided that, even though you are a Jew, we're willing to let bygones be bygones. We'd like you to stay on as the priest."

Joseph was flabbergasted. "But how can I do such a thing?"

"We won't tell."

"But..."

"Look, there's a war on, and who knows what happens after that. The bishop in Budapest has other things to think about. As St. Simon said, 'All my days I have lived among wise men, yet I never heard of anything better for a body than silence.'"

Joseph smiled. "That's poor Rabbi Shimon." The smile faded. "I'm sorry. It wouldn't be right. Thank you for all your kindness, you have all become so dear to me that it hurts to leave you. But I need to go and see if any of my family is still alive."

The villagers did their best to persuade, but when they saw that Joseph was determined to leave, they wished him well and returned to work.

Geza and Lajos called Joseph over to speak in private. Joseph was afraid. Surely these two could kill a man—they already had. And they had a special grudge against him. He had made them own up to their guilt in the killing of the Gypsy. And he had told them their guilt was permanent.

"Father, can you come out to the farm with us?"

Joseph's throat tightened. "As I said, I'm not a priest."

"But we need you, Father. We need to ask a favor of you."

They seemed sincere. How could he deny sincere men a favor?

When they got to the farmhouse, Lajos sat down to entertain Joseph with bachelor hospitality, while Geza went off. He soon returned, dropping an old-fashioned leather drawstring bag on the table.

"We'll talk plain with you, Father, it's the only way we know how."

"I'm not a priest. You mustn't call me Fa..."

Lajos held up his hand. "Geza and me, we want to buy forgiveness for killing the thief in our fields."

Joseph said, "Boys, boys, haven't you listened to my sermons? You can't buy God's forgiveness."

"We listened," said Geza, "and we heard you quote some saint about how some men 'buy Paradise in a single hour.'"

"Well, yes, but that's with an *act* of great courage and kindness, not with money."

"We don't have much opportunity here for acts—maybe we never will. But you're going away to be with the Jews. You'll probably have the opportunity with them; they're in real deep shit. Oops." He covered his mouth. "Anyway, here. Take this money. Act for us." He pushed over the leather bag.

Joseph undid the strings and looked inside. He gasped. There were coins, gold and silver, bearing the imprint of the Austro-Hungarian Empire. "This is a small fortune!"

"We came by it honest," Lajos said defensively.

"It's good money," said Geza with pride. "None of this paper stuff that's worthless as soon as the next clown crosses the Danube."

"But this is your nest egg," said Joseph. "I can see these coins are from the time of the Empire. Your parents must have left it to you as inheritance."

Lajos shrugged. "Sure, but there's mo..."

Geza gave his brother a good kick and cleared his throat. "We make enough to live on," he said, "and put some by for a rainy day, too. And in all the years since Papa and Mama died, we've never really needed to buy anything."

"We already have enough farmland," said Lajos.

"Besides," said Geza, "one or the other of us might get married, and you could just imagine what a woman would want to spend it on."

"Please take it, Father Istvan," said Lajos. His brother nodded vigorously.

Joseph left town a few days later, but not on the train. The villagers pointed out many hazards he would do well to avoid. First of all, he did not have appropriate papers. Also, he didn't know Budapest, where fighting still raged in the streets. It made sense to go back to Janace, definitely liberated, where his relatives were likely to return.

Two farmers with a load of pear liquor took him across the Slovak border at a backwoods crossing. Once in Slovakia, Joseph paid a fellow with a broken-down cart to take him within a few miles of Janace. Finally he reached the town. Joseph's first stop was at the home of the old Mayor. The people who answered the door were short with him. The Mayor was long dead.

"How terrible," said Joseph. "He was a fine man. God rest his soul."

Joseph headed for the Jewish part of town. He passed a familiar corner, which had been the site of the ritual bathhouse. Now there was nothing, not even a hole. Why had it been destroyed? The building had served as a community bath for Jews *and* Gentiles, since most people did not have indoor facilities.

He did find the Great Synagogue. There were boards nailed over the stained-glass windows. Over the door there had been a marble slab carved with the Hebrew words, "I have put God before me always." Now there was a crudely painted sign, "National Feed and Grain." Joseph didn't have the stomach to enter the building.

From there, it wasn't far to his own home. He stood outside the little cottage to stare incredulously. How could the house still be standing, without Sari?

The little yard was strewn with garbage and the paint on the wood trim was peeling. He had a momentary pang of guilt, as if he should have been maintaining it these past years. Still, the house seemed to welcome him, as if he were just returning from his usual round of farms and distilleries.

The door was answered by a skinny man with a big belly. "What do you want," he growled, blowing a wave of alcohol at Joseph.

"I...I'm the owner of this house, that is, before..."

"You don't own this stinking dump. I do."

Joseph frowned. "I don't know who you dealt with, but let me assure you, I paid off the mortgage in '34. A copy of the deed is in the records at city hall."

A slovenly woman, her front teeth missing, came to the door. "What's going on?"

"This Jew here says he's the owner of this house."

"The hell he is," said the woman. Her nostrils turned up. "What did you come here for? Why didn't you stay where the Germans took you? Go back. Go back to Poland where you belong."

The man had moved behind the door. He returned with a large knife. "Get out of here. Get out of my house. Why don't you just get out of our country."

Joseph wanted to say that his family had lived here, in the same town, for generations. That with all due respect, he could tell by their accents that it was they who were the newcomers. "I just want to go in for a minute," Joseph said. "Please?"

The man nicked him under the chin. "There's nothing here for you. Nothing."

Joseph pressed the cut to stop the bleeding. His chin was rough. Now that he could be a Jew again, he was regrowing his beard. But were there any other Jews here? Even the Gentiles were strangers to the place. And he, what was he? Shunting from place to place, he realized he was a complete alien in the town of his birth.

Where to go now? The House of Study of course. Citizen or stranger, that was a place a Jew was always assured a welcome. There had been many Houses of Study in Janace, but he went to the one that had been like a second home to him.

It was dark inside, the electricity must have been cut off long ago. His eyes adjusted to the thin light of winter afternoon which trickled through the small windows.

There were people in the room! Jews. He wanted to weep with relief.

"Ah, a ninth for the afternoon prayers," said an old man. They would wait for a tenth, so that they might have a proper communal service.

Joseph looked from face to face. Eight old men; he didn't know any of them.

"Mr. Wassermann!" said one decrepit ancient.

Joseph scanned the fellow's face, but saw nothing familiar.

"Don't you recognize me, sir? I'm Klein. Klein the butcher."

Joseph shook his head slowly. "No, it can't be. I remember Klein, but he was hospitalized before the deportation." It went without saying that no one had survived the slaughter at the Jewish hospital.

"That was my father, may the Lord avenge his blood. I'm Jonathan, the apprentice butcher."

Joseph's mouth fell open. Young Jonathan had been seventeen when he was conscripted into slave labor. This man was *twenty years old?*

He looked again at the eight men, now with great care. The wizened faces, the bent backs, the palsied limbs, the toothless mouths. *They were all boys.*

"If we get a tenth, you will lead us, Mr. Wassermann?"

Joseph nodded. They were deferring to him, because he was by far the oldest man there, but he knew he looked younger than any of them. Oh, God, his heart cried, what have you done to the flower of Israel?

To avoid staring at the gnarled young men, Joseph looked around him. The House of Study didn't look too bad. It had never been very fancy, and the few ornaments, such as the silver finials on the Torah scrolls, had been sold long ago to provide for the destitute.

Apparently someone had tried to make a bonfire of the holy books, but soon grew weary at the thought of burning such a huge number— crammed bookcases covered the walls from floor to ceiling. Water, whether from an attempt to put out the fire or from the leaky roof, had done more damage to the books. Still, there were enough precious volumes left in good condition that a Jew could lose himself in the deep and endless pleasure of the study of Torah. Joseph ached to open one.

But the others wanted to talk. The Russians had taken Poland, they said, and the Germans were closing the camps, covering their tracks.

The camp closings weren't good news for the surviving Jews. They were being forced to go on long marches without food or water, but with severe beatings. Considering the condition they were in, and the winter, few would survive.

"What about Budapest?" asked Joseph. "I have kin who may be alive. You all remember my sister-in-law Kitty and her husband, Halter the mechanic. And my brother's wife Aranka, and their youngest, Judith."

They did remember them, and most of them had relatives with similar stories of escape to Hungary. "But one can't get hopes up too high," said Klein. "The Germans wouldn't give up on the Budapest Jews even when Poland was cut off. They've taken 27,000 Jews that they've rounded up, and they're marching them to the Austrian border."

"But that's more than a hundred miles. And it's winter. And what good does it do the Germans when they get there?"

No one answered. They were, all of them, long past the days of "how could they do such a thing? And why?" or "but it doesn't make any sense."

But the need for hope rose like a seedling out of a crack in concrete. "They say there are 140,000 Jews still in hiding in Budapest. About half are baptized Christians, but that still leaves the possibility that our relatives are alive."

The men told stories that made the refugee Zlotnik's saga seem like a spring picnic. But it was Joseph whom no one believed. It was the first part of his story that defied credulity. They had never heard of anyone who had survived the deportation from Janace.

All the men had trickled in these last two weeks. There were a few others who weren't present, Reform, secularists, and men who had lost their faith. There was a Gentile man who went to the train station every day in hopes of finding his Jewish wife and their children. Good Catholics, they had been protected by the Church for a while, but were later deported. Every day the Christian man was disappointed. No women had returned, and certainly no children.

Most of the men had no money, so they shared whatever food they could come by. They were all looking for jobs, but the Gentiles wouldn't talk to them, much less hire them. They slept in the Jewish cemetery, in the mausoleums built above the graves of the Grand Rabbis.

"Why not here in the House of Study?" Joseph asked. The poor had always found a haven there.

Young Klein licked his lips. "There are local hoodlums who come in for 'fun.' Last week they killed a man. Hershel Weiss, the housepainter."

They waited until the sun dipped below the windows. It was the cutoff for the afternoon service and no tenth man had arrived. They were forced to pray individually.

Joseph left the House of Study as gloomy as the last of the day. He couldn't bear to sleep in the cemetery; he intended to get a room in a boarding house. The truth was these half-dead youths made him unbearably depressed.

Snap out of it. Melancholia was a sin. A Jew always had God's work to do. Tomorrow he would spend some of the Andras brothers' money on materials to repair the House of Study. They'd get some solid boards and iron locks to keep out intruders, and maybe get the electricity turned back on. And food, of course.

"Psst. Mr. Wassermann."

An unfamiliar voice. Joseph turned sharply. He didn't see anyone.

"Down here."

He looked down. Way down, to waist level.

There was a tiny, filthy creature he could barely identify as human.

"Blessed is the Lord our God, king of the universe, who varies his creation," said Joseph, uttering the blessing on the sighting of dwarves.

"You don't recognize me?" A full set of white teeth flashed in the dying light.

The smile, the words, the tiny stature, were childlike. But there was something adult about it, too. The creature's matted hair extended from a receding hairline. The only dwarf he knew had gone in the train.

"Give up? It's me, Kalman Meisels!" It was the teacher Meisels' boy, the student of Rabbi Axelrod, the one who had run into the woods.

"You're alive," said Joseph, his voice choking with astonishment and joy. "What about the other one, the boy who fled with you?"

"He died," said Kalman simply. "There were others too, in the woods. Kids and grownups. They all died."

"You survived, but not the others? How? Why?"

"Oh, that's simple. They just didn't know how to be hungry. I do."

Joseph thought of the Meisels and their terrible poverty. The children had gone hungry, even in good times. What they must have suffered in the ghetto!

Poor Mrs. Meisels. The prayers she must have cried out. Why merciful God, why do you let my children go hungry? And all the while God had his reason.

"I'm real good at going hungry. I'm real good at a lot of things," Kalman said cheerfully. "You could hire me, Mr. Wassermann. I could be, like a scout."

He *was* a child. Joseph picked him up in a huge embrace. The boy was so dirty that he smelled like mushrooms. It didn't matter. Joseph was happier than he had been since the last time he had held his Sari.

"You little devil," he said lovingly, "why didn't you come to the House of Study? They needed a tenth for the afternoon service."

"I don't qualify. I'm not bar-mitzvah yet."

"You're not thirteen?" Despite his tiny stature, Kalman seemed way too old to be a child according to the Law.

"No sir. I won't be thirteen until after the High Holidays. My Torah portion is *Lech L'cha*."

Lech L'cha. Go forth. "And the Lord said to Abram *go forth* from your country, from the land of your birth, from your father's house, to the land that I will show you."

Joseph's spirits bounded. How much more of a sign did you need?

Tomorrow they would get Kalman a haircut and some clothes. Then they would go to city hall and get proper identification papers.

And the day after that, they would leave Janace forever.

CHAPTER FORTY-EIGHT

Budapest

Chaos and ruin were everywhere. Kitty was now certain that Sender was dead, so who cared if the whole world was destroyed.

Her two suitcases and their contents fetched less than a week's worth of food. Kitty survived on tiny pieces of meat that Mitzi sniffed out in the wreckage of bombed buildings. She wandered the streets, oblivious to the fall of both snow and bombs.

On a deserted, rubble-strewn street, Kitty slipped on the ice and fell face down. She decided not to get up. She would just lie here until cold or hunger overtook her. Sender was gone and her sisters were gone. Nothing else mattered.

Mitzi nudged her nose under the collar of Kitty's coat, licking and tickling. "Stop it," said Kitty addressing God as much as Mitzi. But Mitzi was pulling her towards a man.

"Miss Julia," he whispered, glancing around him, furtive as a rodent.

"It's actually Kitty Halter. Excuse me, I never learned your name." He was the watchman at Mordecai Fried's apartment who had lived for a while at her flat.

"You don't have a place to stay." It wasn't a question. "Come. I know an apartment that hasn't been bombed. And they're not raiding for Jews anymore."

The flat was filthy and horrible and packed with Jews. It wasn't like Fried's apartment, nor like her own in the red-light district. There was no light and no air and no children. And no food.

The people looked as if they had been exhumed. One man had been forced by a cruel but greedy rescuer to live naked among pigs. He continued to identify with swine. A woman and her teenage son had hidden for months in a coal bin. A young couple had lived for a year in the broken oven of a commercial bakery.

Although she had nothing, the apartment's residents eyed her jealously. They made mean comments about the dog, but Kitty knew who they meant by "the bitch." Kitty promised Mitzi that they would just rest there a short while until they had warmed up and gained a bit of strength. Then they would go.

Poland

The Soviet soldiers who liberated the concentration camp were not soft men. For a thousand years their ancestors had lived on the frozen breast of Mother Russia. Stalin's gulag and the heritage of serfdom haunted them. They had known hunger and had seen starvation. Even in triumph over Germany, their rations were meager.

So it was to their own astonishment that, as soon as they entered the camp, every single soldier threw up his breakfast. Vomit made no difference; there was nothing in the world that could make the camp smell worse than it already did.

The Colonel was the first to recover. He was the leader of the liberating force and an honored soldier. Had he chosen to wear his medals, they would have tilted his uniform jacket to the left. He wiped his mouth and walked deep into the camp.

The Germans had left in a hurry. All over the grounds smoldering fires indicated their attempts to destroy the evidence of their crimes. Everywhere there were smoking pyres of half-burned document files, record books, and bodies.

At the gates, bludgeoned inmates mutely told the story of how the Germans had forced any Jews who could walk to march away from the camp. But the Nazis hadn't made a dent in the mountains of corpses that lay exposed to the witnessing heavens.

In the eerie quiet, punctuated now and then by the cries of his soldiers, the Colonel made his way to a row of barracks. He hesitated at the first, as if he should knock. The door creaked open. The smell hit him first, an odor he would carry in his nostrils for the rest of his life. His eyes adjusted to the embalming gloom.

Inside the barracks, on the wooden triple-layer bunks, and lying on the floor, were hundreds of corpses. Some were shrouded in the inmate pajamas but most were naked. The Colonel's face burned at the exposure of the men's pubic hair and wasted genitals. Everywhere in the world they covered the dead, except here.

Legs and arm bones were connected to the shriveled torsos by mere sinews. The skulls were barely attached to the bodies. Heads were thrust back, jaws lay open, dry eyeballs stared unseeing at the ceilings.

The bodies were in various stages of decomposition. To keep his sanity, the colonel tried to busy his mind with plans for burial.

When he realized the not-so-obvious, he cackled with crazy laughter.

The men were alive.

At least some of them. Not all, not by any means. Some of them had been dead for days, but others were still in the process of dying. Death here was not like it was in other places. It was not a single, stunning event, but a long, lazy process.

The Colonel bent over to get some blood back in his head. What was he supposed to do? He was a soldier, and a soldier obeyed orders or gave orders. Neat, clear, exact. What order should he follow? Which to command?

He would choose one. One corpse or one man, whatever the roll of the dice. The lot fell to a man on the edge of a top bunk. The Colonel and he were head-to-head. There was no sign of life on the man's face, but while the Colonel continued to stare, a vein throbbed in the man's neck.

The old soldier waited patiently for further movement. He decided the single beat was a fluke, the man was dead. Then, another flutter. Was it possible for someone to have a heart rate this low?

It seemed silly, in retrospect, but the Colonel said, "Do you understand Russian?"

The semi-cadaver nodded slightly.

The Colonel jumped. "Stay here," he said absurdly, "I'll get you some food."

"No," the man whispered. "Can't eat."

"Soup! I'll get you soup!"

"No. Stay with me."

The Colonel's reached for his canteen. "Here, drink water." His hands had stopped shaking, because now he knew what to do. He raised the man's head on his left arm and brought the canteen to his parched lips.

The man took a tiny sip, but then coughed terribly. "Can't swallow anymore."

The Colonel put the canteen down and removed his arm from under the man's head. His sleeve was covered in lice.

"Tell me," whispered the corpse-man, "are there still Jews alive? Does the Jewish people live?"

"Yes," said the Colonel, looking around nervously, as if they could be overheard. He cleared his throat. "But what can I do for you? And what, what is your name?" Preserving the man's name was the closest he would come to saving his life.

"Tefillin. Do you know what they are?"

The Colonel turned pale. Yes, he knew. Once, only once, when he was thirteen years old, his grandfather had taken him into a closet and taught him how to put them on. He remembered how even after all these years. Even after his name had been changed, even after his connections in high places had excised the designation "Hebrew" from all of his documents.

"The loose board, under the first bunk near the door," said the man.

The Colonel found the tefillin, a complete pair. Carefully, he placed them on the man's head. He wound the straps around the man's left arm the correct number of times, but the arm was so thin that the leather ribbons curled down to the floor.

The man smiled slightly. "Thank you. I promised a lady, once. My sister-in-law.

"My name is Thomas Gantz."

The Colonel wrote down everything.

Afterwards, Thomas Gantz smiled again and closed his eyes. He seemed to rest, satisfied. The Colonel watched as the throbbing in Gantz's neck slowed down to nothing at all.

Central Hungary

The sky was beautiful, strewn with the millions of stars that God had promised Abraham would be the number of his progeny. It could have been paradise, except for one thing—it was cold, cold as an ice pick through the heart.

Sender knew paradise wasn't hot, but this was ridiculous. He turned just the slightest bit, and the ferocious pain that resulted confirmed that he was, indeed, alive.

Thank you God, for saving me. I think.

He tested his mobility. He could move his left arm, but if he so much as twitched the fingers of his right arm, it felt as if his head were being ripped off.

On one hand and two knees, he began to creep. He moved very

slowly, but he was in no hurry. He had no idea where he was going.

The peasant woman found him, collapsed, when she came to gather her eggs. It had taken him nine hours to crawl to the henhouse, a distance of fifteen yards.

The woman tried her best to nurse Sender, but every time she touched his head, however gently, he would faint. When her husband came home to dinner, he examined Sender and declared him a Jew. Jews always had nice clothes like that.

"The Jewish gentleman is lucky," the peasant shouted in Sender's ear, as if his problem was deafness. "There's a Jewish doctor nearby. Just came back a week ago."

The peasant and his wife put Sender carefully into a wheelbarrow and rolled him to a tiny infirmary. Sender wanted to ask the couple their names. Perhaps he could return some day and repay them for their kindness, but it hurt too much to talk.

The doctor was in worse shape than Sender. He could not have weighed more than ninety pounds. After he cleaned and stitched the head wound, Sender fell asleep.

By the time he awoke, another day had passed. The doctor told him that the gray glove had saved his life. When Sender had reached up to touch his wound, the kidskin had sealed it like a skin graft. Then, the extreme cold froze the glove in place.

"You ought to count your lucky stars, comrade. You could have bled to death from that flying shrapnel."

"Shrapnel? Hardly. A Russian shot me with a pistol at point-blank range."

"You're mistaken. All you have are surface wounds, and maybe a few chips of the skull. A bullet would have pierced the bone. You would have died instantly."

"Maybe the bullet was defective. You know, Soviet workmanship."

"The Russians fought this war with all their hearts," the doctor snapped. "Even if the bullet was a dud, you'd have far more serious wounds than you do."

"But I tell you, it happened. This Russian shot me in the temple, yet I live."

"The odds against that happening are billions and billions, almost incalculable."

Sender thought of God parting the great waves of mathematics for him, the way he had parted the Red Sea for the Children of Israel.

"The Russian shot me for being a Jew."

"I find that hard to believe. We owe the liberators everything."

There was a photograph of the doctor on his desk. He was young and plump, and was with a prosperous looking older couple, obviously his parents.

"Why did you come back here, Doctor?"

The physician looked at him in genuine surprise. "It's my obligation. This is my home. These honest country people are like my family."

Sender wondered why, if the locals loved him so much, they had failed to hide him in any of the isolated barns or in the thick woods.

According to the radio, the bombing of Budapest had all but ceased. The doctor lent Sender the fare to the capital. He looked relieved to see the wounded man go. Even in this rural and sparsely populated place, two Jews were at least one too many.

Budapest

At the Red Cross office, Joseph did all the talking. Kalman spoke only Yiddish, Slovak, and a little Hungarian. The Red Cross people spoke German.

The first difficulty they ran into was nationality.

"Jewish," answered Joseph, on behalf of himself and the boy.

"Jewish is not a national identity," the clerk replied firmly. They argued for a while and then the clerk wrote down "Czechoslovak."

The next point of contention was whom they were seeking.

"Two sisters-in-law," said Joseph. "Aranka Wassermann and Kitty Halter."

"In-laws are not relatives," said the clerk.

"Oh. Kalman is seeking Alexander Halter. He's a...a foster brother."

"Foster brothers aren't relatives either," the clerk snapped. "Don't you realize that there are millions of people all over Europe who are desperately seeking their kin? Why do you people always think you're entitled to something special?"

Joseph hated to lie. "I have a sister and...and a brother who changed his name!"

The clerk picked up a pen. "All right. Spell out their names."

"Mrs. Renee Fruchter, and Mr. Zlotnik."

"His first name?"

"Uh, Judah."

"And where are they located?"

"Palestine."

The clerk threw his pen down. "We don't deal with Palestine."

"You don't?"

"No. Now if you were Muslim we could connect you with the Red Crescent." It was clear he wished they were Muslim, or something else. Anything but what they were.

"But don't the Jews of Palestine have a first aid service?" It seemed impossible that they wouldn't. Even the Jewish community in little Janace had had one.

"Yes, the Red Shield of David. But it isn't recognized by international bodies."

"Why not?"

"You'll have to leave now, Mr. Wassermann. We have a lot of work to do here."

The nun said, "We are very proud of Christina, now that she's a postulant."

"Yes," said Kitty pretending agreement. What was that? She should have paid attention to Sari when she talked about that convent stuff.

Whatever a postulant was, she hoped it put Judith in a good position. Her "sister" Julia was quite desperate for food and shelter.

Kitty had stayed at the apartment much too long, but this morning was the last straw. One of the men had proposed that they slaughter Mitzi for meat.

Two nuns seated Kitty in a room opposite a door with a grid in it. Judith was brought into the next room and they spoke through the grid. Judith wore a nun's habit but her veil was not as severe as the headdresses of the regular nuns and Kitty could see she had grown into a lovely—plump—young woman.

"Oh, Judith, you look wonderful."

"You must call me Christina."

Kitty looked behind at the two nuns who had accompanied her. "Don't worry about them. They're busy playing with my dog."

"It doesn't matter anyway. When I take my vows I'll be Sister John the Baptist."

"What? Judith, don't you know? The war is over."

"Yes, I know. What difference does that make?"

"What difference! You don't have to pretend anymore. You can be a Jew now."

Judith's face turned ugly under the graceful veil. "Why would I do that? The Jews are dead, or good as dead. They're finished. They have no future."

Kitty was dumbstruck. "But Judith, a *Christian*? Think! You are probably the only survivor of your family. Think of your martyred mother."

Judith's mouth pinched like a clip. "Why should I?"

"Judith, a Catholic nun? Really. You don't believe any of their stuff, do you?"

"Yes, I believe. I believe it's safe in here, and there will always be something to eat. I believe there isn't a Jew in Budapest who is eating as well."

How cold this girl had become. Kitty could be cold herself, however. "The way it looks now the Russians will be taking over. If they do, it won't be so good for Catholics."

Judith's spittle flew through the grid. "Anything is better than to be a Jew."

Kitty couldn't stand to be there another minute. She pushed her chair back from the door, grabbed Mitzi's leash from a startled nun, and ran out of the convent.

She was hungry and lonely and cold. Her God had betrayed her. But she had never betrayed him.

Mitzi was reluctant to go into the devastated neighborhood. It had been severely bombed, and all its buildings, homes as well as shops, had been abandoned. Feral creatures, some human, slinked around, sinking their teeth into whatever they could.

"Please sweetie, try and find us something to eat," Kitty begged.

A roar sounded behind them. Mitzi jumped under Kitty's coat for protection. The shell of a building, severely damaged by previous bombing, had collapsed upon itself.

When the dust settled, Kitty approached the heap of rubble carefully. There was little chance they'd find something edible; scavengers had stripped these buildings bare while they were standing.

Mitzi barked, and wagged her tail furiously.

"What's the matter with you, girl? There's nothing here but crumbled mortar."

Mitzi pulled against the leash with all her might.

Kitty pulled it back, trying to direct the dog away from the collapsed building. Mitzi pulled harder. Kitty slackened the leash; she wasn't going to strangle her only friend.

Mitzi bounded into the center of the mess. She snorted like an asthmatic, and dug furiously. Kitty had never seen the animal so overwrought. There must be one hell of a meaty bone under all that dirt.

Mitzi stopped digging only to sniff, stopped sniffing to dig. Kitty got down on her hands and knees and lifted bricks and other debris too heavy for the little dog to move.

Now Mitzi howled like a wolf. She beat her paws furiously.

A corner of navy-blue cloth protruded from the dirt. Kitty tugged at it. So soft.

A piece of clothing? Mitzi had stopped digging and was now turning round and round as if she had eaten some madness-causing plant.

Kitty cleared more dirt away. It was a man's coat. And there was a man in it.

She abandoned the coat and dug, in white heat, at where the man's head ought to be. Mitzi joined in, and they exposed the man seconds later.

It couldn't be, it couldn't be, it couldn't be.

Almighty God, King of Hosts, Eternal One, surely it could not be.

It was Sender.

CHAPTER FORTY-NINE

The violet-blue eyes blinked calmly. Kitty. Kitty kissing his face with her warm, living lips. Was this paradise at last? No. It was still extremely cold.

Sender hadn't said a word, and his head was bandaged, but Kitty knew he was all right. She busied herself happily in excavating him.

Now nothing in the world would ever go wrong!

Slowly, she registered a familiar and not unpleasant odor. Light citrus, refreshing. What was that again? Oh, yes, "4711." Kitty had worn the scent as a girl. It was the only fragrance Sari considered appropriate for an unmarried woman. Later, Sender bought her more provocative perfumes. Now, even if 4711 had been her favorite, even if she could afford cosmetics, she would never put a bottle of it on her dressing table, not with that label declaring it "made in Germany."

But here in the middle of nowhere she was smelling—gagging on— 4711?

As the peculiarity of it hit her, so did a giant meaty fist. The punch on her shoulder forced her around. Bending over her was a man the size of a grocer's icebox, mean as a beaten mutt, holding a gallon bottle of 4711 by its neck.

A Russian. In their unquenchable thirst for alcohol the Soviet soldiers broke into pharmacies and "liberated" bottles of scent. This man had gotten lucky and found one of the large urns of 4711 from which women refilled their flacons.

A mere flip of the Russian's wrist sent Kitty flying across the ground. She had always been small and skinny, but since her expulsion from Miss Pallfey's she had shrunk. Her collar bones were visible through layers of clothing.

Effortlessly, using one hand, the bear-soldier pulled up her coat and skirt and pulled down her underpants. Oh God, as if it weren't enough to be raped in front of Sender's eyes, her filthy panties were exposed.

To have her husband miraculously restored to her, and then have their love assaulted the very same hour! It was an obscene joke. It was not to be borne.

The soldier had to drop the cologne bottle to keep control. He was infuriated by the strength of her resistance. To have this little toothpick of a girl thwart his will! Drunken lust turned to rage. He smacked her across the face. Kitty could hear the crack of her nose even before she felt the pain.

"You...you..." the Russian sputtered. "You piece of dirt, you ought to be grateful any man is willing to fuck you. *You're ugly. Sin ugly.*"

She *was* ugly. Ugly and filthy. Anything she had had of beauty had always been coaxed, contrived, applied. Now she had nothing left. She didn't own a toothbrush, a lipstick, or a comb. The roots had grown out in her hair. She reeked of her own dried urine. Thinking Sender dead, without a job or a home, she had lost the will for beauty.

She *was* ugly, ugly and disgusting.

His head slammed down on hers and the blood poured down her face and inside her throat. At least she couldn't smell the 4711 anymore.

She waited for the sickening slide of his member against her bared thighs. But she felt nothing but the oppressive weight crushing her body like a burden of shame.

Dead weight.

Using all her strength Kitty managed to roll the soldier off her. Panting with exertion, she looked up. Sender loomed above her, ghostly and weaving, holding a piece of decorative masonry, a gargoyle dripping blood.

Her man had killed the Russian.

"Sender," she exulted. It was a fairy tale. The brave knight destroyed the evil dragon to save the lovely blond damsel he loves. "Oh Sender. My hero!"

"What are you talking about?" Sender breathed, "I've killed a man."

Kitty scrambled to her feet. "And a good thing, too."

"Good?" He looked at her as if she had proposed a bouquet for Hitler. "I killed a human being. I destroyed the image of God."

Kitty took offense. "This is one Talmudical passage I know. 'If your enemy comes to kill you, rise up earlier in the morning to kill him.'"

"Once you've taken a life you become stained with blood forever," Sender said.

Kitty stopped her sharp response as it was forming. In five minutes they had gone from the most sublime moment of their lives to bickering like a bored old couple.

"Well, let's give thanks to God that none of his comrades were around to see it." He had to agree with *that*.

"God saw."

"The bodies of the dead cover this planet like a quilt. Why would God mark this one, killed in innocent defense?" Gently, she added, "He knows you did the right thing."

Sender sighed in resignation. "Anyway, we need to bury him."

"No we don't. They can't trace it to us. He was drunk, he fell and hit his head."

"We need to bury him because God commands it. Every human being, even the worst criminal, deserves a decent burial."

Kitty closed her eyes. Calm yourself, she thought. "I don't have the strength to move my own legs, much less that Goliath's body, and I don't think you do, either. What happened to your head?"

Sender touched the bandage and winced. "I'll tell you la..." He jerked himself back from the brink of fainting.

"We'd better get out of here," said Kitty.

It was hard to tell who was carrying whom. Kitty, her broken nose bleeding, her thin frame almost too frail to support her own coat, or Sender, with blood soaking through his bandage. Only Mitzi, dragging her leash, was carrying her own weight.

They came to a wide boulevard, utterly deserted. Standing in the middle of the street they peered into the ravaged distance.

"Look, something's coming."

Sender squinted. "Oh no. It's a Russian jeep." Sender ducked behind the remnant of a building. "Russians are bad. They've always been bad luck for me."

"Alexander Halter! What are you talking about? 'There is no luck in Israel.' You said so yourself." But Sender would not leave his hiding place.

She didn't care. She loved him, but she just couldn't endure any more. Kitty walked out into the street, Mitzi following.

The staff car was full of soldiers, their legs dangling out the sides. They were not drunk. As they approached Kitty, the car slowed down to a crawl, but it didn't stop.

"Please, please," Kitty called out, running after the car as it passed her. "*Khleb*! Bread! A crust of bread. Please, something to eat."

She was crying now, and clinging to the jeep like a woman trying to keep a man from leaving her. "Please, for the love of..." She was about to say God, but the Russians didn't believe in God, "...for the love of humanity. A piece of bread! Anything, anything to eat!" This is what had become of her. For a piece of bread, she'd do anything.

The car wouldn't stop. Kitty was sobbing so hard, was so hysterical, that she was almost caught in the wheels of the jeep. Tears, blood, and snot ran down her face.

"Look what's become of me," she said bitterly. "See what's become of the Jews."

Something moved the officer in the staff car. Maybe it was Kitty's words, or the blood pouring from her nose. Perhaps he had seen himself what the Germans had done to—God's people. Because *it* was real, *they* were real, whether God was real or not.

Or, he may have been moved by Mitzi's soulful eyes staring up from her filthy, matted fur. For whatever reason, the Russian took pity.

He shouted out a street address. A key ring flew through the air like a shooting star. Kitty jumped to catch it, missed, and fell down. But Mitzi retrieved the keys.

"Apartment 3-A," the Russian called out, as the car picked up speed.

"Thank you, thank you," Kitty called out, blowing a kiss, even though she knew she looked a mess. The soldiers on the back of the staff car whistled and waved.

Kitty ran back to Sender's wall, holding the keys up in triumph.

From her walks with Mitzi, Kitty knew the location of the building, an imposing area of Pest. It took hours to get there. As they approached they saw that the entire neighborhood had been spared bombing, as if it had been nestled in a protective box.

Apartment 3-A extended over all of the third floor of the most majestic building on the block. There was no mystery about who had lived there, or why the Russians had possession of the keys. A bronze plaque proclaimed the tenant as the minister of propaganda for the Hungarian fascist government that had just been deposed. Despite trembling hands, the keys unlocked the door with a satisfying spring of the tumblers.

The apartment was equal in luxury to the Pallfey house. It showed evidence of having been abandoned in a hurry. Closet doors gaped and drawers were left open, their contents spilling out. Valuables were gone, but an abundance of goods lay abandoned. The power and the electric water heater had been left on. But the most fantastic thing about the flat was the wonderful aroma that penetrated even Kitty's broken nose.

The kitchen, the domain of servants, was located at the far end. In the center of the room was a massive table, and on it, an enormous wooden bowl. It was this bowl that was the source of the delirium-inducing fragrance that reached all the way to the front door.

Yeast.

The dough in the bowl had been left to rise before the residents of the apartment bolted. In an ironic reversal of the Passover story, where the Israelites left Egypt in such a rush that their bread had no time to rise, the dough abandoned by the fascists rose and rose, displacing the towel that had been draped over the bowl, overflowing onto the table, threatening to pour over to the floor.

Kitty and Sender grabbed pieces of dough and stuffed their mouths. After a few handfuls they managed to control themselves. Sender lit the oven and Kitty pinched off roll-sized pieces and placed them on baking pans.

They scouted for other food while the bread baked. There was lots more flour, and potatoes and turnips. The icebox was empty but as it was winter, a pantry set out on the kitchen porch was full of raw meat.

Kitty reached in for some beef. Sender stayed her hand. "No. Now that we have enough food to sustain us we mustn't eat non-kosher meat."

"You want to throw away this treasure?" she asked incredulously.

"The Torah says 'the flesh of prey you shall give to the dogs.'"

Kitty gasped. How could she have been so thoughtless? Poor Mitzi had eaten a bit of the raw dough, but only because the good creature was starving. It was one thing for her and Sender to eat whatever could be swallowed, but Mitzi had been raised on the choicest tidbits. How she had suffered, having thrown her lot in with the Jews!

And what a debt they owed the little dog, the very debt of life. Thanks to her unique talent—the ability to memorize Sender's smell from his pillow and sense it under rubble—they had been able to bring him, literally, up from the grave.

Kitty took the chunk of meat—almost as big as Mitzi herself—and placed it before the dog. Mitzi waited politely, then approached daintily to eat.

They found big bins of onions and sacks of sugar, the only food that was immediately edible. Dipping the onions in sugar, they savored a dish of exquisite pungency and sweetness. Kings had never eaten better.

Soon the rolls were baked. They washed ritually, said the blessings and ate. It seemed as if they could never eat enough of the bread, nor bless it enough.

After their dinner, they took long baths in the heated water. The master bedroom was much too intimidating to sleep in, and it only had one bed, albeit an enormous one. They found a servants' room with two cots and a padded sewing basket for Mitzi.

They fell immediately into an exhausted stupor, but both Kitty and Sender woke before dawn. It was then that they could finally tell each other of all that had happened since the day they were parted.

That morning Sender insisted on going out to find work, despite Kitty's protests that he wasn't well enough. The minister had left few clothes behind, but there was shoe polish and hair pomade and a clothes brush that did wonders with the cashmere coat. While the minister's hat would have been too large for Sender, the bandages filled it out. He creased it to a rakish tilt.

Walking out the door, Sender felt confident. A mechanic's skills would be valued in rebuilding a war-ravaged city. But late in the afternoon Sender returned, his shoulders slumped with fatigue.

"No work. Everywhere I went it was the same story. The garages are surrounded by circles of wrecked vehicles, they're desperate for men who can fix them, but as soon as they figure out I'm a Jew…"

"Take heart. Tomorrow you'll have better luck," said Kitty.

"No. No luck for Israel, remember? But I found something that does give me hope. A Jew was buying a can of benzene at the last garage I went to. He said there was a place now for organizing, Jews helping Jews. He took me there and I signed us up. I looked at their list to see if there is anyone we know on it. There wasn't, but maybe later. Maybe someone survived. More and more people are showing up every day."

"And this office is what, political, or like the Red Cross? Where is it?"

"No, it's not affiliated with any group. It's just survivors who've banded together, because no one else will help us. No one but ourselves. They call themselves *Sh'eyrit Hapleyta*. It's a Hebrew pun, 'the surviving remnant,' and also 'the saving remnant.'"

"Oh, Hebrew. So they're a Zionist organization."

"What else is there Kitty? What other hope is there for the Jews? Haven't we tried everything else? What haven't we done to please the Gentiles, to calm their hatred? What is it we haven't done, offered, sacrificed, just to live? They will never let us live in peace. We've got to go and be our own masters."

"You're right, Sender. Even now, when you'd think they'd be gorged on Jewish flesh to the vomiting point, even now they're ravenous.

"While you were out, I found a radio in the music room. I was listening today and the new housing minister said, '*Certain elements* had better not attempt to regain property seized before the war. If they do, they can well expect a violent reaction.' Can you imagine? And that was the new, *leftist* minister."

Sender frowned. "At the Sh'eyrit they said housing was the worst problem. I was thinking we could put up some people here, but I didn't want to volunteer the apartment without your permission, Kitty."

"Of course we can. We must. Besides, it's not even our apartment. I bet the last real owners were Jews."

Sender squirmed on his chair. "There's something else from the Sh'eyrit I have to show you." He took a piece of paper from his breast pocket. "It's a letter for you."

Kitty sprang up. "What? From whom? Where did you get this?"

"This is a copy of a letter, apparently circulating in various cities. It's addressed to you, and your sisters and a few other people. But I can't read Russian script, and neither could any of the other people there."

Her heart pounding, Kitty began to read. "I cannot identify myself, but my name is called in Israel, Dov, son of Jonathan the Levite. I am witness to the last will and testament of Thomas Gantz...

Kitty read through to the end. "For months I have fended off death, living only for the news that the Jewish people survives. Having heard this news now, I make my peace on this earth. Forgive me for my sins against you, dear family. Shalom."

"May God bind his soul in the chain of life," Sender whispered.

"Wait, there's a postscript from the man who found him and wrote this letter.

"If there are any survivors of Thomas Gantz who might read this letter, I make a request of them. Just as I have fulfilled his last wish, fulfill, if you can, my own.

"Those of us Soviet Jews who have survived the Nazis are not fated to be with you, my brothers. We are fated for absorption into the Party and the State, and we are lost to the Jewish people. But know this: all that is left of our soul goes with you.

"Be brave, O Israel, be fruitful. God bless you forever and ever, Amen."

By the end of the first week, the apartment was full to bursting. However, unlike the situation during the war, some of the tenants were earning their keep. Many men and women—all the survivors were single—managed to find work despite prejudice.

One of them put Sender in touch with a Jew who, back when he had been ordered to turn in his truck to the authorities, had preferred to let it roll off a cliff. He found the rusted heap and paid Sender to fix it. Accomplishing this small miracle, Sender's reputation attracted more work.

Many more men than women were returning. The women in the apartment, all young widows, were beset by suitors and each of them quickly accepted a proposal.

One evening an elderly Jew carrying several large shopping bags came to the door. Kitty and Sender exclaimed simultaneously, "Mordecai Fried!"

"Blessed is he who arrives," Sender welcomed with the ritual greeting.

"Blessed are they who are found! It's a sign and a wonder: a married couple reunited after all of this. You're the only such couple I've heard of."

"How did you find us, Reb Mordecai?"

"The Sh'eyrit, of course."

"Excuse our manners," said Kitty. "Please have a seat. And how is your family, Mr. Fried? I know they got out."

Fried put down the bags, whose metal contents clinked. "Thank God. They are in the best of health. My daughter is married now, and we are expecting another grandchild in the summer, God willing. America has been very good to us."

"America? You came from America?"

"Yes. With a shipload of food from our brothers there."

"But there's still a war on. How could you get through?"

Fried shrugged. "If God wills it, even a broom can shoot. Anyway, Mrs. Halter, I've come to deliver a message to you."

"From whom?" Who on earth was still alive?

"Reb Joseph Wassermann, may his light shine."

"Where did you see him? He must come here at once!"

"Oh, no. We met in London."

"London!" Kitty swallowed hard. "Was he by himself?"

"No, he was with a little fellow, one Zalman Meisels, I think."

"That's Kalman," said Sender in wonder, "the second of the Meisels boys."

The fact that these two unlikely people were traveling together on the far end of the earth meant that none of their families was left in Janace. Despite this terrible implication, it was wonderful to hear that Joseph and Kalman had survived.

"What a comfort, to know they have found a haven in England."

"Not haven, but underground station. Reb Joseph says they will soon be gone."

"Gone where?"

"To the Holy Land, of course."

"Palestine!"

"Just as soon as they can bribe and trick their way past the British blockade. Can you believe it? That old man and that little boy—they're going to take up arms and fight for a Jewish state.

"The message Reb Joseph sends you is: *'Come home.'*"

CHAPTER FIFTY

The bags left behind by Mordecai Fried contained cans of fish. Well, the pictures on the labels looked like fish. The contents, "tuna" were a mystery to all the tenants.

Their diet was still severely limited. Kosher meat and poultry was impossible to come by; few surviving ritual slaughterers had returned to their work. Fresh fish and eggs were scarce as rubies. People dreamed of a can of sardines in oil.

"I can't imagine this tuna is a kosher fish," said one tenant, "if it's a fish at all."

"Mordecai Fried is a saintly man," Sender insisted, "he would never bring us non-kosher food." Still, he looked worried as he inspected a can. It was impossible to tell from the illustration whether the tuna had fins and scales, as kosher fish must.

"My father, may God avenge his blood, owned the biggest store in Debrecen," said one woman. "He never carried any such thing as tuna. The Americans think we're stupid refugees. Maybe it's something even a Gentile wouldn't think of eating."

"Like what?"

"Like...like cat."

This notion took root, and the rumor would spread throughout Europe.

Kitty stepped in. "Sender, please open a can. I'm going to try it."

They stared. Kitty had a reputation for boldness, but this was beyond the pale.

She picked up a fork and spoke sternly to the assembled group. "Once, Mitzi uncovered a dead horse under the snow. I ate a chunk of raw, frozen horse flesh. 'Tuna' couldn't be worse than that." But once the tin was open, she hesitated. It really didn't look or smell like fish.

Kitty put the can down on the floor. "Here, Mitzi." The dog looked at the proffered can, walked around the assembled tenants and, seeing she had no more business in the place, returned to her spot in the kitchen.

"See," said Kitty. "If that were cat, wouldn't a dog have torn at it?"

"Well that dog is spoiled. She has the run of the meat pantry. She has no natural instincts left," said the woman from Debrecen.

They all frowned, trying to imagine Mitzi hunting anything.

Kitty made up her mind. She said the blessing for foods that don't fit into other categories, "You are blessed, O Lord, our God, king of the universe, who creates all." Then she stabbed a chunk of the tuna, popped it in her mouth, chewed, and swallowed.

The group waited, holding its breath. She repeated the motions, slower this time.

"This cat," she announced, "is absolutely delicious."

An old rabbi joined the tenants. He was truly old, not like the unnaturally aged people seen among "the remnant." The rabbi had lost his whole family: a wife, seven married daughters, sons-in-law and grandchildren. He had survived for a single goal: the revival of Jewish family life.

Ordinarily, rabbis performed marriages only for couples who had civil licenses, but with the authorities in chaos, the old man agreed to marry the couples in a purely religious ceremony. He wrote out a marriage contract for each couple, and a new one for Sender and Kitty, as well. Husband and wife couldn't live together without such a contract.

For the marriages to be consummated, the women would have to immerse in a ritual bath. For the Halters, too, resumption of intimacy required Kitty's ritual immersion. The trouble was that the main Budapest ritual bath—if it still stood—was in a part of the city where heavy fighting still raged between the Russians and die-hard German forces.

After much discussion, they resolved to try to reach the bathhouse. Except for the old rabbi, who was needed to determine if the bath was still fit, the women would be going alone. Any man would be taken for a combatant and shot by either side.

On the designated morning the men went off to work. Their faces were grim; they didn't know if they would next see their sweethearts as wives, or at all.

One of the women brought home a find from the market, fresh farmer cheese. They spent the rest of the morning making noodles. The cheese, sugar and cinnamon, and the dreaded "cat," would make a fine wedding feast. If they returned.

The women took turns bathing in the apartment's plentiful hot water, because one had to be perfectly clean before immersing in the ritual bath. Each woman packed a bundle of necessary items. There was a hand-held lamp and a flashlight in the pantry, and the rabbi took these along. It was the first day of the Jewish lunar month, a semi-holiday and an auspicious time for weddings, but it meant that there would be no moonlight.

When they left, it was still afternoon, but so gray and cold that it felt like the sun had set. As they moved along, the crackle of gunfire grew louder. When they saw flashes too, the rabbi made them stop until the danger passed.

The bodies of soldiers were scattered on the streets. At first the women skirted the corpses, out of horror and respect, but soon the bodies grew so numerous that they stepped right over them.

Gunfire flared. The rabbi called a stop. Kitty looked down at the dead soldier in her path. He was lying face-down in the street, his body already frozen, his possessions looted. A wallet, open and empty, lay near him.

Kitty picked it up. Perhaps there was identification in. The dead soldier should have a name, a nationality. But the wallet was empty. She unsnapped the change purse. Inside were two small copper coins from some unidentifiable currency.

Two pennies. Renee's last words to her jangled in her ears like change: "Put these or their equivalent in the charity box at the ritual bath."

Beautiful, martyred sister, I won't forget this time.

The rabbi indicated that they could proceed, but a women called out, "Not me. I've got to stop." They all paused while she leaned against a wall, panting. "I'm sorry," she said, "I don't know what's the matter with me. The marches I went on...I was able..." she wheezed, "but now..."

"Don't worry about it," said Kitty, smiling encouragement at. "Take your time. We can't immerse until after nightfall anyway."

Suddenly one of the dead bodies on the ground came to life. A soldier sprang up like a Jack-in-the-box, a German soldier with a rifle.

"Jews!" he roared. "How the hell did you escape? Well, not for long. Hands up! Line up against that wall, swine!"

They did as they were ordered.

So, they had not survived the fate of their people after all.

"Please, kind sir," said the old rabbi. "The war is over for all intents and purposes, what use is there..."

"The war is not over! And it isn't over until the last of you vermin has been exterminated. For the Fuhrer we will fight to the last man." The soldier didn't mention that he had shamelessly faked death to avoid fighting the Russians.

"Sir," the rabbi continued quietly, "have you no mother waiting for you in Germany? Surely she wants you home as soon as possible."

"Shut your Jew-yammering," the young soldier screamed. He jabbed his rifle into the old man's ribs. "How dare you address me like that? That Jew-talk isn't even proper German." He raised his rifle. "There's nothing that's going to save you now."

Just as he was about to pull the trigger, the woman from Debrecen ran from the wall. She zigzagged down the street, hiding and stumbling.

The first bullet, which had been designated for the rabbi, was shot at the woman instead. It missed, ricocheting from a wall. As he aimed again, Kitty looked down on the ground and saw another soldier, a really dead one. She picked up his rifle, aimed for the corner, the neatly indicative corner that was peculiar to the German helmet, and shot.

The soldier turned to face Kitty. Anger, hatred, and arrogance vanished from his face.

His most fervently held convictions were replaced by the most important and surprising fact of the entire war.

He'd been shot to death. By a Jew. By a woman. By a Jewish woman.

The party resumed its trek. Kitty thought: I wonder what Sender was talking about? It didn't feel so bad to kill a man. In fact, it felt a lot like hitting the bull's-eye in target practice on Count Pallfey's estate. Was she wrong to feel this way? Was it a sin?

She turned her gaze to the back of the woman walking ahead of her. It was the woman from Debrecen. Really, thought Kitty, the least she could have done was thank me for saving her life. Irritated, she pulled ahead.

As she passed her, Kitty looked at the face of the other woman. Immediately, she averted her eyes in shame. The woman had not thanked her because Kitty had done her no favor. The woman from Debrecen had wanted to die.

The little party reached the street of the ritual bathhouse. There was rubble in the gutters but most of the buildings were intact. In the distance, artillery sounded, like a thunderstorm passing.

The rabbi and the women said in their hearts: don't get your hopes up. Almost every Jewish institution in Europe was in ruins. The synagogues and community centers had been burned to the ground, the cemeteries desecrated. If the Germans or the Arrow Cross had entered the bathhouse, then it too was surely demolished. Even casual vandalism would have defiled the bath, making it useless.

But a ritual bathhouse had something no synagogue did: anonymity. Because it shrouded the sacred bond of marriage in modesty, and because it had no Christian equivalent, the ritual bath was invisible to the rest of the world.

The rabbi found the key to the building in the hiding place where it had been since the day the authorities had put an end to all Jewish religious life.

The electricity, of course, was off. The rabbi raised the lamp. Everything was still, but was it the stillness of sleep or of death?

The bath house was magnificent. The interior was adorned with the curved lines and brilliant enamels of Art Nouveau, and Turkish-flavored mosaics. The light of the lamp revealed one preserved wonder after another. It fell upon a stack of towels, each impossibly white and fluffy. Fringed chaises invited after-bath relaxation. A mirrored counter offered lotions and scents to apply after bathing. There were charity boxes on the counter, too. Kitty put her two pennies in.

But all the luxuries meant nothing. Was the bath itself still ritually acceptable? The rabbi removed his shoes and socks and went down the steps to the edge of the water. He moved the flashlight around in inspection as Kitty held the lamp up.

The rabbi turned the flashlight off to save its power. He looked up to the glazed tiles of the ceiling and began to cry. Tears flowed down his wrinkled face, over his slowly growing white beard, and plopped audibly into the water. He could barely contain himself long enough to declare the pool valid, but declare it he did.

"Kosher."

The women would take turns immersing. Each required another woman to see that she dipped without touching the sides of the pool, and with every hair submerged. The rabbi sat in the dark waiting room reciting the Book of Psalms from memory.

Kitty, appointed monitor, was still huddled in her coat, since there was no heat, but the naked woman before her stood still as a stone. Using the flashlight, Kitty inspected the hands of the woman from Debrecen to make sure that no dough had gotten under her nails. There was an angry mark on the woman's forearm.

"I tried my best, but it wouldn't scrub off," she raised her arm, showing the tattooed numbers.

Kitty patted it soothingly. "That's all right. It doesn't count."

Kitty bent down and checked the soles of the woman's feet, seeing that no debris from the floor had stuck to them.

"Looks just fine," she said, thumbs-up.

The woman started to cry. "I can't do it. I can't go down."

"Sure you can. Just hold on to the rails. I'm right here, watching you."

"No. Look." She pointed at her abdomen.

Of course Kitty had noticed it before. A grotesque mass of scar tissue extended from her breasts to the pubic area, as if she'd birthed a monster by Caesarean section.

"They did experiments to me in the camp. I can't have any more children. I told Henry. I told him everything. But he still wanted to get married. He insisted."

"Absolutely right. He's lucky to get you. Pretty, smart, from a fine family."

The woman turned, took the first step down to the pool, then stopped.

"I can't do it. I can't."

Kitty seized her shoulders, turning her around. She looked ferociously into the woman's eyes.

"Listen to me! Every woman who is here tonight—every woman, and especially you—is going to get pregnant this year. And we are all going to have perfect, beautiful babies, and raise them to be wonderful Jews. Every one of us, and our husbands, will dance at our children's weddings. And we will stuff ourselves with food, and we will bless God for our good fortune. *Do you understand?*"

Kitty had shaken her so hard, that the woman slipped onto the second step. In fear of Kitty—a *violent* woman—she got to the floor of the bath. Kitty cocked an eyebrow to the ornate ceiling.

I dare you to make a liar out of me, God. Dare and double dare.

The woman from Debrecen dunked under the water. It was proper and right.

"Kosher!" Kitty declared.

"Blessed is the Lord, our God, King of the universe, who has sanctified us in his commandments, and commanded our immersion," the woman recited.

"Amen," said Kitty.

Now the woman was silent, as she prayed. In the ritual bath, prayers are as powerful as they can ever be. Moments before the possibility of life, they equal the last confession before death.

She immersed.

"Kosher."

And again.

"Kosher."

The woman from Debrecen came up out of the water. "Your turn, Kitty."

After Kitty's preparation, the woman from Debrecen checked her as she had been checked. Kitty felt ashamed. Not because she was naked—they had all been naked—but because she was whole. Wasn't she supposed to be the least attractive one?

"How old are you?" the woman asked suddenly.

"Twenty-four," said Kitty. It felt like a lie.

"I'm nineteen."

The woman lifted Kitty's hair from her neck to inspect for loose hairs. "So pretty," she said. Kitty had bleached her hair back to blondness.

"You don't have to compliment me, I'm not a bride."

"Oh, but didn't you always feel like a bride, when you came from the ritual bath? I always did. I always felt, when I was with my husband that night, like it was the first time. Oh! Oh, no." The woman slapped her hand over her mouth.

Kitty went down quickly. Before her wedding day, since Mother could not, Sari and Martha had advised her about the ritual bath. Sari had emphasized the holiness of the experience, but Martha cut her off. "Do your immersion speedily, Kitty, and don't pray too long. God has all the time in the world, but the matron doesn't. She has a family too, and she's waiting to get home. Besides, God knows what you mean."

Considering that Martha's quick prayers were the more quickly answered, Kitty had followed her custom rather than Sari's.

"Kosher," said the woman from Debrecen.

Kitty said the blessing and immersed again. *Please, dear God...me and Sender...*

Of course God knew what they wanted, no point wasting time on that.

And please, all these people too, especially this woman. Make her new again, a bride, and make her love her husband...and please, make my words to her come true...

She emerged from the water.

"Kosher," said the woman from Debrecen.

In she went again.

Please protect all the remnant of my family. Joseph and the little Meisels boy, and the women in the apartment, who are my sisters now, and all the House of Israel.

Please don't be angry with us anymore, but open your heart to us again, because we are your people and you are our God. Just as Sender and I will always love each other, your homely little people and you will always be together.

Remember the promise you made, that you would bless us so greatly that all the horror will vanish from our minds, as the pain of birth vanishes for a new mother.

I've got to go now. Yours always, Kitty.

When she rose, the water tickled her healing nose, so that she laughed.

"Kosher!"

THE END

ABOUT THE AUTHOR

GILA BERKOWITZ is a veteran author and journalist. She was a reporter for *Reuters* and the *LA Times* and has contributed fiction and non-fiction to magazines ranging from *Good Housekeeping* to *Playboy*. Berkowitz taught at Stanford University, where she was a Knight Fellow in Journalism and received the Dreyfus Writing Award. Her best-selling first novel, *The Brides*, was optioned for television and translated into three languages. She divides her time between New Jersey and Jerusalem.